NASH

By Daniel Scavone

For information, or to order additional copies, please contact:

Beacon Publishing Group
P.O. Box 41573 Charleston, S.C. 29423
800.817.8480| beaconpublishinggroup.com

Publisher's catalog available by request.

ISBN-13: 978-1-949472-48-6

ISBN-10: 1-949472-48-6

Published in 2022. New York, NY 10001.

First Edition. Printed in the USA.

NASH

TABLE OF CONTENTS

NASH

THE KURDISH PRIDE GANG

Bobby Linder nodded in agreement when the bartender at Edgefield's, Lucy "No Panties" Macey, asked him if he wanted another beer and a shot of Dickel. Bobby was watching the burning of the Cathedral of Notre-Dame in Paris on the television. He had been to Paris once, just after he dropped out of his freshman year at Belmont University in the spring of 1973. Bobby had just made $500 selling a song to RCA that he had written in one of his music writing classes, and he figured he could do more of that without having to sit in school. Besides, the draft had just ended, and that was why he had gone to college in the first place. He visited his high school friend Austin Benton, who was living in Paris and playing in a band capitalizing on a minor craze for American country music. Bobby hadn't done much sightseeing in Paris, but one day he did get ice cream at Berthillon and strolled along the Seine to the cathedral. He remembered overhearing an English-speaking tour guide tell a crowd about holy relics in the church, including a piece of the cross and crown of Jesus Christ. At the time, as he licked the melting vanilla ice cream on the top edges of the cone, he wondered how the guide knew it was the real crown and cross of Jesus. Now as he sat at Edgefield's watching the fire, he wondered what happened to those relics. His thoughts were interrupted when the television station switched back to its regular programming of Dr. Phil.

"Are you kidding me?"

"Here you go Bobby," Lucy said, placing the glass of beer in front of him while filling the shot glass with Tennessee whiskey. Lucy had gotten the nickname No Panties, or NP for short, when she once quipped that she never wore any to work in case Brett Eldredge stopped in. She wanted to be ready.

"Thanks, NP. Can you believe this? One of the iconic wonders of the world, been around for ages and ages, going up in flames, and they switch to Dr. Fucking Phil. For the love of God." Bobby drank the whiskey shot but left the perspiring glass of beer alone.

"Could have been worse. The Talk is on channel five." Lucy's slight grin of yellowing teeth gave no hint of the beauty she was thirty years ago. That was about the time the seventeen-year-old met a recent army recruit not much older in her hometown of Hattiesburg, Mississippi. Married a few months later and a few months pregnant. The couple lived on base at Camp Shelby for about a year, until the second time soldier boy beat her. Later that night, Lucy woke him up with his own pistol to his head. She told him, in no uncertain terms and with quite a few less than complimentary adjectives, that she was leaving with the baby and, if she even thought he would contemplate coming after them, she would shoot him in the temple, cut his head off, and shove it up his ass—no matter how long it took her to get it up there. Now soldier boy may not have been the brightest of military men, but he did feel that both his head and his anus could be used for better purposes. He nodded slowly in agreement. Lucy collected the whole one hundred twenty-five dollars in his wallet, the baby, and the keys to their eight-year-old Chevy Impala. Lucy did have a problem once she and her baby were in the car: her evangelical parents had disowned her on account of the unwed conception. She had nowhere to go. Lucy decided to head to Nashville simply because country music made her happy.

Bobby lit a cigarette. A key to making Edgefield's his bar of choice was they still allowed smoking. At one time it was never a problem in East Nashville, but now that the area had become hip, these bars were rapidly giving way to artisan restaurants and five-dollar coffee shops. "These daytime talk shows make my head hurt," Bobby said. "Can we put some music on or something?"

Lucy, seeing that there were no objections from any of the other afternoon drinkers, lowered the sound on the TV and clicked another remote, which caused "Goodbye Earl" by the Dixie Chicks to resound through the bar's speakers. Bobby began to speak to no one in particular. "I co-wrote two songs on their first album with Robyn Lynn Macy. Never thought any of their stuff was worth a damn after she left."

Lucy had heard the story before, but she couldn't resist. "I don't know about that, Bobby. They became awful big a few years later when Natalie Maines joined 'em."

Bobby took one final puff off his cigarette before snuffing it into an ashtray advertising Stoker's chewing tobacco. "Popularity isn't the definition of quality, my dear NP. If it were, Kim Kardashian would be our generation's Statue of David."

As she had done, many times before, Lucy let it drop.

Bobby took a sip of his beer and didn't notice the two mustached gentlemen who had just entered the bar. They were members of the Kurdish Pride Gang, and they were not there for a drink and leisurely conversation. "OK, Motherfuckers! Don't anybody move a goddamn muscle!"

Bobby looked up to see a Glock 19 pistol pointed at him and his handful of fellow patrons. A quick look over at the man's partner revealed a large switchblade. The gunman demanded that everyone except Lucy move to the wall opposite the bar and lie on the white and green vinyl floor. On his way over to the wall, Bobby wondered what these two were doing so far away from their turf in Little Kurdistan in South Nashville. He and the others did as they were directed and lay down with their feet against the wall and their arms stretched out Superman style. The guy with the switchblade stood over them as his partner focused his attention on Lucy. "OK, bitch. Do as I say, and we all get out of here OK." He pulled out a crinkled, yellow plastic Piggly Wiggly bag and handed it across the bar to Lucy. He pointed to the cash register. "Fill it! Hurry the fuck up!"

Bobby smelled something awful and realized that the fellow next to him, not a regular at Edgefield's and probably not one to be in the future, had soiled himself. The thief watching over the customers found this amusing enough to notify his companion: "Hey Olan, this one here shit his pants!" The thief bent down to talk to the subject of his recent entertainment, an overweight, red faced gentlemen in his early fifties, who at this moment was more concerned about gasping for air than the load in his chinos. "Sorry, I didn't bring a spare diaper with me, poopy pants!”

Olan, not happy his partner had used his name, said, “Stop goofing around!”

“Yeah man,” Bobby heard himself say. “Everyone is doing what you guys want. Why don’t you just leave him alone?”

Now the thief was OK with Olan’s comment, but not so much with Bobby’s. He stood up, walked over to the pool table, and selected a cue from the wall. With a one-handed swing, like a field hand with a scythe, he hit Bobby across the face. Bobby’s head went numb for a moment until he felt warm liquid in his mouth and saw reds spots hit the tiles.

“Anything else you want to say, motherfucker?”

Bobby raised his right arm and waved his hand ever so slightly with his index finger pointed, in that never fully confirmed universal symbol that everything was fine. “Two Pina Coladas” by Garth Brooks began to play. Olan, the plastic bag now filled with the register’s proceeds and held firmly in his hands, turned to his companion to tell him it was time to leave. The thief bent down and took the watch off Bobby’s wrist.

“Don’t worry about that stuff! Let’s go,” Olan yelled. Behind him, Lucy grabbed what she referred to as “the disagreement solution,” more commonly known as a crowbar, from a shelf beneath the register; she laid a solid one across the back of Olan’s head that made Bobby’s whack seem like a head pat. Olan dropped to the floor, and the gun flew out of his hands, spinning like a boomerang into Bobby’s right hand as if directed by a guardian angel.

Other than a slow, guttural moan emanating

from Olan, you could hear a pin drop. Olan's companion and Bobby stared at each other for a few moments, neither moving a muscle. Finally, Bobby pointed it at the thief's head. "Gun beats knife, asshole." The thief backed away. Bobby turned his attention and the gun to Olan. "Why don't you hand the bag back to the nice lady?"

Olan stretched out his arm and did as he was told, careful not to look into the eyes of Lucy, who was hoping for any excuse to give him another beating.

Bobby turned back to Olan's sidekick. "Watch, please."

The thief tossed the watch to Bobby, who caught it with his free hand. Bobby stood up and asked, "What's your name?"

"Excuse me?"

"What's your name, dipshit?"

The thief nervously looked over at Olan. Olan nervously nodded.

"Royar."

"Royar?"

"Yes." Bobby got up from the ground. Careful to keep the gun trained on the two recent guests.

"Shoot 'em Bobby! Shoot the fuckers!" Lucy yelled.

"Now as tempting as that option may be, that wouldn't be very hospitable. Now would it, Royar?"

Royar shook his head.

Bobby put his hand to his lip, pulled it away, and took a quick look at the blood. "So, what does Royar mean?"

Royar said something in a low voice.

"Excuse me?"

With his head down, Royar spoke louder. "I think it means when the sun rises."

Bobby nodded. "Ah, when the sun rises! Beautiful name!" Bobby pointed down at the man Royar had made fun of for defecating himself. He had still not gotten up, and his face clearly showed regret for having come in for a drink in the first place. "Now Royar, if you want to see the sun rise tomorrow, why don't you apologize to my new friend here?"

"I'm sorry," Royar said.

"Much appreciated." Bobby looked over at Olan and asked him to stand next to Royar. "Now boys, to make this gentleman not feel so bad, I would like you to join him."

Olan and Royar looked confused.

"Let me clarify. I could take Lucy's suggested course of action and shoot both of you in what everyone here I am sure would agree was self-defense, or I could just have her call the police and let them decide what to do." Bobby tapped his forefinger against his lips. "Or third, both of you could shit your pants in sympathy with my friend here, and I will send you on your way." Bobby allowed himself a little smile as he pointed the gun in their direction. "Your choice, boys."

Olan and Royar looked at each other in disbelief. Lucy came from behind the bar to stand next to Bobby with her arms folded. "I just have to see this."

Bobby raised his voice. "I don't have all day, gentlemen."

Olan's face tightened as it was clear he'd elected for option three. Royar soon joined him, both of their faces contorting in an attempt to forget about the pistol being pointed at them in order to concentrate on the matter at hand. Olan was turning red, and Royar, with darker skin, a more purplish hue. After a few flatulent misfires, it was clear from the movement in his pants that Royar had met with success.

"Come on, Olan," Bobby said, "we know you can do it!"

It was unclear if Bobby's prompting helped. Olan's eyes were closed, and his face was the picture of pure concentration and deep strain. After a few bowel noises that, if a vote were taken among the spectators, would certainly have ranked as rather impressive, Olan's eyes widened as a feeling he was unlikely to have had since the age of two rushed over him. Then his body relaxed, like someone who thinks his car may have been stolen in a large parking lot but suddenly finds it. Lucy and some of the spectators clapped, which, in retrospect, Bobby found a bit questionable. It wasn't as if either Olan or Royar had correctly answered a question on Final Jeopardy. In any event, the assignment had been completed. Bobby motioned with the gun toward the entrance.

"Boys, that was well done. But the party is over. Time to go. Now we'll keep this little story to ourselves, but if we see either of you two in this neighborhood again, I guarantee you will wish you could soil your pants every day. Do we have an understanding?"

Olan and Royar nodded and, without waiting for any further instruction from Bobby, quickly made for the exit.

Lucy, arms folded, shaking her head, looked over at Bobby. "Well, ain't that the shit."

THE BOY FROM INDIANOLA

Lauren Culiver put the unsatisfactory cowboy boots back into the shoe box. It was the seventh pair of boots the man had tried on. This guy is worse than the women, Lauren thought. But Lauren smiled at the customer. "You know, I think I have just the pair for you. I'll be right back." Lauren hustled into the stockroom, brushed her shoulder length brunette hair out of her face, put the rejected pair back in its place, and climbed a wooden ladder to retrieve the next. Back on the showroom floor, she started speaking before she reached her destination. "This is one of our finest pairs. Genuine American alligator. Detailed single welt construction and beautiful leather soles." The customer watched while Lauren pulled a boot from the box and spun it around in her hand like it was a movie star pausing for photographs on the runway. She bent down and began to put the boot onto the customer's foot. Overall, he was heavy, and his legs were no exception. The customer was not making any effort to be helpful. Lauren repeated the exercise with the other foot. The customer stood up and took a few steps to a small mirror near the floor.

"They look just great on you," Lauren said while calculating the six percent commission on a $725 sale. The customer turned around to check out the back. Lauren thought that if he didn't by these boots, she might have to kill him, "Look awesome on you from back there as well."

The customer proceeded to pace across the floor several times. Lauren watched each lumbering step like she was being hypnotized by a metronome. While staring at the points of his new leather, he spoke. "I'll take 'em."

"Excellent! Let me rebox them and ring you up."

It had been a good day at the boot store—Lauren had made $196 between her wages and commissions—but it was nearing seven o'clock, and she needed to get home and change. She hopped into the 2011 metallic blue Ford Focus her dad her given her before she left Naperville. On Tuesdays, she sang from ten to ten forty-five at The 5 Spot, but if you were one minute late, Reggie Harris would have your head…and your time.

Lauren lived in an apartment above the Lipstick Lounge on Woodland Street. The Lip, as they called it, was a popular lesbian bar with a good mix of straight locals in East Nashville. Lauren didn't go that way, but the rent was cheap, the place was clean, and the bar had a great brunch on Sundays. Sometimes she practiced her singing on their popular karaoke nights, and it didn't take long for her to get used to the women's pick up lines, which were not much different from the men's in straight bars, albeit a little less conceited.

Even before she jumped into the shower, Lauren washed her hands, physically and mentally removing any scent from the dozen or so feet she touched that day. Naked, she dried her hair in the mirror before getting dressed. Once attired in a white shirt, blue jeans, and black leather boots she had gotten at a discount from her employer, Nashville Boot Co., she grabbed a strawberry yogurt out of the refrigerator only to notice it was two days past the expiration date. Lauren wondered, is it really bad, or is Chobani full of baloney? She opted for the latter, mostly because it was the only thing left to eat.

Her phone buzzed; it was her mother. She decided not to answer. No matter how nice the conversation started, it rarely ended well. "Are you tired yet of this singing idea? Did you ever think of going back to U of I? I saw Michael at the supermarket the other day. He asked how you were doing. He looks great. Had a nice suit on and all." It was just typical mother stuff, but typical mother stuff usually drove Lauren batshit nuts. She needed to prepare her setlist for tonight and preferred to do it with her blood pressure at a somewhat normal level.

Lauren pulled her guitar out of its case. It was a Gibson Montana Hummingbird she purchased during her junior year in college on her first trip to Nashville. It was part of the money her parents gave her for the semester's tuition at University of Illinois, but once she hit Music City, that ship sailed. She was with a couple of girlfriends on a weekend trip during winter break. Bar after bar, club after club, as Lou Reed once sang, "She couldn't believe what she heard at all, she started shaking to that fine, fine music." She always wanted to be a singer, but after that trip, the timeline got moved up.

Every time Lauren picked up that electric acoustic guitar, for a moment it was like the first time she played it at Corner Music. Her heart beat just a little faster. Her green eyes became more focused. The guitar was cherry sunburst in color, mostly mahogany, with an aged Sitka spruce top and a rosewood fretboard. She liked to run her hand along the neck length as she settled the curve of the body into her thigh. Her mind cleared. A few quick picks and strums to check the tune. Beautiful. Lauren leaned over to a small table next to the sofa for her song list. She tucked it into the guitar case. She liked to get the feel of the crowd before deciding what to play. She got that from her father, a schoolbook salesman for thirty-eight years who once told her, "Lauren, if you want to make someone happy, you have to be able to read 'em first. Otherwise, you might as well be just shooting watermelon seeds out your backside." It wasn't exactly Winston Churchill, but Lauren got the point.

The Commander hated it when you were late. Lauren knew that. Not that anything at The 5 Spot ever started on time, but it was one of his pet peeves. Late once and you wouldn't be playing there for a bit. Late twice and you wouldn't be playing there ever. Lauren was late once with a flat tire, but it didn't matter. As the sign on the door of the Commander's back office said: NO EXCUSES. "Sorry, sweetheart," he told her. "I don't want to hear it. I was in a Humvee in Afghanistan back in '02 during Operation Enduring Freedom. It was enduring, all right. We got a flat on the road to Kabul. Seconds later our Humvee was hit by gunfire from a Russian AK-47 with armor piercing bullets by some raghead behind a small mound. Do you think that motherfucker felt bad that we got a flat? I was shot in the arm and my side." The Commander showed her his arm and pulled up his shirt. "My three army brothers with me were not as fortunate. I played dead until the bearded son of a bitch approached, and then I shot the sand monkey in the face through the broken glass." Lauren felt that the comparison of getting a busted tire on Gallatin Avenue in Nashville and having an old boyfriend come to fix it was not exactly akin to fighting off the Taliban, but she thought it best just to let it drop.

Reginald Harris, as the Commander was known back then, grew up in Indianola, Mississippi, about three hundred miles from Nashville as the crow flies but thousands of miles away in most other respects. A small, majority Black city—childhood home of B.B. King and birthplace of Albert King—Indianola was also the location of Club Ebony, a hole in the wall of hole in the wall nightclubs opened in the forties, which had featured not only the two aforementioned performers but virtually every major Black blues singer worth a listen. It was also the home of Indianola Academy, a private segregationist K-12 school founded shortly after Brown v. Board of Education and attended by virtually every child of the town's minority white population and virtually none of the majority Black. The Commander left high school on his seventeenth birthday to join the marines, by this time a six-foot-four set of muscles with feet. When asked about his time in the service, being in Afghanistan and getting shot, he always had the same reply: "It was the first time in my life I routinely had three squares." Back in the states after his tour of duty, the Commander stayed in the marines for a few more years at a base in Chattanooga helping train new recruits the best ways to kill. It was there he met his first wife, Kayla, and they eventually settled in Nashville. Starting out as a bouncer at The 5 Spot, the Commander worked his way up to bar back and then bartender. When the longtime owner, Pops Milligan, got terminally ill, he told the Commander he could have the bar if he took care of Pops's wife until she died. Pops's kids were not too happy about that, but Pops thought fuck 'em since they hardly ever set foot in the bar except for a free meal or drinks. The Commander took good care of Pops's wife until she passed a few years later. Then in his early thirties, the Black kid from buttfuck Indianola was now the owner of one of the most iconic spots for up-and-coming musicians in Nashville—or the country, for that matter. That was over two decades, six kids, and two broken marriages ago. But The 5 Spot was still alive and well, a beacon to all things genuine music.

Thursday nights at The 5 Spot usually featured a number of one-hour performances. Lauren arrived at about 9:15, and the first act was already playing. It was a band from Austin that Lauren had never seen before. Jammed onto a stage not much larger than your average closet, they consisted of a singer, drummer, electric guitar player, electric cello player, and a large, bearded, shirtless guy in overalls with no shoes or socks who played the fiddle, banjo, harmonica, or washboard, depending on the need. A little hickish, Lauren thought, but damn good. That was the positive and the negative about being a musician in Nashville. Everyone was damn good.

Lauren found a spot in a corner and pulled her song list from her guitar case. The crowd seemed upbeat and into the Austin band. As a solo singer with an acoustic guitar, she didn't want to bring the crowd down too much. Maybe start out with Gretchen

Wilson's "Redneck Women" or Carrie Underwood's "Undo It." Lauren had a new song of her own she had been working on about a group of old friends getting together on a hot summer night called "Drinkin', Smokin', and a Little Bit of Dopin" that she wanted to try out if the feeling was right.

Lauren didn't see the Commander approach, frowning like he had some bad news to tell. But his voice told a different story. "Hey, darlin', you're looking mighty fine as usual."

Lauren smiled that half-fake smile all women do at an uncomfortable compliment. "Why thank you, Commander. You are looking rather spiffy yourself." Lauren thought, spiffy? Really?

"Thanks, hon. You're on in five; be ready."

Onstage a few minutes later, Lauren looked over the crowd. She was trying to decide if this was a pure party crowd or one that went a bit deeper, one that focused on the words or the way the chords twisted and turned. She decided to open with Steve Earle's "Copperhead Road" to find out. The crowd responded well. She followed that with Sam Hunt's "Leave the Light On," and the bar was hers. One exception was a rather large redheaded dude who insisted on making obscene gestures every time she looked in his direction. Lauren put an end to that in between songs by pulling her zipper down and asking him if he wanted to come onstage and give it a go since his performance in the audience was so impressive. He half-heartedly shook her off and proceeded to retreat to the back of the bar.

"Sometimes it takes being an asshole to deal with an asshole," Lauren said as she zipped up her pants. "At least that's what my mama told me." The crowd loved it.

SHOES SAY A LOT
ABOUT A MAN

It had been a good show, and Lauren was happy. Her phone buzzed. It was a text from Jimmy Collino. He was at Dino's, a beer and burger dive within walking distance of The 5 Spot. Jimmy and Lauren had been going out on and off for about two years. God forbid the jerk at least walked over to meet me, never mind catching my show, Lauren thought. But then she reasoned she probably shouldn't be too upset; Jimmy was the one who introduced her to the Commander. Jimmy was, after all, an up-and-coming music promoter, and, in a city where it seemed there were more promoters than guitars, he was rather good at it.

Walking in with her guitar, Lauren saw Jimmy sitting at a bar that looked more like a diner counter. He was a picture of darkness in his black boots, jeans, and T-shirt. Lauren walked over and received a quick kiss and the offer of his seat, which was the only one available. When the bartender came over, Lauren ordered a beer and the tastiest greasy hamburger in Music City.

"I reached out to the Commander before I texted you, and he said you rocked it," Jimmy said.

"That's the rumor. You should check it out for yourself sometime." Lauren didn't want to sound too sarcastic, just enough for Jimmy to get the point. He did.

"Come on, L. I was over at the Limelight

pitching some good talent, including you, darlin'. Gigs don't appear out of thin air, you know."

"I know. But you haven't seen me play in at least two months."

Jimmy put on a pouting face and nodded. "When she's right, she's right. My bad. I didn't think I needed to because I know how good you are. Next gig I will be there front and center. I promise." With that, Jimmy opened his arms wide and hugged Lauren.

The next morning at Jimmy's house, Lauren woke up early. She had a ten-hour shift at the boot store, and she had to get to her place first for a change of clothes. Jimmy didn't stir as Lauren quickly got dressed. She put her pocketbook over her shoulder and glanced for a moment at her sleeping partner. She was not sure where this was going, and she had a feeling that soon she would need to address it.

Bobby found himself downtown on Church Street at the Nashville Electric Service building. He hated downtown, nicknamed it Flashville for all the tourists around. He recalled that back in the day, Tootsie's Orchard Lounge, with one light bulb on the ceiling, was lucky to do $500 a day, and homeless people slept in the back at night. Now it could do six figures on a good night, mostly with out-of-state bachelorette and bachelor parties and other visitors. One and done drunken guests. Not that it was all bad. Bobby got robbed more than once back in the eighties and had his car stolen to boot. But the stuff coming out of the old honky-tonks was what made country music what it was today. Now downtown was filling up with themed restaurants of the biggest stars.

Nashville Electric Service had shut off his electricity because he was three months delinquent on his bill. He did not forget to pay it, but it had not been a top priority. He waited six dark days until he received his next royalty check. It was a good one from some work he had done with Faith Hill back in the nineties. He could have paid at one of the kiosks NES had in various locations around the city, but he needed to argue about the reconnection fee they always tried to smack him with. He would usually pretend to be hard of hearing, and the customer service representatives would get so exasperated, they would give up on the reconnection charge just to get him out of there.

After a success at NES, Bobby decided to go boot shopping. Not that his current pair were all that bad. He certainly had more wear and tear on a lot of other wardrobe pieces that could have used replacing, but Bobby was always a fanatic about nice shoes. His daddy once told him, "You can tell a lot about a man just by looking at his shoes. Whether he is doing well or not, a worker or a lazy son of a bitch, even if he's a cheater. It's all right there in his shoes."

Nashville Boot Co. was located on the edge of the Gulch in the hippest neighborhood of the city, just outside of Pie Town, a formerly seedy area recently rebranded due to its triangular shape between three major roadways. The hookers and the heroin dealers were gone, but there was still a bit of an edge to the residents and businesses of the area. Bobby parked right in front of the nondescript white brick building and walked inside to the heavy smell of various leathers filling his nostrils. Cowhide, alligator, crocodile, lizard, ostrich, buffalo, elk, elephant, eel, stingray…name a beast, and it probably was a boot. Bobby took it all in as he looked at the long rows of hide, each pair shiny, neat, and ready to be called out.

"Hi! May I help you?" Lauren was wearing the same smile she had for all the customers.

"Uh, yes thanks. Any good deals on nice boots today?" Bobby smiled.

"We only carry the very best boots, so they are all good deals, I think," Lauren said as she smiled back.

"Well then," Bobby said, "are there any really good deals that are better than all the other good deals?"

Lauren put her index figure to her chin and pretended to be deep in thought. Then she pointed the same finger at Bobby. "You know what? We accidentally got a double order of beautiful Lucchese black crocs. I think I can talk the manager into giving you a break on them, if that is something that interests you."

Bobby, lost for a moment in her green eyes, replied, "Love to see a pair of the black crocs. Size eleven."

Lauren went to the back, came out with the boots, and opened the box. She took one out, held it up, and said, "Let's try them on." Lauren began to walk over to a nearby chair but was stopped by Bobby's comment.

"I'll take 'em."

"But you haven't even tried them on yet."

"I've been wearing size eleven Lucchese boots for nearly fifty years. Foot hasn't changed. They will be fine."

Lauren shrugged in a moment of surrender. Not the first weirdo she'd sold a pair of boots to. "Of course! I'll box them up for you."

"No need for that." Bobby put his right foot on his left knee and pulled off his old boot. He did the same with the other foot. He took the box from Lauren and put the new boots onto his bare feet. He pulled his wallet out and looked at his new footwear. "How much are these?"

"Eight hundred plus seven percent sales tax," Lauren said.

Bobby counted out nine hundred dollars, pretty much wiping out his recent royalty windfall.

"I'll put your old boots in the box and get your change," Lauren said.

"No need on either. If I thought those old shit kickers were any good, I wouldn't have come in here in the first place. Keep the change." Bobby smiled and proceeded to walk out.

Lauren stood dumbfounded for a moment. She had gotten tips in previous jobs as a waitress but never selling shoes. "Hey, sir!"

Bobby, with the door half open, turned around.

Lauren held up the money. "Thanks!"

Bobby decided to make one more stop before heading back home. Music Row was the epicenter of country music. In the former houses transformed into offices or in small, nondescript buildings, multi-million-dollar decisions were made each day about what songs would be hits and who got to play them. Bobby drove into West Nashville and around Buddy Killen circle, a grassy knoll where Division Street and Sixteenth Avenue North met. Named for the now-deceased head of the largest country music publisher in the world, the circle contained the Musica sculpture: nine large, dancing nudes holding aloft a female figure with a tambourine. When the sculpture was unveiled, some in the city complained about the nudity and could not understand what it had to do with music. When Bobby first looked at the statue years ago, its figures moving so freely, he had a hard time figuring out how someone couldn't get it.

Bobby pulled onto Music Square East and parked in front of Sidewalk Music, one of the major country music companies in the country. It was run by Eddie Fontana, a former New Yorker who came down a few decades ago for what was supposed to be a temporary assignment for his former employer, RCA. Eddie ended up starting his own company a few years later. He was a fat kid growing up but Bronx tough. Anyone who made fun of his weight usually was subjected to a sound beating. He loved music and loved making a buck. He started out at RCA at nineteen visiting music stations throughout the Northeast using payola to get songs played on the radio. He was particularly good at it. Eddie's first boss told him he was more important to getting a record up the charts than the musicians. He also had a penchant for wanting to be somebody. Once, when asked by Country Music People Magazine if he missed New York, Eddie said, "I miss a good bagel once in a while, but if I had never come to Nashville, I never would've gotten high with Willie Nelson. If you never got high with Willie, you haven't lived."

Eddie and Bobby met each other in the early eighties when Bobby was hired to write and produce songs for several RCA artists. Eddie had signed up and comer Keith Whitley, and Bobby's first assignment for the label was to work with him and come up with a good intro single. Unbeknown to Eddie, Mr. Whitley really liked his booze, so sometimes the scheduled sessions took place, and sometimes they didn't. Bobby was hesitant to let Eddie know. He had never been one to squeal, and as the new guy on the block, Bobby didn't want anyone to think he couldn't handle a fickle musician. After a month of wrangling, Whitley recorded a single that Bobby thought worked. Bobby decided to arrange it as a ballad because that required fewer studio musicians; expenses had become an issue after half the sessions had to be cancelled due to Whitley's absence. Bobby brought the recording to Eddie's office. After thirty seconds of listening, Eddie shut it off. "The words are good. As for the music, we might be able to sell it to surgeons who want to use it for anesthesia. You need to raise the gas, man. Whitley is a wild cowboy, not a pansy." Over the next few weeks, Bobby rejiggered the song, sometimes laying tracks in Whitley's absence. Eddie liked the new version and it was released, almost instantaneously shooting to number one on the charts and igniting Whitley's mercurial career, which unfortunately ended not many years later with his death, as he was unable to wean himself from the bottle. With the success of this song, Bobby began to understand why people referred to Eddie as the God of the Salesmen.

Besides having a strong business mind, Eddie was a well-known producer in his own right, and he and Bobby collaborated on a number of successful albums. In the eighties, the Nashville country culture lived hard and fast. As many deals were cut in the bars near music row as in the boardrooms. Drugs were big then, and Bobby remembered many all-night producing sessions with Eddie and he snorting cocaine off the studio soundboard. When Eddie started his own company, he slowed his drinking and stopped the drugs. Eddie realized, after two childless, failed marriages and his workaholic ways, that something had to give. Bobby didn't.

The lobby of Sidewalk Music was filled with flowers and large photos of some of their famous artists. Garth Brooks and Faith Hill stared down at visitors from behind the front desk.

"Good afternoon," the receptionist said. "May I help you?"

"Yes. Does Eddie Fontana happen to be in? I am an old friend and business acquaintance of his."

"Is he expecting you?"

"No ma'am. I think if he were expecting me, I wouldn't be asking if he were in, now would I?"

The receptionist kept the frozen smile on her face, but she flushed a little. "I'm sorry, sir, but Mr. Fontana doesn't see visitors without an appointment." She paused before shooting the arrow. "We have all kinds of people coming in all the time saying they are his friend. Many he has never met."

Bobby looked down at his new boots and leaned on the reception desk. "Ma'am, do we really need to do this? Nothing in your life is going to change if you pick up that little phone of yours and tell Mr. Fontana that Bobby Linder is here to see him." Bobby moved in a little closer, pulled out his phone, punched up a number, and showed it to the receptionist. "Now I don't know what size bitch pill you took this morning to make you be this way, but if you don't tell him right now, I am going to call him myself and let him know the little difficulty I am having here."

When Bobby walked into the opulent office, Eddie was already standing with his arms open. His white hair had receded a bit more since the last time Bobby had seen him, and he had gained a little more weight, which was pushing the limits on his Brunello Cucinelli blue jeans.

"Bobby, where have you been, muthafucka!" Eddie walked over an gave Bobby a hug. Eddie was right. Bobby hadn't been around much in the past few years. It depressed him. Once you had something good and it's gone, there is no fun reminiscing.

"I was in the neighborhood, so I wanted to stop in and say hi."

"Sit, please." Eddie opened the humidor behind his desk and offered Bobby a cigar. Bobby declined but accepted a glass of A.H. Hirsch bourbon.

"So really, how have you been?" Eddie said. "You look a little gaunt. Everything OK?"

"Everything is fine." Bobby smiled.

Eddie was glad to move on. "Good. Good. I've been busier than a hooker at an evangelical convention. This business is getting tougher by the day. Competitors always trying to poach talent. You should be glad you left it."

Bobby took a sip of the bourbon. "I didn't leave it. It left me."

Eddie shifted in his seat. "Now, you did have a number of self-inflicted wounds, you have to admit that."

"Yup, I sure did. But I haven't touched a drug

in four years, and I have cut my drinking down to probably the average of most writers and producers in the biz. But my phone still ain't ringing."

"This game has changed so much since you and I started." Eddie stood up behind his desk. "Sometimes I can't tell the difference between country, pop, and rock and roll songs no more. There are even collaborations now between country and rap. They call it hick-hop. How about that shit?"

"You're saying I'm a dinosaur?"

Eddie sat on the corner of his desk. "I'm not saying that. What I am saying is that the game is totally different than when you learned it. What you know about this business in the past is not as relevant as what you currently don't know. And even if you did learn it, you wouldn't like it."

"How did you survive?" Bobby asked as he twirled the glass of bourbon around in his fingers.

"I never left it. This business is not like riding a bike. The ability to do it is constantly changing."

Bobby smiled and popped the question he had planned to ask. "I guess the prospect of getting any future work is out of the question."

"The margins on my business are not enough to swear by. I would love to work with you again, but it is just not feasible. I probably got one or two more years left where I can keep it afloat. But I tell you what. If you want to write some songs, I will have my folks take a look at 'em. If you feel you know some talent, we will look at that as well."

"My folks? We? What happened to you and me?"

"Figure of speech. You know what I mean."

Eddie reached into his pocket and pulled out a roll of cash and began to peel off some hundreds. "In the interim, why don't I give you a couple of bucks for inspiration."

Bobby stood up. "Thanks, Eddie. I don't need your money. You know, one thing I always liked about you was that you never failed to surprise me. When we worked all those years together as partners or when I found out you were using some of our joint work as your own to build cash to start your own label, you never failed to surprise me. But you know what? Your evaluation of country music changing so much that I can't do it anymore is pure bull. A good song is still a good song. And a good performer is still a good performer. The rest is all just window dressing."

Eddie sat back down in his chair. His oversized face grew beet-like, his voice a few octaves lower. "You know what your issue is? You don't know when to stop. I am right that the business has changed. There is no denying that. You just haven't been around to see it. But I was also trying to be polite. You say I used our joint work behind your back? You got some balls. You know how many times I had to make excuses during our pitches when you were not there because you were stoned or drunk out of your mind some place and no one knew where you were? And do you know how many times I gave your ex money because you squandered it and she was too broke to even buy food for the kids? And do you think the rest of the biz didn't know about all your antics? Christ, I am probably the only one you know who would even talk to you! And you want back in? You must be fucking nuts!"

Bobby got up, finished the bourbon, and put the

glass on Eddie's desk. "You know, everything you said is true. I messed up a lot of things in business and my personal life. But you know one thing no one can say about me? Everything I did, I did to myself. I never cheated anybody." Bobby turned to walk out.

"Fuck you, Bobby! Don't bring your sorry ass in here again!"

Bobby stopped and turned around. "I give you credit for crawling your way to being a big honcho. But this is what I think of it." With that Bobby unzipped his pants and proceeded to liquidate yesterday's alcohol consumption onto Eddie's Peshawar rug.

HOT CHICKEN

Bobby woke up that unusually hot Fourth of July to the noise of a lot of people on South Eighth Street. Normally his was a quiet neighborhood of small, one-story homes, but today was the hot chicken festival at East Park. The event brought thousands of people to the small park to sample the Nashville creation of spicy fried chicken usually served on white bread with pickles. Bobby enjoyed the festival although he was not a big fan of the fire truck parade held in the morning beforehand. As if there wasn't enough noise with all the people coming in, some genius had to throw in some trucks honking their horns. As the parade started on nearby Woodland Street, Bobby put his headphones on, turned up the sound on his stereo, and listened to Johnny Cash's *At Folsom Prison*. Bobby had seen Cash as a kid when his father took him to the Grand Ole Opry back in the sixties. When Cash sang "Ring of Fire," Bobby's hair stood up on the back of his head. He'd never heard anything so perfect.

About an hour later, Bobby figured the chicken festivities should be in full swing. He lit up a Camel cigarette and crossed the street to the park. After purchasing a Yazoo beer, he headed over to the hot chicken area. Bobby was a bit amused at the number of hot chicken vendors. All the big names were there—Bolton's, 400 Degrees, Pepperfire, Hattie B's, Prince's—plus a few others. Bobby never really saw much difference between the vendors, but he was partial to Prince's, if only because they were the originators of the genre. Give credit where credit is due.

Chicken in hand, Bobby walked over to the stage to catch a bit of the musical acts. He saw some familiar faces along the way giving a nod or wave but not stopping to chat. Most of the bands were local artists doing the gig for free to garner some attention. When he got to the stage, a rock cover band was playing. The name BLOSSOM was emblazoned in a lightning font across the bass drum. They were playing The Georgia Satellites' "Keep Your Hands To Yourself." Bobby thought their instruments were probably thinking the same thing.

Lauren was really pissed at Jimmy. He told her just yesterday that she was booked to play the Hot Chicken Festival.

"Jimmy, what for? We don't even get paid for that one."

"It is important to give back to your community once in a while, hon. People support those they like. Also, Johnny Horton from the city council asked me if I could round up a couple of performers for the event. His brother is a minority owner of the Titans. I figure we may be able to score some tix in return for this favor."

"Football tickets, really? I was scheduled to work Saturday, and now I have to get out of it. It is going to cost me to do this gig."

"It will all work out, darlin', I promise."

"Well, I better see your butt in the audience. I ain't gonna be the only one making sacrifices here."

"Of course, babe, I'll be there."

"And one more thing."

"Yes?"

"For future reference, please remember that I don't even like fucking chicken!"

Lauren was scheduled to go on about one o'clock. She parked more than four blocks away because she couldn't find any spots closer. Lugging her guitar in the already-ninety-five-degree heat, she had pleasurable images of castrating Jimmy. At the park, she went backstage and found the music organizer, a seventeen-year-old who introduced himself as the nephew of Johnny Horton and who had more pimples than holes in a sponge. With a cigarette in his mouth and oversized Ray-Bans on his cratered face, the organizer told Lauren she would be going on in about twenty-five minutes. He pointed to a cooler of bottled water and told her there was a small, air-conditioned trailer she could hang out in. Lauren decided there was something creepy about this kid, so she politely declined his invitation and waited on the side of the stage, where she caught a glimpse of the act and the audience. The band onstage depressed her a little more, as she thought their musical skills belonged at a tween boys birthday party. Looking out into the audience, she felt most of the crowd seemed more interested in the chicken, beer, or popcorn than the music. Lauren could not find Jimmy. After a few minutes of increasing depression, she did spot someone she recognized. She walked over to waste a few minutes.

"Hi. I think I sold you a pair of boots a few days ago, no?"

Bobby wiped his face to clear off the residue of his lunch. "Uh, yeah, hello."

"Well, how do they feel?"

"How does what feel?"

Lauren pointed at Bobby's feet. "The boots, man! The boots!"

"Oh, Jesus! Sorry! I was having a senior moment. They are fine, thanks."

"Great. Thanks again for the tip. That was cool."

"No problem." Bobby looked down at his empty plate. "Would you like some chicken or something?"

"No thanks. I hate chicken." Lauren turned to go. "I gotta run. I'm on in just a few minutes. Just wanted to say thanks again."

Bobby held up his beer and smiled. "Break a leg!"

Lauren smiled and hustled away.

Bobby looked down into his cup and thought about his last comment. Break a leg. Really? That was the best he could do? What a putz.

After Blossom broke down their gear, which took as least twice as long as it should have, Johnny Horton's nephew appeared onstage with the same cigarette and sunglasses. "Ladies and gentlemen, how about one more hand for Blossom!" He was met with a lackadaisical response. Undeterred, he continued. "And now, folks, one of our very own, right out of East Nashville, please give it up for Ms. Lauren Culiver!"

Lauren smiled as she came onstage with her guitar and gave the not very enthusiastic crowd a brief wave. When she reached the center microphone, the Horton nephew was still there clapping and staring at her. Lauren, smiling right through him, whispered,

"Get the fuck off. Now." He stopped clapping and disappeared.

Lauren figured since she wasn't getting paid and wasn't thrilled about being there, she would at least try out some of her own material and see how it worked. She started with "Hole in My Soul" about her little sister lost to leukemia when Lauren was twelve and her sister was ten. Then she tried out "Two Clowns One Circus" about the state of politics in Washington. Next, she lightened things up with "You Want to Put It Where?" The crowd reacted better than she anticipated, but she thought it best to get back to what they expected, so she delved into some of the more popular country tunes of the last twenty-five years. She talked a lot between numbers, sometimes engaging in small talk with the audience. She even brought a teenage girl onstage to sing Miranda Lambert and Carrie Underwood's "Somethin' Bad." By the closing number, Lauren had the crowd, which was much bigger than when she first got onstage, singing and clapping along. She crossed paths with Horton's nephew on the stairs getting off the stage, but he had smartened up and avoided eye contact.

Her throat was bone dry, and she went over to the cooler to grab a water. As she was taking her first sip, a voice said, "Hey, that was great!"

Lauren whipped around, grabbing her chest and coming face to face with Bobby. "Jesus Christ!"

"Sorry," Bobby said. "I just wanted to say you are pretty impressive. Musically, lyrically, and with your stage presence."

Lauren wondered if her new friend was legit or just another old geezer hopelessly trying to get into a young woman's pants. "Thanks. I haven't done an afternoon gig in a long time. I'm glad you enjoyed it."

"Seriously. I've worked with a lot of talent. I think you have the basics to build on."

Lauren started to think the old geezer theory was more likely. "Are you in the music biz?"

"Yes. I mean I was. Producing and writing. Over twenty-five years."

"Why'd you quit? Tired of it?"

"No, I loved it. But I loved booze and drugs more. I've been clean for a while now, but apparently I'm still persona non grata."

"Well, I'm glad you got yourself together." Lauren picked up her guitar. "Nice seeing you again." She gave a slight wave and began walking away.

"Hey, would you mind if I checked you out? I mean your show—when you play at a club or bar."

Lauren looked down at the ground.

Bobby raised his hands. "Don't worry, I am not a stalker or anything."

Lauren looked up and smiled. "Sure. I play The 5 Spot most Thursdays, but I don't even know your name."

"Bobby. Bobby Linder."

Lauren nodded and continued to walk away. Then she turned around. "Hey, Bobby! Nice boots."

Lauren had barely made it out of the stage area when she heard a familiar voice. "Hey, hot stuff!"

"Jesus, Jimmy, I'm glad you could make it."

"Sorry, babe. I was promoting a band at The High Watt last night, and it went later than I thought it would. I didn't even hear the alarm. Anyway, I talked to the stage manager, and he said you killed it, but he didn't think you were too friendly."

"Who are you talking about? Horton's nephew? That creepy kid? He makes me want to take a shower."

Jimmy smirked. "Anyway, you did great. Why don't you come over to my place tonight and we'll order some Chinese food? I got a few song ideas I've been working on for you, and I want to run some potential gigs by you."

Lauren smiled and shook her head. "Just when I think I can't take any more of your crap, you pull me back in."

Jimmy grabbed Lauren's guitar, gave her a kiss, and they walked off together.

BEWARE OF SNAKES

It was still very warm when Bobby got back to his house. The old window air conditioning unit was not doing much more than regurgitating the air from outside. It didn't matter. He was still excited by Lauren's performance. She was far from perfect, maybe just a bit better than mediocre, but he had seen this before. The building blocks were there. They just needed to be cleaned up and put in the right order. He couldn't stop thinking about it. He knew he could help.

Bobby's thoughts were interrupted by his cell phone. He reached into his pocket, pulled it out, dropped it, cursed, and answered the call. On the other end was his ex, Sarah Parkinson. She had changed back to her maiden name immediately after the divorce fourteen years ago. Not that it wasn't amicable. Bobby was so drunk or high most of the time that he gave Sarah whatever she wanted. And she wanted a lot. The house in Belle Meade, the two kids, the dog, the Mercedes, the Jag, and his retirement account. Bobby kept the rights to his songs and his clothes. Soon after, Sarah sold the Tennessee house and moved back to her hometown of Austin, Texas, where Bobby had first met her in a club when he was producer of that evening's act. By the second set, Sarah and Bobby were having sex in the women's room. But in emotional years, that was eons ago. They had two kids, both girls, who were now grown. Jessica, just married, lived in California, and Emily, who just graduated college, was still living with Sarah in Austin. Bobby didn't get to talk to them often, but he missed them terribly. They didn't miss him as much.

"Hi, Bobby. How are you?"

"Fine. What's up?" Bobby knew this call was not likely to be a friendly catch up.

"Glad you are well. Just wanted to let you know, Emily got a job in Houston, and I thought maybe we could help her out with the apartment."

"We," Bobby said, "would love to help Emily out, but you have all the money."

"You don't need to get sarcastic. I just thought you would be happy to help your daughter get started, that's all."

Bobby was angry, but Sarah had a point. He would be happy to help Emily. But he had nothing to give. Sixty-eight years old and broke. Embarrassed of himself.

Sarah continued, "I guess you're still not working?"

"I'm working on a few things." Bobby felt he had to hit back. "What about your friend?" When Sarah moved back to Austin, John Clauser, a former studio musician Bobby had used often, moved back with her. Bobby never used his name. "Can't he help some?"

"It's not his kid."

"It's not his car, house, money, or wife either."

"Never mind. I'm sorry I called."

Bobby thought about saying "me too" before Sarah hung up, but he did not want to be a jerk. He knew Sarah was far from perfect, but nobody was more responsible for his current state of affairs than he himself. "I'll see what I can do," Bobby said.

After the call, Bobby sat down on the couch. He pulled out a cigarette but was too depressed to grab a lighter. He hated being in this position and knew only he was to blame. Bobby was worried because he was unsure how much longer he could go on like this. He lay on the couch and stared at the ceiling until his depression mercifully pushed him into a deep sleep.

The following week on a break from work, Lauren was having a cup of coffee at the Frothy Monkey. She had to give Jimmy some credit. He had lined up a couple of nice gigs for her, including a night at the Exit/In with some musicians he knew who were currently out of her league. But where she and Jimmy were going on a personal level was getting complicated. Just the other night, one of her girlfriends asked if she and Jimmy were a couple. She wanted to say that they had been a couple for almost two years, but she wasn't sure that was true. Lauren had this feeling that there was no progression, like they were stuck in the early dating stage. They had separate apartments, slept together two or three times a week, ate dinner here and there, saw a movie on rare occasions. Yes, they were both involved in Lauren's musical efforts, but for the most part, that was strictly business. Not that Lauren was itching to get married, but she just couldn't read Jimmy's level of commitment. There was boyfriend Jimmy and businessman Jimmy. Sometimes she couldn't tell which was which. She had a gig that night back at The 5 Spot. Jimmy said he was coming. On her way out of the coffee shop, she promised herself to have a talk with him.

When Lauren arrived at The 5 Spot, the Commander was in true form. He was yelling at one of the bartenders who had just dropped a case of Yazoo beer, sending suds across the bar floor and onto clean glasses prepped for the evening. "Jesus Christ, I don't think you need a college degree to properly carry a fucking case of beer. But you do need to be able to do it to be a bartender around here! Apparently, contrary to the belief of many, this shit ain't free. Clean it up, and let's see a goddamn good night at the registers for Christ's sake!" Lauren decided to hold off on saying hello to the Commander until he calmed down. She stayed at the opposite end of the bar and ordered a water from another bartender who also was making best efforts to stay out of the calamity.

Lauren learned that one of the acts was a no show, so she would have two forty-five minute sets. She had never played that long, so she was going to have to pull out virtually every song in her playbook. The bar crowd seemed mellow, but the place was quite full for a Wednesday. Suddenly a recognizable voice filled her ears from behind: "What, I don't even get a check-in anymore?"

It was the Commander. She apologized and said she'd thought he was busy.

"I can multitask, sweetheart," the Commander said as he moved on toward the kitchen. "I can multitask."

Lauren took the stage to muted applause. She opened with Gretchen Wilson's "Redneck Women," which brought the audience to life. A heavyset, clearly drunk young girl with short, black pigtails in a red and white stripped dress that didn't do much for her figure jumped onstage for Deana Carter's "Strawberry Wine." Lauren was caught by surprise, but the girl had a nice voice, even though her eyes were barely open, and the song elicited the loudest applause of the first set. After the first set, Lauren grabbed a beer at the bar and acknowledge the few who came up to say they were enjoying the show. Then a newly familiar face appeared.

"Ah, my stalker!" Lauren quipped as she took a sip of her beer.

Bobby laughed. "I just wanted to see if the talent I saw in the park last week is for real."

"And?"

"Indeed, it is. I did notice, though, that you didn't play any of your own songs."

"Ah, they need some more work, so I don't like to torture paying customers."

"Feedback is valuable. You can't tell what works or what can make it better without some input."

Just then, Jimmy appeared. He didn't even acknowledge Bobby. "Hey babe, just finished a few calls." He gave her a quick kiss on the lips.

Lauren was getting a little annoyed by all of the unannounced males popping up. "Jimmy this is…" Lauren paused, trying to recall Bobby's name. "Bobby?"

Bobby nodded.

"Bobby, this is Jimmy."

Bobby said hello; Jimmy nodded.

"Bobby's a writer and producer too," Lauren continued.

"Poor bastard," Jimmy quipped. "Represent anyone I would know?"

"Not recently. Been out of the game for a bit."

"What about last century?"

Lauren slapped Jimmy on the arm. "Don't be so rude."

"It's OK." Bobby kept his smile. "He's not that far off. It's been longer than just a bit. But, at one time or another, I did write or produce some songs for Randy Travis, George Strait, Billy Ray Cyrus, Faith Hill—before Tim McGraw, Lee Ann Womack, Garth Brooks, Alan Jackson, and maybe a few others this old brain can't recall right now."

"Wow." Again Lauren wondered if this guy was for real.

"What did you say your name was?" Jimmy asked.

"Bobby Linder."

Jimmy smiled and put his hand up to his forehead before pointing at Bobby. "I think I heard of you, man! You were a bigwig hooked up with Eddie Fontana back in the day. You ended up getting screwed up with some demons, no?"

"Jimmy!" Lauren turned to Bobby. "I am so sorry."

"Hey, like I said before, Jimmy is not too far from the truth. No worries. I best be going. Getting past my bedtime. Just wanted to repeat that I think you got what it takes to go far in this business. Keep working on it."

Before Lauren could reply, Jimmy jumped in. "She knows that. We both know it. And I intend on getting her there."

The Commodore approached. "OK ladies, let's break up this sorority party. Lauren, you're back on in two minutes."

Lauren told Bobby it was good seeing him again, gave Jimmy a kiss, and went onstage to set up.

Jimmy looked at Bobby, his eyes narrowing. "Don't even think about it."

For a moment, Bobby was taken aback. If it were a few years ago, he might have said to Jimmy, "If I did think about it, you little shit, you'd be collecting tips in a club bathroom in no time." Instead, he heard himself say, "No worries, my friend. No worries." Bobby nodded and left for home.

Lauren's second set was even smoother than the first. Encouraged by Bobby's comments, she threw in a few of her songs, which seemed to go over better than she expected. Afterwards, she grabbed a beer from the bar and joined Jimmy at a table in the corner.

Lauren's smile faded as she saw that Jimmy's usual after-performance happy face was missing. "What gives with that look? I thought I was rather good up there, if I say so myself."

Jimmy didn't look up. "Do you think I do a good job managing you?"

"Yes."

"Do you trust my abilities?"

"Of course I do."

"Then why are you talking shop with a has-been?"

"Are you serious? I sold him a pair of boots a few weeks ago, for Christ's sake. Then he was at the park concert and asked if I had any gigs coming up. That's it."

Jimmy shook his head. "That's it? You think so? You happened to be the one to sell him a pair of boots. Happened to run into him at the park. He happened to walk in here tonight. You really believe that?" Jimmy took a deep breath, leaned in closer to Lauren, and spoke in a lower voice. "Lauren, as we move you up the musical ladder, there will be snakes everywhere. And the snakes won't care about a thing in the world except what is in it for them." Jimmy reached for Lauren's hand. "That's what is different about us. We're a team—professionally and personally. We care about each other and only want what is best for each other." Jimmy let go of Lauren's hand and leaned back in his chair, running his hand over his hair. "This guy Linder, he's a train wreck. He couldn't get a job in this city if it was volunteer work. He's probably latching onto you with some ridiculous hope of riding you back into the limelight. But the time for that guy has long been over. Think about it. A guy who wrote for the likes of Garth Brooks and those others, chasing you down at a free gig in a park. He would only bring you down with him." Jimmy leaned forward once again. "But if you want him instead of me…hey, I never wrote anything for Garth Brooks. Just say the word. I will still love you."

Lauren's mind was racing so fast she felt a bit dizzy. Then she heard her own voice. "No, you're right. I guess I'm at that stage where if anyone tells me I'm good, I'm easily sucked in. Bobby seems like a nice enough guy. A lot of what he said seemed to make sense, but maybe that's because I wanted it to. I mean, the time I've spent with him probably doesn't total half an hour. Maybe running into him three times in such a short period is a little creepy."

Lauren decided to skip her earlier plan of

bringing up the status of their relationship. At least for now. Jimmy's concerns seemed valid, and she reasoned you don't expend that energy on people you don't care about.

"There you go." Jimmy grinned. "Now my girl is talking sense! Let me just finish my beer and we'll get out of here."

"Leave now and I'll fuck your brains out."

Jimmy's full beer remained at the empty table until the bar closed.

BAD NEWS COMES IN BUNCHES

Bobby woke up with his mouth as dry as summer in the Mojave, and his nose felt like it had been stuffed with cotton. Before he could even open his eyes, the light hurt. Wincing, he realized he had left the curtains of the floor-to-ceiling window in his Four Seasons hotel room wide open. It was like he was being interrogated. Slowly he sat up. His head throbbed. The night before trudged through his mind. He had been backstage at Farm Aid in Tinsley, Illinois, on the outskirts of Chicago, with Eddie Fontana. They went to this event every year in part to support acts they produced and in part to schmooze possible new ones. Recently they had gotten wind of the fact that Kenny Chesney, a rising star who had won his first Country Music Association Entertainer of the Year Award the year before, was not happy with his current producer. Bobby had managed a few weeks earlier to convince Chesney to meet confidentially with him and Eddie during Farm Aid. He called up room service for a bottle of bourbon and some aspirin.

Bobby sat up, put his face in his hands for a moment, and looked at the radio clock next the bed. It was eleven-thirty. He was supposed to be meeting with Eddie and Chesney at Manny's Deli at twelve. Fuck! Bobby didn't even bother to put his whole body into the tub; he just stuck his head under the shower. Thinking about last night, he remembered taking a break from the concert and going to an early dinner with Eddie, Emmylou Harris, and her manager. He put back a couple of bourbons and probably a bottle of wine, but that wasn't unusual. He remembered returning to the show, but that was about it. Bobby dried off, took a quick hit of mouthwash, and got dressed. No time to shave. A bellman knocked on the door with the bourbon and aspirin. Bobby scrambled for his wallet and gave him a tip. He opened the bottle and swallowed down some aspirin before making his way to the lobby, where he grabbed a cab for the three-mile ride to Manny's. It was sunny, and Bobby was angry he forgot his sunglasses. It was as if somebody was sticking a hot poker into his eyeballs. To make matters worse, the taxi's air conditioning wasn't working, and Bobby felt a little sick. The cab pulled in front of Manny's, which was located in a nondescript strip of stores in the South Loop. As usual, the deli was packed, but Bobby spotted Eddie and Chesney right away, in conversation at a table in the far back. He took a deep breath, put a smile on his face, and approached the table. As Bobby got close, Eddie looked up, and one might have thought he had seen Death himself. "Hey, boys!" Bobby said as jovially as he could muster. "Sorry I'm late. Got a call from Doug Morris over at Universal. The guy wouldn't let me get off the phone." Bobby held his hand out to Chesney. "Hey, Kenny. Great to see ya." Eddie's mouth was still slightly agape. Chesney returned the handshake and just nodded. Bobby continued, "I'm just going to grab a coffee. Anybody want anything?" Eddie and Chesney shook their heads.

As Bobby started to walk away, Chesney quipped, "You might want to do something about your jacket."

Bobby turned around. "What, you don't like it?" He put his hands on the lapels. "I just picked it up from Barney's last time I was in New York."

Eddie pointed to the pocket on his own jacket. Bobby looked down at his tan sport coat. There was a dark red wine stain about the size of a fist. Bobby couldn't believe he missed that. "Jesus Christ. I forgot some drunk bumped into me last night." Bobby took the jacket off, put it over an empty chair, and proceeded to go get his coffee.

Upon his return, only Eddie was at the table. "Where is Kenny? In the loo?"

Eddie stared at his plate. "He left."

"He what? Why?"

Still not looking up, Eddie replied, "He left, Bobby. He said he just remembered he promised to lend Mayer one of his guitars and had forgotten to give it to him." Eddie tapped his fingers on the white Formica table. "Personally, though, I do not think that was it."

"Well, what then?"

Eddie looked up and raised his voice to a harsh whisper. "Have you taken a good look at yourself? You're unshaven, your hair is crazy, your eyes are redder than an inflamed asshole, your clothes are disheveled, and your breath smells like booze. In sum, you are an overall mess! Did you think Chesney was going to deal with this nonsense?"

Bobby glanced at the ceiling and took a deep breath before he spoke. "I think you are exaggerating a bit."

"Exaggerating!" A few people turned to look at

Eddie, and he lowered his voice. "Are you kidding me? I lost track of you at the show last night. I found you about two in the morning in a truck behind the stage doing lines with some roadies. You could hardly speak. I got you a cab and paid one of the roadies who at least was only half in the bag a hundred bucks to get you back to your room. We were supposed to be working last night, Bobby. That is why we are here." Eddie placed his index finger onto the table. "And you know this isn't the first time. People are beginning to talk, and I am at the end of my rope."

"You're right, you're right. I was just trying to unwind after a long day, and I went a little over the edge. I will maintain going forward."

Eddie stood up. "You need to get some help. Now. No more of this behavior. I will do whatever it takes to help you, but if anything like this happens again, you and I are finished." Eddie threw his napkin onto his plate and walked out.

Bobby yelled to him, "Chesney is kind of a dick anyway!" He grabbed his jacket off the empty chair, dipped a napkin into a glass of water, and vainly tried to get the wine stain out.

The plane ride back to Nashville was not the most pleasant, but it would not be the worst. Bobby agreed that he would get some help, and the Farm Aid concert was not a total bust. They did manage to reconnect with a few current and former clients, and although they never did get another shot at Chesney, an up and comer by the name of Jason Aldean, who had been there to watch the show and do some prospecting of his own, asked them for help producing his upcoming album.

Still, the conversation on the flight was sporadic and a bit strained.

It was raining back in Nashville, where Eddie was picked up by his new and third bride, Cathy Chicowski, who was twenty years younger. Bobby grabbed a cab for the ride home to Belle Meade. Bobby loved that house. He and Sarah used to ride through Belle Meade when they first got married, imagining that one day they could own a home among the bankers, entertainers, record executive, and other powerful folks of the Nashville social scene. Even then, neither Sarah nor Bobby were fully convinced that they would do it. Bobby was not even totally convinced he wanted to. But it seemed Eddie and Bobby could not write good songs fast enough, and the only thing that held them back was the time they spent producing songs and albums. The money was there, so what the hell? Besides, Sarah really liked it there.

The cab pulled into the circular drive and dropped Bobby off at his front door. He couldn't wait to see the girls. The door opened, and through the screen Bobby could see six-year-old Jessica waving and three-year-old Emily jumping up and down. Things hadn't been that great between Sarah and him lately, but that was forgotten at this moment.

Once inside, Bobby scooped Emily up while Jessica repeatedly asked him what he got her on the trip. The trio went into the kitchen where Sarah was leaning against the island holding a glass of white wine. Bobby greeted her and gave a quick kiss. Bobby knew that look. No smile, no grimace.

"When you're done with the girls, can we talk?" Sarah asked more as a statement of fact.

Bobby told the girls to get ready for bed and he would give them each a present from his suitcase when they came back down. He turned his attention to Sarah. "Right now? No 'how are you?' Or 'how was your trip?' I had a very difficult past few days. Can I at least have a drink first?" Bobby went over to a kitchen cabinet and pulled out a bottle of bourbon.

"I need a divorce, Bobby."

Bobby moved to another cabinet for the glass and went to the refrigerator for ice.

"Did you hear what I said?" Sarah said.

"Yes, I heard you." Bobby took a long sip.

Sarah put her glass down "Well?"

Bobby let out a short laugh. "I've been in the house for five minutes after busting my ass twenty-four seven for the past few days so we can continue to live in this house and drive those overpriced cars you see out there. Are you fucking kidding me?" Bobby finished his bourbon and poured another.

Sarah shook her head and folded her arms across her chest. "I do not do this lightly. I did not just think of this as you pulled into the driveway. You are drunk constantly, if not stoned on something else. You come home at all hours if at all, and most of the time I can't even reach you. It is not a good environment for the girls."

Bobby raised his arms and twirled around the large kitchen. "This is not a good environment? Doesn't look like Tijuana to me!"

"You know that is not what I'm talking about."

Bobby moved in front of Sarah. "Then what are you talking about? Exactly what?"

Sarah looked straight at Bobby, her voice

rising. "I don't love you anymore."

Bobby stepped back and slowly nodded. "What about the kids? Any thoughts on that?"

"The kids will be fine. They are used to you not being here even when you are."

Bobby pointed at Sarah's face. "That's an exaggeration!"

"Is it? Tell me the last time you spent twenty-four hours in this house. Tell me the last time you went a day here totally sober. The kids are getting older now. It is not good."

"I had a talk with Eddie. We agreed on getting help with my drinking and other activities."

"It doesn't matter."

"Why?"

"I'm seeing someone."

The room fell silent for a moment, and then Bobby slammed his hand on the kitchen island. Sarah jumped, and some of her wine spilled onto her clothes.

"Jesus Christ, Bobby." She went to grab a hand towel and walked toward the living room; Bobby followed her.

"You give me a high and mighty lecture about my behavior and how it affects the kids. Meanwhile you're fucking around."

"I am not fucking around."

"Oh really. Then what do you call it? Playing doctor?"

"I'm not talking about this with you anymore until you calm down." Sarah walked out of the room. Bobby wanted to follow, but something told him not to. Back into the kitchen, he filled up his glass with even more bourbon than before. Taking a long sip, he mumbled to himself, "Linder, you sure are having one bad fucking week."

THE SUPERHERO

The Commander hated Halloween. Only other day of the year he hated as much was St. Patrick's Day. Something about those two days made normally sane adults turn into maniacs. Yes, they were usually two of the biggest-grossing nights of the year for The 5 Spot, but the headaches the Commander had to put up with offset any gain. Drunks, fights, yelling, vomit, men groping women, women groping men. A giant pain in the ass. But having a big crowd on those days was important for the bar's reputation, so the Commander reluctantly pulled out all the stops. He would have not one but three popular Nashville bands that night—the Smoking Flowers, the Minks, and the Black Gypsies. He spent a few thousand on decorations and even tolerated the obligatory costume contest, which was usually won by the woman wearing the least.

When the Commander first started in the marines, he was a bit of a wild child and had difficulty with military discipline. He spent more time than most doing various exercises and extra duties as punishment. One excruciatingly hot day in Parris Island, South Carolina, a few weeks into basic training, his sergeant really let him have it. He was awakened at three in the morning, two hours earlier than the rest of the recruits. He had to run barefoot six miles in the dark woods. Upon returning, he was forced to drink a gallon of water and was then thrown into a spinning clothes dryer for five minutes. Upon release, he had to run another six miles. Finally, he was forced to crawl in a sandy mud pit, under barbed wire, for about sixty yards. Near the end of the pit, his drill sergeant grabbed the back of his head and pushed his face hard and deep into the mud. For a moment, the Commander thought he was going to suffocate before his face was yanked out of the mud. The sergeant edged in close and said in a surprisingly calm voice, "Son, you see, what the smart ones realize is that life is nothing more than a series of negotiations. Now you can go on being an ignorant, stubborn horse's ass, and life will be awful rough for you well after you leave the marines. School, work, marriage, it's all just a series of negotiations, son. No more, no less." The Commander never forgot that advice.

Over at Edgefield's, as the evening was winding down, Lucy announced last call to the remaining patrons. There were few if any who needed another drink, but that did nothing to curb the final requests. It was Halloween, and it seemed to her that at some point during her life, when she wasn't playing close attention, the adults had hijacked the holiday from the children. Maybe it was because prior to the days of helicopter parents, kids were allowed to go out at night with their friends, unsupervised, roaming the far corners of their neighborhoods to collect candy or possibly create mischief at those houses who were chintzy with the good stuff or pretended they weren't home. There was laughter, yelling, endless talking, and flirting as they passed each other on sidewalks filled with devils, hippies, cowboys, princesses, and superheroes. Complete and utter freedom, in the dark no less. Lucy was amused at some of her patrons, well into their forties, fifties, and sixties, dressed in costumes and drinking heavily with the hope of creating that feeling of their childhood Halloweens long past. She played along, wearing her Dorothy from The Wizard of Oz costume, the same one she wore every year.

"Hey, NP, you ever going to wear a different costume on Halloween?" a regular asked.

"Only if you stop wearing your dick mask every day." Lucy smiled as if Brett Eldridge had walked into the room. Anyone with fifteen feet of her analysis roared.

Lauren came barging into Edgefield's with two longtime friends, Amy Hertzinger and Kayla Walker. Lauren hardly went to this bar, where the crowd was a bit older, but it was a rare night. She was off from work the next day, Jimmy had a meeting downtown with a new club owner, she had no gig, and she hadn't seen Amy or Kayla in months. They had been to several bars in East Nashville, and Edgefield's just happened to be another one they were walking past. The trio hadn't planned on getting into costume, but Amy, on her way out the door from work at a large construction firm, tossed a few hard hats, orange and yellow work vests, a few tools, and some tool belts into her car. A few fake mustaches from a local costume store coupled with some tequila shots, and they were ready to go.

The women just caught the last call and were enjoying their drinks. It was late, and a few men wandered about, desperate to find a pick-up before closing time. Some tried hitting on the construction trio, but once a woman is in her mid-twenties, her many prior experiences give her an ability to rebuff advances better than a missile defense system. Lauren and friends were feeling no pain, and with whatever brain function she had left, she realized it was about time to head home. A minute later, Amy put an end to that thought. Squinting on account of the large crowd, the light, and the alcohol, she asked, "Hey, isn't that Jimmy over there?"

Lauren and Kayla looked in the same direction as Amy but couldn't quite ascertain the same observation. "Can't be," Lauren said. "It must be someone that looks kinda like him. Jimmy's downtown on Second Avenue."

"Well, if it's someone that kinda looks like Jimmy," Amy said, "the guy looks more like him than him."

Lauren stepped past a woman dressed as an ear of corn for a clearer look. Sure enough, sitting near the pool table, was unmistakably Jimmy. Even though he was dressed in what looked like some sort of superhero outfit, Lauren recognized his familiar gestures as he spoke to a woman dressed in a pink flamingo outfit. A pink flamingo with a nice cleavage. Lauren's mind seemed to erupt into many directions, like fireworks exploding over the Cumberland River. What about his meeting downtown? Was it canceled? Why hadn't he told her? Who was he talking to? What was with the costume? Yeah, who was he talking to? The ladies were not sure what was going on, but all three knew something was.

"Maybe we should just leave," Kayla said. "We're all a little toasted. I know I'm not thinking very straight right now."

If Lauren heard Kayla's suggestion, she didn't acknowledge it. She proceeded to walk in a straight line toward Jimmy as if the bar held just him and her.

"Oh, this is going to beat going home to watch James Corden," Amy blurted to Kayla.

Jimmy did not notice the individual walking in his direction. It may have been the mask he was wearing, a la Ninja Turtle, which made his peripheral vision not up to snuff. Or maybe it was the conversation he was engaged in, detailing his work in the music biz to an enraptured listener.

Lauren spoke first, though not much. "Hey."

When Jimmy turned his eyes upward to the voice, there was a moment's delay before the vision in front of him connected to his brain. The face didn't match the voice. But then it did. He wanted to stand up, but it seemed that someone just put a piano on his chest. "Hi! I didn't think I would see you at Edgefield's."

"Obviously."

Jimmy vainly tried to defuse. "Lauren, this is Faye. Faye, Lauren."

Lauren forced a quick smile toward the flamingo and then turned her attention back to her superhero. "I thought you had a meeting downtown?"

"I did. It was cancelled. So I figured I would go out since it was Halloween and all."

"Didn't feel like giving me a call?"

"You told me you were going out with some friends. A girls' night."

Lauren thought about giving Jimmy an inch but decided against it. In retrospect, she somehow knew this was coming. "Ah, OK. That seems to make sense…if I was brain dead."

The flamingo decided that the room was getting a bit too warm. She told Jimmy it was great talking to him, gave a brief smile and nod to Lauren, and left to join her friends talking to brothers dressed like the Black Keys. Neither Lauren nor Jimmy acknowledged her leaving.

"By the way, who or what are you dressed as?" Lauren asked.

"Excuse me?"

Lauren pointed up and down at Jimmy. He was wearing brown pants, a brown shirt, a brown bedsheet for a cape, and an eye mask. "Who are you supposed to be? The costume?"

Jimmy breathed a sigh of relief. It seemed to him that Lauren might not be as upset as he first thought. "Oh. I didn't have a lot to work with." Jimmy smiled. "I'm Night Owl from the Watchmen comics."

Lauren nodded. "Ah, for a minute there, I thought you were just a giant piece of shit." She turned and walked away.

Jimmy managed to get up and cut in front of Lauren just before she reached Amy and Kayla, neither of whom had blinked since this episode started. "Lauren, I think you are way overreacting."

Lauren's face reddened. "Am I? Really? I walk in here to find that you weren't where you told me you were going to be, dressed up like who the hell knows what, talking to some woman. You knew I was out for Halloween; I presume your cell phone was working. I can tell you mine was, but it didn't ring."

"OK, you're right. I should have called. It was just a spur of the moment thing. And I know it looks a little bad, but I came in for a drink and just met that girl a few minutes before you came over."

Lauren showed a slight grin and placed her hands on her hips. "You must think I am really goddamn stupid. Who gets dressed up in a costume to just have a drink? I think it is even worse that you did that and met some chick for the first time than if you went behind my back with someone you'd been seeing. Think about it. You would rather go out by yourself and talk to strangers than see if I were around—which you know I was."

Jimmy shook his head. "It's not like that. I...." Before Jimmy could finish, the music stopped and the lights came on. A general moan came from the crowd.

Lauren held up her hand in front of Jimmy. "Please, no more. I'm going home." Lauren moved past Jimmy to Amy and Kayla, who closed ranks and escorted Lauren outside.

"Are you OK?" Kayla asked.

"I don't know," Lauren said. "It's such a messed-up situation with him."

"Hey, frankly I think that was awesome," Amy said. "Jimmy had that coming for a long time."

Kayla looked at Amy and started laughing.

"What, that's funny?" Amy said.

Even Lauren had started to laugh.

"What the fuck guys?" Amy said. "Am I missing something?"

Apparently during the crush out the door, Amy's fake mustached had fallen off and stuck on her crotch. Amy looked down to where the others pointed, shrugged, and they proceeded laughing down the street.

PERFECTION, PERSEVERANCE & ANGST

Bobby went to the Topgolf driving range to hit some balls. Back in the day, he used to be a member of the Belle Meade Country Club, the ritzy course where all the bankers and music executives played the game of staying atop the social ladder. The club was another thing he had to give up after the divorce; he simply couldn't afford it any longer. Bobby was never any good at the game, but it always helped relieve his tension. He didn't mind the driving range. Topgolf had come a long way since back in the day when the only amusement was trying to hit the poor bastard in the cage-covered cart picking up the balls. Now they had multilevel, climate-controlled tee boxes. Not to mention, you could grab a cocktail and some cigarettes while hitting. Sometimes they even had live music. It sure beat riding a bicycle at the gym, although that was something that never had entered Bobby's mind.

With a beer in one hand, a basket of white-dimpled orbs in the other, and a Camel between his lips, Bobby took the stairs to his usual hitting bay. He pulled out a five iron from his well-worn golf bag and began swinging. No warmup necessary. Thwack! The ball sailed up and out in an arc that reminded him of the Roman candles he used to hold and fire as a kid. On those Fourth of Julys, the Linders were part of an annual multiblock party in their small, mostly middle-class town of White House, about twenty miles outside of Nashville. The parents would spend days prior preparing fried chicken, ribs, biscuits and gravy, corn bread, and various family specialties. Everyone would feast, and then the parents would settle in with some bourbon or spiked tea while the kids were given various fireworks to go play with and cigarettes to light them. It was quite a sight, adults sinking into a comfortable state of stupor while ten-year-olds ran around puffing on cigarettes and shooting off fireworks into the air or at each other. The sounds and sights of summer in middle Tennessee.

Thwack! Bobby's mind eased with each swing. He didn't think about the fact that he hadn't seen either of his kids in over a year or how he could help Emily with her new apartment. Thwack! He didn't think about Eddie, Lauren, or the fact that he could not find a way to get back into the music business. Thwack! He certainly didn't think about Sarah, the fact that he was alone and hadn't had sex with anyone but himself in a long time. Thwack! All he thought about as the cool fall breeze whispered over him was getting the little object into the air, straight and far. Ignorant bliss. Sometimes it is OK.

Lauren woke to her phone vibrating. Due to her inebriation the night before, she wasn't sure, but she thought this was not the first time her phone had gone off that morning. She grabbed the jeans she had taken off just a few hours earlier and pulled the phone from the back pocket. It was Jimmy. Everything from the previous evening at Edgefield's came flooding back in an instant, startling her from semi-consciousness to acute awareness. She tossed the phone onto her bed and fell back onto the pillow. Screw him, she thought. Running around town in the stupidest costume ever while flirting with other women when he knew she was free. Not even a frigging call. He looked happy too. The phone vibrated again. Lauren put the pillow over her head for a moment and then pulled it off. She grabbed the phone and sent a text to Jimmy. "Stop calling me. If I wanted to talk to you, I would have answered the phone the first time. The tenth time is not going to make a difference."

Jimmy texted back. "But I think we should talk. I am sorry if I upset you. But I think you are misinterpreting an awful lot. Call me. PLEASE."

Lauren almost went down the rabbit hole. Maybe she had overreacted. She did have a lot to drink, and she had told him she was going out with friends. Now that they were both sober, maybe she should at least give him another chance to explain what happened last night. But then Lauren got that feeling in her stomach, that rare feeling you get once in a while when you sense the absolute truth of a situation. Something just wasn't right. The more she thought about it, she wasn't sure if it ever was. Lauren texted him back. "I am not calling you. I am not texting you. Just leave me the hell alone. If you bother me one more time, I'm going on Facebook to tell everyone you have a tattoo of Minnie Mouse on your ass."

When Jimmy was a freshman in college, he joined a fraternity. On the final night of pledging, it was customary for each new member to get a tattoo of the fraternity's Greek letters on the outside of their right thigh. Jimmy drank too much and passed out prior to the tattoo ritual. As a result, the other members decided to give him a slightly different permanent remembrance of the evening. Needless to say, as to Lauren's last text, there was no reply from Jimmy.

Lauren lay back on her bed, staring at the ceiling. Tears were welling up in her eyes, and she tried to stop them. She hated feeling sorry for herself. It was all in vain. Lauren tossed the covers and her pillows onto the floor, curled up into a ball, and stayed like that well into the afternoon.

After Bobby finished the bucket of golf balls, he went downstairs to get another beer and sat outside on a bench to enjoy the unseasonably warm weather for the first day in November. A single black ant scurried across his shoe. Bobby wondered where it was going all by itself. His Motorola flip phone rang. He hesitated to answer, because if it was his ex-wife, he knew it would be a complete blow to his current relaxed mental state. He looked at the number and did not recognize it. Bobby thought it might be spam, but the phone rang too often to ignore. "Hello." For a moment there was silence. If this was a robocaller, Bobby was ready to hit him with every curse word known to man and maybe a few newly invented. "Hello?" he repeated.

"Oh, uh, hi. Is this Bobby Linder?" A female voice.

"What do you want?" Bobby said, barely containing his annoyance.

"This is Lauren Culiver. You saw me play at East Park and came to my show at The 5 Spot."

Bobby stood up. His voice became calmer. "Oh, yes! Hi, Lauren. Sorry, I thought you were a sales call. Of course I remember. Your manager didn't seem happy that I was at your show."

Lauren remembered Jimmy had been less than enthralled meeting Bobby. "Yeah, he's like that. That's one of the reasons I'm calling."

"How did you get my number?"

"I Googled it."

"You actually found my cell phone number on Google?"

"There is little about you I couldn't find. I saw you really did write for all those stars."

"Note to self. I need to Google me."

Lauren let out a short laugh. "I was wondering if some day you would have time for a cup of coffee. With your experience, I would love to pick your brain."

"Of course. But don't pick my brain too hard. Not sure if there is much left."

"I'll try not to. When would be a good time for you?"

Bobby looked at his almost finished beer. "Time is all I got, hon. Why don't you pick it?"

"How about Bongo East tomorrow morning around ten? I don't have to go to work until the afternoon."

"Perfect. Is there anything you want to focus on?"

Lauren thought for a moment. "Just help make me a superstar. I want to be the next Emmylou Harris."

"Ah, I see we are aiming low! See you tomorrow at ten. Oh, there is one thing I want you to think about."

"What might that be?" Lauren asked.

"Let me know what the best thing about you is and what you think is the worst. It does not necessarily have to be related to your music."

"Why?"

"You want my help, right?"

"Yes."

"Then let me ask the questions."

Bobby couldn't leave Topgolf fast enough. He couldn't believe his luck. He had a gut feeling about Lauren's potential from the first time he saw her play, but after the conversation with Jimmy at The 5 Spot, Bobby thought it was just another wasted hope. He didn't know what had happened between Lauren and Jimmy, and he didn't care. Life puts you in situations, some good and some bad. Sometimes you have that choice, and sometimes you don't. Bobby learned long ago that you deal with it, one way or another. He'd won this coin toss. The key was to make the most of it. It would take some thought.

As soon as Bobby got home, he went over to some shelves near the television in the living room containing books, files, knickknacks, and a few empty beer bottles. He pulled out two binders and a few files that contained songs, some finished and some incomplete. It was a real mishmash. A few were neatly typed while others were quickly scrawled with a pen, pencil, or marker. Some were written on lined paper. Others on napkins and even one on a used paper plate. These were unused songs Bobby had written going back to his days at Belmont. Bobby poured a deep glass of bourbon and spent the next few hours reviewing the songs. Some he crumpled up and threw into a corner, confused why he even considered saving them, but there was a small handful he put into a pile for consideration. He read those over twice more and cut the pile in half each time. Still seeking a song that might work for Lauren, he came up blank. He grabbed a pen and envelopes from unopened bills. Bobby went into his kitchen and sat down at the table. It was the first time he had tried to write a song in more than ten years. He sat there for over four hours. He got through one complete song and parts of two others. They weren't great, but they weren't bad. But that wasn't really the point. The valve had been reopened. It might take a while, but the good stuff was bound to come out.

Next, he gave some thought to what type of band should be behind Lauren. He hoped he still had enough goodwill, if not juice, to get some of the good musicians he still knew to back her up. On the short list were a drummer, bass guitarist, keyboard and piano player, and a fiddler, of course. He couldn't write quickly enough. Then he stopped. Maybe he was getting ahead of himself. All she'd said was that she wanted to sit down for a cup of coffee. Bobby leaned back on his couch and took a long sip of his third glass of bourbon. He looked up at the ceiling. He knew he did not have a lot of shots left. Bobby remembered that Lauren did say that she wanted Bobby to make her a superstar. "Fuck it," Bobby mumbled to himself. He sat back up and continued working until morning.

After a brief nap, he shaved for the first time in a few days and put on jeans, a button down shirt, and the boots he had bought from Lauren. He searched in his dresser and found the Rolex he hadn't worn since his divorce. In his closet on the top shelf, alone, was his black, fur felt Stetson cowboy hat. He wore it only on special occasions but decided this qualified. Bobby pulled it off the shelf, put his nose to the felt, and inhaled. He went to a mirror and positioned it on his head, careful to make sure it was perfectly centered.

Bobby decided to walk the half mile from his house to Bongo East, which was near the Five Points area of East Nashville. The trees were just at the end of their full autumn colors, and his feet crunched against the leaves that had already surrendered to their final fate. It was a bit cooler than normal, and Bobby loved how fresh and clean everything seemed.

When Bobby got to Bongo East, Lauren was there, and she waved to him from her table. Lauren already had her coffee and a bagel with blueberry cream cheese. After a quick hello, Bobby grabbed a black coffee and returned.

Lauren hurriedly swallowed a bite of her bagel. "Hey, thanks for meeting with me."

"Of course. Thanks for asking me."

Lauren smiled and shrugged. "OK. So, what do we do next?"

Bobby looked down at his coffee and laughed. "Remember what I said?"

Lauren thought for a moment. "Let you ask the questions?"

"Exactly. Before we know what to do next, it's important we know where we need to start. Did you give any thought to my questions?"

Lauren leaned back in her chair and folded her arms across her chest. "Yes, and it wasn't easy."

Bobby looked at her, slightly amused. "Well?"

"Which one do you want me to start with?"

"The worst thing about you."

"I have to pluck hair around my nipples."

Bobby laughed. "Let's be serious."

"Hey, if you ever plucked hair around your nipples, you would know how serious it is! But OK, I think the worst thing about me is I never can let things go. I wish I could. I've tried all my life, but it's no use. If something is bothering me, I can't get past it."

"So?" Bobby said. "A lot of people are like that."

Lauren looked at Bobby sternly. "I mean ever. Once a really popular girl in my high school told me that my ponytail made me look like the cartoon character Twilight Sparkle. To this day, I have never worn a ponytail again. If I screw up a song onstage, I can't sleep that night, and sometimes I will think of that performance weeks later and have trouble sleeping again." Lauren shook her head. "And if it involves someone I really care about, like a friend or boyfriend, forget it. I replay almost every word of each discussion over and over to see what is possibly wrong." Lauren looked at Bobby's blank face. "What? I bet you think I am nuts."

"No. No, I don't. We can use that. Songwriters and performers who have a lot inside, especially angst, can use that to their advantage. The more you can break through to your audience's feelings versus just having them listen, the more successful you will be. Think of your favorite songs. Most of them will be ones that bring back a memory or produce an emotion."

Lauren spun her coffee cup around in her hands. "Well, I am glad this angst or whatever you want to call it may be good for something other than taking a few years off my life."

Bobby chuckled. "Now, what is the absolute

best thing about Lauren Culiver?"

"My periods are shorter than average."

"Again, let's be serious, please."

"I am serious. If you were a woman, you would be very jealous of that fact."

Bobby waited.

Lauren reluctantly continued, her voice growing more serious. "All right. Not easy for me. With all my angst, I do not usually think about how great I am. But I did put a lot of thought into it. I narrowed it down to two possibilities. Is that OK?"

"It depends. What are they?"

Lauren took a deep breath and leaned forward. "First, I am never satisfied until whatever I am working on is perfect. Second, when I want something, I mean really want something, I will not stop until I get it."

"That is incongruent."

Lauren looked puzzled. "Come again?"

"You can never be perfect. If you think like that, you will never succeed. You can be excellent. You can be great, and you can pursue perfection, but you can't be perfect. Maybe there are brief moments of perfection but not on a consistent basis. Many of my songs that have become hits, I look back on them and think it would have been better if I used this phrase rather than that, or the musical arrangement could have used another horn or more bass in the guitar. Striving for perfection is OK. But not letting go of something because it isn't perfect will always be a problem. You can always improve something."

"Now I am completely confused." Lauren sat back in her chair, arms crossed.

"Have you ever heard of the law of diminishing

returns?" Bobby asked.

"No. I guess I dropped out of college before they got to that."

"It refers to the point at which the benefit gained by trying to improve something is less than the amount of energy or money invested in it."

Lauren brushed back her hair. "Would it be like why I told Jimmy to get lost because the amount of effort needed to work on the relationship probably would not be worth the result?"

"Something like that, I guess." Bobby adjusted his Stetson. "I like the fact that you say when you want something, you keep at it until you attain it. I saw that in you the first time we met, in the boot store, and when you performed in the park. That's good. The music industry is a killer business. Sometimes even the best get crushed. You need to know how to get back up again and again. Now we can use your striving for perfection because it will make you consistently look to be better. But you need someone to tell you when enough is enough. Combine that with turning your angst into a positive, and we may be onto something." Bobby took a sip of his coffee.

Lauren got up, came around the table, and stood next to Bobby. Bobby was puzzled. "What are you doing?"

"Well, if we have to put together my angst, perfectionism, and unstoppable perseverance, we can't sit around here all day, now can we?"

BECCA

The times changed depending on work schedules, gigs, and the like, but for the two weeks following their discussion at Bongo East, Lauren and Bobby met every day. Bobby called in a chit from an old friend, Clint Higanbottom, an artist manager at Warner Music Nashville, who allowed them unlimited use of a conference room, even giving them an access card so they could get in after hours. At first, they didn't go into specifics, just hours upon hours of discussion on the direction Lauren wanted to take her music, her writing skills, and the image she wanted to project. They decided that she needed to incorporate much more of her own music when she played, and it had to be top notch. Lauren showed Bobby some songs she had been working on, and he was more than a bit impressed. Bobby thought the tone and composition of the music would be critical.

As for image, Lauren insisted on just being herself. "OK," Bobby replied. "And who is Lauren Culiver?"

"I guess it depends on the day of the week and what is going on in my life."

"Exactly, and that is why everyone needs an image. As your fan base grows, they expect certain things from you. No one goes to see Metallica to hear love songs. You need to be consistent. You can change over time like a Dylan or a Prine, but that is a long process. On a day to day or even year to year basis, a lot of what you do onstage and in song has to be consistent."

"Sounds pretty boring to me," Lauren moaned as she took a bite of a doughnut she stole from the coffee room.

"Don't confuse repetition with consistency. Have you ever seen Bruce Springsteen?"

"Do I look like I live under a rock? Who hasn't seen The Boss?"

Bobby put his elbow on the table and his chin on his fist. "Well, if you were to describe his show, what would you say?"

She stood up and gave her best Springsteen imitation. "'It's heart-stopping, pants-dropping, hard-rocking, booty-shaking, love-making, earth-quaking, Viagra-taking, justifying, death-defying, and legendary.' "

Bobby laughed. "Very good. I guess you notice he mentions it at all his shows. You want to know something? I heard him say that at his shows before you were even on this earth.

In the end, he is known as a pure, hard driving rock and roller in blue jeans and a T-shirt. But he has done ballads, country, acoustic, folk, and even Irish songs with great success. But when people think of him, they think of that rock and roller in the blue jeans and T-shirt.

"I think what you are trying to say more or less is that you have to crawl before you can walk."

"Exactly!" Bobby said, slapping the table. "Basically, let's try to stay in a lane at first, and when we get a lead, then we can move a bit to the left or right."

"But I'm not exactly sure what my image should be."

"It's already in you," Bobby said. "We just need to pull it out."

One morning, a women Lauren had never seen before walked into the conference room unannounced. She appeared to be in her late fifties, red hair blown out a bit excessively, even redder lipstick over quite a bit of makeup. Even so, there was something attractive about her. She wore a silver Star of David necklace over a gold lame blouse and black bell-bottomed slacks with gold high heels. Before Lauren had a chance to fully take it all in, the woman held out her arms and said, "Bobby Linder, you old, raggedy ass sonofabitch! Get over here and give me a hug." She smiled a warm smile as Bobby jumped up and complied, even giving her a quick squeeze on her backside. The woman made a show of slapping Bobby's hand away and turned to Lauren. "This hound dog has been trying to get in there ever since I was a young lass."

"Becca," Bobby said, "this is the young lady I was telling you about, Ms. Lauren Culiver. Lauren, this is Rebecca Silverman. Known to everyone simply as Becca."

Before Lauren had a chance to respond, Becca walked over and gave her frozen face a kiss on the cheek, the smell of Black Orchard perfume overwhelming Lauren's senses. "So good to finally meet you. Bobby talked about you in such high terms I just couldn't wait."

Lauren looked from Becca and Bobby. "Pardon

me, but I am completely confused."

Bobby jumped in. "Becca is the maker of stars. Shania Twain was a struggling nobody in country music going into her thirties before she hooked up with Becca. Boom. Then the magic happened. Next thing you know, Twain is the best-selling female artist in country music history and one of the best-selling music artists of all time. And that is just one of many, many stories of her success."

Lauren looked at Becca, who just shrugged, nodded, and smiled. All Lauren managed to say was, "How?"

Becca sat down next to Lauren and grabbed her hand. "I am what is known as an image consultant, honey."

"Best in the business!" Bobby chimed in.

"Will you just hush now!" Becca exclaimed. Bobby put his fingers to his lips as Becca continued. "Look, Lauren. I didn't start out as a country music expert. I still ain't exactly one either. I grew up as a Jewish girl in the town of Brookline, just outside of Boston. Lucky if I could spell country. But I do have a bit of a gift, all us women do, of knowing what and how to please people. Sort of a gift and a curse, isn't it? I have been in the business for over thirty years, and with several superstars under my belt, I am still here."

"But why me?" Lauren said. "I certainly ain't no superstar, star, or even a planet for that matter."

Becca laughed and took hold of Lauren's hand. "Honey, I've known that pain in the butt across the table for an awfully long time. I can tell you one thing about him above all. He knows talent, and he knows how to make the most of that talent. He has produced records and written songs across a wide spectrum, but they fit just perfectly with the artists in question. Now I hadn't heard from our boy over here in a long time, but out of the blue he called me as excited as I have ever heard him. I just figured he either finally lost his mind or he is really onto something. So we will have to find out now, won't we?"

Lauren put her head back and laughed. "Why, Mr. Linder, you sure are something!"

Becca wasted little time. "I see you have your guitar with you." She pointed to a spot in the middle of the room. "Why don't you stand over there and let me hear something?"

"Now?"

"Good a time as any."

"Can I just stay seated here?"

"Do you sit down when you play a gig?"

"No."

"Then no. You can't sit down. My job is to make you look good. The less guessing I must do, the better. If you stand while you play for a crowd, then I need to see how you stand. I need to see where your eye contact is, what your hair looks like, what would look good on you, are you blinking too much, and so on and so forth."

"I get it. I get it." Lauren got up and grabbed her guitar in the corner. "Any requests?"

Becca thought for a moment. "How about Sara Evans's 'Born to Fly'"?

Lauren nodded, tuned her guitar, took a deep breath, and began the song with its ten second intro, which in Evans's version is a single drum tapping the same beat Lauren tapped on the body of her guitar before starting the lyrics. Lauren had always liked the song but previously never paid much mind to the words. Not only did she realize how good they were, but they spookily applied to her present situation. She wondered if Becca somehow knew this. As she played, she looked at Bobby and Becca but couldn't get a read on their reactions. They were staring at her intently, as if she were telling them something tragic had happened to a member of their family. Just concentrate on the song, Lauren thought, just the song. Lauren closed her eyes and sang. She thought about Evans's lyrics, the impatience, wanting to do more now, and how waiting was not an option. Tired of the shoe store job and playing gigs that sometimes cost her more than she got paid. Hell, yeah! She was born to fly!

When Lauren finished, there was a moment of silence. Then Becca turned to Bobby and said, "I certainly can see what you do." She turned back to Lauren. "You have talent, young lady. Let's see if we can get the world to know."

For the next two hours, Becca had Lauren play the same song over ten times. Each time, Becca had Lauren focus on one thing—how to hold the guitar, moving around the stage, eye contact, smiling, being angry, being loose, and being sexy.

"I don't want to be judged on being sexy as part of my performance," Lauren said.

"Honey, with a beautiful body like yours, you really have no choice," Becca said.

Bobby nodded in agreement.

Around noon, Becca suggested they go out for lunch. Bobby said that he wanted to stay behind because he was working on getting some studio musicians together for a session with Lauren, but he urged them to go without him. Becca and Lauren took the short walk from the Warner studio to the Union Common Restaurant on Broadway. The manager, a short, well dressed, heavyset man slightly older than Lauren's new acquaintance, greeted Becca right away, giving her an exaggerated kiss on the cheek; he seemed genuinely glad to see her. Becca asked for a private spot, and the manager sat them in a high-backed booth away from the bar and most of the other tables. Becca ordered a Manhattan, but Lauren, though desperate for something to calm her nerves, decided it best not to join in for appearance's sake and asked for ice water.

Lauren started to comment on how cool the restaurant looked, but Becca cut her off. "So tell me, what is going on with you?"

Lauren sat back in her seat. "So much for chitchat, I guess."

"Honey, if you want some chitchat, I host a poker game every third Friday of the month. But bring some coin, because the table isn't free. Right now, my job is to help Bobby figure out what to do with you."

Lauren nodded. "OK, what do you want to know?"

Becca took a sip of her drink. "Well, for starters, what makes you tick? What do you want? What bothers you?"

"Essentially, I guess, I really enjoy singing. When I do it, I feel whole."

"Why?"

"Why?" Lauren let out a short laugh. "Let's see. I work in a shoe store, I am basically broke all the time, I am not in any sort of relationship, and I can't get my hair to stay straight.”

"It's an escape for you?”

"Maybe. But I think it's more than that. Even if I ran my own business, had money, was married to the greatest guy in the world, and possessed the best hair in Nashville, I still would enjoy singing the most.”

Becca smiled. "That's good. Because even if you make it in this business, there is more bullshit than you can imagine. If you do it for any other reason than making music, then in the long run, it will bring you down hard, and I do mean hard, physically, emotionally, and mentally—regardless of how much money you make.” Becca lit a cigarette, which caused a little concern to Lauren because she was certain this was a smoke free establishment. Becca continued, nonplussed. "You mentioned relationships and referred to marrying a great guy. Yet you seem to give off a bit of a lesbian vibe when you sing.”

Lauren's eyes widened. "What? I am not gay! Or at least I never thought I was!” Then she added, "Not that it is a bad thing. I live above a lesbian bar, for Christ's sake. Play there sometimes. Nice people.”

"Well, there you go. They must have rubbed off on you more than you realize.” Becca raised her hands to her face, moving her fingers rapidly. "Maybe lesbian fumes went through the vents to your apartment, changing you.”

"Very funny.”

"Seriously, though, there are plenty of female gay listeners, which is fine. Gayness does not distinguish between music genres. The problem is there are not a lot of lesbian country artists. Not nearly as popular as in rock or pop.” The pair was interrupted by the waiter. Lauren ordered a chicken salad and Becca a club sandwich. Becca continued. "Anyway, you are a very pretty girl, and regardless of talent, it is a bullet we need to use, be it for the pole or the hole."

"Wow, you don't hold back," Lauren said.

"Personally, I don't have time for it."

After some additional conversation about Lauren's plus and minuses, Becca thought it only fair that Lauren learn a little more about herself. Growing up, she hated that she was an only child with overbearing parents living in an entirely Jewish orthodox community. "Could the men do anything more to make themselves look less attractive?" She was in the first class of women at Columbia. " I was a virgin when I went in but not when I left, unlike many of my colleagues at Barnard." Her first job was with McKinsey, but they only let her go on calls with a male who always got team lead. "Yet, despite clear obstacles to not having one, and contrary to Mr. Freud, I never desired to have a penis." At the end of her second year, when a guy in her group got the largest bonus, winning a huge client with her idea, she quit. "Like Bobby's former partner, Eddie Fonatana, after college I got hired to travel around to radio stations in New York trying to get them to play certain records. Sometimes it was as easy as tipping the deejays a few shekels or maybe showing a little leg, but every once in a while, and it was a rare once in a while, I would come across a radio station owner or significant deejay who really cared about the music and the person behind it. I liked them the best. With those folks, I only promoted those performers I really thought had the right stuff, and I was usually right. I started to figure out what worked and what didn't work. Next thing I know, I fall for some hick record executive up from Nashville trying to promote country music in the big city. He failed miserably, but I followed him back to Nashville, where he recognized all my talent and got me a job promoting up and coming local musicians. I took to that like a fat man to a cheesesteak. I was exceptionally good at reading people and being able to promote their strengths. Soon record companies started to see how the adjustments I made to newcomers really helped them to the next level. Where with a lot of hard work, and not just a few sharp elbows, this little Jewish girl from New England became the image maker in Music City helping to shape country music."

Lauren and Becca laughed their way through the rest of lunch. Lauren was happy because she knew Becca was the real deal. Becca was happy because she knew Bobby was right: Lauren had something there. Besides, they both were starting to really like each other.

THE AMAZON OF DELIVERY

Eddie Fontana sat in his doctor's waiting room getting more upset by the minute. His appointment was for 8:30, and he was still waiting to be called at 9:10. These cocksuckers thought no one else had anything to do. He'd given this bastard front row tickets to Trace Atkins at the Ryman a few months back when he'd called. Give me another request, motherfucker, see how that works out, Eddie thought.

Eddie was more than a bit uptight. He'd noticed he had been forgetting things lately. Not just where he parked his car, but what kind of car he had in the first place. Two weeks ago, he forgot how to drive home from work, something he had been doing from the same location for twenty-seven years. He managed to find his way back to Sidewalk Music and did not recall the route home until he awoke on his office couch at three in the morning. Scared the hell out of him, as did the tests his doctor had ordered. Last time he was there, he'd taken some sort of test where he was asked a bunch of questions supposedly to evaluate his mental skills. They wouldn't tell him his score but did suggest an MRI of his brain over at Vanderbilt hospital. Eddie got a call yesterday asking him to come into the doctor's office for the results. He didn't sleep all night.

A thirty something, overweight, redheaded nurse in blue scrubs walked into the waiting room. "Mr. Fontana?"

"As far as I know." Eddie wondered why the

same nurse asked him this same question every time he came to the office.

"This way, please." Once again, Eddie wondered, as there was no other way to go. But instead of leading him into an examination room, she led him into the doctor's office, a sprawling and surprisingly messy room of mahogany shelves filled with medical books, journals, and papers. Eddie's heart beat a little faster. This was not normal. Who likes not normal?

"Please have a seat. Dr. Larson will be in shortly. He is just finishing up another examination."

Eddie nodded and sat down in one of the worn leather chairs facing the doctor's desk. There were a couple of expensive looking airplane models on a shelf, which Eddie thought was a bit odd. On another shelf was a picture of the doctor with what Eddie assumed to be his wife, apparently on vacation. Eddie guessed it was Tuscany because of the cypress trees in the background. Eddie had been there years ago on a honeymoon with his second wife, a marriage that didn't last much longer than a one hit wonder. There was also a picture of the doctor's three children on his desk. Eddie could not help but notice the large gap in the front teeth of his middle child, a daughter of about fifteen. Eddie wondered why a doctor would let his daughter walk around with a space that you felt like putting your finger in to plug it up. He hoped they got the kid fixed. There was a fine line between sexy a la Lauren Hutton and looking like you had a tooth knocked out. They'd be using her mouth as a bicycle rack. Eddie chuckled at his own joke. Just then the doctor walked in with a file in his hand.

"Good morning, Mr. Fontana. How are you?"

Eddie felt uneasy; the doctor's tone of voice was lower and slower than normal.

"I don't know, doc. Why don't you tell me?"

The doctor sat down in his chair behind the desk and got right to the point. Looking through his horn-rimmed mahogany glasses, he said, "Not great, Mr. Fontana, I am afraid. I still want to verify by sending you back to Vanderbilt Medical to a neurologist for further evaluation. But from what we have seen so far, I think you may be in stage two for dementia on the Reisberg Scale."

When describing this moment later, Eddie always referred to it as an out-of-body experience. As if he were in the corner of the room watching the doctor deliver the news to someone he didn't know. It wasn't as though there was no feeling. It was more of a cold numbness. After a moment, Eddie heard himself try to be lighthearted. "Stage two? What happened to stage one?"

The doctor had absolutely no change in demeanor. "Well, in stage one, there is no impairment that can be detected. It can be confusing, I know. In addition, it is a bit of a misnomer, because you really do not have dementia at all. There are actually seven stages. The first three stages of the scale are just a precursor. It is not until stage four that one is considered to have what is called early-stage dementia. Then, over time, the disease gradually accelerates in the body in the final stages to mid, middle, and late-stage dementia.

Eddie felt a sorrow for the doctor having to deliver such bad news, as he'd probably done so many times before. It was probably why he sounded so detached. One would have to be unless you were one cold son of a bitch. Eddie felt lightheaded, and his mouth felt like a sandpit. He asked for a glass of water, and the doctor pulled a bottle out of a small refrigerator near his desk.

"You wouldn't happen to have any bourbon to go with this, would you, doc?"

Without smiling, the doctor shook his head.

"OK, now for the sixty-four-million-dollar question." Eddie took a deep breath. "How much time do I have?"

"That's a tough question. In general, most patients do not die from the disease itself. It is more the result of factors of the disease like not eating or the inability to cope with physical problems or infections."

With a little less patience, Eddie asked, "OK, then, I guess what I need to know is how long before I don't know what is going on?"

"Again, a precise answer is difficult. In most cases, it takes five to nine years for a stage two individual to reach stage five, which is where you would have major memory deficiencies such as where you are, where you live, phone number, things like that. But the period can be drastically different for each individual case. In later stages, you would also need help with daily activities such as eating and dressing. I can give you some reading information that goes into detail on all the stages."

Eddie did not hear the last sentence. "I am just in stage two, and there are stages that are worse? Jesus Christ!" Eddie got up from his chair. The doctor, now more than a bit unnerved, said he would get the dementia reading materials. When the doctor returned to the room, Eddie was nowhere to be found.

Bobby had not felt this good in a long time. Lauren and Becca had hit it off and were a good fit to work together. He was also beginning to round up some top studio musicians who agreed to work with Lauren from time to time in the studio and maybe at some small shows, either as a long-ago favor owed to Bobby or as a gamble on bigger reimbursement if something actually hit. In addition, he had been working on some original songs with Lauren. Bobby could see she was an incredibly talented songwriter. This was good because he also realized in working with her that he was too out of touch to write a song in today's world. Loretta Lynn once said that good songs are about truth because a lot of people are living that. More people were living Lauren's life than his.

Bobby stopped into Edgefield's. He had not been there since the robbery attempt. Lucy and the rest of the regular misfits were happy to see him. Lucy gave him the first beer and shot on the house. He had a few more. A man walked in who Bobby had never seen before. He was a stocky, short fellow wearing horned rim glasses and sporting a bushy, light brown mustache just beginning to turn gray that matched the few strands left on the top of his head. He was wearing a tan khaki shirt that seemed a bit too small, and he walked with a slight limp. He sat next to Bobby, giving him a nod. When Lucy came by, he ordered a beer and a cheeseburger. As the food arrived, Bobby asked the stranger if it would be OK if he smoked. The man replied, "I don't care if you burn." He gave out a chuckle, as did other patrons who overheard the remark. Bobby was debating whether to call the guy out when the stranger added, "Only joking, my friend. Better to laugh than cry, eh?" He reached into his pocket and pulled out a pack of Marlboros. "Here, have one of mine. Mind if I join you?"

"Two's a party," Bobby replied as he accepted a cigarette from his stool neighbor.

"Name is Frank Bartleby. Sorry for the quip if you were offended."

"Nope," Bobby lied. "Not sure I have seen you here before."

"You haven't. I'm from Atlanta. I sell medical supplies. Just came out of the Nashville Rehabilitation Hospital over there on Cleo Miller Drive. Thought I would stop in for a quick bite and a pop. Heading to Memphis next."

"That can't be easy. I mean all that traveling. Neither of us are young pups."

"Actually, I love it, man. I pretty much make my own schedule, and, not to sound like a dime store novel, but I really enjoy the open road."

Bobby nodded in agreement. "I get that. Must not be married, I guess."

"I was. Twice actually. First one left me because she said I wasn't around enough. Broke my heart, really. But we both knew I couldn't change. Second one was on account the wife found a picture of me in a compromising position in the backroom of a strip club."

"Wow. I guess I have three questions on that one. Who took the picture? Why in hell would you keep it? And, if I may also ask, why would you tell that story to a stranger you just met?"

"An old buddy of mine took it while I was on calls in Cincinnati. He's a crazy bastard. As for your second question, I thought about that a lot but, unfortunately, not until after my wife tore it up in my face. I can't decide on whether it was sheer stupidity, or, in the back of my mind, I wanted her to find it. Don't get me wrong; at first I was devastated. But how happy could I have been to be getting a steamer from a stranger in the back of a sleazy strip club and memorializing it?" Lucy came back with Frank's cheeseburger. He took a bite and continued. "I mean I am not a big believer in fate. You make your own fate."

Bobby slowly nodded. "You make your own fate. I like that. Problem is, now I have no one to blame for some of the calamities I've been through."

"Hey, man, it's just a part of life. But you can't focus on the bad stuff. Just on how to make things better when things are tough and enjoy the high moments when you get 'em." Frank looked at the food in his hands. "Jesus, this is a good burger."

"You sure have a glass half full view of life," Bobby said.

Frank put his burger down and wiped his hands on a napkin. "What is the benefit of looking at it any other way? I would rather have a false sense of happiness than a true feeling of dread. And in answer to your third question, I would think this story is safer in the hands of a stranger than an acquaintance. You will never see me again." Frank ordered another beer and asked Bobby if he could buy him one.

"I can't recall ever declining such an offer," Bobby said.

Frank signaled Lucy for a second beer and

continued. "What do you do, may I ask, or are you retired?"

Bobby took a last hit off his cigarette and spewed the smoke toward the ceiling. "I guess you can say I am semi-retired. I've been a song writer and producer here in Nashville since my college days."

"Did you ever work with Stephen Foster?" Frank asked.

Another smattering of laughter arose from the surrounding peanut gallery. Bobby leaned back on his stool. "Jesus, I didn't realize I was part of a comedy routine."

"No, seriously," Frank said, "that is really cool. Being part of the Nashville music scene. Bet it beats selling medical supplies."

Bobby pointed at Frank. "Glass half full, remember?"

"Touché."

Frank's quick pop lasted almost three hours as he and Bobby talked about everything from their divorces to the upcoming presidential election, wet versus dry rub on spareribs, and Hank Williams versus Bob Wills. The late afternoon sun peered through the front door when Frank said he had to go if he wanted to get to Memphis before dark, a feat Bobby knew was logistically impossible. Frank's undersized shirt now had the addition of a few ketchup stains. He shook Bobby's hand and thanked him for the conversation. He then suggested to Bobby that he should consider the words of Henry Thoreau: "Live in the present, launch yourself on every wave, and find your eternity in each moment." With that, Frank walked out the door, lifting his hand over and behind his head in a final salute to no one in particular.

Lucy walked over to where Bobby was sitting. "Well, that sure was one nut job."

Bobby looked at the door. "I'm not so sure, NP. I'm not so sure."

Lauren was not having one of her better days at work. First, she had a bit of a tiff with a customer who returned a pair of boots, saying that they didn't fit right. The problem for Lauren was they looked like the guy had just finished panning for gold in the Yukon. Then, while carrying four boxes of boots, she stumbled over a discarded boot on the floor. After a ten-foot stretch of attempting to keep her balance, she went sprawling across the floor, boxes and all, her face stopping just inches from a mirror where she saw her glossy dusty rose lipstick smeared across her face. Now, with just forty-five minutes left in the workday, she was working with a massively obese woman in a plaid house dress who was insisting on trying on boots that in truth wouldn't fit on her arm.

"Ma'am, I think we may want to try another style. I don't think these are going to look good on you," Lauren said politely while trying to stuff the customer's ham hock into the boot but not having much luck getting it past the ankle.

"But I have an old pair just like these at home," the woman replied without giving much assistance to Lauren's efforts.

Lauren thought the woman might be confusing the boots with a pair of waders, but she kept her calm. "I think they shrunk the calves of these boots over the years without letting anyone know," Lauren lied. The woman nodded in agreement. After unsuccessfully trying a few more boots, the woman settled on a pair of sandals.

On the way home, Lauren stopped at Publix and picked up a frozen pepperoni pizza and a bottle of diet herbal Dr. Enuf for dinner. Considering the type of day it had been, upon reaching home she found herself laughing over the fact that someone had parked in her reserved spot in the Lipstick Lounge parking lot. She parked in a far corner of the lot and, upon entering her apartment, heard a vibration coming through the floor from the bar. Lauren correctly guessed that it must be karaoke night. She poured herself a glass of pinot grigio and sat on the couch with her mail, which consisted of a postcard from a state legislature candidate she had never heard of, an electric bill, a coupon from Wendy's, and a catalogue from Lulu's clothing store. The heading on the catalogue said it contained "in style fashion trends in dresses and shoes for trendsetters worldwide." Lauren thought about it for a moment and doubted she was a trendsetter. After browsing through the catalogue, where the models were prettier than the clothes, she put the pizza in the oven and pulled out her guitar. She played nothing in particular as her mind drifted. She was getting a bit worried. Since she broke up with Jimmy, she really had not had many gigs. Her weekly gig at The 5 Spot was still there as long as she didn't aggravate the Commander, but she had always left the other bookings and confirmations to Jimmy. Now when she called up, they either asked what happened to Jimmy or didn't return her calls. She began to wonder if she was being blacklisted. In any event, she could have used the practice, and she certainly could have used the extra cash.

The phone rang; it was Bobby. He wanted to know if she had time to come over to Warner Studios to continue work on some songs. Lauren told Bobby she was exhausted from a long and miserable day and hadn't eaten yet. She could tell Bobby was disappointed. She felt bad knowing how much he was doing for her. "I have a pizza in the oven. Why don't you come over here, and we can work on them for a little while?"

"At your place? Sure that's OK? I don't want to intrude."

"What's the difference? We're just knocking around ideas. A seat is a seat."

"OK, I guess. What's your address? I know you said you live somewhere on the Woodland."

"You know the Lipstick Lounge?"

"The lesbian bar?"

"Yes, I'm in the apartment above it. The entrance is in the back. And before you ask, no I am not."

About a half hour later, Bobby appeared at her door. "You're just in time. I was about to eat the pizza without you," Lauren said. "I apologize for the mess. I haven't had time to clean the past few days."

"No worries. Makes my place look like a convent." Bobby looked at the floor. "Is that music coming from downstairs."

"Yup. Karaoke night." Lauren handed him a slice of pizza on a paper plate and a beer.

Lauren and Bobby spent the next few hours working on some songs. They had just about completed one called "Man Up or Stand Down," about a husband suspected of cheating by his wife. Lauren liked to play a speedy version on her guitar, but Bobby thought it needed to be slowed down. "We got some good lyrics here. Let the people have the time to hear 'em."

"Doesn't the singer have a choice in how to sing a song? Especially one she co-wrote?"

"Yes, but you also have to consider how it is going to blend in with the musical composition. Plus," Bobby added, "what makes you think I can't sing?"

"Oh, so you're a singer now?"

Bobby was unflustered. "I've been known to carry a tune or two back in the day."

"Oh, really?"

"Yes, really."

Lauren stood up and patted herself on her backside as if to wake herself up. "OK, Mr. Presley, let's go."

"Where?" Bobby asked, more than a little bewildered.

"To a proving ground." With that, Lauren grabbed Bobby's hand and led him downstairs.

The Lipstick Lounge was packed. Onstage, two women were singing karaoke to "Islands in the Stream." They were slightly above awful, but they seemed not to care. The crowd was overly generous in their applause. Bobby quickly figured out why they were there. "Oh, no. This is not happening," he yelled to Lauren above the din of the crowd.

"What happened to Mr. I've Been Known to Carry a Tune?"

"The key to that remark was 'back in the day!'" Another woman had come onstage and begun singing Miley Cyrus's "Wrecking Ball."

Lauren squirmed closer to Bobby's ear. "Come on, it'll be fun. One song each."

Bobby bit his lip and looked around. Gay men and lesbians never bothered him. He was in the music business and had plenty of friends of that persuasion. He just couldn't remember a situation in which he was the only straight person in a packed room. Especially one where he was a lot more sober than they were. He turned back to Lauren. "OK, you're on. One song each. Whoever gets the biggest cheer gets to decide the speed of 'Man Up or Stand Down.' Deal?"

Lauren didn't hesitate. "Heck, yeah." They both made their way through the crowd to the deejay booth. Bobby asked for the book of available songs and studied it closely. Lauren ordered two shots of Jack Daniels from a waitress who passed by. After about fifteen minutes and two shots later, Lauren asked Bobby, "Are we gonna sing or just stand here looking pretty?"

"Hey," Bobby said, "I am very particular about what I sing."

Lauren rolled her eyes.

"Ah," he said. "I found what I was looking for."

Lauren asked what it was, but Bobby did not reply as he pointed the page out to the deejay. Bobby then attempted to hand the book to Lauren.

"Nope, don't need it."

"Oh, a little cocky, don't you think? OK then, after you."

"Oh, no you don't, Bobby Linder. Tonight, you are my guest. You came to my apartment, drank my beer, and I treated you to some shots. You first."

Bobby took a deep breath. "OK, fine." He

turned to the deejay, who nodded and signaled that Bobby was next. A woman was just finishing the song "California Gurls." Bobby hopped onto what passed for a stage, but if it were any smaller, it would have qualified as a pedestal. Grabbing the microphone, Bobby surprised Lauren by beginning to speak before the deejay started the music. Bobby's initial "If I may have everyone's attention," was met with a few jeers and boos, but interest seemed to grow as he spoke.

"As most of you may have surmised, I am not a lesbian." Lauren's eyes grew wider. "In fact, I am not even gay." There were a few murmurs in the crowd, but for the most part, there was silence. "However, I'm not sure what happened when I walked in here. Something just came over me." Bobby pointed toward the deejay. "Maestro, if you please!" As the music started, Bobby opened with the initial lyrics, "Let's go girls, come on!" It was Shania Twain's "Man! I Feel Like a Woman." In the crowd, hands and fists were raised in the air with yells and howls of approval. Lauren broke into laughter and clapped along. Bobby's singing left a lot to be desired, but the crowd loved it, joining in unison with every oh, oh, oh. Bobby brought the house noise level up a notch when, during the jam portion of the song, he imitated Twain's exact moves in the video, including unbuttoning his shirt and showing his shoulders, playing with the microphone, and rubbing the brim of an imagined top hat. As the song ended, Bobby climbed off the stage to an extended ovation.

When he reached Lauren, she immediately asked through the din of the crowd, "Let me guess. You wrote that song, didn't you?"

"Nope." Bobby smiled. "Co-wrote."

Lauren smiled and shook her head. "Very clever."

"Sometimes it's not all in the message but the way it's delivered."

"Oh really? I will keep that in mind." Lauren had originally told the deejay she was going to sing Natalie Imbruglia's "Torn," a tune she had performed to receptive audiences in the past. However, she went back to the deejay and called an audible. Lauren hopped onstage, nodded to the deejay, and grabbed the microphone as if it were a lifeline out of quick moving waters. The tune was another Shania Twain song, "That Don't Impress Me Much." Even though Bobby had been working with Lauren for a couple of weeks, he was impressed by the power in her voice. She moved sinuously around the closet size stage as if it were a stadium. In the middle of the song, she jumped off the stage onto a table with the help of some of the women who were sitting there. She pulled off her white blouse to reveal a tan sports bra, not missing a beat. At this point, it seemed to Bobby that everyone in the bar was singing along. He joined in as well. At the close of the number, the crowd roared its approval. The crowd had liked Bobby as well, but he realized the tone was different. In Bobby's case, it was more of a "hey, you are clever and funny." In Lauren's case, it was "that was damn good." Lauren climbed down off the table, and in between pats on her back and smiles in her face, she made it back to Bobby. Out of breath, she asked, "How was that for delivering the message?"

Bobby nodded. "I must admit, yours was like Amazon Prime; mine was Pony Express all the way."

"I hope we don't use that in a song; that was

pretty corny."

As they walked out, Bobby couldn't be happier. You can give advice and suggestions day into night and night into day, but nothing beats instinct. And it was becoming clear and clearer that this girl had it in spades.

THE MEXICAN CONNECTION

Lauren had a conversation with Bobby about her need for some paying gigs. Initially, Bobby was a little perturbed. He was already putting in an enormous amount of time for no money working on songs, productions, and image. He had gotten them a nice place to work and people volunteering to help. The fact that Lauren let her personal life interfere with her booking manager had nothing to do with him. He thought Lauren and Jimmy should have set some guidelines and kept business and personal matters separate. Amateur mistake. On the other hand, the conversation did show Bobby that she now trusted him and was relying on him. He liked that feeling.

Bobby spent most of a morning on the phone calling up some venues he thought could be a good fit for Lauren. Problem was, anyone he ever knew who managed those clubs was long gone. After three hours, he was batting zero. In trying to think about who could help, he knew Eddie Fontana was the man. Eddie was a pro at working the managers to get gigs for his up and coming performers, whether it was a spot on a national television show or a small bar in Nashville. Bobby uncomfortably recalled the last time he had seen Eddie, when he had urinated on his expensive office rug. But this would not be the first time Bobby had to approach someone with his tail between his legs. In truth, half the conversations in the music business were kissing a backside or having your backside kissed. In a way, the biz was one big ass kissing fiesta. You just tried to be the ass more than the lips.

Bobby called Eddie's cell phone, desperately thinking of the appropriate message to leave. To his surprise, Eddie picked up.

"Eddie?"

"I think so, unless my mind is so bad now, I forgot my own goddamn name."

"Hey, this is Bobby."

"Ah, the one who left a gift on my rug. Now that I remember."

"I am really so sorry, Eddie. I was going through a bad time."

"Oh, really? I just got some bad news from my doctor. Should I have shit on his desk?"

Like an old married couple, it seemed that not enough damage could ever be done to totally break the relationship apart, no matter what it might have seemed like at its darkest moments. Soon Eddie was spilling his guts about his diagnosis, and Bobby was genuinely saddened. In fact, he had decided not to even ask Eddie about the gigs, but Eddie knew Bobby better than Bobby knew himself.

"Come on, spill it," Eddie said. "You have never spoken to me for five minutes without asking for something."

Bobby was going to dispute that but upon reflection thought that there might be some truth to it. He began to tell Eddie the whole story about how he met Lauren and what he was trying to do. About three minutes into the story, Eddie told him it was one of the most boring stories he had ever heard, and could Bobby please get to the point.

"I am trying to get her some decent gigs around the city. Nothing too big."

"I will see what I can do. No promises, but I am sure we can come up with something."

"Thanks, Eddie. I really appreciate it, man. And again, sorry about the rug and all you're going through right now."

"That's OK. But I did have to get rid of the rug. Could not get the awful smell out. Jesus, what the hell are you eating?"

"I owe you."

"Yeah, yeah. Just do me a favor; let's keep our disagreements to yelling, and you keep your schmeckle in your pants."

A few days later, Eddie's assistant called Bobby and gave him the names of club managers to speak to. Bobby was assured they would be receptive. The assistant also told Bobby to let Eddie know how the gigs went. If they were successful, he had one or two larger venues in mind.

The assistant had been true to her word. That afternoon, Bobby called up the four managers, and every club promised to find Lauren a spot in the upcoming weeks. As he hung up the phone on the last call, Bobby shook his head and smiled. "Eddie's still got it."

As the sky darkened, Bobby drove over to Nashville Boot Co. to tell Lauren the news. She would soon have a turn at The High Watt, The Basement, Station Inn, and The Blue Room. Lauren thought he was joking. "You're just hilarious, Bobby."

"You really think I would drive over here for a joke this stupid?"

Lauren stared at him for a moment.

"And, if we can knock it out of the park," Bobby said, "we are likely to get bigger venues, like the Cannery Ballroom and possibly the Marathon Music Works."

Lauren continued to stare at Bobby in disbelief. "Mr. Linder, if you are playing with me, I really think I will have to kill you. Seriously."

Bobby was deadpan and straight-faced. "If I am kidding, I'll buy you the gun myself."

Lauren jumped into Bobby's arms and kissed him square on the lips.

On his ride home, Bobby started to think that maybe he was on the way back. Originally, he'd taken an interest in Lauren because he knew she was good, and he simply wanted to help where he could. Frankly, he had nothing else to do. Now he began to wonder if, maybe through divine intervention, what started as simply trying to help someone was leading to something bigger for himself. He seemed to be reconnecting with old contacts in the business and discovering new ones. Plus, his activities with Lauren seemed to be producing positive results on all fronts. Bobby certainly wasn't religious. With the exception of Jessica's wedding, he couldn't remember the last time he had been to church. But there was something unexplainable about the past month or so. Things were going too well in the world of Bobby Linder. Granted, he was still extremely low on funds, and he didn't have a full-time paying job, but he was feeling as happy and energized as he had felt in a long, long time. Sweet karma.

The first club to get back to Bobby with a date for Lauren was The Blue Room. The Blue Room was part of a combination record store, record label, and performance venue. The record store and label were known as Third Man Records, all started by Jack White, the lead singer and guitarist for the White Stripes. Although a small venue, The Blue Room was well known in the Nashville hipster music scene, and some buzz from there carried a lot of weight. The date to play was three weeks out. Before the gig, he wanted Lauren to work with some studio musicians, something she had never done in earnest. Bobby felt that even a few musicians would give her show more pop.

The first person Bobby reached out to was Dave Hanson, a studio drummer and band fill-in who was as respected as any musician in Nashville. It would be unlikely for someone of his caliber to work with a newbie like Lauren, at least not for free. But not only had Bobby and Hanson known each other a long time through their respective music circles, but they'd done a stint in drug rehab together and grown close. Although they didn't speak often, they'd never lost contact. They liked to tease each other about whose wife raked who over the coals the most in their respective divorces. Bobby thought if he could get Hanson on board, it would be easier to rope in two or three more musicians. The conversation went well. After a couple of laughs over their Hiroshima nuptials, Bobby began to fill Hanson in on Lauren. As in his conversation with Eddie, Bobby didn't get far.

"Let me guess," Hanson interrupted. "You need a drummer."

"Yes, maybe for a few brief practices and a

night at The Blue Room."

"Let me also guess: you want this done gratis?"

"I can give you a piece of the door, but to be honest, I don't expect it to be much. It really is for exposure."

"Maybe we can ask one of our wives to chip in," Hanson quipped.

In the end, Hanson agreed to give Bobby two practice sessions and an initial gig in exchange for drinks. Most importantly, Hanson knew a bassist and a fiddler who were good up and comers, young, hungry, and in need of exposure. Bobby pinched himself.

Bobby also wanted to see if he could wrangle a keyboard player. He would have loved a full-blown piano, but it was a little too early for that, and besides, some of these stages would be tight enough as it was. He was hoping to get Miguel Lopez, a keyboardist extraordinaire. Bobby had used him on many recordings and was never disappointed. He had heard, however, that Miguel had recently retired, having married the former wife of the head of a major record label. Word was that Miguel was blacklisted after that, probably in large part because his new wife and her previous husband were white, multi-generational Nashvillians, and he was Mexican. On the bright side for Miguel, word was that his new wife had gotten a huge windfall from the divorce. Miguel was a bit of an eccentric, and Bobby had not spoken to him in years, so he thought it best to try and talk to him in person. He called Hanson back and got Miguel's address but also a warning: "Be careful with this one; that boy is a walking firestorm." Bobby scrawled the address on the back of a water bill, took a shower, and put on better clothes than he had been wearing. Miguel lived not far from where Bobby had lived in Belle Meade when he was married. On the drive over, he drove by the park where he used to take the girls when they were little. Bobby noticed that the trees were past their foliage peak and realized Thanksgiving was right around the corner. He had loved Thanksgiving when the girls were younger. For all her misgivings, Sarah was a great cook. Before his parents had passed, when he was still on speaking terms with family members on both sides, and his mind wasn't engulfed in some chemical substance, everything about the day made him feel comfortably warm. The food, extended family, football on the television, and even Arlo Guthrie singing "Alice's Restaurant," which he made his reluctant daughters sit and listen to with him each year—all of it left him with a feeling of inner happiness he rarely felt on other days.

Bobby pulled onto Honeywood Drive and soon found himself heading up the long driveway of the address Hanson had given him. Bobby prayed it wasn't a mistake. A large Spanish style home with a terracotta roof sat on what Bobby estimated to be at least five acres. Bobby pulled around a circular driveway in front of the house. He got out of the car quickly, lest he change his mind. Shortly after he rang the bell, a woman of around fifty answered the door. She was dressed more casually than Bobby expected, although she still projected an air of stylishness with a prettiness that made it clear she must have been a bombshell back in the day. Her shoulder length blonde hair was pulled back into a ponytail. She wore a blue bandana print Chloe blouse tucked into a pair of Gucci blue jeans. On her feet were a pair of Christian Louboutin leopard sandals; there was a small tattoo of a dragon just above her powder blue, manicured toenails. Bobby apologized for showing up unannounced and asked if Miguel Lopez lived there, as he was an old friend. The woman invited Bobby in and introduced herself as Cynthia, Miguel's wife. Looking at Cynthia, Bobby thought Miguel did not just marry above his pay grade but married into the CEO corner office.

Bobby declined the offer of a drink as Cynthia escorted him through a foyer with a herringbone floor and a floating spiral staircase and then through a maze of rooms, some the size of Bobby's small rented house, until they reached the sunroom looking out onto the pool and an expanse of manicured gardens. There was a short Latino guy with curly hair piled high and a graying goatee lying on a floral lounge chair. He was wearing a gray tank top with the inscription Yippee Ki Yay Motherfucker written across the front, gold running shorts, and black socks with no shoes. He was reading a copy of Meditations by Marcus Aurelius. It was Miguel Lopez just like Bobby remembered—a lot going on. Miguel was so entranced by the book that he did not hear the pair come in until Cynthia announced the visitor. It took Miguel a moment to connect the dots. A smile broadened over his face.

"Mi compadre!" Miguel exclaimed. "Hace tiempo que no nos vemos! Long time no see!" Miguel popped up and gave Bobby a long hug.

Bobby grinned. "Let's just say I hit a few roadblocks. So good to see you, man."

Cynthia interrupted. "Are you sure you two lovers don't need anything?"

Miguel asked her to grab a few beers as he escorted Bobby to some nearby chairs. He told Bobby he had heard about his divorce and rehabbing but kind of lost touch with the scene as he hadn't been playing over the past year or so. As Cynthia came in with their beers, Bobby looked around and joked that he wouldn't be playing much either if he were in Miguel's current situation.

"I know, right? Not bad for a beaner. One moment I am in the studio all day and playing gigs at night just to pay the rent, and now I just hang in this place with my hot mamacita." Miguel pointed his index finger at Bobby. "But seriously, I was tired of the same old stuff, man. Day in and day out. I was about to call it a day even before I met Cynthia. It has changed so much, our business. So much more about the show, less about the music and what is in here," Miguel said, slapping his chest.

"I know. I am the opposite, though; I have been blocked every turn. Feel like a dinosaur. The business has become a one-horse pony. Same ol' same ol'. Someone like Blake Shelton farts on a record, and they will push it until it sells a million."

Miguel nodded in sympathy, stood up, walked over to a drawer, and pulled out a joint. "You still smoke?"

"Love to but better not. Rehab told me it could be my gateway back."

"Bummer, man. It's my gateway to total relaxation, but I understand." With that, Miguel lit the cigarette, took a long hit, and sat down next to Bobby. "So, man, what brings this unexpected, albeit pleasant, visit?"

Bobby explained his work with Lauren. He said it gave him a sense of purpose. "After my divorce, last rehab, and constant rejections from the business I was in all my life, I felt like I was in a never-ending whirlpool. I don't want you to start playing the violin or anything, but I honestly did not know if I could go on. Coaching this young woman, someone I probably wouldn't have given a second look back in the day, has really lifted me. Plus, the more time I spend with her, the more I think she has what it takes. Economically, I'm still living on fumes, but right now I'm feeling pretty good." Bobby then laid it on the line and said he had come to ask Miguel for help on a few sessions but understood if he couldn't.

Miguel took another hit off the joint, looked up, and pushed the smoke slowly out of his mouth toward the oak beams in the ceiling. It was quiet for a good thirty second before Miguel broke the silence. "I came to California from Puebla, Mexico, with my parents and older sister when I was seven. No one in the family spoke English. My father worked the lettuce fields in Salinas, and my mom was a maid in various fleabag hotels. My sister and I never went to a real school in the States. It was my sister who taught me how to read. We had no TV, but we did have a radio. I learned English listening to the Bakersfield sounds, the likes of Merle Haggard and Buck Owens. My mom also had a side job cleaning the Fox Theater after shows. I was about ten, and I found out George Jones was putting on a show there. I begged her to take me. She snuck me in and had me hide among some costumes behind the stage. When the music started, I felt a chill run down my spine. I can hardly describe it to this day. I knew I just had to see what was happening on the stage, so I crawled out from behind the costumes and kind of peeked around some equipment boxes just offstage. There was a piano being played right in front of me. I couldn't see the guy playing it because the back of the piano was closest to me, and the lid was up. I had never seen an actual piano before. It was the most beautiful thing I had ever heard. It was so smooth and, combined with George's voice, perfeccion! I don't think I moved or even blinked the entire set. After they were done, the piano player stood up. He was wearing sunglasses. As the crowd continued clapping and the band left the stage, I saw two guys lead him off, and I realized he was blind. Dude, the man was blind, and he was playing sounds from heaven. Later I would find out he was the famous Hargus "Pig" Robbins. Now my parents had no money for a piano, but for my next birthday, I got a used electronic keyboard. Played it ten hours a day, every day. By the time I was fourteen, I was playing in local bars. And you know what? Every time I was onstage, I got that feeling in my spine. And I did every time I played—until recently. Just stopped getting the feeling, man. If you stop getting the feeling, then what is it for?" Miguel took one more hit of the joint and placed it in an ashtray filled with several weed butts.

Bobby nodded. "I hear you, man. I was not as fortunate as you to be good at playing. I mean, I can play a little guitar and piano, but nothing that would even get me hired at a hillbilly wedding. But like you, I loved it since I was a kid. That's why I took to writing songs, because I had to be in the game somehow. Maybe it's because I am in a different position than you, I don't know; I mean, I have to find something to do to survive, I guess, but this Lauren kid, there is something there. Every once in a while, when she hits it exactly right, I get my own feeling in the spine that you are talking about. I thought you might get a kick out of it."

Miguel looked out the window as if he saw something far in the bushes. "I am going to need a keyboard."

"What?"

"I got rid of all my instruments. Even Cynthia's baby grand. If you want me to play, I am going to need a keyboard."

Bobby laughed and reached over to give Miguel a hug. "I'll find you a keyboard, you crazy wetback. Now why don't you pass me that joint and tell me all about Cynthia."

THE WORD

Bobby arranged a rehearsal with the band on the following Sunday, knowing some of the members were likely to have studio work or gigs during the week or on Saturday. He had to schedule it for the evening because Miguel said he meditated religiously on Sunday afternoon: "My mojo is completely wrecked for the week if I don't." Bobby insisted that he and Lauren work every day beforehand to make sure they were prepared for these pros and could make a good impression. He suggested to Lauren that they stick to covers at first so the band could get into a groove with her before they ventured into original work.

As Thanksgiving and the holidays approached, Lauren was busier than ever with expanded hours at the boot store and working with Bobby, but she didn't mind. Bobby suggested she call in sick the Saturday before the rehearsal, but she told Bobby she was a terrible liar. Bobby said that somewhere down the line, she was going to have to make a choice, and if she were serious about her music, some sacrifices would have to be made.

"I get it, Bobby. You know I love music more than anything, but I also love having a roof over my head."

"Did you know when Dolly Parton first started out, she slept in her car?"

"Really, I'm supposed to sleep in my car?"

"I'm just saying. You are incredibly good, but

it is not just about being incredibly good. You see the talent here in Nashville. There are busboys in this town that people in most cities would line up around the block to hear. You have to want it more than anyone else."

Lauren put her head down, and her hair fell in front of her. Her shoulders started to shake. "Are you ok?" Bobby asked.

Lauren just shook her head.

"What's the matter?"

Lauren lifted her face. Her cheeks were red and wet with tears. "You do realize I dropped out of college to do this? I used the tuition money my parents gave me to buy my guitar. I came to Nashville with my last $300. My first day here, I got a job in that barbeque joint on Fourth Street. When I filled out the application, I didn't have an address, so the manager was kind enough to let me sleep in the back of the restaurant for the first two months I was there. The deal for my rent was to kill any mouse I saw. Then there was an older waitress whose husband had just died of cancer. She let me sleep on the couch in her little house next to the airport. At night it was planes overhead and her crying in the bedroom, but I sure appreciated having a place to stay. I used to get up and go into this little shed in the back yard so I could practice my guitar without disturbing her. Anyway, I got good enough to get some gigs and got a better job at the boot store, where I'm their best salesperson. I got a car and my own place. And oh yeah, now I got me an aging producer who says he can make me a star. I would say I have done OK, so please don't tell me I need to want it more. I think I want it just fine."

Bobby had been in enough arguments to know when it was time to wave the white flag. Especially since he now knew who was wrong. She wanted it just fine.

Bobby could not use any space at Warner for the Sunday session as all studios and practice rooms were spoken for. He reached out to Eddie, who said they could use a studio at Sidewalk Music if they didn't leave the place a mess and if Bobby promised not to bother him for at least a few weeks. Hanson introduced Bobby to the two young musicians, the bassist Henry Taylor—a Rastafarian from Jamaica and son of a minister who got hooked on country music when he went to college at the University of Texas on a soccer scholarship—and fiddler Wyatt Prescott, a Nashville native whose great grandfather was Vassar Clements, the Father of Hillbilly Jazz. Miguel came in straighter than Bobby expected for that time of the day wearing a gray pea cap, a green tank top that read "Don't Blame Me. I Didn't Vote for the Pussy Grabber," Bermuda shorts, and sandals. Bobby had forgotten about having to secure Miguel a keyboard but located one in the studio. Lauren came in all excited and wearing more makeup than ever. Bobby introduced Lauren to the band members. After some small talk to ease Lauren's nerves, Bobby asked her to pick a song she would like to start out with. He suggested she choose something slower and skip playing her guitar so the band could get the gist of her voice. She suggested Deana Carter's "Strawberry Wine" and looked at the band to see if they knew it.

"Lauren," Bobby said, "these guys can play any

song you can think of, even ones not written yet."

As the band tuned up, Bobby told Lauren to try to relax, as if it were just the two of them. "These guys aren't here to judge, only to help."

The heat was turned off on the weekends, and it was chilly in the studio this late November evening. Lauren felt cold, and regardless of Bobby's advice, she was still nervous as the band began to play. Lauren closed her eyes and took a deep a breadth. She felt the first few words fall into her ears as if someone else were singing. It comforted her, and she felt stronger as her emotions filled out the words of the song. As the song closed, Bobby saw the musicians nod to one another, a good sign.

Hanson clicked his drumsticks together. "Very nice! I'll put that against Deana herself."

Lauren picked up her guitar, and they proceeded to play a wide range of country tunes. The band got a big kick out of her rendition of Marty Stuart's "The Whiskey Ain't Workin'."

Lauren quipped, "That's the first time I did that song away from my bathroom mirror."

Toward the end of the session, after about twelve songs, Hanson ordered pizzas, and Miguel primed everyone's appetite with a joint most cigar stores would have been proud of. The musicians sat around with Lauren offering suggestions on tone and pace. Afterwards, Lauren played three of her own songs solo with her guitar. Bobby handed out sheets with the lyrics and asked the band to think about incorporating musical compositions for them. The upcoming Thursday was Thanksgiving, and the group agreed to meet again the following Sunday. The only problem was that Bobby had not yet secured a place for them to practice. Miguel told the group that Cynthia was on the board of trustees at Belmont, and the university had lots of studios in its music department; he was sure she could work something out for them.

After the band left, Lauren could not get the smile off her face. "That was just awesome. Those guys were fantastic. Thanks so much, Bobby."

"No, thank you. Those guys now realize you are the real deal, so they'll come back." Bobby asked Lauren what her schedule was for the week. She told him she was heading back to the Chicago suburb of Naperville on Wednesday to see her parents.

"It's either this one or Christmas, and at least at Thanksgiving I don't feel as guilty if I want to kill someone," she said. "Besides, I could use a couple of good meals cooked by someone else. But I'll be back by Saturday, if not before. What are you up to for the holiday?"

Bobby hadn't given it any thought, and even if he had, he probably wouldn't have had a plan. "We'll see. I've been so busy; I haven't been able to focus on that yet."

Lauren nodded and forced a smile. She buttoned up her Levi's jacket and grabbed her guitar. She bent down to where Bobby was seated and gave him a kiss on his cheek. "Thanks for tonight. Really. It means a lot to me."

Bobby just smiled in return.

It was colder than normal when Bobby awoke on Thanksgiving morning. He read a text from Miguel saying if Bobby had no plans, he should come over for dinner; Cynthia's sister and a few neighbors would be there too. Bobby politely declined. Even though he'd been divorced for years, he still felt uncomfortable at social gatherings. Looking into the mirror in his bathroom, Bobby realized he hadn't shaved in a few days. His hair was uncombed, and he was a bit concerned about how bad he looked. He took some time to shave, showered, dressed, and headed over to the Biscuit House for breakfast. There was a handwritten note on the door saying they were going to close at noon for the holiday. Bobby was greeted by Marie, a heavyset waitress in her forties who, from the shoulder down, looked like she worked at the shipping docks on the Cumberland River. But she was always pleasant and knew Bobby well from his visits over the years. She interrupted herself waiting on another table to yell at Bobby, "Take a seat wherever you feel like, hon. I'll be right with ya." The special was chicken fried turkey, but Bobby wasn't that desperate. He ordered some eggs and shrimp grits with coffee. The cup felt good in his cold hands. Marie came over to ask how everything was and what he was doing for Thanksgiving. He lied and told her he was going to a friend's house. He didn't need the sympathy. Marie volunteered that she was having Thanksgiving dinner at her apartment with her two sons and her new boyfriend. Bobby wished her luck.

From a small TV near the cashier, Bobby could hear the sounds of the Macy's Thanksgiving Day Parade in New York. He had always wanted to go as a kid. Watching it on a black and white television, he would stomp around the house pretending he was the drum major of a marching band. A couple in their twenties called Marie over to tell her their scrambled eggs were not warm enough. Marie took them away and returned a few minutes later with what looked like a fresh batch. After breakfast, Bobby said goodbye to Marie and walked outside. To his surprise, it had gotten colder. He put up his jacket collar. A homeless man approached Bobby in the parking lot and asked if he had any spare change for breakfast. Bobby almost always ignored these advances, but he thought on Thanksgiving that would be bad karma, so he gave the man five dollars. The man quickly left the parking lot, apparently no longer interested in breakfast.

Bobby drove past Edgefield's, but a sign on the door indicated the bar would not be open until 6 p.m. The sign also said, "Happy Thanksgiving." Bobby thought anyone reading that sign would be much happier if it just said "Open." Back at home, he put the television on low and called his daughter, Jessica. They wished each other a happy Thanksgiving, and Jessica said she just found out she was pregnant. She sounded happy, and Bobby was happy for her. But he also felt vacant, not like he was hoping to feel at the announcement of his first grandchild. He told her he would plan to come out to California sometime soon. Jessica didn't reply. After goodbyes, Bobby called up his younger daughter, Emily, but she did not answer, and her voicemail was full. Reasoning Emily was likely to travel to Sarah's for the holiday, he was not thrilled with now having to call his ex-wife's home in Austin to try and reach her. John Clausin answered the phone. Bobby realized that it was the first time he'd heard the man's voice since Jessica's wedding. Bobby wasn't sure why it was so unexpected. He also hated the fact that his heart was beating fast and he felt flushed. The conversation was brief but cordial. Clausen told Bobby that Emily was out but would be sure to tell her about the call. Clausen wished Bobby a happy Thanksgiving. Bobby couldn't return the favor and hung up.

Bobby poured himself a bourbon and raised the sound on the television. Some announcers were discussing the upcoming Lions versus Bears football game. He switched the channel to an infomercial on a cordless, bagless vacuum. The phone rang, and Bobby answered without looking at the number. "Emily?"

It wasn't Emily but Miguel making a last-ditch effort to get Bobby to come for dinner. Bobby stared at the wall behind the television and realized for the first time how badly it needed to be painted. He told Miguel yes, he looked forward to coming.

"Why did you make me ask you twice? Now get your white turkey ass over here by three."

Bobby hadn't been to someone's house for Thanksgiving since he went to Sarah's sister and brother-in-law's house years ago in an upscale area of Austin; they made fun of him for wearing jeans and a sweater. "I told you," Sarah had said, annoyed. "What you are wearing isn't appropriate." Recalling this put Bobby in a bit of a tizzy, because Cynthia and Miguel's abode made Sarah's sister's place look like an outhouse. Bobby got his best suit out of the closet. It hadn't been dry cleaned in a while, but he took an iron to it, and it looked OK. He grabbed a shirt he wore on special occasions—there hadn't been one in a while— and a Brooks Brothers tie Jessica had given him for his sixtieth birthday. When he arrived at the house for dinner, Miguel answered the door. He was wearing sandals, shorts, a shirt that read "I Just Look Illegal," and a pea cap. Miguel took one look at Bobby and asked, "You coming from a funeral?"

"Jesus Christ." Bobby tore his tie off. "How about a little hint on the dress code?"

Cynthia and the rest of the guests were more dressed up than Miguel, but nothing more than sweaters and jeans. It had been years, Bobby thought, and Sarah still screwed him up. Cynthia surprised Bobby with a quick kiss on the cheek and introduced her neighbors, Frank and Susie Haggerty. Frank, a bald, stocky guy, was an executive at Pinnacle Bank, and Susie was a substitute schoolteacher. The other couple, about ten years younger than the Haggertys, were Russian, Aleksei and Natalia Vasiliev. Natalia was a doctor at Vanderbilt Hospital. Bobby never found out what Aleksei did. Cynthia introduced Bobby to her sister, Debbie Pitman. A slight but buxom woman in her early fifties with shoulder length brunette hair and a dark complexion, she was her sister's opposite, though just as attractive in her own way. Debbie had been married and divorced without ever having kids. She had moved to New Orleans when she got married and her new husband joined his family's oil refinery business. Soon after, Debbie discovered she couldn't have kids and became rather depressed. In an effort to help her husband, whose business had hit the skids during an oil glut, she decided to start a business. She opened a sidewalk stand selling kolaches, a delicious, slightly sweet-based pastry usually filled with sausage, cheese, or fruit. Originally from Czechoslovakia, these little bits of heaven had made little headway outside of Texas; they were the best kept secret of the Lone Star

State. Soon Debbie's kolache stand turned into a small corner store, then shortly after that, two stores, then more than a few dozen. In the interim, Debbie caught her husband in a fling with a former high school sweetheart and gave him the boot.

At dinner, Bobby sat in between Natalia and Debbie. He was a bit concerned about talking to Natalia because every time he tried to include her in the conversation, Aleksei stared at him in a manner that made Bobby more than a little uncomfortable. On the other hand, Debbie was easygoing and funny. She smoked at the table, which even Bobby was hesitant to do. Dinner was spectacular by anyone's Thanksgiving standards: turkey, country ham, stone crabs, and an assortment of sides Bobby didn't get to sample all of. After dinner, they all slipped into the sunroom for drinks. Bobby felt great. Cynthia brought out a game called Catch Phrase!, where your teammates try to guess a word in a limited amount of time. They decided on men versus women. Everyone found it hilarious, and the more liquor they had, the more hilarious it became. As the neighbors started to depart for the evening, Bobby thought he should leave as well, but Debbie implored him to stay, saying she didn't want to be a third wheel for the rest of the night. Shortly thereafter, only Cynthia, Miguel, Debbie, and Bobby remained, and somehow, a Courvoisier or two later, it was only Debbie and Bobby.

Bobby awoke the next morning, still groggy, and stared out a window that he realized was not his. Rolling over, he saw Debbie still in a deep sleep. It all came back to him. Quietly dressing, he went into an adjoining bathroom, splashed water onto his face, and used his wet hand to comb his hair. Back in the bedroom, he was torn between waking Debbie or letting her sleep. To just leave seemed rude, so he sat on the bed, leaned to her ear, and gently spoke. "Hey, Deb, I am heading out."

Debbie slowly turned toward his voice and smiled. "Hi. What time is it?"

"I have absolutely no idea."

Debbie laughed and rubbed her eyes. "Well, that was some Thanksgiving."

"Yes, it was," Bobby said. "I enjoyed it."

"Good. And listen, we're certainly not sixteen anymore, so you don't have to say you'll call me."

Bobby just nodded.

"But," Debbie continued, "if you are ever in New Orleans, please stop in for a kolache."

Bobby promised he would, gave her a kiss, and left.

In the kitchen, Miguel was sitting in his underwear reading the Daily Tennessean. "Hey, there he is," Miguel said.

"Hey, Miguel, I am really sorry, man. The booze must have gotten the better of me."

"No worries, man. Cynthia said Deb hadn't been laid in a long time, so you did her a favor."

"Jesus. By the way, where is Cynthia? I need to thank her for dinner and make sure she doesn't want to kill me."

"Again, all good, dude. Cynthia went to play tennis. She left you a care package there on the island." A large Tupperware container, tied with a bow, was filled with leftovers from last night's feast. "Dinner, some lovin', and leftovers," Miguel continued. "I'd say you had a rather good twenty-four hours."

Bobby picked up the Tupperware and patted Miguel on the back on his way out of the kitchen. "Certainly could have been worse, my brother."

Having left Nashville a little later than usual, Lauren didn't get into Naperville until after 9 p.m. Her mother called several times to see where she was on the road, and her message changed from "We're waiting for you for dinner" to "We'll save you something." Naperville, located about thirty miles from downtown Chicago, was one of the wealthiest mid-sized cities in the country. Naperville had always been predominately white but recently had seen a large increase in its Asian population due to an influx of tech companies in and around the city. Lauren's dad viewed this as both a plus and a minus: "better schools but worse drivers." Lauren never liked Naperville. Niche.com had rated the city the best place to raise a family, and Kiplinger's had ranked it as the number one place for early retirement. To Lauren, it was like living in Whoville without all the magical stuff. Thirty-nine square miles of plain vanilla. An alternate version of *The Truman Show*.

Lauren pulled onto Santa Maria Drive, one of the nicest streets in town. Her dad, David, was an engineer who'd struggled financially when Lauren was young but later patented a device that tracked kids' phones, which led to his developing products that tracked a lot of things—your luggage through baggage at the airport, your car with a valet, your dog, and if you wanted to pay extra for the watch, your spouse. The proceeds made for a more than comfortable life for the Culivers. Lauren's mom, Louise, worked as a librarian for the town's public library, which, of course, had a five-star ranking from Library Journal.

It was dark when Lauren pulled into the driveway, but the outside of the house was brightly lit. She had struggled to get along with her parents in recent years, but there was something about her childhood home that was always comforting.

Lauren hadn't been back since last Easter, and her parents were happy to see her. Her mom, a terrible cook, reheated some kielbasa and sauerkraut. It was already overcooked, so the microwaving did not help the cause. Nevertheless, Lauren and her parents had a lively conversation with updates on local matters such as the divorce of the Hopkins, who were longtime residents down the street; apparently Mr. Hopkins had had an eye for the wife of the street's newcomers, the Vincenzos. Furthermore, Mr. Culiver noted, the annual Fourth of July celebration would no longer include fireworks, after a very heated public debate about the possible harmful effects from the smoke. Mrs. Culiver asked if Lauren was still dating Jimmy, and she said yes. She didn't feel guilty about the lie, as she had already told them Jimmy was a medical resident at Vanderbilt.

"When are we going to meet this fella Jimmy? He sounds charming."

"He's terribly busy at the hospital, Mother. They make them work like a hundred hours a week. I hardly get to see him anymore."

"Well make sure you try—wouldn't want that one to get away. If you continue in the music business, at least you'll have someone to fall back on."

Lauren decided not to go there. She had come

to learn that nothing was going to change how her parents felt about her choice of careers. She could either accept that or live in a constant state of animosity toward them, and she just didn't want that negativity on her plate. What was the harm of a little lie to shorten certain conversations? In fact, Lauren did not bring her music up at all—not collaborating with Bobby, not the studio sessions, not the upcoming gigs. She did tell them she was happy working at the boot store and doing well.

Thanksgiving morning was clear and brisk. Lauren went for a run in the neighborhood. She needed to get some energy out. Back home, she saw that her brother, Michael, had arrived. He was three years older, married with two young kids—a three-year-old and a one-year-old—and lived in an upscale apartment near Lincoln Park in downtown Chicago. He was a lawyer, and his wife, Sharon, a hedge fund manager. Lauren always had a close relationship with her brother but thought his wife was totally stuck up. From the very beginning, Lauren found it odd that Sharon hardly acknowledged her parents when she visited and almost completely ignored Lauren. A few years into their dating, Lauren told Michael she thought Sharon was so consumed with her own perceived presence that she was still in shock every time she went to the bathroom. After that comment, Michael wouldn't talk to Lauren for over a month. Since then, Lauren had had a grin-and-bear-it relationship with Sharon, with the occasional fantasy of pushing her out of a moving car. Lauren gave them both a hug, and Sharon complimented Lauren on her hair, saying it was a much nicer look than before.

Lauren made some cornbread from a box, which had somehow become her responsibility over the years. Michael oversaw the turkey after wrestling it a few years back from Louise's overcooking. Sharon volunteered to be the supervisor but didn't come out of her room until well into the afternoon.

The children were fed early and given to the couple's nanny to entertain. Thanksgiving dinner was going well until Michael began questioning Lauren about her music.

"How is your music stuff going?"

"My music stuff is just fine."

"Are you making any money at it yet? You've been doing it for a while now."

"I'm not in it for the money."

"Does it interfere with your career?"

"Michael, I sell boots."

It almost ended there, and things might have turned out well and good, but Sharon decided to join the conversation. "Do you think you'll ever get over the hobby? Maybe focus on something more fulfilling than selling shoes?"

Lauren wasn't sure why she responded the way she did. Because of the questions? Sharon's amazingly neutral tone of voice? The smile on Sharon's face, with just a bit of stuffing stuck to her front teeth? In any event, respond she did.

"Sharon, you really are some cunt."

At first, everyone stared at Lauren in disbelief. Even Lauren thought that she might have gone too far.

"Lauren!" Louise said.

But Lauren's self-doubt rapidly faded. "I am sorry, mother. But she is definitely a cunt. No matter how offensive the word—and I personally find it very offensive—this woman is it. A cunt, pure and simple. Anyone who is honest could see it after spending ten minutes with her. An unadulterated, grade A, prime cunt."

Michael stood up and slammed his fork on the table. "Are you goddamn kidding me?"

Sharon ran off crying into a bathroom. David looked down at the table.

Lauren's mother pointed down the hall to the bathroom. "Lauren, go in there and apologize to Sharon. That was completely uncalled for. Plus, need I remind you there are children in this house! Frankly, I am shocked that someone who grew up in this family could speak like that."

Lauren pushed her chair back and was rising to leave when she heard a voice at the other end of the table. "But Lauren is right."

"Dad!" Michael exclaimed.

"I am sorry, son, but Lauren is right. I've been holding it in for a long time out of respect for you and the grandkids, but Lauren is right."

Lauren stared at her father in shock. Her father smiled back. "The woman is a pretentious, uh, whatever Lauren said."

"David!" Louise said, incredulous.

"Come on now, Louise. You know it too. The woman acts like the Queen of England, and we are the peasants. She's always nitpicking at something, especially Lauren, and that is our daughter. It needs to stop."

Lauren smiled at her father. She was reminded of the time in fourth grade when she got into trouble because her classmate Cindy Glaser told the teacher that Lauren was chewing gum in class. Lauren yelled at Cindy that she was a tattle tale. When David got home that evening, Lauren was sitting at the kitchen table writing her detention assignment: "I will not chew gum in class," one hundred times. After she told her father the story, he told her to write, "Cindy Glaser is a tattle tale" one hundred times, and he signed it. When she handed it in, the teacher's eyes widened, but she never said another word about it.

In the end, Michael and Sharon left in a huff, but not before Sharon turned to Lauren on the way out and shouted, "And I could have helped you so much!"

Lauren could only roll her eyes.

Lauren apologized to her parents for wrecking Thanksgiving. Her father said not to worry about it, that Michael would get over it and maybe even have a chat with Sharon about her behavior. Even Lauren's mother reluctantly agreed that Sharon "could be a bit of a tart at times." The next morning, Lauren had a quick breakfast, gave her parents a hug, and headed home. There was a lot to do before the rehearsal on Sunday.

GOING ALL IN

Miguel's wife, Cynthia, outdid herself. She secured the use of Ocean Way Studios for the rehearsal. Owned by Belmont University, Ocean Way wasn't your typical college music studio. Located deep in Music Row, the building was a 175-year-old church converted into three music studios about twenty-five years ago. Since then, anyone who was anyone in country music had cut an album at the studio, not to mention many artists in other genres. Cynthia reserved Studio A, the largest space, which was situated in the church's former sanctuary. The stained-glass windows and overarching wooden beams still gave the aura of a holy place—if no longer for religion then for music. Bobby and most of the musicians had been in Ocean Way on many occasions for actual recordings, but it was Lauren's first time, and she had difficulty containing her excitement. When she saw the many gold and platinum albums on the wall that had been recorded there, she felt dizzy.

One of the songs Lauren and Bobby had written was called "No Use Talkin' Because I'll Still Be Walkin'"; it was about a woman intent on leaving a longterm relationship after finding out her lover has been having an affair with her best friend. Wyatt had been playing with it during the week and had come up with an upbeat tempo that the band agreed matched the vibe of someone trying to be strong and positive in a difficult situation. After rehearsing the song a few times, Lauren and the band really started to mesh. At one point, Wyatt with his fiddle and Miguel on electric piano got into a long riff that had Bobby staring in disbelief.

They spent some time working on the other original songs before closing with a song Miguel thought perfect for Lauren, Steve Earle's "Guitar Town." They changed some of the words to reflect Lauren's gender—such as "rockin' daddy" to "rockin' mama"—and everyone agreed it was a good choice. It worked.

Despite the fact that she wasn't in front of a live audience, Lauren had never been so excited playing music. The acknowledgement of these experienced musicians gave her the confidence to push a little harder, stretch a little further. Bobby thought they were close to ready for the clubs. He wanted to get a feel for how many members of the band would be willing to carry on. After the session, while Lauren was in the ladies' room, Bobby thanked the band for all their help and asked if any of them would be interested in moving forward to play some club gigs. Henry and Wyatt eagerly said yes. Hanson, who originally agreed to just one gig, was not as enthusiastic.

"Bobby, I think your girl Lauren has a lot of talent," Hanson said. "I would love to help out when I can. But most nights, I need the paying gigs. As you are aware, I'm still payin' off the old missus."

"I'll pay you," Bobby blurted out. "I'll pay all of you."

Hanson chuckled. "Now I don't want to get all personal or nothin', but how you gonna do that?"

"Don't worry about it. It'll get done. Not saying

you'll get rich, but you'll get paid same as you would if you was playing regular studio or club gigs."

Hanson looked down and coughed. "OK, I'm in. I hope you don't think I'm being difficult."

"Not at all," Bobby said. "We all have to take care of numero uno. I get it." Bobby turned to Miguel, who was sitting in an aluminum folding chair smoking a cigarette directly under the "Absolutely No Smoking" sign. "What about you there, my compadre?"

Miguel took a long hit off his cigarette. "I don't know, Bobby. Playin' these last few times, I'd forgotten how much I love it. That being said, I also wanted to move on, man. As Ralph Waldo Emerson once said, 'Unless you try to do something beyond what you have already mastered, you will never grow.' I'm getting old, but I still want to grow. I don't want to wish I had done things only to run out of time."

Bobby wanted to convince Miguel that playing with Lauren would be different, because Miguel would be a crucial part of launching a career instead of just walking into a studio and being told what to play. But Bobby knew better than to push. "Sure, Miguel, I get it. But if you change your mind, we would love to have you."

In the end, Miguel agreed to come to the last practice before the club gigs. He also said he would help Bobby find another keyboard player, although Miguel was quick to point out the new player would likely not be as good as he was.

"I already know that" Bobby said.

A week before Christmas, Jimmy came out of the offices of the Big Machine Label with a smile. He had just scored a contract for Slow Bourbon, a band from Lexington, Kentucky, that he had been promoting. He had initially caught them in a dive bar when they first arrived in Nashville and thought he could do something with them. They had a handsome lead singer with a voice to match, and the music was tighter than most bands just starting out. They were completely clueless about the workings of the Nashville music machine and were grateful that Jimmy offered to help. They'd quickly become popular throughout the city, and after scoring a gig at Luke Bryan's restaurant, 32 Bridge, they happened to be playing one night when Bryan was there. He liked them so much that he asked if they would open for him on a quick tour around some smaller venues in the South in preparation for a large national circuit. The tour had not even started yet, but word got out, and the recording companies came calling. Jimmy had been struggling to crack into the big labels as a music manager, and he figured this just might be his chance. He had been busting his hump in Music City for over five years since leaving his hometown, Gainesville, and it felt awesome to finally break through.

Both of Jimmy's parents were professors at the University of Florida. Jimmy was not much of an athlete, but he was handsome, with high cheekbones and jet black hair. He was quite the charmer and had a lot of friends. Unlike his parents, Jimmy wasn't much with the books, flunking out of the university and then a local community college. He was a decent drummer and got some gigs with bands at local bars around the Gator campus. There was one band he joined that was better than most; they called themselves Ellipsis. They became the biggest thing in Gainesville. High on the local success, they headed for Nashville and hopefully the big time. It wasn't long before Jimmy realized the only similarity between Gainesville and Nashville was the ville. He saw high school bands that were better than Ellipsis. Waiters, construction workers, taxi drivers, cooks, dog walkers, and various oddballs and misfits from North, South, East, and West bumfuck all converged on Music City with the same dream. Problem was, most were good, really good. Jimmy knew his band was out of its depth. But he also knew he wanted to stay in music; he loved it, and he was growing fond of Nashville. Jimmy sat down one day in the two-bedroom dump he shared with his depressed bandmates and tried to make a list of things he was good at. In the end, he could come up with only one: I, Jimmy Collino, could talk my way out of hell even if Satan were blocking the gate.

Shortly afterwards, Jimmy had the idea of going into management of musicians rather than being one. Eventually all the Ellipsis band members went back to Gainesville except Jimmy. He spent the next few months familiarizing himself with every possible musician and singer in the city. He researched the record labels and their key executives. He hopped from club to club, handing out business cards to owners or managers, saying he had hot acts for their establishments even though he initially had none. Eventually he began to get some local musicians to promote because they recognized he had ingratiated himself with club owners and was therefore rather good at getting them work. Just maybe he could bullshit Satan. Yet he hadn't had serious success with record labels until Slow Bourbon. He was hoping that this success would allow him to expand his reach to better clients.

Jimmy initially met Lauren at a country music contest in Riverfront Park held by a local radio station. She wasn't the best act on the stage; many of the more polished performers had been playing the Nashville scene far longer than she. Jimmy was the first person ever to approach Lauren about helping her with her career. She was a little leery because she knew most of the people in the contest were better than she was. At first, she thought it was really no more than a slick pickup ploy. In truth, Jimmy wasn't so sure it was more than that either. But over the next few months, Jimmy showed up at her small gigs in churches and at charity events and gave her some tips that she found valuable. He also got her the gig at The 5 Spot. One night in a parking lot after a gig, he went for it and kissed her. She didn't protest. Soon they were growing close, and Jimmy found he cared for Lauren more than he had for any other woman. He thought they had a great relationship other than the fact Lauren was not happy about his late hours at clubs and his flirtatious ways. For Jimmy, though, flirting was just part of the business. He spent most nights in clubs schmoozing musicians, club owners and managers, and sometimes the audience. In retrospect, Jimmy would admit he went too far. He knew Lauren was right to reject him. But he also still cared for her very much, and he realized he had made a serious mistake. Even though Lauren wanted nothing to do with him at this point, he had no intention of giving up on her.

Bobby climbed up into the small attic of his house. He opened an old wooden chest that had been left there when he first bought the place. Inside was one of his old boot boxes. Bobby blew the dust from the top and opened the box. Inside was a lone piece of paper. A certificate, to be precise. In the years before Bobby got divorced, he used to hide money in his home office. Bobby had kept the stash hidden from his wife to buy booze and drugs during the heyday of his habit. When Sarah announced she wanted a divorce, he began to stash away more. When he thought he wouldn't be able to hide the cash from the nosy divorce lawyers, he went to a Charles Schwab office and purchased seventy-five-thousand dollars' worth of Microsoft shares, primarily because it was the only company that came to mind. He asked Schwab to ship the certificate to his office so he wouldn't have to keep an account on record. When he bought the stock ten years earlier, it was at about seventeen dollars a share. Now it was trading at close to ten times that much. Initially Bobby figured he would just lie low with the certificate until the divorce was finalized and then cash it in to continue his drug induced fiesta. But his last attempt at rehab took hold. After that, he intended to use the funds to get him through old age and hoped to have a little left over for his daughters when he left the earth. He almost broke it when Sarah asked him to help out with Emily's Houston apartment, but he knew how much Sarah had gotten in the divorce; despite her protest, there was more than enough money for the apartment. But since he started working with Lauren, he felt more energized than he had in a long time. Before Lauren, he would drag himself out of bed just before noon most days, find himself at Edgefield's around two o'clock, grab a cheap to-go dinner around seven, eat and watch television for about an hour before falling asleep on the couch, and then start the same cycle again the next day. These days, however, when he went to bed, his mind was usually racing with ideas for Lauren, and he couldn't wait until morning to get up and begin working. To hell with it, he thought, holding up the stock certificate in the dim attic light. If he had to live on the streets when he was eighty, it would be worth it. That afternoon, Bobby cashed out his Microsoft shares and put the proceeds in the bank. The teller, accustomed to Bobby's pleas over the years to waive overdraft fees, looked at him suspiciously. Bobby smiled and told her he had made the money from his night job as a gigolo. The teller was not amused.

Bobby decided to switch venues for the first club gig and booked Lauren at The Basement at Eighth Avenue South ten days out. The gig was on a Tuesday, which was billed as new band night. The Basement was popular among knowledgeable music goers interested in new stuff, and although the space itself was small, it was usually packed with people on Tuesday nights. Thanks to Eddie Fontana's recommendation and the reputations of the studio musicians in Lauren's band, the manager was giving her the eleven to midnight slot, which was prime time.

The final rehearsal was to be the Sunday before The Basement gig, back at Ocean Studios. Bobby invited Becca because he wanted to get her impressions on the overall look and feel of the band. That Sunday, it rained hard. Bobby was aggravated that he had left his umbrella at home; he could not find a parking space within two blocks of the studio. He arrived soaking wet. Everyone else, umbrellas in hand, arrived dry, and of course Becca appeared as if perfectly attired for a night on the town. Miguel arrived with a young keyboard player, Toby Hunter from Kansas City, whom Miguel had mentored. Toby was thin, with recessed cheeks and a blonde goatee that looked like it needed some work. But he was soft spoken and had deep blue eyes and a serious look about him that made him seem older than his thirty or so years on the planet. If Toby could play, Bobby would be satisfied, because with the exception of Hanson, the rest of the band was in line with Lauren's age. Bobby handed out a playlist that he calculated would take up the full hour on The Basement stage, including some in-between-song tuning and talking. There was some old country, new country, a folk song or two, and a few originals in the middle of the set—Lauren's own compositions and those co-written with Bobby. They agreed to keep "Guitar Town" as the closer. Bobby wanted to open with something that blew the crowd away at the get-go, a song that showcased the band and showed Lauren's toughness. Miguel suggested "Dead Flowers" by the Rolling Stones. Bobby thought it was brilliant: country music by a great rock band. Becca interrupted to tell a story: while she was a student at Columbia, the Stones were in New York for a concert, and she wound up spending the night with Keith Richards. "I guess I always had this thing for ugly lead guitarists." The story broke the band's serious mood, but everyone agreed it was worth it.

The band practiced for well over three hours,

and Bobby thought that Toby was awfully good. Becca gave some good advice on where the musicians should be positioned and paid particular attention to Lauren's movements and demeanor. "Lauren, you don't have to look and act like you're so nice all the time," she yelled. "Your audience is there to hear good music, not to make a friend. Worry only about how good you're performing." Lauren responded by really getting into her songs, and she moved around like she owned the place. Bobby now felt the new and improved Lauren was ready to get back in front of audiences.

After practice, Bobby told everyone how much he appreciated their time, reached into his old green canvas backpack, and pulled out some envelopes. He started with Hanson and proceeded to hand them out to the remaining band members. When he got to Miguel, Miguel said that if Bobby tried to give him an envelope, he would give Bobby a beating right on the spot. Bobby decided not to test him. Lauren stared at Bobby in shock as he handed her an envelope. She looked inside to see five hundred-dollar bills. All the other envelopes contained the same amount except for Becca's, which held one thousand for her previous work.

"Again, it's not much," Bobby said. "You deserve much more, and hopefully we can get the ball rolling for bigger slices."

Bobby thanked Miguel and Becca and bid them goodbye. The rest of the band members thanked Bobby as they packed up and left. When everyone was gone, Lauren had not moved from the spot where Bobby had given her the envelope.

"You need a ride?" Bobby asked.

"No." Lauren walked over and sat down in a

chair. She didn't seem right. She was slightly bent over, staring at the floor.

"Are you ok?" Bobby said.

Lauren looked up, angry. "No, Bobby. I am not OK." She waved the envelope in the air. "What is it with this money?"

"What about it?" Bobby asked. "I just wanted to give a little thanks for the time and effort these people put in. They could have made a lot more playing around town."

"I'm pretty sure you don't have enough money to be handing out cash-filled envelopes. And anyway, this is about me, Bobby. All of this depends on whether I make it or not. You didn't even consult me. What do you think these people must have thought?"

"About what?"

"About the fact that you were giving out cash and promising more. What do you think they must have thought about me for letting you do that?"

"But you had nothing to do with it."

"Do they know that? Or do they think I'm taking advantage of some old guy who doesn't seem to have a pot to piss in?"

Bobby was more than a bit taken aback. He walked over to Lauren, who had tears on her face. "Lauren, I was just trying to help."

"I know, Bobby. I get it. But I'm not sure you do. Look, I appreciate everything you've done for me. Really, I do. But at the end of the day, everything we are doing is going to be a reflection on me. I would not have wanted you to use your own money like that and to promise more. It just makes me feel shitty. Real shitty."

Bobby knelt on one knee in front of Lauren and spoke softly. "You're right. I wasn't thinking. I should have consulted you. I guess I was selfish. Working with you has made me feel so good, I just want to make sure it continues. But also, I really believe in you, Lauren. And please don't worry about the money. Having it sitting in a bank does absolutely nothing for me."

Lauren smiled and wiped a tear away. "You're an incredibly good person, Bobby Linder. But promise me that from now on, we talk about everything first, OK?"

Bobby smiled. "Yes, ma'am."

Lauren smiled back. "All you men are so clueless."

KNOCK THEM OUT

Lauren walked into The 5 Spot to have a talk with the Commander. She needed to tell him that she was going to miss some of her weekly gigs because of the schedule Bobby had planned. She was a bit nervous about how he was going to respond. She also felt bad, because the Commander had been the first to give her a respectable gig. Loyalty was something Lauren always had been keen on—both giving and receiving. She asked one of the bartenders if the Commander was around, and he just nodded toward the back, where the office was. Lauren walked through the kitchen, and as she got closer to the office, she heard an unmistakable voice yelling into the phone.

"That's the second time in two months you overcharged me for the Bud Light. One more fucking time, and every night here is going to be Coors Light night. I hope we are on the same page."

As Lauren stood at the door, the Commander waved her in and pointed to a cracked leather chair against the wall in front of his desk. She overheard an apology coming from the other end of the line. The Commander brushed it aside, the anger in his voice rising a notch.

"I don't need goddamn apologies. I need correct invoices!" The Commander had made himself clear and promptly hung up the phone. Within seconds, it seemed he had completely moved on. "Ms. Culiver, what a nice surprise. What brings you into my humble abode?"

Lauren was not sure if the fuse was still lit. "Is this a bad time?"

"It usually is," the Commander said, stone faced.

Lauren proceeded to get up. "I'll come back."

"And interrupt me twice? Why don't you just sit your pretty self-down and tell me what's on your mind."

Lauren sat down again, more nervous than when she'd first walked in. "I just wanted to say how much I appreciate your letting me play here every week. It has really helped me get so much better—"

The Commander spun a finger in the air, signaling for Lauren to get to the point.

"Well, I've been working with a guy named Bobby Linder, and—"

"He's got a bunch of gigs around town to showcase you," the Commander interrupted.

Lauren looked more than a bit taken aback.

The Commander continued. "You're also likely to be booked at The Blues Inn, The Station Inn, The Basement, and The High Watt. And you have some premium players backing you up."

Lauren was at a loss for words. Even she did not yet know of the other possible gigs.

"Lauren, I am in the Nashville club business. It is my job to know what is going on."

"Uh, OK. So I'm guessing you know why I'm here."

The Commander shrugged. "I'm guessing you came here to tell me you're quitting The 5 Spot."

"No!" Lauren said. "Not unless you want me to.

I love it here. But I do need to take a few weeks off for these other gigs. I was hoping you wouldn't hold it against me. And that you might let me come back."

The Commander looked down at his desk and chuckled. He looked back up at Lauren. "Hey, I know I come across as a tough s.o.b. sometimes. I have to be. I am a Black man in the South who came from nothing, and I don't want to go back. But no one understands more than me the importance of grabbing the ring when you can. Now you got this guy Bobby Linder hustling for you. He's been out of the picture for a long time, and I know he has had his troubles. But back in the day, he really knew his stuff. If he has a hunch about you, I wouldn't bet against him. Plus, the musicians in your band wouldn't hang around if they didn't think you were the real deal. Not to mention I hired you. Do you need some polish? Yes, but I can see why Linder is taking a shot. There is something about you. Now don't go telling anyone I'm a big softie, but nothing makes me happier than seeing people who start off in places like mine succeed. I appreciate you coming to tell me what I already knew; that's classy. You are always welcome back here."

Lauren felt a wave of lightness spread over her. "Thank you. Thank you so much. Whatever happens, I promise I will be back." Lauren couldn't stop smiling and staring at the Commander.

"Uh, is this a magic moment?" the Commander said. "Because unless it is, I have work to do."

Lauren snapped to and stood up. "Sorry. Thanks again. Can I give you a hug?"

"Don't push it," came the stone-faced reply.

It was Tuesday at 7:30, and Bobby had arrived early, but The Basement was already packed. "New Faces Night" didn't start until 8 p.m. Bobby introduced himself to the manager, a thirty something stoner whose father owned the place. Bobby checked out the stage to determine where to position the musicians in Lauren's band. Bobby watched the first act, Feast of the Seven Fishes, who were more of a punk band than anything else. Not Bobby's type of music, but they had their moments. Around nine, some of the band members started to stroll in. First Henry and Wyatt, then Toby, and finally Hanson. The group hung near the bar having a few beers. American Girl, a Tom Petty cover band, was now playing. Bobby looked nervously around the club for signs of Lauren as he checked his cell phone. The Basement continued to grow more crowded, and Bobby wondered how that was even possible. At ten o'clock, Bobby got a tap on his shoulder. It was Lauren.

"Man," he said, "you had me worried. Where were you?"

"I don't like to get to my gigs too early," Lauren said. "It gets me nervous."

"Good, no worries. I think my heart attack is subsiding." Bobby ordered her a Yazoo draft.

After a few more drinks, as the band onstage closed its set with "Don't Do Me Like That," the manager came over and took Bobby and the band backstage to a room not much bigger than a walk-in closet. It was especially crowded because a three-person honkabilly group scheduled for the ten o'clock slot was still inside.

"Ok, boys!" the manager shouted. "Get out

there and keep 'em happy. Make sure you are done by nine-fifty."

Bobby was relieved that they were leaving, because the trio smelled as though they had been practicing in a cow pen.

The manager turned to Bobby's band. "Ladies and gents, you will have ten minutes to get your shit together onstage. Then you have an hour to show 'em your best. Any questions?"

The entire band shook its head. There really wasn't much to set up. Every band used the same drums, keyboards, and amplifiers. Only the guitars and the occasional fiddle or washboard were proprietary. On a small shelf were a bunch of empty beer and soda cans. There was one lukewarm beer left. Hanson picked it up. "Well, boys, we might want to drink a bit slower."

Lauren was silent, and Bobby worried her nerves might be getting the better of her. He told her a story about meeting his childhood idol for the first time. About two years after dropping out of college, Bobby was hawking songs to any label that would listen on Music Row. Close to exasperation, he got a call from Capital Records asking to meet with him about some songs he had sent a few months earlier. He almost missed the 9 a.m. meeting because there was a Godfather marathon on television, and he didn't get to bed until after 2 a.m. He woke just twenty minutes before the meeting and arrived a few minutes late wearing the same clothes he'd worn the previous night. He knew he looked rough when the receptionist asked to see his ID, and then the secretary who was escorting him to the meeting room asked if he'd like to use the men's room to freshen up. Bobby was supposed to meet with a Mr. Golden, but when he walked into the room, he saw a worn-out forty something with a beard and a black cowboy hat.

"It was goddamn Merle Haggard," Bobby said. "I had a poster of him in my room all through high school. I honestly thought I was dreaming. Even Merle had his doubts. I remember he looked over at Golden and asked, 'Are we sure this is the fella?' Anyway, Mr. Golden introduced Merle and himself and said Merle liked some of the songs I had been sending in. Merle nodded and said, 'Yup, I certainly do, son. Some clever lyrics there. This one song you wrote, 'Traveling with Mr. Lonely,' how do you think that should be played?' I looked behind me to see if he was talking to somebody else. I said something to the effect that I was no expert on the matter, but if I had to give an opinion, it would be a slower ballad. He pointed to a guitar in the corner and asked me to give him an idea of what I was talking about. I nervously grabbed it and said I would fashion it a bit like his earlier hit "Branded Man." Now I can play a half decent guitar, and usually not embarrass myself with my chops, but my nerves weren't helping. After about two minutes of my playing and singing, Merle held his hand up for me to stop. He said my voice sounded like a rooster with its testicles in a vise, but he thought my musical concept for the song was right on. Merle agreed to record it. In addition, Capital Records signed me on as a full-time writer for its roster, which in the late seventies was the bomb."

"That's a really cool story," Lauren said, "but why are you telling me this?"

Bobby pulled out a cigarette, lit it, and watched the smoke swirl into the ceiling fan above them.

"Because if you have a talent, I mean real talent, the people who are experts in that area will recognize it, no matter how you may try to mess it up. I was late for the meeting and looked like death warmed over. But I knew the song was good, and in the end, that was all Capitol Records and Haggard cared about. Now you have the talent, and I am not the only one who has told you that. So you go out there tonight, and just do you, and everything will fall into place."

Lauren smiled and nodded.

The honkabilly group finished, and Bobby and the band rushed past them to set up on the very tight stage. Bobby told Lauren to stay back, as he didn't want her onstage until the set was about to start. Hanson bitched a bit about the drum set while Henry and Wyatt connected their guitar and fiddle to the amps. Toby tuned the keyboard to his liking, and Bobby tested and adjusted the microphone to Lauren's height. Bobby checked his watch. He looked to each member of the band, and they all nodded back. Bobby walked offstage to Lauren, who already had her guitar slung over her shoulder.

"It's time," Bobby said, "for you to begin to make yourself somebody."

Lauren took a deep breath and felt surprisingly calm. She walked past Bobby, and on her way to the microphone acknowledged the band with a quick smile and a slight bow. Lauren plugged her guitar into an amplifier, swinging it in front of her body as she looked out over the semi-interested crowd. The moment reminded her of going to the Brookdale Racquet Club pool in Naperville as a child. When she would walk in and see all the kids swimming, laughing, and yelling in the water under the warm Northern Illinois sun, it always brought her a feeling of happiness and comfort.

Bobby waited nervously stageside, wondering what was going on. He didn't have to wait much longer.

"Hi, I'm Lauren Culiver. And I am here to knock you out."

Bobby's eyes grew wide. Lauren had never tried out that line in rehearsal. Nevertheless, Lauren proved it more right than wrong. Her voice was as good as Bobby had ever heard, she moved around the small stage like she had been there one hundred times before, and she interacted with the audience like she knew them all personally. The band reacted by stepping up their game. The bar was empty as everyone had eyes on the stage. At the end of the set, the audience was so insistent for more that the manager hopped onstage and asked Lauren and the band for one more song. They had nothing prepared, so Toby came out from behind the keyboards and joined Lauren in a duet of "Jackson."

When they came offstage, Bobby was so happy that he gave Lauren a hug and lifted her off the ground. She was sweaty, but Bobby couldn't have cared less. "You were just awesome! I mean in every way." Bobby turned to the band with the same effervescence. "Spectacular, boys, simply spectacular."

The manager came over and asked Bobby to give him a call to set up a date to play The Basement East, which was four times the size of The Basement. The band had a couple of drinks at the bar, trying to review the set but routinely getting interrupted with compliments from audience members. As Bobby watched a couple congratulating Lauren, he smiled but couldn't help worrying a little. Some of what Lauren had done on the stage was never discussed in rehearsal, but it all worked. Bobby wondered how much longer before the student became the teacher, how much longer he'd be around. He erased the thought from his mind and made an effort to just enjoy the moment.

Back at her apartment, Lauren's heart was still beating fast. She poured herself a glass of wine, lay down on her bed, and stared at nothing in particular. She put her hands over her face and let out a yell. After all the hard work, all the doubt, all the naysayers, maybe, just maybe, it would all be worth it. It was late, but she still called her friends Amy and Kayla and gave them a blow-by-blow recap of the show. By now it was almost three in the morning, and after three glasses of wine, Lauren still wasn't tired. She wondered if Jimmy knew of her success that evening. She had to admit, as much of a jerk he sometimes was as a boyfriend, he deserved some credit for how well she'd done.

Lauren twirled her hair nervously as she dialed. After three rings, she decided it was a bad idea and hung up. Less than a minute later, she received a text: "Hey, did you just butt dial me?"

For a moment, Lauren thought about answering yes, taking the easy way out, but she couldn't. "No. I had a good night at The Basement. Just wanted to let you know."

"I know."

"You do?"

"A good buddy of mine, remember Frank Fanning? He was there and texted me. Said you were playing with a band and were great. Congrats."

Lauren smiled and typed. "Thanks."

"That's it? That's the only reason you texted?"

"Yes." Lauren lied.

"I miss you."

"You must be drunk."

"Yes, but I still miss you."

Lauren wasn't sure she should type what her fingers were typing. "Sometimes I miss you too."

"Sometimes? I guess that's a start." Jimmy added a smiley face emoji and a thumbs up.

Lauren was afraid of going a bit too far; it might be the wine talking. "Well, I'm tired."

"Should be, it's after three in the morning. Coffee sometime?"

"Maybe."

"Again, at least it's a start!" Jimmy followed up with the same two emojis.

BUCK FIGHT

Bobby woke to the buzz of his phone. It had been like this for the past few weeks. After the initial show at The Basement, the buzz grew quickly. Shows at Station Inn, High Watt, and The Blue Room were packed with enthusiastic crowds. Last night they had played The Basement East, which supposedly held four hundred people, but Bobby thought there were at least six hundred packed in. It was on a Sunday, no less. The good news for Bobby was that the money coming in almost covered his band expenses, so his personal dip at this point was minimal.

On the other end of the line was Todd Olinhauser, owner of the Cannery Ballroom. Olinhauser also owned The High Watt, where Lauren had successfully played a few weeks earlier. He was a little hesitant to book her at the Cannery, which held about a thousand people, but then he had gotten word of the sold-out Basement East show. Bobby thought Olinhauser's offer might actually begin to put him in the black when all was said and done. Still Bobby knew there was work to do. The Basement East was their largest venue to date. This was a whole new level. Regional and up and coming national acts played the Cannery. Bobby called Lauren to tell her the good news; she didn't answer, so he left a message. He reached out to the other band members, who were excited by this development. About an hour later, Lauren called back, also thrilled.

"Bobby, that is just fantastic."

"I know. Great stuff. Glad you got the message. Where were you?"

There was a long pause. "I was doing my laundry and left my phone in a different room. Does it matter?"

"Of course not." Bobby wondered why he asked the question in the first place. "I just got a little concerned because I know you usually don't work on Mondays. My bad."

"I can take care of myself, Mr. Linder."

"Duly noted. I'm going to arrange a date for another rehearsal. As you know, this venue is a lot larger and is going to require some adjustments."

"You got it, manager man. Gotta run. I still have laundry to do up the wazoo."

Bobby was a bit taken aback by Lauren's apparent lack of concern. This was a big step up, and she was usually so into it. He was hoping to discuss a few ideas with her, but he decided it could wait. "I wouldn't want you showing up in dirty clothes."

Lauren laughed. "OK then, keep me posted on the rehearsal. Love ya, bye."

When Bobby hung up, he had an odd feeling he couldn't put his finger on. He'd had the same feeling a few times over the years, and it was never good. But there was no time to dwell on it now. He took out a pad and paper and began scratching out some ideas for the upcoming show.

At rehearsal five days after the Cannery Ballroom invite, the band assembled back at Ocean Way Studios. Lauren's promise at The Basement show to knock out the audience seemed to take hold as the group smelled the blood of growing success. The musicians had all been involved on both sides of the fence—acts going up and acts coming down. The acts going up were more fun and usually paid better. Lauren came into the studio walking brusquely, the puppy dog eyes of previous rehearsals long gone. There was no sense of nervousness, only an aura of contentment. She was wearing a new, light brown Stetson hat that was half cowboy, half fedora.

"Hey, boys, what do you think?" Lauren asked, pointing to the hat.

Wyatt, who had been quietly developing a crush on Lauren, was the first to reply. "Looks awesome, Lauren. Gives you a bit of the outlaw look."

Hanson chimed in: "Now you can tell the audience you're there to kill 'em, not just knock 'em out." The rest of the band agreed. Bobby was going to suggest asking Becca if it was a good look, but it was clear Lauren was a big fan of her hat. No need to make an issue of it. Besides, Bobby thought, this growing confidence was good; Lauren would need it as the challenges and opportunities grew bigger and tougher.

At about ninety minutes, the set at the Cannery Ballroom was going to be longer than previous engagements, so they needed to introduce a few more songs into the set. As Lauren became more comfortable on the stage, Bobby noticed that the crowd really got into her more upbeat country numbers that came close to rock crossovers. They added songs to the setlist like Trisha Yearwood's "She's in Love with the Boy," Runaway June's "Buy My Own Drinks," and Carrie Underwood's "Undo It." They even added an up-tempo ditty Lauren had written called "It's Gonna Shake You Up (When I Break You Up)," which was about a woman leaving a bad situation. During rehearsal, they experimented with Lauren playing a handful of numbers on an electric guitar. The band agreed that it was a definite plus.

The night of the Cannery Ballroom show was colder than usual for February in Nashville. In fact, there was a rare forecast of snow later in the evening. Bobby got into his car for the ride to the gig and cursed the weakness of his car's heater. He blew smoke into the air all the way to the establishment. Inside, Hanson asked Bobby if he wanted an edible.

"You do know I'm in recovery, right?" Bobby said.

Before Hanson could apologize, Bobby grabbed the piece of cherry taffy out of his hand and popped it into his mouth. Recovery or not, Bobby needed to calm his nerves.

Most of the band was hanging around backstage, and Becca, who had come to see the show, looked completely out of place in her Chanel dress. She helped Lauren put on her makeup. It was about forty minutes until showtime, and the crowd was already thick. When Bobby went to the bar to grab a beer, he noticed a familiar face at the other end. It was Jimmy. Bobby's heart pounded faster. The last thing he needed after all this work was for this clown to come in and mess things up. Without a moment's hesitation, Bobby hustled through the crowd. Tapping Jimmy on the shoulder, Bobby exclaimed, "Hey, friend."

"We are?"

"Why are you here?"

"Same reason you are." Jimmy sipped his bourbon. "To see Lauren play."

Bobby was trying his best to remain calm. "Do you really think that's a good idea? Lauren has worked awfully hard to get to this point, and I know she had to work through a lot to get past your breakup. Tonight is especially important."

"I know." Jimmy smiled. "I wouldn't have come if she hadn't invited me. Can I buy you a drink?"

Bobby did not wait for a reply and headed backstage. He couldn't imagine Lauren would have asked Jimmy to the show. He debated whether to indulge in the pleasure of kicking Jimmy out himself or to have the bouncers do it. Bobby came up behind Lauren and Becca, who were discussing the pros and cons of putting some sparkle on Lauren's face, with both agreeing that the main downside was finding sparkles on your clothes for weeks thereafter.

"Hey, Lauren," Bobby said. "What's his face is at the bar. He said you asked him to come."

Without turning around, Lauren replied, "If you mean Jimmy Collino, I did. We were chatting the other day and—"

"Chatting?"

Lauren swiveled around to face Bobby. "Yes, chatting. He said he would like to see my new show sometime, and I thought this was as good a time as any."

Becca, sensing this conversation was about to go deeper, said she needed to use the ladies room and excused herself. Bobby pulled up an empty chair, sat down, and took a deep breath. "I thought you guys had broken up. From what you told me, he put you through a lot. Do you think it's wise to let him in at this point when things are going so well?"

"First of all, Bobby, I am not 'letting anybody in' as you call it. I've known Jimmy a long time. He was helping me out with my music long before I met you. Not that I am not greatly appreciative of what you have done and are doing. But I thought I owed it to him to see how I'm doing, and maybe, just maybe, how far I've come without him. I can handle myself, OK?"

Bobby put up his hands as he stood. "OK, OK. Just voicing a little concern, that's all. If you feel good about it, that's all that matters."

"I feel good about it." Lauren turned back to the mirror to finish her makeup.

Bobby watched the Cannery Ballroom show from the very back of the room. Now that the venues were getting larger, he wanted to see if the act was effective from a distance. It was. Besides the band being tighter than ever, Lauren took her performance to another level. It seemed she had morphed into a singer with a little bit of Dolly, a dash of Emmylou, and a drizzle of Janis. She owned the stage. Any self-doubt was long gone. On the contrary, if she told the audience she could fly, they would believe it. And she would too. After the "Jackson" encore, the audience refused to quit calling for another song. Lauren surprised Bobby by coming back onstage solo to sing an acoustic version of the Kenny Chesney song "You and Tequila." The crowd ate it up.

On his way backstage, he ran into Becca, who said, "I don't know what you've done with this girl over the past few months, but you got dynamite in a bottle there, and I think it's going to explode anytime now."

Backstage the excitement was palpable. Just a few weeks ago, Bobby had to plead with some of the band members to stay on; now they could think of no better place to be. Lauren was smiling while talking to Olinhauser, who asked her to consider another performance in just a few weeks. Bobby came into the room clapping loudly and yelling about what a great show it was. Olinhauser ordered some liquor to be brought in, on the house. A few friends of the band were allowed in. A few minutes later, Jimmy appeared. Bobby watched closely as he gave Lauren a congratulatory kiss and meandered over to speak with Hanson. Lauren came over to Bobby.

"Hey," she said, "I think I'm going to just grab an Uber home. I'm shot."

"What happened to your car?"

"It's here. I'm just too exhausted to drive it right now. Jimmy said he'd drop it off later with my guitars."

There were so many things Bobby thought of saying, but this was what came out: "I can drive you."

"Thanks, Bobby, but I just need to be alone and decompress. Stay here a while and enjoy our success." Lauren smiled as she pointed back and forth between them.

After Lauren left, it was clear that this party would wind down when most parties with musicians and their friends do, which is when the booze runs out. It would be a while, because Olinhauser had been especially generous.

Jimmy approached Bobby. "Hey, man, I hope there's no hard feelings with me being here."

"Why would there be?"

"Well, it seemed to be an issue when you approached me at the bar, and I know you're aware I was dating Lauren as well as helping her with her career. I know you two aren't dating"—Jimmy chuckled—"but I don't want you to feel like I'm butting in. Lauren and I go way back, and I'm simply happy to see her doing well."

Bobby was having none of it. "I think your definition of helping someone with their career is different than mine."

Jimmy's smile disappeared. "For some reason, I am getting the feeling you don't like me."

"You must be clairvoyant."

Jimmy put his hands into his pockets and shrugged. "Any reason?"

Bobby moved in closer. "Yeah, I have a few. First, from what I know, you never gave much of a damn about Lauren and even less about her music. You were fooling around on her behind her back, and more people have seen talking clams with feet than saw you supporting her at her shows. And now that she's on the move, really on the move, you pop in and hop on."

Jimmy looked down at the floor and let out a small laugh. "You know what I think there, Robert?"

Bobby could almost feel his blood pressure rising. No one had called him Robert since his mother died.

"You say I couldn't give a damn about Lauren," Jimmy said. "That's priceless. I think it's you that couldn't care less about Lauren. You view her as your ticket back in. You've been a washed-up drug addict and a has been in our business for years, and this is your last great hope to rejoin the big time club. As Lauren moves up, and she will move up, if you think she's going to pin her ultimate success on you, then you will soon get an awfully rude awakening."

Bobby took a deep breath. "Get the hell out before I do something you're going to regret."

Jimmy raised his hands in the air as if to surrender and backed away. "OK, OK. Sorry to step on your dream, man." He turned around, waved to everyone behind him, and walked out.

Bobby lay in bed, but sleep was impossible. It had been such a great night for the show, but all he could think about was his conversation with Jimmy. Maybe Collino was right. Was he being selfish? Now that Lauren was getting some notice, should she be with someone more connected to the scene? Was he kidding himself? Who was he really doing this for? Daylight crept in through Bobby's curtainless bedroom window, and he hadn't slept a wink.

His initial thought was to head over to Lauren's to have a heart to heart, but he was too confused at the moment to know what exactly to say. Bobby took a long shower; the warm water cascading over the remnants of his long, gray hair felt good. Afterwards, he dressed and headed out the door for the Biscuit House. Bobby had forgotten it had snowed a few inches the night before, something many Nashvillians enjoyed due to the rare nature of the event. Not Bobby. He was never a fan of the cold. He had once even thought of moving back to Florida, but half the population was too old, and the other half seemed like they were running away from something, only to find the road didn't go any farther. He didn't feel like getting his feet cold and wet, so he eighty-sixed the idea of walking and went back inside to get his car keys.

At the Biscuit House, Marie waved him over to one of her tables. "Hey stranger, where you been? I was getting worried about y'all."

Bobby was not in the mood for talking, but poor, heavyset Marie was just so genuine and upbeat, he had to respond. "Sorry, Marie, I've just been busy. It's good to see you again."

Bobby was hoping they could leave it at that, but it was not to be. While pouring Bobby's coffee, Marie went into unsolicited detail, in an unfamiliar tone, about finding out her most recent boyfriend had cheated on her. "Son of a bitch was foolin' around all day I was at work, then I'd come home, and he'd ask me what I was making for dinner. When I found out what he was doing, I waited for him to ask me what was for dinner. When he did, I started beating him over the head with a spatula. I said, 'Here's your dinner!' He ran out of the house so fast, he didn't even bother to put shoes on."

"Gee, Marie, I didn't think you had it in ya."

Marie looked at Bobby, and her grimace turned into a smile. "We all have our limits, Mr. Linder."

Bobby had a few more cups of coffee as he waited for ten o'clock to roll around, when Edgefield's opened. His mind was going in too many directions to focus on much else.

At the bar, Lucy was happy to see him. She complained that business was slow on account of the ongoing gentrification of the neighborhood. "Those rosé drinkin' cappuccino sippin' fuckers just don't seem to be into this place."

"So maybe you need to get some pink wine and a cappuccino machine," Bobby said.

Lucy leaned on the bar in front of Bobby. "If I do that and maybe ban smoking, which they also complain about, would you still come in?"

"Not a chance."

Lucy raised her hands into the air. "Case in point. I am stuck between a rock and a hard place."

Bobby drank heavily that morning and well into the afternoon. Even Lucy commented that he was going too fast. Bobby switched from beer to bourbon around noon. About three o'clock, Lucy threw a cheeseburger in front of him.

"I didn't order this," Bobby said.

"I know," Lucy said. "I think you should eat something and maybe go home and relax a bit."

During the subsequent negotiation, the parties agreed that Bobby would eat the burger and go home if Lucy gave him one more drink. Once outside, Bobby forgot where he had parked his car. He walked around for twenty minutes until he found it where he had parked it that morning—right in front of the Biscuit House. Bobby cursed as he fumbled the keys out of his pocket and dropped them into the snow. He pulled the car out, unaware he had bumped into the car behind him. Going west on Woodland on the way home, his phone rang; pulling it out of his pocket, he saw it was Lauren. Before he could answer, he ran up onto a curb and dropped the phone as he tried to get the car back onto the street. Unfortunately, a fifty-five-year-old oak tree was having none of it. The airbag smashed Bobby's nose, but in his daze, he didn't realize blood was pouring down his face onto his jacket and pants.

He could still hear his phone ringing but didn't know where it was coming from. A Black woman tapped on his window, asking if he was OK. He stared at her blurry figure and then caught the flash of red and blue lights in his sideview mirror. A police officer pulled open the driver side door.

"Hey, buddy, you OK?"

Bobby tried to regain his composure. "Yeah, I think so. I skidded on the ice."

"Sir, the inside of your car smells like a Dickel distillery. Think that had anything to do with it?"

An ambulance arrived, and the medics checked Bobby for injuries, finding none except for a broken nose. When they were done, the police officer started a field sobriety test, which ended rather quickly when Bobby slipped and fell while trying to stand on one leg. The officer gave Bobby a blood alcohol content test, and that was that.

Down at the police station, Bobby was thrown into a holding cell while some paperwork was completed. He stared at the cement wall in front of him; it had the markings of graffiti that was constantly being erased and redone, like a boxing match that just won't end. One scrawl said, "FUCK EVERYTHING." That had Bobby's mind going in a bunch of directions for quite a while. Bobby was not sure how long he was in the cell as he fell in and out of sleep. There was noise at the steel door with the bullet proof window as the arresting officer entered the room. He took Bobby to a different room, where he was given a summons to appear in court to face a DUI charge. The officer said he would not hold Bobby overnight if he could get a ride home. Bobby was unsure who to call. Certainly not any members of the band. Eddie was out of the question because Bobby needed to keep intact whatever remained of his reputation. He decided to call Miguel, and before Bobby could tell him what he was charged with, Miguel said, "I'll be right over."

While waiting for Miguel, Bobby was surprised when he caught a glimpse of the clock and saw it was after 11 p.m. When Miguel arrived, the officer brought Bobby out to the waiting area. Miguel was wearing a T-shirt with the slogan "I can't breathe," and the room suddenly reeked of marijuana. The officer gave Miguel a look but decided not to pursue the matter since he was taking Bobby off his hands.

Once they were in Miguel's car, Bobby cleared his throat. "Thanks for picking me up. I'm really sorry for you having to come out here."

"No problem, bro. Cynthia was having a ladies gourmet night, so it was kind of good to get out of there."

Bobby touched his face. "My nose feels like shit."

"You look like shit," Miguel said. They both laughed.

Back at Bobby's house, Miguel got some ice and wrapped it in a dish towel for Bobby's nose. Then he pulled a joint out of the pocket of his army fatigue jacket as Bobby sat with his head leaning on the back of the couch and ice on his nose.

"So, what's going on, man?" Miguel asked. "Why the self beatdown?"

"Let's just say I had a lot of self-reflection."

"And from the looks of it, a lot of bourbon."

Miguel offered Bobby the joint, but he waved it

away. "I think I may have hit my body damage quota for the day."

"Seriously, man. What gives?"

Bobby lifted his head off the couch, and with the ice still on his nose, turned to Miguel. "I called you because I know you are solid and would keep it on the down low. I'm embarrassed by the whole thing. Frankly, I got to thinking that maybe I'm not the right person for Lauren. Let's face it, man. I've been out of the biz for a long time. There are a lot of young bucks in this town more tuned in than me. Lauren has been making decisions on her own that have improved her performances more than my suggestions have." Bobby rested the blood-spotted towel in his lap. "I guess I must be feeling sorry for myself. You must think I'm a putz, eh?"

"I've always thought you were a putz." Miguel smiled at Bobby, took a puff of the joint, and placed it in a nearby ashtray. "Look, I'm not here to song and dance you. I'm your friend, but I ain't no liar. Yeah, you got some issues. It's clear you miss the old days, and you are enjoying working with Lauren; it brings you back a bit. Sometimes do you push a little too hard, or get a bit too picky and act a little like Mr. Big Music Executive? Yes, you do. And if you asked me, yes, I think part of your working with Lauren is selfish. If she makes it, you get some respect back and maybe even a bit of a livelihood."

"Wow," Bobby said. "Should I come in closer so you can twist the knife easier?"

Miguel didn't miss a beat. "I also wonder if it makes you feel good because Lauren is so young. I mean face it, man, you and I are deep into the back nine of life. To be around youth, to be reminded of what that was like is a good feeling. I get that. I get all of it. And you know what? So what? We're all selfish. We all sometimes act bigger than we are. Who wouldn't trade everything to be younger? So put all that stuff behind you." Miguel inched his chair closer to Bobby. "This is the important thing. I've watched what you've done with Lauren. There are few, and I mean very few, people in the industry who could do what you've done. She is on an upward trajectory, and there is no, and I mean zero, indication that she's stopping. You say Lauren has her own ideas? That just means you're a good teacher. Stop beating yourself up, man. As this thing gets bigger, do I think people are going to try and snatch her away? Of course. That's a dirty side of this business that has been around since the first caveman sang a song. You need to have confidence in yourself, brother. You are the man." Miguel patted Bobby on his knee, stood up, grabbed the joint out of the ashtray, and took a last hit. "OK, are we good here?"

Bobby smiled and threw an ice cube from the towel at Miguel. "We're good."

"Well then, my job is done. Peace out."

AWOL

"Hey, snoozy. Wake up. It's almost eleven o'clock."
Lauren opened her eyes to the voice. Jimmy was
standing over her with two cups of coffee. He was
barefoot, wearing his black jeans but no shirt. Lauren's
mind ran through the events of the last night. She
recalled taking an Uber home because she was too
exhausted to drive, taking a shower, and getting ready
for bed. And then the knock on the door. It was Jimmy
with the keys to her car. Why she asked him to come
inside, she didn't know.

Lauren sat up, and Jimmy passed her a coffee.
"Thanks," she said.

Jimmy sat down on the edge of the bed. "Your
milk smelled a little questionable, so I used the Coffee
Mate. I found it with the cleaning supplies under your
kitchen sink."

"Hey, don't knock it. I'd put that stuff up
against Ajax any day." Lauren took a sip of her coffee,
still trying to sort out how she felt.

"Hey, I know I mentioned it last night, but you
were spectacular."

"Thanks." Lauren looked down at the flowered
sheets covering her legs. "Jimmy, do you think it was a
good idea?"

"The Cannery Ballroom? Why not?"

"No. Us. Last night. This. You here, sitting in
my bedroom with coffee."

Jimmy smiled. "I would like to think so. To be

honest, I didn't expect it. But I'm glad I'm here. I missed you, Lauren."

Lauren put her coffee on the bedside table and fell back onto the bed. "Uh, I don't know. I just don't know. I mean, I don't want to sound like a bitch. I'm not talking about the stupid things you did when we were together. It's just that I'm in a different place now. I forgive you for what happened between us. But I don't know what I want going forward."

Jimmy put his hand on Lauren's leg, which was covered by the sheet. "I get it. You have a lot going on. There's a lot between us to add into the mix. But if I can offer a suggestion, why don't we take it slow? I won't crowd you. I'll respect whatever decision you make. But I hope you don't shut me out completely. People change." Jimmy stood up, took his shirt off the bedpost, and put it on.

Lauren sat up again and wrapped her arms around her knees. "Look, I don't want to give you a let's-be-friends spiel, but let's respect each other and play it by ear. I promise I won't shut you out."

"Deal." Jimmy put his shoes on and gave Lauren a light kiss. After coffee, he left, and Lauren put her face into the pillow and let out a scream.

Wyatt Prescott, wearing an old Charlie Daniels shirt under his jean jacket, walked into The Violin Shop, about a mile southwest of Music Row, to get the horsehair replaced on his fiddle bow. He was greeted by Fred Woodward, a graying man in his mid-sixties, who was fond of wearing black. Fred was the longtime owner of The Violin Shop and a former fiddler for Emmylou Harris and the Hot Band. Wyatt told Fred he would wait around for the replacement. Fred handed it off to one of his employees, known only to Wyatt as Brian, a heavyset, laid back gentlemen with a college degree in instrument repair from Minnesota State College.

Wyatt always enjoyed looking at the many violins hanging in neat rows on the wall—a beautiful marriage of spruce and maple wood. Wyatt was always patient when someone asked him the difference between a fiddle and a violin: "If he's wearin' a tuxedo, it's a violin; if he's wearin' blue jeans, it's a fiddle." But today, as he was admiring the various instruments adorning the walls of The Violin Shop, Wyatt was having difficulty keeping Lauren off his mind. It was more than just admiration for a fellow performer or a pretty woman. He really liked her and wanted to know her better than just playing gigs together. On one hand, he didn't want to risk blowing up the mojo of the band by creating an uncomfortable situation, but on the other hand, he just couldn't live with the status quo. He was angry with himself because his feeling were in such turmoil that he was almost getting sick to his stomach around her.

Wyatt was a tall, good-looking guy with blonde hair, green eyes, a goatee that didn't quite seemed finished, and a solid chin. He'd had more than his share of girlfriends over the years but none that stuck too long—both a fringe benefit and a disadvantage of being a good musician in Nashville. But even in his best relationships, he didn't feel the way he felt about Lauren, and she didn't even know about it.

Wyatt was rustled from his thoughts by Fred, who had come back out with the restrung bow. "What don't you grab a fiddle and give the bow a test drive?"

Wyatt nodded, looked at the wall, and grabbed one that caught his fancy.

"Nice choice," Fred said. "That's a 1997 Eggimann."

Wyatt nodded again, trying not to let on he had no clue what that meant.

Wyatt played a few fiddle portions from Alison Krauss's instrumental "Cluck Old Hen." "Nice job, Fred. Bow is perfect. By the way, how much for the fiddle? I've been thinking of picking up another one."

"That one's a beauty. For you, I can let it go for about twenty-four thousand."

"Twenty-four thousand!" Wyatt laughed and gently placed the fiddle back on the wall. "I ain't there yet, my brother. But someday, with a little luck, just maybe."

As hoped for, Bobby got an offer for Lauren and the band to play the Marathon Music Works from Chris Cobb, one of the co-owners. The catch was that the gig was on Saturday, just five days away, because of a cancellation by an Austin band whose lead guitarist busted his ribs in a motorcycle accident. Bobby was a bit hesitant because Marathon, with a capacity of 1,500, would be their largest venue yet. He didn't want to stall the band's momentum with a poor turnout.

Cobb was quick to dismiss Bobby's concerns. "You have the hottest local band in Nashville right now. That's why I'm calling you. I put Lauren on our website, and it'll sell out in a day."

Bobby cautiously agreed to the date and called up Lauren and the band members to schedule a rehearsal. Not anticipating a show so soon, some of the band members had side gigs that they couldn't break. The best everyone could do was midnight on Thursday. The rehearsal went well, with Lauren having enough confidence to add one of her own songs, a ballad called "Should'a Ducked," which was about a cowboy who dies by hitting his head on a tree branch while riding his horse and daydreaming about his girlfriend. They also added Dolly Parton's "Tennessee Homesick Blues." They put a fiddle solo in there for Wyatt, and he nailed it. After the rehearsal, Lauren went over to Wyatt to tell him how great the solo was. Wyatt asked if Lauren wanted to grab a beer.

"It's two-thirty in the morning," she said. "Nothing's open."

"Maybe Saturday, after the show?"

Lauren smiled. "Sure. If it goes well, maybe I'll buy drinks for the whole band!"

Wyatt nodded and forced a smile.

On Saturday morning, Bobby desperately wanted to sleep in, knowing it was going to be a long night, but he was too amped up. Shortly after 6 a.m., he got up, made some coffee, and put on the news. According to CBS This Morning, a Swedish seventeen-year-old named Greta Thunberg had been named Person of the Year by Time Magazine. But the story focused more on how the president of the United States, who was also a finalist for the award, was mocking her selection. Bobby was worried about the mind of that man. After his second cup of coffee, Bobby's phone buzzed with a text from Wyatt. Sorry Bobby, I won't be able to make it tonight. Something came up. -W

Bobby stood up, began pacing the floor, and dialed Wyatt's number. It rang six times and went to voicemail. Bobby tried again. And again. Bobby decided to go over to Wyatt's place and see what was going on. Just as he grabbed his jacket, he realized he had no idea where Wyatt lived. For a moment, Bobby stood paralyzed. Then he placed a call to someone who maybe could help.

Hanson answered groggily. "What the hell, Bobby?"

Bobby got directly to the point. "Wyatt, where does he live?"

"Wyatt Prescott?"

Bobby raised his voice. "No, Wyatt Earp. Of course Wyatt Prescott. For Christ's sake, where does he live?"

"Thirty-First Street North, near Centennial Park. I think his building is called West End Village or something like that. I was there once after a gig. I remember it being on the third floor because the elevator was down, so I had to take the stairs. I couldn't tell you exactly which apartment, though. Is Wyatt OK?"

"I hope so," Bobby said. "But if he is, I may kill him."

Bobby hung up. Having lost his license for six months on the DUI, he called an Uber, paced, and tried calling Wyatt one more time. When the Uber driver arrived, Bobby blew out of his house so fast even the Uber driver—a Black man in his mid-thirties who had recently moved from Owensboro, Kentucky—was startled.

"Are you OK, man?" the driver asked as Bobby

rolled into the back seat.

"I don't know. Please drive."

The driver started his route, checked on Bobby in the rearview, and tried to relax his uptight passenger. "My name is Owen, and I'm from Owensboro, so that's easy to remember."

"I'm sure I won't forget it, Owen," Bobby replied curtly.

Owen took Bobby's tone in stride. "You're my last ride for today. I worked the overnight shift. Mostly driving drunk tourists from Broadway back to their hotels. If they can remember their hotels. I dropped one cat off at the Omni downtown about three this morning, and about an hour later, I get a pickup call from the same hotel. The guy had been walking around trying to find his room for forty-five minutes before security finally confronted him and figured out from the room key in his wallet that he was at the Marriott all the way up in the West End."

Bobby cracked a brief smile. "Now that's what I call a good night. Wish it were me. I have to go around chasing people so things don't get messed up."

Owen stopped at a red light and turned around to face Bobby. "Sorry to hear that, man, really. But it will get better. I believe that. God doesn't give us more than we can handle."

Bobby looked out the passenger window as the car drove west on Route 41 past the football stadium and over the Cumberland River. "I wish I could be that sure of it, my friend."

"It's true. Believe me, I know."

Bobby was becoming a little annoyed with the conversation. "And why is that? You got a flat on Route

70 during rush hour, but you were back in business by dinner?"

Owen smiled, and Bobby felt a little guilty about being so rude. "Sorry, man. I got a lot of crazy stuff on my mind."

"No worries," Owen said. A few minutes later, he pulled up to the West End Village Apartments.

"Thank you," Bobby said, taking a twenty dollar tip out of his wallet.

"If you're not going to be very long," Owen said, "I'll wait for you. My apartment is back toward where I picked you up."

"I don't want to inconvenience you."

Owen smiled. "My pleasure."

"Thanks. I hope to make this quick." Bobby hastened himself out of the car, but once inside the building, he had no idea which apartment was Wyatt's. He went to the management office to see if anyone could direct him, but it was closed. Bobby took the stairs up to the third floor where Hanson said Wyatt lived, but there were at least twenty doors along the tan, carpeted hallway. Bobby knocked on the first door. A heavyset gentleman in an open bathrobe and tighty-whities answered the door. "Can I help you?"

"Uh, sorry to bother you. Just wondering if you knew a Wyatt Prescott who lives on this floor. He's a musician, blonde hair, kind of a pitiful goatee."

The gentleman looked up as if the answer were somewhere on the ceiling. "Sorry, I don't know a lot of people in the building. I like to keep to myself."

Bobby was not the least bit surprised. He apologized again and went to the next door. This time he was greeted by a redheaded woman in her mid-fifties. Not necessarily unattractive, she wore an overabundance of makeup and large, gold earrings that seemed to be causing some stress to her earlobes. She was wearing jeans and a red sweater, which amplified her abundance of breasts. She was holding a small gray dog that might have been the ugliest animal he had ever seen. The dog let out a low growl.

"Oh shush," the woman said. Then she smiled at Bobby. "Don't mind him. He minds company much more than I do."

"Really sorry to intrude, ma'am. I'm looking for a good friend of mine, Wyatt Prescott. Lives on this floor, but I'm not exactly sure where."

Bobby was about to describe Wyatt, but the woman beat him to it. "The good-looking blonde hair fella? Plays the fiddle?"

"Yes, that's him!"

The well-coiffed woman peered out into the hallway and pointed. "I believe he's in 314."

"Thanks so much. Really."

"No problem," she said. "Would you like to come in for a cup of coffee?"

"You are truly, kind, ma'am. But I need to run."

The women nodded and smiled just slightly, but Bobby was already on his way to Wyatt's door. He knocked loud enough for everyone on the floor to hear. There was no answer. Bobby tried again and then began talking to the door in something between a whisper and a normal voice. "Wyatt, it's Bobby. Come on and open up. I don't know what's going on, but talk to me, man." Bobby waited and then leaned the top of his head against the door. "Listen, Wyatt. I am not leaving. This is too important. We have come too far with this thing.

I am going to sit here by your door until you open it." With that, Bobby slid down the door and surveyed the hall. The heavyset gentleman with his bathrobe was outside his door. Bobby was in no mood. "What are you staring at?" The gentleman quickly retreated back into his place. As Bobby put his arms on his knees and his head in his arms, he heard the unlocking of the door behind him. He shot up so fast he pulled a muscle in his back. "Ah, Christ."

Wyatt stared at him. "Are you OK?"

"I don't know. Am I?" Bobby tried to forget about the pain in his back. "Why don't we get inside and talk about it?"

Wyatt nodded, opened the door wider, and turned back inside. Bobby followed close behind, one hand clutching his lower back. Wyatt sat down in a white bean bag chair. Bobby didn't think they still made those. He sat on the couch.

"Would you like a cup of coffee?" Wyatt asked.

"No thanks. I'm wired enough. But buddy, can you tell me what's going on? Are you OK? Is there anything I can do?"

"Yeah, sorry to bust up your day. But I just can't do the show tonight."

Bobby took a deep breath. "Wyatt, it does more than just bust up my day. Tonight is big for us. It means a lot going forward. Is something seriously wrong?"

Wyatt stared down at his feet. "You're going to think I'm overreacting."

Bobby rubbed his chin with an index finger and thumb. Speaking softly, he said, "I promise I will not think you're overreacting. But this is especially important. A lot of people are depending on you, and it's too late for a replacement. So please, please tell me what is happening."

Wyatt was clearly upset as he met Bobby's eye. "I fucked up with Lauren."

Bobby had no clue what Wyatt was talking about, so he just waited for him to continue.

"I really have fallen for her over the past few weeks," Wyatt said. "I asked her out for a beer at our last practice, but she wanted to go home. I suggested maybe another time, but she seemed to prefer going out with the whole band. In other words, 'Forget about it, Wyatt, you are barking up the wrong tree.' What a dork I am."

"So then what happened?" Bobby asked.

"What do you mean?" Wyatt asked, incredulous. "Nothing happened. That's the point. I can't face Lauren now. I made a pass, and she said no. It will be embarrassing for both of us."

Bobby leaned back on the couch and shook his head. "Let me get this straight. You asked Lauren to go for a beer after practice, which had to be close to three in the morning. She said no, as would any sane person at that hour, and then she left the door open for some other time—but maybe with the rest of the band."

"Exactly."

Bobby stood up and moved closer to Wyatt. "Are you kidding me? First, if you wanted to ask her out, that is the lamest way to do it I ever heard. I bet you ten to one that she has no idea you even like her in that way. In other words, there's no need to be worried about her feeling awkward, because Lauren has no idea of what to feel awkward about. Therefore, you are in the same position as you ever were. Jesus! And one more thing: she just got out of a pretty volatile longterm relationship. So this might be a bad time. Don't assume she wouldn't be interested at a more appropriate time."

"You really think so?"

"Absolutely," Bobby said, although in truth he thought Wyatt was a little too backwoods for Lauren. "However, there is some truth to the old saying, 'don't shit where you eat,' but I'll leave that up to you."

"So what do you think I should do?"

"I'd sit on this thing with Lauren for a while. Believe me, if it's meant to be, she'll let you know when she's ready. In the meantime, please come back to the band. We need you, and frankly, no one would be more upset to lose you than Lauren. So what do you say?"

Wyatt leaned back in his chair and stared for a few moments at the GloFish in a small aquarium across the room. "So what time should I be there tonight?"

Bobby made a fist and punched the air. "Ha! That's my boy! I knew your brains would kick in." Bobby stood up. "We go on at nine. Be there by seven-thirty."

Wyatt nodded, hugged Bobby, and thanked him for coming. As Bobby walked down the hall, he couldn't believe the poor, lovesick bastard bought the line of shit he'd just slung. He just hoped it stuck, at least for a while.

In the lobby, Bobby was ready to call another Uber, but when he walked outside, there was Owen, seated in his car where he'd dropped Bobby off.

"Hey, man, thanks for waiting." Bobby jumped into the back. "I really didn't expect you to stay this long."

"When Own makes a promise, Owen keeps a promise."

They drove for a while in silence, Bobby awash in relaxation and relief he had not felt since waking up. He thought back to his earlier conversation with Owen, and though Bobby wasn't a religious man, he was curious about what Owen had said. "Hey, Owen, how do you know God doesn't give you more than you can handle?"

Owen looked in the rearview mirror. "Well, it wasn't because of a flat on Route 70."

"Really sorry about that," Bobby said. "I was in a bad place."

Owen waved it off with a flick of his wrist. "I used to be a welder at Titan Contracting, one of the larger employers in Owensboro. Pay was good and I enjoyed the work. In case you haven't figured it out, I'm gay. Being Black and gay in an industrial contracting company, I didn't have a lot of friends, but except for one time when somebody wrote faggot on my locker, no one bothered me. One year I was planning a trip to see my older sister in California, and I wanted to make some extra cash, so I decided to moonlight for a taxi company on weekends, seeing as Uber had yet to arrive in our neck of the woods. Was doing it about a month or so when I picked up this kid about twenty on Frederica Street, a popular area of restaurants and bars for the college kids. Anyhow, it was late, and he was a little drunk but still polite. Told me about how he missed his parents and little sister back in Lexington. When we arrived at his apartment, he reached into his pocket for his wallet and panicked. He'd left it back at the bar, which was now closed. The ride wasn't that far, so the fare wasn't large, and I felt sorry for him—he looked like he'd just lost the family dog. I told him not to worry about it. I said I'd be happy to take him back to see if we could get someone to open up the bar, but he said he'd just call them in the morning. He said he didn't have that much money in his wallet anyway. But he was insistent on paying me. Said it would really bother him if he didn't, and he would just run inside and get some money from his roommate. Sure enough, he came back a few minutes later with his roommate. He came over to my window and joked that his roommate came along to make sure he didn't go buy more beer. I started to laugh, and that's when I felt this blow to my face. One of them yelling that they hated fucking queers. When I went to cover my face, they dragged me out of the car."

Bobby was stunned. "That's awful. What did they do?"

Owen let out a soft laugh. "Let's put it this way. I was in a coma for eleven days. Cracked skull, fractured vertebrae in my lower back, and this scar below my eye isn't a birthmark."

"Jesus!"

"Yes, Jesus. They say after you go through something like that, when you wake up you forget what exactly happened. That wasn't the case for me, though. I remembered every second of it. After I got out of the hospital, I was paranoid, man. There I was, in the town I grew up in, never been one hundred miles out of, and I was literally afraid to walk around the block."

Bobby rested his forearms on the passenger seat in front of him. "What did you do?"

"I was too scared to go anywhere. I tried to go

to the supermarket and broke out in a cold sweat. I quit the taxi gig, and I called in sick so many times to my welding job that I got fired. Basically, I stayed home and did bad stuff. First just pot, then coke, and finally crack. That did me in. Lost my house, car, basically everything. Within a few months, I went from totally secure to panhandling on the street. Tough to be a panhandler when you're afraid of people."

"Anyway, it was a rough few months of mostly sleeping in a park. One day this woman approached me, a young white women, couldn't have been more than thirty. I'd seen her pass by the park a few times. I couldn't take my eyes off her face; just something about it was calming. She walked with a limp, which I later found out was from a car accident when she was a child. Anyway, she asked if I wanted to go to this shelter that provided food and might be able to get me someplace to stay until I could get back on my feet. I'd heard those places were dangerous, so I said no. But over the next few days, she persisted and promised me this one wasn't dangerous at all. So I agreed to take a look, figuring at least I'd get a good meal and maybe they'd give me a few bucks; I hadn't had crack in a while and was dying for a hit. Anyway, when she took me to the shelter, I realized it was for children. I was angry and embarrassed. I think I even cursed at her. But she was so calm. Didn't take any offense at all. She said just because this mission was for kids didn't mean they would refuse to help me. I was awful hungry. She took me to her office and told me to wait while she got me a plate of food. I still remember it: meatloaf with gravy, baked beans, and mashed potatoes. Within a few hours, she arranged a place for me to stay with some volunteer. He was an older man, about your age, no offense."

"None taken," Bobby said.

"He gave me my own room, toiletries, even some of his clothes. He didn't talk much but never asked for anything in return. Made sure I had three squares a day. He went to work during the week and trusted me with the house. One day when he was gone, I went into this small study where he sometimes worked at night. There were pictures on the shelves of young kids and one of a woman. I thought either he had gotten divorced or that was a sister and her kids or something. One night we had this terrible storm, and it knocked down a big maple tree in his front yard. Just missed the house. I told him I'd help him clean up. We were out there with axes and saws for hours. It was hot. I mean that weight-on-your-back Kentucky hot on a clear summer day. He hardly spoke as he cut and chopped away, and hours after we started, he didn't seem to be any more tired. Just to break up the monotony, I asked him about the pictures. I said something like, 'I saw that picture in your study. Beautiful children. Related?' He stopped swinging the axe, and for a second I thought he was going to chew me out for snooping. Instead, he sat down on one of the logs. He looked at me, but past me, if that makes sense. He told me those were his kids. He said the picture of the woman was his wife. He proceeded to tell me he'd had an argument with her over keeping the kids quiet while he was trying to watch a football game. She argued with him, saying that kids were kids, and it was a ridiculous request. It got heated, and she said she was going to take the kids out to the mall so he could watch the game and hopefully calm down. On her way to the mall, a pickup truck ran a red light and hit the car broadside. Everyone was killed on the spot except the youngest, who hung on for two weeks before succumbing to her injuries. He told me the story in a monotone voice, then he got up, asked me please not to inquire about it again, and went back to chopping the tree. That moment changed me forever. I was thinking this man probably blamed himself for losing everything, and I mean everything, and he had not only managed to carry on but had opened his home to complete strangers in need while I continued to pity myself. He had the courage to care and to help others even though so much of his own life was destroyed."

Bobby was so entranced by the story that he didn't realize they had just pulled in front of his house.

"Sorry I went on so long," Owen said.

"No, man, are you kidding? You need to finish."

Owen nodded. "I'll try and make it quick. Don't want you sitting out here all day listening to me run my mouth." Owen got out of the car, opened the rear door, and leaned in toward Bobby. "That woman who took me to the children's mission and that man who took me in saved my life. Now did they come into my life through coincidence or divine intervention? I guess that one is a matter of personal opinion, but as for me, my faith in a higher power was strengthened. I am not a big believer much in coincidence. I decided right then to start anew. Shortly thereafter, I came to Nashville, got a job as an assistant cook in a restaurant downtown, and began driving a bit for Uber. I met someone about a year ago, and we couldn't be happier. I try to spend a little time at this mission on the north side to give back a little."

Bobby got out of the car. "That's quite a story, Owen."

Owen chuckled. "Well, sir, the point of my overlong story is, sometimes things that we think are really bad maybe ain't really that so."

Bobby nodded and watched as Owen got back in the driver's seat and drove away.

MOVING ON UP

Marathon Music Works, part of a block-long brick complex and former home of the long defunct automobile manufacturer Marathon Motor Works, was packed tighter than the backside of Nicki Minaj's leggings. The buzz around Lauren and the band was palpable. Becca was sitting with Lauren backstage, but unlike previous meetings, where it seemed Becca's job was to offer instructions, the two now chatted and laughed as one drank a beer and the other a Manhattan.

Bobby was more than a little relieved when Wyatt, the last band member to arrive, appeared.

"We cool?" Bobby asked.

Wyatt just smiled and nodded.

It was time to play and play they did. The roar after the opening number shook the stage. The band fed off the energy and delivered again and again. Even Bobby, side stage, was rapt. Lauren, sweat seeping into the threads of her red blouse, seemed to be in a new zone. Her voice was sharper and more forceful, her synchronicity with the band right on, and her connection with the audience tight.

Becca walked up to Bobby and yelled into his ear above the music. "Mr. Linder, I think it's time to take this show on the road!"

Even after the "Jackson" encore, the audience refused to surrender. The band came back onstage and did a version of Harry Nilsson's "I'd Rather Be Dead (Than Wet My Bed)," a song they had rehearsed only once, as a goof. The crowd ate it up.

Backstage after the show, there was a lot of high fiving and laughter. What made it better was when Chris Cobb came in and handed Bobby a check for $18,000. Things were starting to get real. Bobby found himself looking out for Jimmy and was relieved he was nowhere in sight. Wyatt seemed relaxed around Lauren and was talking in a group with her. Becca came over to Bobby and said, "I was serious about what I said earlier."

"You really think we're ready?"

Becca's eyes grew wide. "Were you watching what I was watching tonight? The time for foreplay is over."

Early the next morning, Bobby's cell phone rang. He ignored the call, but it rang again.

"What!" Bobby yelled into the phone.

The woman on the other end was nonplussed. "Please hold for Mr. Fontana."

Bobby sat up in bed.

"Bobby, this is Eddie. We need to talk."

Bobby asked Eddie if they could meet the next day because he had to pick up his car at the repair shop. Eddie said he would send a car to get Bobby and have the repair shop deliver the car to his home. That's when Bobby knew the meeting was important.

At the offices of Sidewalk Music, the receptionist who had given him such a hard time during his last visit was all smiles and immediately dialed one of Eddie's assistants to say that Bobby was there. Very shortly, a twentysomething woman in jeans and a Dierks Bentley T-shirt with a seriousness beyond her years arrived to take Bobby to Eddie's office but not before asking if he preferred sparkling or flat. Knowing that Eddie kept some of the finest bourbon in his office, Bobby declined.

Unlike Bobby's last visit, Eddie was not waiting with open arms but sitting behind his desk, looking older than before. The Peshawar rug Bobby had disgraced was gone. Eddie looked up from his desk but did not stand. "Please sit, Bobby," he said, motioning to one of the chairs in front of his desk.

Although it was only ten o'clock in the morning, Eddie pulled a bottle of bourbon and two glasses from a drawer. He poured them each a drink. Bobby had no idea what Eddie wanted to talk about, but he was worried he or the band had done something to anger one of the owners or managers of a club Eddie had gotten them into.

"Hey," Bobby said, "before we start, I just want to thank you, man, for getting me in with the clubs. I do not know if you've gotten any feedback, but we drew big crowds, and it was a great launching pad. I really can't thank you enough."

Eddie waved him off. "Ah, it was just a few quick phone calls. Don't thank me; I'll probably forget you did anyway."

Bobby winced, recalling Eddie's dementia diagnosis. "It's getting worse?"

"It is what it is, man. But if you hear I'm lying in bed somewhere drooling and shitting my pants, you come put me out of my misery, OK?"

Bobby forced a smile and nodded.

"Anyway," Eddie said, "I hear this woman Lauren Culiver is lighting up the town."

"Yeah, she's doing really well. She's come a long way in a short period of time."

Eddie took a cigar out of a humidor and offered one to Bobby, who declined. Eddie lit his. "You should pat yourself on the back on that one. If not for you, she probably would have been playing honky-tonks until she cranked out a few kids."

"I'm not so sure about that, Eddie. You spend a little time around her, and the talent is obvious."

Eddie took a long puff on the cigar. "A lot of people have raw talent. The trick is polishing that talent so other people are willing to pay to partake in it. That's what you and I have been doing our whole careers. But I didn't ask you here to debate the key to musical success. I think I can help Lauren and you onto bigger and better things."

Bobby smiled and tapped his hands on his thighs. "I appreciate it, Eddie. But you've done a lot already. I enjoy the work I'm doing here. I don't think I'm at the stage where I need a partner."

Eddie coughed and leaned forward in his chair, the smoke from his cigar melding into the wrinkles of his face, which had grown more serious. It was a look Bobby had seen many times over the years; it meant Eddie was getting to the crux of a matter. "I didn't mention the word partner. Did I?"

Bobby looked out the window at the limbs of a blackjack oak tree just beginning to bud. "No, you didn't. But we worked together for a long time, and I've seen this movie."

Eddie looked down at his desk. "Bobby, I'm not sure how much time I have before I'm a bumbling idiot. You and I have been through a lot, and regardless of some issues over the years, it has been more good than bad. When you got heavy into drugs, I should have done more to help you. But you were right last time you were here. To some degree, whether I wanted to admit it or not, I saw our work as an opportunity to grow this label on my own. And maybe I did use some of our joint work while you were off the wagon. I can't change what happened. But I can try to make up for it."

Bobby felt himself growing more anxious. "What are you saying?"

"You know we produce and record Faith Hill. She's going on tour in a little over a month. Although she packs 'em in, I think I can convince her that some young blood like Lauren might be good for both of them. As Lauren's audience grows, they'll get to know Faith, and vice versa."

Bobby was stunned. Faith usually toured with her husband, Tim McGraw. "What about Tim?"

"We think she needs to do a solo trip once in a while to solidify her own identity."

"How do you know Faith will like Lauren?"

"Because I asked her manager to check out the show at the Cannery. He gave it three thumbs up. I think between him and me, we can get Faith on board."

"What's in it for Sidewalk Records?"

"Not much at this point. We put you on the payroll as a talent scout, but you get to keep all the profits from anything having to do with Lauren and the band. This includes the Faith Hill tour and any records you decide to record, less expenses, of course."

"You're telling me that you're going to hook Lauren up with the Faith Hill tour, I'm going to join Sidewalk Records, and I can produce her records and keep the profits?"

"I believe that is what I said."

Bobby held his hands open. "Why, Eddie?"

Eddie slowly rose, walked around his desk, and stood in front of Bobby. "It sounds like a cliché, but son of a bitch, what they say is true. When you know you're going down, a lot of things you thought were important mean a lot less. I know you love this business, and I know from last time you were in here and what you're doing with Lauren that you desperately want back in. And I know I screwed you over at times. For my own peace, I need to make it up to you. Please allow me to do that."

Bobby looked up at Eddie and for the first time saw fear and sadness in his eyes. It frightened him. He held up his glass and forced a smile. "OK, Eddie, let's do this."

The day after meeting with Eddie, Bobby went back to Sidewalk Records to iron out the details of their new arrangement. With a small office, an advance, and a new credit card, he called a meeting with Lauren and the band at Café Margot in East Nashville. It had been one of his favorite places for years, but he hadn't been back in a long time because he could no longer afford it. He even invited Becca and Miguel, thinking he could use their input. He hadn't told anyone anything about the particulars of the meeting other than that it would be some important stuff.

Bobby got a table upstairs, and as they had cocktails and shared appetizers of monkfish medallions, grilled quail, and cheese cannelloni, he thanked everyone for all the hard work they'd put in to get to this point. He paused, pulled a piece of paper out of his pocket, and looked it over. Bobby told the group he just needed to see if there was anything else he'd wanted to say. "Oh, yeah, I almost forgot. If it is ok with Lauren, we're getting signed to Sidewalk Records, and we're going on a national tour with Faith Hill in about a month!"

After a brief pause, Lauren yelled it was fine with her and a roar went up from the table. It was so loud that the restaurant owner, Margot McCormack herself, came out of the downstairs kitchen along with the maître d' and some waiters to see what was going on. Hanson got up, put his hands on Bobby's cheeks, and gave him a kiss on the lips. Lauren danced on a chair while others shimmied and high-fived around the room.

When the excitement subsided a bit, the band began to bombard Bobby with questions.

"When does the tour start?"

"Where are we going to play?"

"Are we flying or busing?"

"Do we get our own rooms?"

"Easy, easy," Bobby said. "I don't have a lot of specifics just yet. Sidewalk is still working out our contract and our pay with Faith Hill. But what I can tell you is, if we make a record with Sidewalk, we don't have to split profits with the label, just expenses. I know we don't have a lot of time, but I think we need to work on Lauren's songs and cut a single and an album quickly so that we can promote them on this tour."

"Wow," Miguel exclaimed. "The record company wants none of the profits. Never heard of that before."

"What did you do, Bobby?" Becca said. "Bend over for Eddie Fontana?"

Over the laughter, Bobby said, "Let's just say we're old friends and leave it at that."

Becca suggested that they consider giving the band a name.

"Like what?" Lauren asked.

"I don't know," Becca said. "Maybe Lauren Culiver and the Nash Band?"

Bobby braced himself for the usual debate that came with naming a band, but Henry Taylor, the least talkative of the collective, said, "That's perfect." There were nods all around.

Within a few days, Sidewalk had negotiated with Faith Hill's people the compensation for Bobby and the band, and it was more than enough to make everyone happy. More importantly, they no longer had to work side jobs, so they could concentrate on solidifying their songs. The tour was to start in Austin in less than five weeks and end in Washington D.C. six weeks later, including stops in Toronto and Vancouver. Bobby informed the band that they would have between fifty minutes and one hour to perform during each show, depending on the venue and their starting times.

Bobby thought it best to spend the next few weeks polishing original songs and then recording them a few days prior to the tour. At Sidewalk, they now had full access to a practice studio and a recording studio, not to mention unlimited access to donuts in the kitchen from Five Daughters Bakery, a Nashville staple.

Lauren and Bobby spent hours before and after rehearsals working on songs. Sometimes Josh Cooperman, a thirty-something superstar writer hired by Eddie, stopped in for a bit and made suggestions. In just the past two years, Cooperman had written hits for Eric Church, Kenny Chesney, Sam Hunt, and Florida Georgia Line, to name a few. Normally writers were skittish when someone stepped into their territory, especially if they were critiquing your work, but Bobby quickly saw that this guy had the goods. Sometimes just changing a word or a phrase in a song could make a dud into something special. It was a gift, and not many had it, but Cooperman did. He insisted on taking no credit for his insights. "Just remember me when you make it, Lauren," he said with a smile and a Virginia drawl. Smart man thought Bobby. Sometimes you had to make an investment to get a shot at something bigger later.

In the second week of rehearsing, Eddie's assistant came into the studio and told Bobby that Eddie needed to see him. Bobby walked into Eddie's office, where Eddie was waiting with Faith Hill. Bobby knew Faith from back in the day when he and Eddie had written and produced songs for her early in her career. He quickly saw that the years had been kinder to her than they had been to him. Bobby wasn't even sure Faith would remember him.

"Well, Bobby Linder, it sure has been a long time," Faith said with a smile and a Mississippi twang. She gave Bobby a hug, as if the last time she'd seen him was just yesterday. If she knew the details of his dark years, she sure wasn't letting on.

"Hi, Faith. So glad to see you again. You look great. I cannot thank you enough for this opportunity. It's above and beyond."

"Please, Bobby, this Lauren girl is the talk of the town. If she's buzzing the country scene here, she'll buzz it anywhere."

"I think you'll really enjoy her."

"I'm sure. I was hoping to meet her and the band."

The band was in the middle of a song when Bobby walked back into the rehearsal studio with Faith Hill. The members of the band stopped simultaneously except for Toby, who was looking at the keyboard in the middle of a solo. Wyatt walked over and nudged him, and the keys came to a stop. Lauren's eyes were so wide, one might have thought she was witnessing the second coming.

"Hi y'all!" Faith turned to Lauren. "And you must be the girl everyone is talking about."

Lauren blushed and looked down at the floor. "I don't know about all that, ma'am."

Faith laughed. "Ma'am? I'm not your grandmother." She smiled at the rest of the group. "How are you boys doing?"

They all nodded and mumbled friendly hellos.

"Can you make my day and play me something?" Faith said.

"That would make my day," Lauren said. She looked to Bobby for a suggestion.

"Why don't you play the one we were working on yesterday?" he said.

Lauren nodded. She had recently written "Ghost Lovers." It was about seeing things in travels that reminded her of past romances. It was a slow song, but it really tested Lauren's voice and cadence. Bobby knew the lyrics were a winner. The more people who can relate to a song, the better the job the writer has done. Who isn't sometimes reminded of past loves by places or inanimate objects?

Faith loved it. "I want to give you a hug!"

Lauren beamed.

"Anything to show off the boys in the band?" Faith said.

Before Bobby could make a suggestion, Wyatt called out, "How about 'Luxury Liner'?" It was a Gram Parsons tune made popular by Emmylou Harris. With Lauren's smooth voice carrying over the quick beat, the band smoked it.

When they were finished, Faith clapped and held her arms in the air. "I'm sold!" She went up to each member of the band and welcomed them to the tour. She saved Lauren for last. "Sweetie, you really got it. I'm looking forward to spending some time with you."

"It would be my honor." Lauren's voice was relaxed, but she looked starstruck.

Within three weeks, Bobby and Lauren felt they had eight original songs that were polished enough to record. To round out the album, they decided to add recent fan cover favorites, Cheryl Crow's "If It Makes You Happy" and the John Prine's "Angel From Montgomery." Due to the fact that Lauren seemed to be shaking Music City up a bit, they decided to title the album Troublemaker. Bobby was lucky to snag Sidewalk's top audio engineer, Tommy Lane. The only issue was that Tommy had a two-day window before he started an assignment with Blake Shelton, so things need to go smoothly.

During Bobby's career, the recording studio was one of his favorite parts of the job. Eddie used to call it the place where dreams, music, and money were made or killed. But to Bobby, it was the culmination of everything everyone involved in the business worked for. The songwriter, the singer, the musicians, the producer, the engineer, and the record company all needed to come together and give both their contribution and stamp of approval. The final product was like putting in the last piece of a thousand-piece puzzle.

Most of the band was placed in the live room, or the main room. Hanson and Lauren were placed in separate isolation rooms, as it was important that Lauren's voice be central, and that the drums not overtake her or the rest of the band. They would add in Lauren's guitar to the tracks later. Bobby and Tommy Lane sat in the control room. During the first few takes, Bobby could hear that Lauren's voice was not where it needed to be. When Bobby or Tommy made suggestions, her nervous responses came back rather abruptly, with little change from the previous takes. At this point, the band's cohesion started to falter. Concerned, Bobby told the band to take a break and asked Lauren if she would come into the control room.

Tommy turned to Bobby. "Hey, do you mind if I take this one? You're a little upset. Let me talk to her; she doesn't have any attachment to me. Sometimes that works best."

Bobby shrugged; it was as good an idea as any. When Lauren came into the control room, she was clearly shaken. The confidence she had been exuding over the past month was absent. Bobby excused himself to grab a cup of coffee. Tommy took his headphones off and offered Lauren the chair next to him. She sat down with her arms folded across her chest.

"Bobby thinks you're a little uptight."

"Well, then I guess Bobby is a fucking genius," Lauren said.

Tommy just smiled. "I was the engineer back in '06 for Taylor Swift's first album."

That got Lauren's attention. She sat up straighter.

Tommy continued, "She was sixteen. Cutest thing. She came into the studio shy as a meerkat. Anyway, we start the recording, and about fifteen minutes in, we need to take a break because Taylor felt sick. We had to wait around for about an hour while she puked her guts out. Her producer, a fella by the name of Nat Chapman who still works with her, finally calmed her down. We start recording again, and just a few minutes in, Taylor comes charging out of her booth and runs toward the bathroom. We wait about another half hour, and Nat sends a female assistant into the bathroom to see what's going on. A few minutes later, the assistant comes out and whispers something to Nat. Nat turns around and tells us to go home, that the recording session is cancelled for the day."

Lauren waited for Tommy to continue, but he didn't. "What happened to Taylor?"

"She peed her pants."

"Excuse me?"

"From what I understand, it was like a firehose

went off. We had to call in a janitor to clean up the bathroom."

"Why'd she pee her pants?"

Tommy shrugged. "She was nervous. Can't totally blame her. There will never be a day as big as recording your first record. For a musician, it is your true coming out party to the world."

Lauren lifted her head and peered into the spotlights on the ceiling. "I guess you're telling me it's perfectly normal."

"What? To pee your pants?"

Lauren laughed. "You know what I mean."

"What I mean is, if you made it to this point, professionals who have been in the business a long time have recognized your talent. This opportunity is given to very few people. Better chance of getting struck by lightning. The biggest star in music today doubted herself while everyone around her didn't. The people around her were clearly right. The people around you are clearly right. You are gifted. Now why don't you get out there and do it."

Lauren smiled and nodded. "Thank you. I think I feel a little better."

Bobby walked back into the room. "Everything OK?"

"Yeah. Tommy just told me the story of Taylor Swift peeing her pants during her first recording."

After Lauren left, Bobby turned to Tommy. "I'm not sure what you told her, but none of it was true, was it?"

"Not a lick," Tommy said, putting his headphones back on.

FRENCH WOMEN

The warmer than normal late April sun was just beginning to set on Texas. The Austin360 Amphitheater was less than half full when Lauren and the band were ready to take the stage. That was one of the tricky things Bobby had tried to tell them over the past few weeks. When you are the opening act, the crowd isn't there to see you. In fact, most people walking in are hoping you finish up soon so the real show can start.

"Your job," Bobby told them, "is to make every one of those late arriving bastards regret they missed the rest of your set."

Lauren's confidence, shaken during her initial day in the recording studio, had rebounded. The recording session ended up going smoothly, and even Eddie, who pulled no punches, said he thought the final product was terrific.

Bobby called the band together for one final word before they went onstage. "People, I can tell you, as someone who's had his share of screw-ups and has paid for them dearly, that moments like this don't come around often. This is a once-in-a-lifetime, grab-the-bull-by-the-horns opportunity. And do you know why we get it? Because we deserve it. That's why. And not just because we worked hard. Lots of people in our business work hard. No, we deserve it because we are great at it. It's time to go out there and show the world. Now, I'm not the religious type, but can somebody lead us in a brief prayer?"

Henry Taylor stepped forward, and everyone held hands. "Dear Lord, thank you for this opportunity. Help us demonstrate our full potential tonight. Sprinkle some holy music dust on our souls so we may rise to the occasion. In your name we pray."

The band, sans Lauren, went onstage to a light smattering of applause. Bobby watched from a few feet behind Lauren as she prepared to make her entrance. She was silhouetted in the lights, but he could still make out her jeans tucked into her boots and her hair falling over the back of her blouse. She took a deep breath and walked forcefully onstage. She picked up her guitar off a stand.

"Hi, y'all. My name is Lauren Culiver, and this here is the Nash Band."

A light flurry of applause followed. Lauren was undeterred by the fact that more people seemed interested in the concession stand than in the stage. She turned to the band.

"What do you say, boys? Let's show 'em what we got."

By the third song, many attendees were a lot less interested in food and drink, and quite a few hurried back to their seats. Bobby had been concerned about how the band would look and sound to a crowd ten times larger than any they had ever played to before, but now he was just enjoying the moment. From the looks of it, the band was too. Lauren moved about the stage as if she had built it, and the band followed her lead. By the end of their act, the applause was more than respectable. The band came offstage so ramped up, one would think they'd injected speed. Bobby gave

Lauren a tight hug that left his shirt as sweaty as hers. As the roadies were changing out equipment on the stage, Faith Hill, in a silver lame dress slit up both sides, approached Lauren with a high five and a light hug. "Way to go, girl! I knew from the first time I saw you play at Sidewalk, you had it in you. Thanks for getting the crowd pumped. This is going to be a fun tour."

As the band members cracked open beers and excitedly talked about the show—Hanson was convinced that two girls in the front row were flirting with him—Bobby asked Lauren to come with him to the side of the stage to watch Hill. Lauren stood mesmerized as Hill slid through songs like "It Matters to Me," "This Kiss," and "Breathe." The only thing Lauren uttered throughout the whole show was, "Wow, she is so good."

"She's been famous for almost thirty years," Bobby said. "Now it's like second nature. Notice her style. She knows her strength is ballads. Her voice is so smooth, not aggressive. She does very few hard country songs. Knowing what you are good at is important."

"So I guess that raises the question, what am I good at?"

"That's what we're finding out, but to be honest, I'm having more trouble figuring out what you're not good at. There is little I can't see you doing, from Patsy Cline to the Allman Brothers. In any event, I say we're off to a good start figuring out our sweet spot."

Lauren winked. "Or spots."

The next show, at Red Rocks Amphitheatre in

Colorado, went well, followed by the MGM Grand Garden Arena in Vegas where, with 17,000 seats, the band members had their first experience seeing themselves on two huge screens on either side of the stage.

"Just what I needed," Hanson said. "My big head blown up bigger."

The next stop was the Moda Center in Portland, which was the big warmup for Los Angeles. Bobby remembered a sign that used to hang in an office he shared with Eddie: No matter what type of music you play, never fuck up in New York and LA. The day before the Portland show, Faith asked Lauren to come to her rehearsal, where Faith suggested the pair sing "Back at Mama's House," a duet she normally did with her husband, Tim McGraw. After three takes, Faith said, "Perfect. That song will be about two-thirds through my set. That should give you enough time to rest after your performance."

"Are you serious?"

"Listen, girl, country music is still an old boys club. Don't let anybody kid you. Most of them wear cowboy hats too small for their big heads. I've had to put up with a lot of garbage to get where I am. If I can help a talented woman move forward in this business, nothing will make me happier. I don't look at it as competition; we're on the same team."

"I don't know what to say, Faith. I don't know how to thank you."

"Don't say anything, and don't thank me," Faith said. "Just belt out the song like you just did."

The night of the Portland show, Lauren was so excited she couldn't sit still. She and the band put on their best show yet, and when the duet ended during Faith's set, the crowd erupted in a standing ovation.

Backstage, Bobby was happy and worried at the same time. Everything seemed to be moving so fast. Just a few months ago, Lauren was an unknown playing to small crowds in Nashville honky-tonks, and now she was singing duets with one of the biggest stars of country music. It brought to mind a quote by Henry David Thoreau: "Success usually comes to those who are too busy looking for it." Bobby wasn't about to look a gift horse in the mouth. But he also knew from years of experience that there was something to be said for slow and steady. You catch more on your way up if you have the time to grab it. But sometimes fate is fate, regardless of the most well laid plans. And if fate is on the positive side of the ledger, why complain?

The band got into Los Angeles the day before the show at the Staples Center. Staying at the Marriott Hotel downtown on West Olympic Avenue, Bobby got a call in his room from Lauren asking if he could meet her at the lobby bar. Bobby assumed it would be another meeting to go over the set list. When he arrived in the lobby, Lauren was already sitting on a lounge couch with a glass of wine. Her demeanor was more that of a businesswoman having a cocktail after a long day than a country singer gearing up for the biggest show of her life.

"So," Bobby said, "we excited for tomorrow?"

Lauren smiled and raised a fist. "Oh, yeah!"

Bobby sat down and ordered a bourbon from the waitress. After some chitchat, it seemed Lauren didn't have any particular reason for the meeting.

"So, is everything all right?" Bobby said.

"Yes, everything is great. I mean, why wouldn't it be? Who would have thought we'd have gotten this far this fast?"

Bobby nodded in agreement.

"But I wanted to tell you something so you don't get upset later," Lauren said.

Bobby had a feeling that whatever Lauren wanted to say involved Jimmy. He took a sip of his bourbon.

"Listen, I know you're not going to be thrilled," Lauren said, "but I invited Jimmy to the show tomorrow." Lauren raised her hand. "Now before you say anything, I have given this a lot of thought. I couldn't be more grateful for what you've done for me, and I hope we work together for a long time. But this is my personal life, and what I do with it should be my decision and mine alone. I don't know what's going to happen with me and Jimmy. We've been talking on the phone lately, and we've agreed to take things one step at a time. He's even getting his own hotel room. I wanted to tell you before he got here out of my respect for you. I hope you understand."

Bobby stared at Lauren and smiled. He wanted to tell her it was probably a huge mistake. He didn't know Jimmy well, but he was a quick judge of character, and his judgment told him this dude was bad news. But he knew better than to say so. "Not a problem, Lauren. I appreciate the heads up. I'm sure he's going to love the show."

The next night, the Staples Center was almost full as Lauren and the band were about to go on. Each show seemed to have more people in their seats than the last show. Faith Hill had quipped to Bobby, "If this keeps up, I'm going home." Becca had sent Lauren gifts for the show: a pair of Moussy vintage blue jeans, a white Stella McCartney T-shirt, and a pair of leopard Louboutins. The clothes looked as though they were made for her. The boys in the band couldn't stop staring. The normally quiet Henry Taylor joked, "That's it. I am now officially into white girls."

Onstage, the band continued peaking. Although distinctly country, their sound continued to grow more sophisticated, with blues and rock creeping in. They added Waylon Jennings's "Are You Sure Hank Done It This Way," with the band showcasing their individual talents in solos. Lauren's voice was growing more forceful, and she was developing a good banter with the audience, despite not being the headliner. Her movements across the stage were becoming more aggressive and eye-catching. In all of Bobby's years in the business, he had never seen anything like it. You would have thought Lauren and the band had been playing big arenas for at least a decade. Backstage, the Los Angeles Times was waiting. The next day, in the paper's review of the show, Lauren would get almost as much ink as Faith Hill. The review would end with a line about their duet: "It was like watching the past, present, and future of country music all rolled into one."

During the intermission before Hill's performance, Bobby saw that Jimmy had been invited backstage. He stole a side glance as Jimmy gave Lauren a big hug. Not wanting to end up in another ugly confrontation, Bobby decided to avoid Jimmy. He left the stadium shortly after the show, and on his way back to his hotel, he acted on a tip from the hospitality director backstage, stopping into The Burrow, a small bar and kitchen in the bowels of the O Hotel on Flower Street. It boasted a speakeasy vibe with a mishmash of sofas, chairs, and tables. Bobby sat in a leather chair and ordered a double bourbon and—realizing he hadn't eaten all day—a smoked duck breast sandwich. The bar was half full, and on the sofa across from him sat two well dressed women speaking French. Bobby guessed the older woman was in her mid-forties and the other in her early thirties. The pair were in a pretty serious discussion, and he speculated they were in L.A. on business.

Bobby thought about the time he visited his old high school buddy in Paris, after he dropped out of Belmont. He'd been staying in Paris for two weeks and had bet his friend he would bed a Parisian before he left. He tried hard everywhere—in bars, restaurants, parks, museums, even grocery stores. After ten days of complete failure, he started to worry that maybe a broke, non-French-speaking Tennessean with no worldly experience wasn't what a mademoiselle might be looking for. On the eleventh day, Bobby's luck changed. He had become hooked on the lemon tarts and espresso at the Stohrer patisserie on the rue Montorgueil. On this day, after placing his order, he found himself a few francs short. The girl behind him, a tall nineteen-year-old with brown hair in a pixie cut, blue eyes, and a tan chapeau, offered to make up the difference. Embarrassed, Bobby tried to make her understand that wouldn't be necessary, that he would skip the tart. He quickly found out that the girl, though definitely French, also spoke English.

"Please take it," she said in her accented English. "Otherwise we will be here all day."

Bobby did as he was told and waited for her outside the patisserie. When she came out with her café cream and chocolate éclair, he said he just wanted to thank her again.

"Instead of thanking me, why not walk with me?"

Bobby recalled that she asked a lot of questions. Did he like Paris? How did it compare to Nashville? Did he know any real country music stars? Did he have a girlfriend back home? What did he like to read? They walked up the rue d'Aboukir to the statue of Louis XIV. Leaning against the black iron fence surrounding the statue, Bobby had a chance to ask a few questions of his own. Her name was Isabelle, and she was studying anthropology at Trinity College in Cambridge, England. She was home for a long weekend while her parents were on a trip to Morocco. She liked to ski and play tennis and laughed when Bobby told her he had no desire to do either. Soon Bobby found himself at her parents' apartment on Avenue Montaigne. It was certainly the nicest apartment Bobby had ever been inside and larger than most houses he knew. It was still morning, but Isabelle, disappearing from the living room, came back with a bottle of Sancerre and a marijuana cigarette. She put on a cassette of Miles Davis, and they talked for an hour. She was clearly an avid reader, and Bobby remembers struggling to keep up with the conversation. A bit dizzy from the wine, the weed, the conversation, and the general excitement of meeting Isabelle, Bobby leaned in for a kiss. Isabelle did not resist. Shortly thereafter, she led him into the master bedroom. Bobby asked why not her room, and she said that this was more fun. They spent the entire afternoon in bed except for forays into the kitchen to fetch cheese and saucisson brioche. Isabelle said she was meeting friends for dinner. Bobby thought she might invite him, but she didn't. He suggested they meet again the next morning at the patisserie, but Isabelle declined, saying she needed to get some things done before heading back to England. Bobby realized she wasn't interested in taking things further. He felt like a book she had read and was putting back onto the shelf. So much to do in so little time—to little to bother rereading the same thing again.

Bobby's friend refused to pay the bet. He didn't buy Bobby's story of going out for coffee and a lemon tart and spending the rest of the day in bed with a beautiful French girl in a magnificent apartment in one of the finest areas of Paris. Bobby didn't care. It had been the single best afternoon of his young life. Now, sitting in the LA. bar across from the two Frenchwomen, it still was.

RUPTURE

Faith Hill invited Bobby and Lauren on her private jet for the trip to the next show, in Vancouver. Bobby declined, wanting to make sure all of the band members made it onto their commercial flight, but he encouraged Lauren to go. Landing in Vancouver, the band checked into the Shangri-La Hotel while Bobby went over to Rogers Arena to scope out the venue. The local hockey team, the Canucks, had a game that evening, so ice still covered the floor. The concert was scheduled for two nights out. Overnight, the setup for the concert would begin; the band would have a practice tomorrow and a brief practice and soundcheck the day of the show. Bobby usually had to wait until Faith Hill decided when she wanted to do her bit, but it was a small price to pay. With the ice floor and no crowd, it was cold in the arena. Bobby went down to the front row behind one of the goals on the end of the floor where the stage would be erected. Looking up at the empty seats in the cavernous arena, he marveled at the ability of some artists to attract a paying, adoring crowds of 20,000. Most of the entertainers he had known seemed to take it in stride, and not necessarily in a conceited way. As a teenager, Bobby had gone to shows around Nashville at places like Ryman Auditorium, but never at a stadium or an arena. When he was in his mid-twenties and had written some songs for Alabama, they invited him to their concert in Dallas at the now-demolished Reunion Arena. It was the first time he had been in an arena that huge. When the band came onstage, the roar of the crowd made the hair on the back of his head stand up, and his skin hot. He felt both fearful and excited. Sometimes he still did.

After taking in the arena, Bobby headed back to the hotel lobby. On the flight, Hanson had been talking up a Chinese restaurant in Vancouver he'd been to a few years back. Everyone was going except Lauren, who had yet to arrive. At Bao Bei in the Chinatown section of the city, Bobby and the band sat at a long table. Everyone agreed that Hanson was right about how good the food was. Over dumplings, fish, beef tongue, prawns, and too many Yanjing beers and Ginjo sakes, Hanson started to rib Toby. A man of few words, Toby usually kept to himself on tour, preferring a book in his hotel room to hanging out with the other band members. Only Hanson's persistent badgering on the flight had convinced Toby to join the group for dinner. Not that Toby was antisocial; it was just a matter of his upbringing. Toby was an only child raised by a single mother. Shortly after he was born, his father left town with a waitress from the local diner. Toby's father was a musician with an overinflated sense of his own talent. He went to Vegas in hopes of making it big but never got past casino lounges. Last Toby's mother heard, the waitress had left him, and he had gone to Oklahoma to be a regional salesman for Sony Betamax machines. Toby's mother never had an interest in marrying again, instead doting on Toby. Although she paid him a lot of attention, she didn't spoil him. She couldn't afford to, anyway. But she read to him often. When Toby could read himself, he spent a lot of time in his room or under the hackberry tree in their yard. In high school, he was the class valedictorian and played piano in the school orchestra. He took a year off after high school to save some money for college and found a job at a banquet hall as a waiter. One evening during a wedding, the band's keyboard player got sick on a bad oyster he heisted during hors d'oeuvres. Bobby asked his boss if he could fill in. The band was glad to have him. It was clear the kid was a natural. Miguel Lopez happened to be a guest at the wedding. Miguel invited Toby over to his house, took him under his wing, and gave him some tips. Miguel got Toby into a good band playing gigs around town and even a few stints as a studio musician. Although he never lost his love for learning and reading, Toby got the music bug and knew that over the next few years, he would more likely be playing in honky-tonks on Broadway than studying at Vanderbilt.

"Hey, Toby, what's your deal?" Hanson said. "Nice looking boy like you. Never seen you with a girl. You go the other way?"

Toby just smiled politely. "No, sir."

"No, sir, what, Tob?" Hanson asked. "No, you don't like girls? Or no, you don't hold onto your ankles?"

Toby's face reddened.

"Don't listen to him," Bobby said. "Just trying to get a rise out of you."

"Actually," Wyatt said, "I think either gay or straight, our boy Toby here would have no trouble attracting 'em."

"And why do you say that?" Hanson said.

"Because we both work out at the same gym. In the locker room, he is known as Toby the Tail."

"What's with Toby the Tail?" Hanson said.

Wyatt held his index fingers about twelve inches apart.

Hanson was incredulous. "Are you trying to tell me that our boy Toby here has a twelve-inch piece of equipment?"

"Shh!" Bobby said. "Keep it down."

Hanson repeated his question in a loud whisper.

"At least," Wyatt replied nonchalantly as he bit into a prawn.

"Oh no, boys. I am not buying it. Maybe if he multiplied it by pie squared."

"Bet?" Wyatt asked, eating another prawn.

"For sure. How much?"

"How about one hundred bucks."

"I ain't looking at another man's junk for just one hundred bucks. Make it five hundred."

Wyatt was quiet.

Hanson smiled. "Didn't think I would call your bluff, did you?"

"Deal," Wyatt said.

"How we going to do this?" Hanson asked. "It's not like I carry around a measuring tape."

Henry reached under the table and pulled off a loafer. "Size twelve. Would that work?"

Hanson and Wyatt agreed.

"OK, Toby let's see it."

Toby, still red faced, shook his head.

"Hey, guys," Bobby said. "No one is pulling their johnson out in the middle of a Chinese restaurant, for Christ's sake."

"The bathroom?" Wyatt asked.

"Now how would it look if a bunch of men from the same table all walked into the bathroom at the same time?" Hanson said.

Shortly afterwards, in an alley behind the restaurant, an extremely reluctant Toby pulled down his pants with one hand and looked up at the sky while holding Henry's shoe in the other. The four other men looked on attentively, as if they were medical students observing a heart operation for the first time. In the end, Hanson was five hundred dollars lighter, and a photo of a surprised man holding a loafer against his member made the rounds on Instagram and in texts and emails for many months to come.

Back at the hotel, as the band headed to the elevator, a surprised Bobby noticed Lauren and Jimmy sitting at the lobby bar. Lauren caught Bobby's eye and waved. He was hesitant to go over but felt obligated at this point. He noticed they both had their travel bags by their seats.

"Hi, Bobby, we just got here. The flight on Faith's jet was fabulous. I wish you could have joined us."

"Us?" Bobby asked as calmly as he could. "Both of you came on the jet?"

Jimmy smiled. "Yeah, it was great. I'd never flown private like that before."

"Well, since you weren't coming," Lauren said, "I asked Faith if it was OK for Jimmy to ride. She said not a problem. In fact, she and Jimmy yapped the whole way up here."

"Do you think that was a good idea?" Bobby said.

"What?"

Bobby resisted the urge to launch into a million

reasons why it was a bad move. "No worries. Glad you made it. I'm bushed. See you tomorrow at rehearsal, two o'clock."

"Leaving so soon? Can I buy you a drink before you put yourself to bed?" Jimmy said, still smiling.

Bobby imagined himself reaching into Jimmy's drink and shoving an ice cube down his throat. "No, thanks. I had more than enough tonight."

Back in his room, Bobby was furious. It wasn't kosher bringing that clown onto Hill's plane. Jimmy was a wildcard. Lauren shouldn't have substituted Jimmy for Bobby, like he was OK with it. He hoped Lauren kept her head on straight. He didn't want this guy blowing it up for all of them. Bobby watched TV for a while but was totally disconnected. He slept little before the gray light of dawn slithered through the curtains.

Bobby arrived early at practice the next afternoon. Faith Hill was just finishing up her rehearsal. Bobby apologized for Lauren assuming she could invite someone else onto Faith's plane.

"Oh no, Bobby, it was great." She smiled. "Jimmy is very funny. I told him whenever he is around and we use the jet, he's welcome."

Lauren arrived at rehearsal in a happy mood. If she grasped Bobby's annoyance from the night before, she didn't show it. Joking with the band and the stagehands, she was very relaxed, as if she were back in the rehearsal studio at Belmont. They rehearsed a couple of songs and ran through the setlist for that evening. After practice, Bobby announced to the group that Eddie Fontana had called that morning to say that their debut album had cracked the top fifty in sales that week.

"We are on the brink of a breakout," he said. "Let's keep doing what we're doing."

The next day, after a final practice and soundcheck, Bobby went back to the hotel and took a nap. Bobby was normally anxious the day of a show, but the night before, he hadn't sleep well. He had a dream his eldest daughter and her husband came to visit him in Tennessee. In the dream, she had two children, a young girl and a boy, and they liked Bobby a lot. They rode on a carousel with Bobby between them. Then they were on a beach, Bobby building a sandcastle with his grandchildren while Jessica sat on a chaise lounge, smiling. They played in the water, hitting a beach ball back and forth, the rainbow colors on the panels of the ball spinning in the hot sun. Suddenly, a rip tide began pulling the kids out. Bobby tried as hard as he could to swim to the rescue, but he seemed to go nowhere as the children drifted farther and farther away, their panicked voices growing faint. Jessica was screaming at him to do something. He awoke with a start. Sweaty but relieved, he went to the small refrigerator, pulled out two miniature bottles of bourbon, and dumped them both into a glass. He realized he hadn't spoken to either of his daughters in months. Remorse seeped into is mind. He'd recently been in the cities where both of his daughters lived, and he hadn't even thought to visit or invite them to the show. "Jerk," Bobby whispered out loud. Later that afternoon, he grabbed his phone and called Jessica. She answered out of breath, explaining she had been outside gardening. Bobby apologized for not calling in such a long time. She mentioned that she was pregnant, and Bobby mentioned the dream about her having children, but he thought it best to leave out the drowning part. Bobby told her about Lauren and the tour and how he was really doing much better now. Bobby thought she seemed sincerely happy for him.

"Jessica, I know I haven't there for you very much for a long time now, and I am so sorry for that. I know I can never make it up to you. To be honest, I don't even know where to start. But I've straightened up, and I was hoping you'd let me into your life, if only for a little bit. When this tour is over, I'd like to come out to California and spend some time with you and your husband. I could even wait until after you have the baby, if you like. I wouldn't be a nuisance, and I'd stay in a hotel so as not to put you out or anything."

Jessica's silence seemed like an eternity to Bobby. Finally she spoke. "You and Mom got divorced when I was fourteen. I maybe saw you four or five times a year for a while, and the last few years, I haven't seen you at all. Even when you and Mom were together, I don't remember you and me doing much. Can't remember you at any of my softball games or high school plays. I never went to a father-daughter dance. Heck, Dad, you weren't even at my college graduation. Mom told me you were so high somewhere, you forgot about it. All of that wasn't easy for me. I still see a shrink from time to time. You are my father, but I am not the girl you remember or imagine. I've moved on. You should too."

Bobby was at a complete loss. He could only mumble, "OK, then. If that's how you feel."

"That is how I feel. Thank you for understanding. I need to go now. It's about to rain, and I have to finish my gardening."

"Bye," Bobby whispered, but Jessica had already hung up. Bobby sat down on his bed. He was sweating and having trouble breathing. He could hear his heart beating. He downed his drink, but it didn't help. Bobby pulled a picture out of his wallet. Sarah had taken it the day they moved into their new home in Belle Meade. Bobby was with Jessica and Emily on the front steps of the house. Jessica couldn't have been more than eight, Emily three. Bobby stared at the photo for more than fifteen minutes. He wondered what the hell happened. He had no clear answer.

Bobby was running late and forced himself to get dressed. When he arrived at the arena, Hanson asked, "What happened to you? You look terrible." Bobby looked around. The rest of the band was already there, as well as Jimmy. Bobby didn't feel like eating but grabbed a bourbon from the buffet table. It was a little more than an hour before showtime. Faith Hill's manager came in and told Bobby that Lauren's set was going to be only forty-five minutes because Tim McGraw had flown in to catch the show, and they were going to do a few songs together, including the duet Lauren had been singing with Faith. Bobby was fine with that, and no one in the band seemed to mind. Lauren and Jimmy were sitting on a couch drinking beer when Jimmy lit up a joint and passed it to her. Bobby didn't think that was such a good idea.

"Lauren, you think that's wise?"

"Come on, Bobby, it's just a joint. I need to relax."

"She'll be fine," Jimmy said.

"I didn't ask you," Bobby shot back.

Jimmy stood up. "I don't care if you did. I'm

telling you she'll be fine, old man."

Bobby moved within inches of Jimmy. "Is that right? I think it's time…."

"Stop it!" Lauren screamed. The room fell silent. Lauren looked at Jimmy. "Sit down. Bobby's right. I can speak for myself." Jimmy held his hands up in surrender and sat. Lauren turned to Bobby. "Listen, has anything gone wrong in any show we've done?"

"Well—"

"Contrary to what you may think, I'm a big girl. Therefore, unless you have some constructive suggestion on our setlist, stage setting, or some other aspect of the show, leave me alone on what I do otherwise. Please."

Bobby slowly shook his head and looked at his watch. "All right, everyone, thirty minutes to showtime." He turned away from Lauren, grabbed another drink, and left the dressing room.

When it was time for the show, most of the tension in the band had dissipated. Lauren seemed calm, and the show went off without a hitch. Not that Bobby knew. He'd found a bar in the arena and stayed there for the duration. He was still at the bar about halfway through Faith Hill's set when he received a text from Lauren: "Can we talk?" Bobby finished his drink, paid the tab, and headed back to the dressing room. Along the way, the concourse was crowded with people going for food, drinks, or the bathroom. Faith's voice boomed louder each time he passed a tunnel into the seating area. He found his way through the maze backstage to the dressing room. Lauren was sitting on a chair drinking a bottle of water. She stood up when Bobby came in.

"Where's the band?" Bobby asked.

"They went back to the hotel."

"And Jimmy?"

Lauren put her drink down and stuck her hands in the back pockets of her jeans. "Same."

Bobby leaned against the table where the food had been.

"Are you OK?" Lauren said. "You seem a bit tipsy."

"I had a few pops, but I'm fine. I presume you want to talk about our discussion earlier."

Lauren nodded. "First, I'm sorry. It was wrong of me to lash out like that in front of other people."

"I get it," Bobby replied. "I shouldn't have butted in. I was just concerned about you smoking a joint before you went onstage. I've seen folks go down that road, and I've gone down it myself. It starts out as 'just a joint,' but it doesn't end well. And as long as we're putting it all out on the table, I know we agreed to stay out of each other's personal life, but Jimmy bugs the heck out of me. I don't exactly know why, but he does."

Lauren looked down at her shoes. "Well, that's the second thing. I think you guys got off on the wrong foot, and if we can have a do-over, I think it would be different. I think Jimmy can add value."

Bobby stood up straight and let out a short laugh. "Did I just hear you right? Jimmy can add value? What are you suggesting? You want him to be part of our team?"

"He has some good ideas."

"Are you serious? Did you actually discuss this with him before talking to me?"

"Jimmy knows me. He's also doing very well in the business now. He's about to go on a regional tour with the band he manages, Slow Bourbon. They've opened for Luke Bryan. Look at all the people who've been helping us in different ways. Becca, Eddie, Tommy Lane, Miguel, Cynthia, the boys in the band. I think Jimmy can help us with the younger crowd."

"I'm too old for you now?"

"Please don't put words in my mouth. I just think some people have insight into certain things. Jimmy hangs out in the same places and listens to a lot of the same music as millennials. I just think he would be an additional benefit. That's all."

Bobby walked over to the chair where he'd left his jacket when he first arrived. He was feeling anxious and dizzy. "No."

Lauren stood up to face Bobby. "No? That's it? I don't have a say in the matter?"

"You had your say."

"I guess I mean a say that mattered." The two stared at each other for a moment, and then Bobby grabbed Lauren by the shoulders and kissed her. Lauren turned her head away.

"Bobby!"

He held on and tried to kiss her again.

"Bobby! Stop it!"

Bobby didn't let go until Lauren kicked him in the leg. Breathing heavily, mouth agape, she back away and sat down in a chair. The air in the room was still, and the music onstage could be heard through the walls.

"I'm so sorry," Bobby said, approaching Lauren. "I don't know why I did that."

Without looking up, Lauren ran out of the room.

If it is possible to sober up on a moment's notice after eight or nine bourbons, Bobby did it. His heart was beating so hard, he was frightened he might be having a heart attack. He sat back down and clasped his chest. His mind was lurching with so many thoughts and yet no thoughts. He noticed Lauren's guitar case in a corner. She never let roadies handle it, joking once that it was the only thing in her life that had never let her down. Bobby opened the case and stared at the guitar, his foggy reflection gazing back at him from the lacquered Sitka spruce.

Back at the hotel, Bobby raced through the lobby and decided to take the stairs rather than wait for the elevator. He knocked on Henry Taylor's door, figuring Henry would be the most discreet member of the band.

Henry opened the door and saw Bobby holding Lauren's guitar case. "Is Lauren all right?"

"Yes. She left her guitar at the arena. Can you let her know we have it? I'll leave it with you."

"Sure, but why don't you just give it to her yourself?"

Bobby felt his face redden. "We had a bit of a tiff after the show. I think it best if we don't see each other at the moment."

Henry nodded and reached for the guitar.

Before releasing the handle, Bobby said, "I would appreciate it if you would keep this between us."

Henry was getting the feeling this was no ordinary argument. He practically had to pull the guitar away from Bobby. "Are you sure you don't want to come in for a drink and talk about it?"

"No, thanks. I think I need to be alone for a bit."

Lauren left the arena dizzy and sick to her stomach. It was raining, and her phone was dead, so she couldn't call a cab or an Uber. One minute you were playing in front of thousands of screaming people, and the next you were alone in the rain, in the dark, in a strange place. She thought of going back inside to borrow a phone to call Jimmy at the hotel, but she wasn't sure if she wanted to get him involved in this mess. Lauren got herself on West George Street heading back to the hotel. She replayed the incident over and over in her mind. She hadn't seen this one coming. What prompted it? Was Jimmy drunk? His breath sure reeked. Had she ever done anything to make him think that would be OK? What did this mean going forward? What would she say to Jimmy? Halfway to the hotel, overwhelmed, she sat on a bench, her tears blending with the raindrops as they fell to the sidewalk. A couple passed by and asked if she was OK. Lauren wiped her eyes, nodded, and made some excuse about having just broken up with her boyfriend. The man gave Lauren his umbrella stating they were only a half block from home. The woman asked if they could call her a cab, but Lauren said that she'd rather walk. The couple smiled and left Lauren in the strange comfort of her solitude.

Lauren resumed her journey back to the hotel. She looked at all the lights in the high rises. They seemed so warm and inviting. Although she really wanted to talk to somebody, she decided not to tell Jimmy about what happened, at least not yet. She needed to sort things out first and feared Jimmy might explode. Arriving back at the hotel, she caught a glimpse of herself in the glass of the doorway. A complete mess. She rubbed her eyes and pulled back her hair, as if it would make any difference at that point. She left the umbrella outside and skirted through the lobby, feeling the eyes of strangers upon her. At the door to the room she was sharing with Jimmy, she took a deep breath and made an effort to compose herself. She opened the door, and the room was empty. There was a note near the TV: "At the bar, come down when you can! Love, J." Relieved to be alone, Lauren took off her wet clothes and went into the shower. The warm water rushing over her head and face calmed her, at least for the moment. Drying off in front of the mirror, Lauren stared at her naked body. The warmth of the shower quickly faded. Going into the bedroom, she put on one of Jimmy's long sleeve T-shirts. There was a knock on the door. Lauren hesitated. She didn't want to face Bobby with some bullshit apology.

"Who is it?"

"It's Henry. I have your guitar. Bobby said you left it at the arena."

Lauren realized she had completely forgotten about the most important object in her life. She opened the door and forced a smile. "Thanks, Henry. That was awfully stupid of me. I had a bunch of stuff on my mind."

Henry could see that Lauren's eyes were red and her skin was paler then normal. He resisted asking what had happened with Bobby. "That was a great show tonight. I feel we get a bit better each time."

"From you lips to god's ears. Let's hope it continues."

Henry said he was heading down to the bar to

meet up with the rest of the band and asked Lauren if she wanted to join him, but she declined. Henry nodded and wished her a good night.

Lauren got into bed and put on the TV; the images and sounds hit her eyes and ears, but nothing was getting through. Soon she fell into a deep sleep and didn't even hear Jimmy stumble in a few hours later.

As the sun began to rise the next morning, Lauren woke up, stared at the ceiling, and for a second wondered whether what happened last night was real. She sat up, and her face flushed with anger. She got out of bed and put on her blue jeans and boots. She took off Jimmy's shirt and replaced it with a bra. Grabbing a blouse from the closet, she heard Jimmy stir.

"Go back to sleep," she said. "I need to talk to Bobby."

Jimmy nodded, rolled over, and went back to sleep. Lauren splashed water on her face, decided not to bother brushing her hair, and headed out.

The knock on the door was so forceful, Bobby thought it might be the police. He opened it warily, and Lauren strode in. "Bobby, close the door."

Bobby did as he was told. Lauren turned to him.

"What the hell was that?" she said. "I mean, where did that come from?"

Bobby sat on the edge of the bed. "I'm so sorry."

"I don't need apologies after the fact. I just need an answer. What the hell was that?"

Bobby looked down at the carpet. "I really don't know why it happened. I was really drunk."

"Bzzz. Wrong answer!"

Bobby looked up, taken aback by Lauren's

intensity.

"I'm not sure what the answer is, but that's not it. Maybe the booze gave you the courage but not the rational."

Bobby spoke softly. "I think I am attracted to you."

"What?"

"I was up all night. In the end, I had to face it. I am attracted to you. Believe me, I get it. It is never going to happen again. But the drink made me lose my inhibitions. I know it sounds so stupid. And I can't tell you how embarrassed I am. We've spent so much time together. And things have been going so well. I haven't felt this much excitement and energy since I was much younger. I guess I tricked myself into thinking I still was."

"Are you saying that when you were younger, you grabbed women and forced yourself on them?"

Bobby shook his head. "Lauren, I've never done anything like that before. Not to make excuses, but yesterday my eldest daughter basically told me she wants nothing to do with me I started drinking right after that."

Lauren knew by the blank look on Bobby's face that he was telling the truth. "Not that that in any way excuses what you did, but I'm sorry."

"Where do we go from here?" Bobby said.

"You tell me."

"I don't think I'm in that position. If you want me out of the picture, I will totally understand."

Lauren sat down on the bed next to Bobby. "Man, this is really hard. Aside from all you've done for my career, I consider you a friend. But you really scared me last night. It was like you were a totally different person. That being said, I'm not one to turn my back on a friend. You have to promise me we are business partners, friends, and nothing else. That other stuff has to leave your mind."

Bobby was quick to agree. Lauren could see he was relieved, as if he'd been told no, it wasn't a malignant tumor.

Bobby quipped, "I would give you a hug, but…"

"Don't even joke, Bobby."

BLACK COUNTRY ROYALTY

There was an eight-day break before the next show, in Chicago. As far as Bobby was concerned, it couldn't come at a better time. The members of the band were flying back to Nashville while Faith Hill was flying to New York for a gig on the Stephen Colbert's show and a round of daytime TV interviews. Bobby was exhausted, having slept little, and was worried about the flight home after his troubles with Lauren. He was relieved when he saw her board the plane with no discernable concern. On the way to his seat, Bobby apologized to Jimmy for his behavior before the last night's show. If Lauren had told Jimmy of the incident, he wasn't letting on.

Shortly after takeoff, Lauren came over to Bobby's seat. He was sitting with Hanson and hoped she didn't intend to resume their conversation from the morning. Instead, Lauren wanted to know what Bobby thought of adding a lead guitarist to the band and having Lauren shift to playing backup guitar.

"I mean, I'm OK," Lauren said. "But let's face it, I'm the worst musician in the band. Not so sure the worst musician in the band should be the lead guitar player."

Bobby agreed it was a good idea, because it would allow Lauren to focus more on her singing and audience engagement. He promised to ask around as soon as they got back to Nashville.

After Lauren returned to her seat, Hanson

looked over at Bobby. "Man, that girl has a strong drive to win. In my experience, all successful musicians have that gene. She seems totally focused on doing whatever it takes."

"I sure hope so," Bobby replied before falling into a deep sleep all the way back to Nashville.

Bobby felt good to be back in Music City. Years ago he used to travel a lot; now he realized he didn't miss that world. Not that he minded new experiences, but Nashville was like a worn pair of pajamas, with good music and good food to boot.

Bobby took an Uber to Sidewalk. He wanted to check his messages and mail. It was after six, so he thought the building would be empty. To his surprise, Eddie was at his desk. Bobby stopped at his door.

"You just can't give it up, can you?"

"What, and go home?" Eddie said. "All my wife is concerned about now is that I don't change the will."

Bobby grinned. "Seriously, how have you been feeling?"

"I forgot." Eddie quipped. "I hear you guys are banging it up on this tour. Good for you. If I feel up to it, I may even catch the show in New York. I have some business there I need to take care of." Eddie grabbed a piece of paper and handed it to Bobby. It was the latest country chart list. "Your group just broke the top twenty-five with a strong arrow up. The song 'Eclipse' is starting to be played on stations all over. You did it, Bobby. I'm sorry I doubted you."

Bobby should have smiled but he couldn't. A quiet thanks was all he could muster.

Eddie was puzzled. "Uh-oh, that didn't sound

very upbeat. What's going on?"

It would be a rare case when someone would tell the top executive of a record company what Bobby had done to Lauren the night before, but Eddie and Bobby went back so far, with so many highs and lows, that Bobby almost took comfort in getting it off his chest. He sat down and proceeded to tell Eddie every detail of the previous evening, at least everything he could remember. Conversely, it would be a rare case for the top executive of a record company to hear a story like that and not break out in a cold sweat about legal liability. But this was a man who knew he was dying and dying from the brain down. He couldn't care less about liability, but he did care about a friend in trouble.

"Jesus, Bobby. That sure was one bourbon too many."

"Tell me about it. But I think it was more than that."

"You falling for this girl?"

"I think it's a lot of things. I let my emotions get the better of me. If not this stupid thing with Lauren, it probably would have been something else. I could feel myself coming apart a bit."

Eddie leaned back in his chair and tried to lighten the mood. "You want to get some help? We can't have you going around grabbing the asses of our artists."

"Let me see if I can work this out on my own. I'm cutting out the booze, for one thing. That's what got me started. You'd think I'd know better. But I have some things I need to face. I promise you, nothing like this will happen again."

"The way I am heading, I probably won't remember what you did in the first place. Seriously, though. If you have a lot going on that's troubling you, you don't have to lie on the grenade by yourself. Since I found out I'm slowly turning into a vegetable, I've been seeing a shrink every week. Hey, I may be from the Bronx, but I am scared shitless. You don't want to end up where you were a few years ago."

Bobby nodded in agreement. "I'll keep it in mind." He got up and thanked Eddie for the conversation. For all that had happened between them, the ups and downs, the fighting, screaming, and betrayals, Bobby had come to realize that Eddie was the person he was closest to.

During the week, Bobby had some musicians come into the Sidewalk studio to audition for lead guitar. Even after all his years in the business, Bobby was still astounded at the talent in Nashville. Yet most of these people were living hand to mouth. Sometimes the difference between success or failure wasn't much more than luck, catching the eye of a record producer or talent scout. Miguel had sent over one candidate who ripped some amazing licks, but at twenty-five, his teeth were beginning to rot, and that scared Bobby off. Eddie had also received a recommendation from one of the club owners. The player was talented for sure, but he was already in his mid-forties. Besides modeling, probably no industry was more age biased than music. If you were good enough, you could stay in until you were old, but only if you got in young; there was no getting in if you were old, no matter how good you were. That's just the way it was. As the old guitarist played, you could see it in his eyes; he already knew what the answer would be. But Bobby had to admire him for his tenacity. Over the next few days, Bobby held at least fifteen auditions. None quite fit the bill. Next up was a twenty-year-old Black female guitarist from Memphis. Bobby gave her credit for walking in with two strikes against her. You had a better chance of finding the Hope diamond at the bottom of the Cumberland River than finding a Black female lead guitarist in a country band. But she had driven over three hours to get there, so Bobby was willing to give her a chance. At the very least, he figured he could offer some tips. She introduced herself as Hope Jones. She wore a pink tank top, cutoff jeans, and black Converse sneakers with no socks. Her hair was in two ponytails with the ends dyed purple. Hope asked Bobby what she should play. Bobby, believing this was going to be a short audition, said she could play whatever she liked. Hope thought for a moment and played the guitar solo from Garth Brooks's "Friends in Low Places." Her chord transitions were smooth and effortless. Bobby was certain she must have practiced that one.

"Can I hear 'Tennessee Whiskey'?" he said.

Without hesitation, Hope began playing—perfectly. Bobby decided to go deep.

"Do you happen to know Marty Robbins's "El Paso"?

Hope nodded and played.

Bobby was astonished. When she was done, he asked, "How in God's name do you know a song written in 1959 that's almost three times as old as you are?"

"My grandfather."

"Your grandfather was into country music?"

"Yes, very much so."

"He played you his records?"

"Sometimes, but most of the time he played them on his guitar."

Bobby's interest was growing. "Well, he certainly did a good job."

"Thanks. I'm not nearly as good as him, though."

"I doubt that. Did he ever do any studio work?"

"Sure, and live shows as well."

Bobby was now all in. "Anyone I might have heard of?"

"I'm not sure. His name is Charley Pride."

Bobby slowly stood up from his seat. "Are you telling me you're Charley Pride's granddaughter?"

Nonplussed, Hope nodded.

"'Kiss an Angel Good Mornin' Charley Pride?"

Hope nodded again.

"Do you have any idea how famous your grandpa is?"

Hope shrugged. "He sure has a nice house."

Bobby decided to have Hope play with the band to see if there was any chemistry. Problem was, Hope had come to Nashville with the clothes on her back and seventy dollars in her pocket. Bobby called up Miguel and explained the situation, hoping Hope could crash at his place. Miguel agreed as soon as Bobby mentioned the Charley Pride connection. Bobby asked Hope if she needed to call her parents. She said no because they knew she would get the job.

"Smart parents," Bobby replied. He scheduled a rehearsal the next evening and had Lauren arrive early to see if she clicked with Hope. Bobby had told Lauren over the phone the guitarist was a woman. Lauren remembered her conversation with Faith Hill about moving talented women along, so she was open to it. The fact that Hope was Black, Lauren could not care less. In fact, if Hope worked out, Lauren decided the first person she would call would be the Commander back at The 5 Spot. Might take the grump out of him, at least for a few minutes. When the rest of the band arrived, Bobby could see some skepticism on their faces. There was only one way to put that to rest. Bobby suggested they play Emmylou Harris's "Luxury Liner," one of the crowd favorites on tour. Hope took it to another level, pushing the energy of the band higher. Hanson, suspicious that Bobby had coached her on that one, suggested Kenny Chesney's "Feel Like a Rock Star," a song they had never rehearsed. After a few false starts, the band got in synch and took off with it. Halfway through, Hope played a guitar solo. Bobby felt a chill down his neck. After they finished the song, Hanson said, "Well, I'm in." The rest of the band nodded in agreement. Lauren smiled and gave Hope a welcome hug. Everyone knew a major missing piece had been found.

In Chicago for the restart of the tour, Bobby was relieved to discover that Jimmy would not be tagging along. His band, Slow Bourbon, was in the studio cutting an album and preparing for a three-week tour. It was the middle of May in Chicago, and the weather was perfect. Early the morning of the show, Bobby walked through Millennium Park and came upon the sculpture called Cloud Gate, a huge, polished, stainless-steel structure in the shape of a kidney bean. Like the hundreds of people walking around the sculpture in an almost trance-like state, Bobby was drawn in by its simple opulence. His reflection distorted against the object as he approached. Walking underneath, Bobby found himself at the omphalos. Looking up, he saw himself in many forms. In the center, he was totally proportional, while all around the sides, there were dozens of Bobby Linders in various shapes and sizes. In a way, it was how he thought of himself—a figure of many different forms, none of them distinct. A bit sadly he wondered, should it be like this at his age?

Bobby was excited about the Chicago show. Hope added a new dimension to the band, although he was a bit concerned about not having a smaller venue to work out any kinks. The good news was that when he showed her the list of songs, she was familiar with all of them, except for Lauren's original compositions. The band had spent the last few days back in Nashville giving her a crash course in those songs, and Becca came to a few sessions to offer Hope some tips on stage presence. Bobby was unnerved when he found out she had never played before an audience of more than a few hundred people. Becca said Hope would be fine and took her shopping after the last Nashville practice. "Hope should be the yin to Lauren's yang. Let me get the girls a new wardrobe for the next couple of shows."

The evening of the show, Lauren was dressed in all white: short shorts, a blouse, and a blazer with matching cowboy boots. The band came strolling in with their usual combination of blue jeans and various colored shirts. Hope came out of makeup wearing black, high heel Louboutin's; shiny, glittery, purple tights; and a tight yellow vest. She reminded Bobby of a cross between Nikki Minaj and Lady Gaga at their extremes. Bobby looked at Lauren and Hope.

"Was this Becca's idea?"

The women nodded in unison.

For a moment, Bobby wondered if Becca had pushed things too far, but then he began to see her way of thinking. They had a twenty-year-old Black female guitarist in a country band. They were making the rules here. Push it all the way.

During the show, it was clear that Becca's concept was working. There was Lauren, the country girl from Nashville, with a smooth voice, an innocent, coquettish smile, and an easy connection with the audience. At her side was Hope, the gritty Black girl from Memphis, with the calm of a road warrior veteran whipping out licks on the guitar with her body and attitude screaming "I don't give a damn if you don't like it." But they did. The band was receiving the loudest ovations of the tour. Lauren was mastering the art of audience control, but she was smart enough to give her bandmates a runway to shine. For this show, they added Brad Paisley's "Throttleneck," with its heavy guitar solos. The crowd ate it up. Everyone on and offstage realized the band had reached a new dimension.

Within days of the Chicago show, their debut album was in the top ten. On StubHub, almost as many people were buying tickets to see Lauren Culiver and the Nash Band as they were to see Faith Hill. In Indianapolis, they had fans waiting for them in the parking lot of their hotel when they arrived. In

Cleveland, Lauren was interviewed on 99.5 WGAR radio. Even the boys in the band were starting to get attention. In Pittsburgh, it creeped Wyatt out a bit when he noticed that the woman in the front row giving him the eye was the same woman who'd been doing so at the Indianapolis show.

The band was playing at the top of its game, which was important, because New York was the next show. Not that New York was anywhere near the center of the country music world, but it was New York—the media and money center of the universe, plus bragging rights. Madison Square Garden, now one of the oldest major indoor arenas, still demanded special attention. Anyone who was anyone in music had played there over the last fifty years. As Eddie told Bobby many years ago, "If you ain't played the Garden, you ain't shit."

The night before the show, Faith Hill invited Bobby to dinner. They ate at Michael's New York on the west side of Midtown. Over plates of lobster risotto and Colorado rack of lamb, the pair discussed old times in the nineties, when Faith was an up and comer, and Bobby and Eddie wrote and produced a number of her songs. Bobby remembered the first time he met her. He got a call from an acquaintance at a music publishing company where Faith was a secretary. The acquaintance had heard her singing to herself, and he thought she had the chops. The acquaintance wondered if Bobby had any songs he could throw her way. Bobby said the best thing would be to meet her, so he could get a better feel for what to suggest. She came into Bobby's office as a twentysomething already married a few years, a marriage that would soon implode under the pressure of success. Bobby recalled how pretty she was and at first wondered if his acquaintance at the publishing house was just doing this to impress her. She was nervous, but there was no doubt her voice was unique, and her guitar playing was solid. At the time, Bobby wasn't blown away. She told him that she had recently been rejected as a backup singer for Reba McEntire. What would he know about singing that Reba didn't? But as a favor to his friend, and because Faith was charming, he made a deal with her. He gave her two songs he'd recently written but had been unable to come up with satisfactory music and vocal arrangements for. He suggested that she work on them for a while and give him a call if she thought she had something. About two weeks later, she appeared in the lobby as Bobby and Eddie were headed out to lunch. Bobby suggested she come back another day, but Eddie, possibly due to her looks, suggested that they hear her out. So back they went into the studio. Bobby and Eddie were stunned. Her vocal arrangements for both songs were perfect, her guitar playing was crisp, and she had good ideas about what instruments were needed to complete the arrangements. Bobby and Eddie decided to have lunch delivered and called some studio musicians to come in as quickly as possible. By two the following morning, they had recorded the two songs, which would be on her first album, Take Me as I Am, which would go on to sell over three million copies. Fast forward a few short decades later, and thst former secretary and her husband owned an island in the Bahamas and ran a large charitable foundation.

"I have to be honest with you," Faith said to Bobby. "When Eddie called me about having your band on our tour, the only reason I considered it was as a favor, in return for you guys helping me when I first started. Even after I listened to Lauren and the band that first time in the studio, I thought they were OK but not blockbuster. No one really comes for the opening act anyway, so I figured this would be my payback to you guys. But wow, Bobby. They are really something. I'm starting to feel like I'm in a competition, and I may be losing."

"I greatly appreciate the compliments, Faith, and the exaggeration."

"I never exaggerate."

Bobby couldn't argue. The band was getting rave reviews for the concerts and their debut album. Just six months ago, he would not have imagined such success in his wildest fantasies. Now was having dinner with Faith Hill in New York, and his band was about to play to a full house in Madison Square Garden. It had been a crazy ride. Bobby joked that in case Faith was wondering, he considered the slate even.

The next morning, he asked Lauren to meet him in the hotel lobby. They were to have a rehearsal at noon, but he wanted to spend some time at the Garden with Lauren first. They entered the arena to find a construction crew putting the finishing touches on the stage. Bobby took Lauren to the middle of the floor, where a few thousand folding chairs were stacked. With her hands in her back pockets, Lauren looked up at the faded yellow and orange ceiling. "Wow."

"Lauren," Bobby said, "you've made it. Take it all in. Enjoy it. I think you're on your way to a spectacular career. But even someone like Faith will tell you the greatest memories are the early ones.

You're about to play to a sold out crowd at Madison Square Garden, smack in the middle of New York City. That's heavy stuff. I hope you never get jaded. I never have."

Lauren shook her head. "I won't. And thanks for everything. I know this wouldn't have been possible without you. And I want you to know that that thing in Chicago—"

"Lauren, please."

"It's important. I want you to know that I completely forgive you for what happened. I know you've been through a lot over the years. As far as I'm concerned, it's water under the bridge. I'll never bring it up again."

"Thanks. You don't know how that makes me feel."

"Then give me a hug."

"Seriously?"

Lauren smiled and nodded. With the sound of construction chatter in the background, they hugged in the empty arena while the souls of the many who had played before whispered in the air.

Bobby called up Eddie to see if he was still coming to the New York show. His secretary said Eddie had been planning on it but had not been feeling well, so he wouldn't make it. Bobby made mental note to check in on Eddie upon returning home.

The show in New York was electric. Hope was now completely comfortable in her role as the bad ass girl of the band. As for Lauren, Bobby could see she had learned so much since the first show in Austin. Her interaction with her band and the audience, sometimes at the same time, was perfect. Watching them play from the side of the stage, Bobby felt overwhelmed with emotion. He hadn't felt this way since the marriage of his daughter. So much work and effort. Never knowing what the outcome would be. But it was not simply good; it was better than good. Bobby felt tears fill his eyes. He tried hard to fight it, but he couldn't. Before long, he was crying.

The band did two more shows, one in Philadelphia and one in Washington, D.C., before heading back to Nashville. Faith had planned to take a month off before finishing the tour with several shows in the South. Lauren and the band were not contracted for that leg. It was probably for the best. They could focus on their growing popularity. One thing was certain—upon landing at the Nashville airport, they were as exhausted as they were happy.

The next day when Bobby went into his office, there was a cake with a number three candle in it, the album's current spot on the charts. Bobby went to see Eddie, but his assistant told Bobby that Eddie had not been in the office in a number of days and would be working from home for a while. Bobby had been worrying about Eddie ever since he didn't show up in New York. He really wanted to go see him, but there was so much to be done. His desk was littered with letters and messages from promoters, television and radio stations, newspapers and magazines. Bobby sat down in his chair and looked at the stacks of paper on his desk. He smiled and thought, I'm back.

STAY HARD

Even though the band was exhausted, the album was quickly rising on the charts, and Sidewalk was anxious to get a video out. On their second day back from the tour, the band shot the video on the John Seigenthaler Pedestrian Bridge, an old truss bridge, more than a century old, that offered a great view of downtown Nashville. That evening, back in her apartment, the travel, performances, and related stress finally caught up to Lauren. She stayed in bed most of the next three days. On the plane home, she had asked Toby for reading recommendations. He had given her a copy of Nietzsche's Beyond Good and Evil. So much for light reading. When awake, Lauren spent much of her time with the book. She had never thought about how concepts of good and evil shift depending upon who is in power. She made up her mind to write some lyrics that dealt with more than short jeans, broken hearts, pickup trucks, and cold beer.

Since Lauren got back to Nashville, Jimmy had been in the studio with Slow Bourbon, staying into the early morning most nights if he left at all, so they had not seen much of each other. They planned to have dinner out that evening. When Jimmy came by that afternoon, Lauren was still in bed. His skin was pale and sweaty.

"Are you OK?" Lauren asked.

"I'm fine, babe. In fact, we're just about to wrap the album up. When we go out tonight, let's celebrate."

Lauren ran a hand through her hair. "About that. I'm still exhausted. I didn't realize how much that tour took out of me. What do you say we order in?"

Jimmy sat down on the bed and grabbed Lauren's hand. Lauren wondered why his hand was cold, but his face was sweaty.

"Are you sure you're OK?" she repeated.

"I'm fine, hon. Just been working hard and was really looking forward to a night out with you." Jimmy reached into his pocket and pulled out a small bottle. "Here, take one of these. You'll feel great. You'll have fun tonight. I guarantee it."

"Oh, come on, man. I was wondering what was going on with you. Are you strung out?"

Jimmy laughed. "No. You sound like my parents, for Christ's sake. It's just Adderall. Gives you a boost, like a good double espresso, that's all. Hey, you're a star now. You want to lie in bed all the time or get out there and enjoy it?"

Lauren shook her head and smiled. "Jimmy Collino, you are something else."

Jimmy dropped the aspirin size white tablet into her hand. Not long afterward, Lauren had to admit Jimmy was right. She was starting to feel better. In fact, she felt awesome. Since she had a few hours before dinner, she was even motivated to write a song, something she had not been able to do since the tour started. With Nietzsche still on her mind, the song mused on influences in our lives that define good and evil. She entitled it "Religion."

That night Lauren and Jimmy had their best time together in a long time. Dinner at The Chef and I, live bluegrass at The Station Inn, and then a drag show and dancing at Club Play. Lauren was a bit taken aback at how many people recognized her. "I told you that you were a star!" Jimmy yelled over the music. Lauren didn't mind being interrupted by fans, but it felt weird that so many strangers knew who she was. She tried not to dwell on it and danced and laughed with Jimmy until the early morning.

Jimmy came into Lauren's bedroom with a cup of coffee, and the smell of it called her back to the real world. "Oh, man," Lauren said, grabbing the cup from Jimmy with both hands. "My head is pounding. What are you doing up and about already?"

"Already? It's two-thirty. I've been trying to get you up since noon."

Lauren's mouth was agape. "You're kidding me." She reached for her Apple watch on the side table. "Wow. Did you get the license of the truck that hit me?" Lauren fell back onto the bed, face first into the pillow.

Jimmy smiled. "Hey, I have to run. Trying to finish up Slow Bourbon's album today."

"How come you're so perky?"

Jimmy reached into his pocket, pulled out the bottle of Adderall, and shook it. "Works like a charm. Want one?"

"No! I think I did enough damage already, thank you."

Jimmy opened the bottle and placed two tablets on Lauren's end table. "Just in case you change your mind."

Despite two more cups of coffee and a long shower, Lauren was still dragging. She was tempted to go back to bed but felt she needed to get out. She decided to take a drive over to The 5 Spot to see the Commander. For all his gruffness, there was something calming about him. When she walked into the club, the head bartender, Stevie Vandaveer, was preparing for the evening.

"Lauren Culiver! Didn't think I'd be seeing you here anytime soon. I figured we were just a speck in your rearview mirror."

"Nope, you ain't going to lose me that easily. Is the boss man around?"

"Yes, he is," came a voice from the back. "Why don't you get your backside in here, Miss Culiver."

Lauren laughed, walked into the office, and gave the Commander a big hug.

"Last time you were here, you were apologizing for having to miss a few gigs. Now look at you, Miss Country Star!" The Commander gave a big smile. Lauren noticed that his upper lip was swollen, and one of his front teeth was missing.

"I hope you don't mind me asking, but what happened to your mouth?"

"Oh this?" the Commander asked calmly. "I happened to be enjoying a cigarette outside the club when some punk tried to skip out on his tab. He bolted past Eddie, our bouncer, at the front door. I was in his way, so he hit me square in the chops!

"Oh my God, are you OK?"

"Right as rain. He got the first punch in. But I got the next twenty. Cops said bar bolting was the guy's specialty. Right now, I understand he's handcuffed to his hospital bed."

"Remind me to pay my tab," Lauren said wryly.

"So tell me why I deserve the honor of your presence. I heard you knocked it out of the ballpark on the tour."

Lauren shrugged. "Nothing really. I just felt like being someplace familiar after all that running around. I've basically been in my bed for the last three days."

The Commander nodded as he sat down. "Ah, I see."

"What does that mean?"

The Commander motioned for Lauren to have a seat. "It's not easy to go from a hundred miles an hour to zero. When I close shop after a busy night, it takes me a couple of hours and a drink or two to unwind enough to hit the sheets. What you've been doing for the last month and a half must magnify that feeling by a thousand. Don't ignore it. Life in the fast lane can do some damage. I know most of the famous musicians in Nashville. Over the years, I've seen many of them develop serious issues, be it body or mind. There is a price to pay for success in your business, and you want to try to pay the lowest price possible. Take care of yourself, and don't get sucked in."

"Sucked in?"

"To the life. Where your time is always somebody else's. Where everyone is kissing your ass, and you think you are an invincible know-it-all. You're a smart woman, Lauren. But I have seen it happen too often." The Commander opened his desk drawer, took out a small box, and opened the lid. "I want to give you something. As you might have guessed, I'm not much of a religious person, but you might not know I am quite spiritual. Over the years, I have collected certain items that I believe have helped me get through life. Remember last year I told you the story of me surviving the Humvee attack in Afghanistan?"

"Yes."

"We had this Chinese gentleman in our infantry assault unit, Huan Gao. He was a martial arts instructor who taught us things such as ground fighting, firearm disarmament, and the principle core values of martial arts. We became close friends. On a morning when some members of the unit and myself were about to head out on a reconnaissance mission, Huan gave me this coin." The Commander held up a copper coin engraved with two crossed swords. "Huan practiced feng shui. When he gave me this coin, he told me that in feng shui, the symbol of crossed swords is supposed to protect one from negative energy. I remember one of my buddies, Jerry Duchla, made fun of it, saying something like he would probably be better off with a rocket launcher. It was later the very same day that the Humvee got attacked. As for Duchla? Two bullets basically took his face off. Those same bullets had to whiz right past my face first. Needless to say, I've kept the coin. Now I want you to have it."

Incredulous, Lauren replied, "Commander, I couldn't possibly consider taking that coin."

"Since my Afghanistan days, I've collected enough spiritual symbols to more than protect me from evils and temptations. You are entering a glorious phase of your life, but not one without serious dangers." The Commander stretched out his arm to Lauren, the coin now seemingly small in his large, thick fingers.

Lauren took it and looked at it closely. She then

grasped it tightly. "Thank you. I will keep it with me always."

"By the way, I hear you're helping my tribe with a dynamite new guitarist."

"Oh, you mean Hope?" Lauren asked. "She's the bomb."

The pair chatted a little while longer, and Lauren promised that after things settled down a bit, she would come play The 5 Spot again. The Commander said anytime, but since she was getting famous now, it would have to be on the down low. The pair hugged again, and Lauren did not feel like letting go. While still in the grasp of the big man, she whispered, "Thank you, I really needed this."

Back at home, Lauren returned a message from Bobby. He had secured interviews for her with Nashville.com and the podcast The Writers Room, with the editor of the Nash Country Daily. Both were scheduled for the next day. "Jesus, Bobby, don't I need some time to prepare?"

"Lauren, you're a natural. It sounds so cliché, but just be yourself. If you want, I can send over a stylist in the morning."

"I would appreciate that. I don't mind being myself if someone disguises me first."

Jimmy called and said he would be working late finishing the album, so he was just going to stay at his place. Lauren realized she had done absolutely no cleaning up around her apartment and spent a few hours attempting to correct the situation. Bobby had told her on the plane ride home that she should expect a large check soon from the tour. She thought about getting a bigger apartment, especially if things started working out with Jimmy. But she did like the neighborhood, a little gritty for sure, but she was not ready to trade it in for the glitz of the Gulch and certainly not the sleepy hamlets of Brentwood, Far Hills, Oak Hill, or even Belle Meade, even if she could afford it. She was convinced that the suburbs, like her hometown Naperville, were where good ideas went to die.

Despite feeling tired and consuming three glasses of wine, Lauren had trouble sleeping. Her doorbell rang at seven-thirty the next morning. Lauren got out of bed, put on her robe, and answered the door. It was Marie Rinzotti, a short, forty something, gun chewing dynamo who could make Frankenstein look like Leonardo DiCaprio. She was the go-to hair and makeup artist for many of the town's music stars. Lauren apologized for answering the door in her robe.

"Don't sweat it, sweetie, at least you put it on. Last week I got called to Trace Adkins's house. He answered the door buck naked, and it was two in the afternoon."

Two hours later, Rinzotti was done, and Lauren was impressed. Her first interview was at eleven o'clock at 417 Union, a popular diner downtown. She could not shake feeling drained. She looked at the two pills Jimmy had left on her end table. She whispered, "Fuck it," and swallowed one.

The interviewer for Nashville.com was already at the diner when Lauren arrived. She usually loved their pulled pork hash and eggs, but she wasn't hungry. The interviewer was young, not much out of college, and was feeding Lauren softball questions. Lauren felt relaxed, and it was easy for her to steer the interview.

In the end, the interviewer asked for her autograph on a paper napkin.

The Writer's Room podcast was not for a few hours, and Lauren didn't feel like going home, plus she thought she could use some fresh air for a change. She took a walk around the park near the state capitol building. In the center of a plaza was a large, bronze statue of Andrew Jackson astride his horse rearing on its hind legs. Both were atop a large, white limestone base with the word JACKSON carved in big, bold letters. As a kid, she remembered seeing the exact same statue in Lafayette Park in Washington, D.C., when her parents took her there on vacation. She recalled her dad saying that the sculptor was commissioned to do one in New Orleans, and over a century later, another was placed in Jacksonville. Since then, every time she saw the statue, she wondered why the country needed four of them, especially since Jackson had fought to save slavery and lost. After all, there was only one Statue of Liberty, not counting the one in Vegas. Looking closely, Lauren could read the remnants of some graffiti. The faded red letters read, STILL?

Lauren took a walk down to the Cumberland River, not far from where she had made a video on the bridge a few days earlier. She watched a barge being towed by a tugboat, heading west. She could see the outline of the tugboat captain in the wheelhouse. Lauren wondered where he was from, whether he was married with kids, whether he missed his family. She felt some remorse that she would never know. When the barge passed, it exposed East Nashville and the football stadium. She wondered who the genius was who decided the monstrosity had to be built right on the river.

Lauren took an Uber to the radio station at 10 Music Ave East, the location of the podcast. On the way over, she received a text from Bobby asking her to stop by Sidewalk after the interview, as it was just down the block. The podcaster, Tim Crosby, was a much more formidable interviewer than Lauren's morning round. A well-educated, handsome, walking country music encyclopedia, he had listened closely to Lauren's album and some recordings of her live shows as well. He knew where she grew up, went to college, the fact that she dropped out, and even about her job at the Nashville Boot Company. Crosby asked about her influences and what she wanted to accomplish. He said he thought she was a cross between Emmylou Harris and Janis Joplin, which made her nervous. Lauren knew she was good, but she didn't think she was that good. The interview lasted for well over an hour, but Lauren stayed sharp. It was clear that Crosby liked her as an artist. That made her feel good.

At Sidewalk Records, Lauren found Bobby at his desk. He smiled when Lauren entered. "I listened to the podcast. Fantastic. Absolutely fantastic. You kept up with Crosby, and he loved you."

"Kept up with him? All I did was answer his questions."

"You would be surprised how many people mess that up."

Bobby opened a drawer and pulled out an envelope with Lauren's name on it. "Oh, by the way, this is yours."

Lauren opened it. There was a check for $78,000. Laura spoke softly. "What is this?"

"Your cut of the tour after expenses."

"Are you serious? I don't think I have \$780 in the bank, never mind this. And what about the rest of the guys? I can't take all this."

" I split everything evenly. Hills's management said we added a lot to the tour, so they gave us a little bump."

"Jesus!"

"And one more thing. I just heard that when Billboard's charts come out on Tuesday, the album will be number one."

Lauren leaned against the wall and put her hands to her cheeks. "This is all just too much. So fast. It seems so unreal. Just a few months ago, I was thankful to get forty-five minutes playing The 5 Spot for gas money. I stopped by there yesterday, and it was like a time warp. Then a day later. I'm giving interviews, getting ridiculous checks, and a number one album. I haven't been able to wrap my head around it."

"I know, I feel the same way," Bobby said. "And I've been here before. It certainly is weird at times and even a little—or should I say a lot—crazy. But enjoy it. You deserve it. Continue to work hard. Don't make the mistake I did thinking it will stay great and you can just coast. Because you can't. Because someone hungrier than you will tear you apart while you're asleep at the switch. It gets tougher to stay hungry when you become successful. You can get soft. Be nice, but don't get soft. You know what the toughest thing in music is if you're fortunate enough to have a strong first album?"

"What?"

"A strong second album. You had your whole

life to turn ideas into songs for the first one. Now we have maybe a year at most to follow it up. So whenever you get the urge, write. We also need to get you on your own tour this summer to support the album and ride the wave from the Faith Hill tour. I'm working on that now."

"It just seems so overwhelming."

Bobby stood and squeezed Lauren's shoulders. "Everything will be fine, I promise. Just remember to take care of yourself and—"

"Don't get soft."

"Exactly."

After Lauren left his office, Bobby wrote a check to his daughter, Emily, in an amount he guessed would cover her Houston apartment rent for a year. He imagined the look on his ex-wife's face when Emily told her about it. He smiled.

FUNERAL FOR A FRIEND

When Eddie Fontana woke up, he was frightened. His heart was beating so hard he could hardly breathe, and he had no idea where he was. Eddie saw his phone on a dresser. Nervously he grabbed it. He needed help but didn't know who to call. The names in the contact list seemed so foreign. As he scrolled, they blurred together, and he grew more anxious. He came across the name Bobby Linder. Sounded familiar. He pressed call and lay back on his bed. He got Bobby's voicemail: "This is Bobby Linder. Please leave a message, and I will return your call. And don't forget to pick up a copy of the great debut album by Lauren Culiver and the Nash Band."

"I'm here," Eddie said. "I need help. Not sure where but I'm here."

Bobby had been on the phone that afternoon with various concert promoters. He was thrilled that he had a warm conversation with Larry Loggins of Loggins Touring Productions. They handled concert promotions for many of the top country acts, including many of Sidewalk's artists. During that call, Eddie's number flashed across Bobby's phone, and he made a mental note to call him when he was done.

After work, Bobby felt good about the day's accomplishments but was exhausted as well. He was tempted to stop into the nearby Hutton Hotel for a drink but forced himself to stay on the wagon. Instead, he made a quick stop at Thai Esane to pick up dinner and a soda. It was raining hard on the ride home, and Bobby started to think now that he had the means, it might be time to get an apartment closer to Music Row. Plus, besides Miguel, he hadn't had anyone over to his place in years. He was too embarrassed by it.

Back at home, Bobby put the TV on in the living room, sat on the couch, and began eating his chicken pad thai out of the aluminum container. There was a story on the news about a robber who had somehow managed to crawl through a heating duct into the ceiling above a downtown jewelry store, where he planned to wait until the store closed. Unfortunately, the ceiling gave way, and he landed right in front of a couple selecting wedding bands. The owner said he had to shoot him because he grabbed some watches and tried to run off. The police were a bit dubious, as the thief was still lying in the broken ceiling debris screaming and holding his bloody leg. The next story was about a new cupcake store opening in Brentwood. Bobby thought that was an interesting transition. While the owner was being interviewed, Bobby could hear Kenny Chesney playing in the store, one of Sidewalk's clients. He realized he had forgotten to call Eddie or even listen to the message. Playing the message, he stood up. As soon as it ended, he called Eddie. There was no answer. He didn't try again. He got into his car and drove to Eddie's house, which was only a few blocks from where Bobby had lived when he was married. It was still raining and almost dark when Bobby drove up the long driveway. Bobby's heart started to pound when he noticed the front door was ajar, but there were no lights on inside. He went inside and called for Eddie. There was no answer. Apparently, his wife was not home either. He checked every room, which was no small feat in a fifteen-thousand-square-foot home. Bobby called Eddie's main assistant and asked her the last time she had heard from him. She said Eddie had not been feeling well the last few days, so she had left him alone, and he never called her. Bobby asked her to reach out to Eddie's wife, Cathy. A few minutes later, Cathy called Bobby and said Eddie had suggested she go visit her sister in Atlanta since he was just lying around the house making everyone miserable. Bobby remained as calm as he could and said Eddie probably was checking out some band at a club and couldn't hear his phone. He told her to enjoy her time in Atlanta, and he would have Eddie reach out to her in the morning. Next, Bobby called the major hospitals in the city. Nothing. Bobby then tried Nashville Chief of Police Clinton Harris, whom every major music label in the city relied upon to keep the dirty laundry of their artists on the down low. After making some inquiries, Chief Harris called Bobby back and said he had nothing but would reach out immediately if he heard anything.

Bobby was now in a full-blown panic. He looked outside. It was completely dark and still raining hard. Where could Eddie be? Bobby got into his car and started to drive to the office, hoping against hope that maybe Eddie had gone there. As he pulled up in front of Sidewalk, his phone rang. It was the police chief. Eddie had been located wandering around the grounds of the Belle Meade Plantation by a night watchman. He was incoherent and was being taken to Vanderbilt hospital. Bobby arrived at the emergency room just before they wheeled Eddie in. He was unconscious on a stretcher. His hair and clothes were soaking wet. Bobby asked an attendant what happened, but there was no response as Eddie was wheeled into an examination room.

Bobby impatiently paced the waiting room for a few hours. Chief Harris sent over an officer to see if he could get some information on Eddie's condition. The doctor told the officer they thought Eddie had had a ministroke, but since Eddie's medical records showed he was on the way to dementia, they were going to do more tests over the next few days. When the officer relayed the message, Bobby broke down. Bobby recalled how he first met Eddie thirty-five years earlier when Eddie correctly mocked the musical arrangement Bobby had done for Keith Whitley's first song. He hoped the God of the Salesmen wasn't fading away.

The officer offered to drive Bobby home, but he elected to stay. Around nine the next morning, an intern gave Bobby some news: the symptoms of the ministroke were subsiding, but they were going to run a battery of tests to see what was going on in Eddie's brain. Bobby asked if he could see Eddie but was told no, not until later in the afternoon, and only if the patient was up to it While waiting, Bobby called Cathy and gave her an update. She said she would be back in Nashville later that day. At around 3 p.m. he was told he could stop in for a brief visit. The attending physician told Bobby that a ministroke, technically known as a transient ischemic attack, had been confirmed by the test. Although the attack was over, the patient could still experience memory loss, poor mobility, and problems with speech and comprehension. More importantly, these ministrokes were a sign that a more serious stroke was possible. They were going to keep Eddie a few days for more tests because his dementia had complicated matters, and it was possible that he was now in stage three of the Reisberg Scale, which was characterized by forgetfulness, getting lost, difficulty speaking, and other noticeable issues associated with the disease.

When Bobby walked into the room, Eddie was sleeping. He looked different to Bobby—in a way, almost unrecognizable. He seemed so much older and unkempt. His hair was uncombed, and his face, which was always clean shaven, had at least a week's worth of white stubble. The lines on his face stood out more than ever.

"Eddie, it's me, Bobby. You had me scared there for a while, buddy. I thought maybe you ran off with some young miss and left me holding the bag." Bobby tried to comb Eddie's hair with his hand. "We can't have Mr. Dapper looking like he just got attacked by a hedgehog. Seriously though, Eddie, I am here for you. I will check in a few times a day. We are going to get through this. You just get some rest." For a brief moment, Eddie opened his eyes, but it was unclear if he recognized Bobby. He fell back to sleep.

About twenty-one hours after Bobby first listened to Eddie's message, he left the hospital. Once in his car, he slammed his fist into the dashboard and rested his forehead on the steering wheel. A nurse heading into work knocked on his window to ask if everything was OK. Without putting the window down, Bobby started the car and drove off. In his driveway, he fell asleep in his car until the next morning.

Lauren was excited. She had gone on a writing binge, penning three songs over two days. Sometimes it would take her weeks to write just one. To top it off, she thought these new songs were some of her best. She couldn't wait to show Bobby at their meeting that afternoon. She needed a nap, but she also needed a shower. Instead of napping, she popped an Adderall from the bottle Jimmy had recently given her and went to clean up.

At Sidewalk Records, Bobby agreed with Lauren. He thought the songs had great potential. "Somehow, over the past year, you have leapfrogged me in songwriting."

"I agree," Lauren joked.

They decided to get the band together over the next week to come up with the arrangements. Bobby told Lauren he was still planning their tour but not for at least five months, as he wanted to let the first record play out and record a second. Plus, he was distracted by Eddie's condition. In the interim, he was planning some television, radio, and podcast interviews for her around the country.

Lauren saluted and said, "Aye, aye captain."

Bobby thought Lauren had lost some weight, and he hoped she was sleeping and eating OK.

"I've been running around like a nut," Lauren said. "I'll try to get more rest. But my butt was getting too big anyway."

Bobby asked Lauren if she wanted to grab an early dinner, but she had already made plans to meet Jimmy for a cocktail at The Fox Bar & Cocktail Club on Gallatin Pike, just outside of East Nashville in an area known as East Hill. Lauren went home to freshen up. She was learning that coming down from Adderall was more like a crash, so she put the bottle into her pocketbook.

When Lauren got to the bar, she was pleasantly surprised that Jimmy was already there. "Well, that's a first."

"Hey, babe, I told you I would try harder."

Over drinks, Lauren told Jimmy about the plans for a tour and a second album. Jimmy smiled but didn't say much.

"Aren't you excited for me?" Lauren asked.

"Of course I am. I'm just worried, that's all."

"Why?"

Jimmy looked down at the table. "I would rather not get into it and get you upset."

Lauren leaned forward. "You think if you leave me hanging like this, I'm not going to be upset?"

"I'm just worried that with Bobby Linder, the whole thing is going to collapse."

Lauren looked at Jimmy a bit shocked. "Jimmy, a year ago I was selling cowboy boots. Now I have the number one country album, and we're getting ready to do another one. I just got off an incredibly successful tour with Faith Hill and will be going out on my own in a few months. I would say Bobby has done a pretty damn good job."

Jimmy leaned back in his chair. "I am not saying he hasn't. But I am telling you there are some people who have a black cloud over their head, and Linder is one of them. He has proven it over and over, and it's tough for a tiger to change his stripes. People all over town have been saying it's only a matter of time before the bottom falls out. You're a pretty big star right now and getting bigger. Do you think it's prudent to have one guy be your manager, co-writer, record producer, record label, and promoter? Don't you think that's a little risky? I know I couldn't do all those jobs at once for you. It would be unfair to you. I'd be spread too thin."

Lauren had to admit that Jimmy might have a point. It did seem like it was an awful lot for one person to handle, and by all indications, Bobby was likely to get even get busier. Lauren nodded. "You may be right. Let me think about it."

Jimmy smiled. "I'm glad. And by the way, I know a great manager."

Lauren changed the subject. The idea of rehiring Jimmy as her manager was too heavy to think about now. She excused herself, went to the restroom, and popped an Adderall. They spent the rest of the night salsa dancing at Ibiza across town.

Over the next week, Bobby split his time working on the new album at Sidewalk and visiting Eddie in the hospital. After a few days, Eddie seemed to be recovering nicely. About a week after the episode, he was eating, joking with Bobby, and bitching with the staff about getting out. He still had his moments of incoherence and forgetfulness, but the majority of the time, Bobby thought he seemed almost as good as normal. On the other hand, the doctors confirmed that Eddie had advanced to stage three of the seven-stage Reisberg Scale, and it appeared that his condition was deteriorating significantly quicker than most people with the disease. They wanted to do more tests to figure out what was going on. To soften the doctors up, Eddie promised to undergo more tests and get some in-home help if they agreed to let him go home and get some rest. As Eddie put it, "I could get more sleep on an airport tarmac than in this hospital, for Christ's sake."

Back at the studio, Lauren had been delivering excellent material. So good, in fact, that Bobby decided to completely surrender co-writing duties. Lauren told Bobby she thought that was a good idea since it seemed he already had so much on his plate and maybe needed more help. Bobby thought the comment was a little odd but let it drop.

For the album, Bobby concentrated more on the musical component. With serious money now coming in, Bobby wanted to bring in additional studio musicians and maybe even some backup singers. Bobby knew that second albums were where many once-promising stars died on the tracks. As he told Miguel, whom he brought in to help with the recording, "I want to blow the roof off this bitch."

Larry Loggins flew in on his private jet from Austin to visit Sidewalk Music and meet Bobby and Lauren. Loggins was a bearded, balding, overly tan, cigar smoking, low talking titan of concert promotions. Bobby had not seen Loggins, now seventy, in over ten years, but he looked as if he hadn't aged a day. He knew his stuff, and if he didn't, he could still sell you on what he wanted. He had seen Lauren perform in Austin. "I was just waiting for the call," he told the pair.

Although Loggins thought Lauren and the band could likely sell out large venues, he suggested they stick to smaller ones, around three to five thousand or so, even if they had to do more than one show per city. His reasoning was that Lauren was still building her fan base, and smaller venues provided more fan satisfaction.

"Would you rather see Bruce Springsteen where the Titans play, or at the Ryman?" he said. "Most important thing you can do with concerts when you are an up and comer is to keep 'em wanting more." He also said it was a lot cheaper to set up and take down in the smaller venues—less lighting, sound, security, and transportation costs.

The three agreed to work together. Loggins would put a team together back in Austin to work on a full-blown proposal. Loggins said he would be in town for a few days to catch up with some of his artists. He said he was going out to dinner that night with Taylor Swift at Rodizio Grill and did Lauren want to meet her? Lauren asked him to repeat what he just said. Without missing a beat or a changing his expression, he did. Lauren let out a scream like a twelve-year-old girl at her favorite boy band concert. Even after all these years, Bobby was amazed at how smooth Loggins was. After the legend left his office, Bobby checked his back pocket to see if his wallet was still there.

Bobby stopped by the hospital on his way home that night only to discover that Eddie had been released earlier that day. Bobby figured he must have driven them crazy enough to let him go. On his way home, Bobby stopped at the old, yellow VW bus hot dog truck, I Dream of Weenie, and ordered two chili slaw dogs and a diet Dr. Pepper. He sat at one of the picnic tables on the grass. It was getting into late spring, and a hint of the upcoming hot Tennessee days was in the breeze. Nearby a couple with two young children were enjoying the evening, the four-year-old running around their table, stopping every now and then at the insistence of his mother to take a bite of his hot dog, while she broke off pieces of another to feed the younger child still in a stroller. The father looked on casually, a bit distant from the activity around him. A stray black and white dog walked by, hoping for a handout, but there were no takers among the tube steak crowd. With its head down, the dog left in search of a better venue.

Back at home, Bobby pulled the mail out of his mailbox. Walking up the driveway, he was looking at his mail, most of it junk, when his cell phone rang. It was Chief Harris. Bobby thought he was calling to say what Bobby already knew, that Eddie was out of the hospital. But the chief's voice was more somber. "Bobby, Chief Harris. I have some bad news."

"Don't tell me Eddie's back in the hospital," Bobby said.

"He's gone, Bobby. My officers on the scene said it appears to be suicide. I am so sorry I must tell you this."

A lot of people have asked Bobby what he did after that call, but to this day, his memory is limited. He remembers a police officer coming to his house with a note Eddie had left for him, still in a sealed envelope with Bobby's name on the front. The officer said that the police chief requested that Bobby keep the note to himself since really it should be retained by the police as part of the investigation. Bobby does not remember sitting in a chair staring at the front of the envelope for over an hour before summoning the courage to open it. Although he read the letter only once, it was quite possible he could still recite it word for word. It read:

Dear Bobby:

Well, we both know I pissed you off many times over the years but look at it this way: this is the last time! Seriously, though, you know me better than anyone. Did you really expect me to stay around while my brain rotted? Or had a more serious stroke and had to be in a wheelchair drooling on myself? We both know that I am much too vain for those options. This isn't something I did on a whim; I have been thinking about it from the first moment I found out from my doctor I would eventually turn into an uneatable vegetable.

Now to the important stuff. As you probably guessed, and sometimes got mad at me for, I am loaded. I mean really loaded. The music business has been particularly good to me. I don't have any kids, my first two wives took more than enough for themselves, I left Cathy plenty of investments and real estate, and, if I could be around to collect, I'd bet she'll be remarried in a few years anyway. Of course, I am giving a good sum to the Dementia Society of America. This thing I got is bad news, man, and I wouldn't wish it on my worst enemy (even the asshole heads of the other record labels). I am giving another chunk to our old favorite Farm Aid. Begrudgingly, I am also giving a bit to the Catholic Church—just in case they are right. If so, I think we both agree I am going to need some help getting into the right club. A good portion is also going to the Musicians Foundation. I made a lot of money off some of them, and I need to pay it back.

But my friend, I did not forget you. As you know,

I own the vast majority of Sidewalk Records. It's now yours. When I first asked you to rejoin the company a few months ago, I knew I was going to do this. I just didn't think I would be giving up the ghost so fast. Don't thank me. I am not going to get sappy because I want to be clear headed when I blow my brains out, but we have been through an awful lot together, my friend. The fact is, when I look back on it, you were the most instrumental person in my success. I was good in the business, we both know that. But you made me the best. Do not think of this as a gift. You deserve this.

Anyway, time to say sayonara. Give my lawyer, Kevin Murphy at Bass Berry, a call. He has all the details on this stuff.

And one more thing—don't fuck it up!

Been Fun,
Eddie

Bobby hadn't taken a drink in over a month. But he knew he was not going to get past this one. When Bobby walked into Edgefield's, Eddie's suicide had already been on the local news.

Lucy and some of the regulars who knew of Bobby and Eddie's friendship offered condolences. Bobby didn't say much, mostly just nodded. By Bobby's second bourbon, Eddie's death came back on the local news, and Lucy changed the channel to The Price Is Right. Bobby told her to put the news back on. "It's all right. It's what everyone wants to see." Bobby wondered what everyone's fascination was with others' misfortune. He was just as guilty, slowing down to look at the scene of an accident or intently reading about horrific crimes in the Daily Tennessean. Bobby thought Keith Urban was on to something in his song "But for the Grace of God," in which he sang about not having the misfortune of a lot of people around him. It made us feel better about our own predicament: Hey, my life is pretty lousy, but at least I didn't get my head blown off in a robbery, poor bastard.

Bobby oiled himself up well over the next few hours, but it didn't help. He felt as bad as when he first heard the news, just drunk. Bobby sadly realized nothing was going to ease the pain. Lucy insisted he not drive home and got him an Uber. Back at home, Bobby went into a closet and pulled out a box he hadn't opened since his divorce. It contained things from his home office in Belle Meade, which at the time of packing he thought he would just put into his next home office. Problem was, he never got one. Opening the box, he found a picture of Jessica and Sarah on swings in their backyard. There was the Nashville Songwriter of the Year Award he won back in 2002. Bobby had been so proud of that. He was nominated for a Grammy along with co-writer Toby Keith a year later. They didn't win, but Bobby said it wouldn't have matched the Nashville Songwriter award anyway, since the integrity of Grammy selections was so iffy. He picked up a tie, a good portion of which was cut off. He smiled. He used to like pulling that out of his desk and telling visitors the story of Eddie, him, and their bank. In the early years of Sidewalk, the company hit a few financial bumps. Eddie decided to ask the bank for additional funds. He asked Bobby to go along for support. Bobby showed up in Eddie's office dressed in a suit and tie. Eddie asked him what was up with the tie. Bobby explained that he wanted to look professional at the meeting. Eddie grabbed scissors off his desk and cut the tie in half. "Fuck 'em. We owe them so much money at this point, they really have no choice but to give us some more if they have hope of seeing anything in return." Bobby just shrugged and wore the cut off tie to the meeting. Eddie was right. The nervous bank officer was only too happy to oblige.

There were a few more family pictures, graduations and vacations mostly, which to Bobby seemed like another lifetime. Then he found what he was looking for. It was a picture of Bobby and Eddie at the Farm Aid concert in Burgettstown, Pennsylvania, about eighteen years earlier. They were there to try and sign the up-and-coming Drive-By Truckers to a long-term record deal, as their current one with a small indie label was expiring. Burgettstown was about twenty-five miles east of Pittsburgh, but it might as well have been twenty-five thousand. Virtually an all-white enclave of about thirteen hundred people, the town had been losing population since the 1940s. It was home to S&T Bank Music Park, but at the time of the photo, before the death of newspapers, it had been called the Post-Gazette Pavilion, a twenty-three-thousand-seat convert venue. Bobby remembered the photo was taken at a small party backstage. In the picture were Willie Nelson, John Mellencamp, Keith Urban, Dave Matthews, Neil Young, and smack in the middle, Bobby and Eddie. In the picture, both had darker hair and more of it. Eddie was wearing his Hank Williams T-shirt, which he called his good luck charm when he was trying to make a deal. Bobby was grinning ear to ear while Eddie stood relatively stone-faced. Looking at the picture now, Bobby could see in both of them what they knew—that they had made it. In the world of music, they were welcome guests in the A suite. It wouldn't be long after that photo that Bobby's life started to spiral into drinking and drugs while Eddie grabbed the golden ring, held on tight, and grabbed a few more. Bobby no longer had any animosity toward Eddie for taking advantage of Bobby's decline. If he hadn't, Bobby realized, it all would have gone to shit as everything in his life did during those years. Things they did together played in Bobby's mind until he was overwhelmed. He closed the box but kept the picture out. The next day, he placed it in a prominent place in the reception area of Sidewalk Music.

Eddie had never been a religious person. He had mentioned to Bobby that his parents were practicing Catholics back in the Bronx, but much to their disliking, Eddie was pretty averse to church. Even when he found out about his deadly illness, a fact that has made more than a few rediscover their faith, Eddie showed little inclination to make peace with the heavens. His lawyer told Bobby the plans for the funeral, which, due to the hole in his head, did not include a viewing. Instead, there was going to be a celebration of his life at the mother church of country music, the Ryman Auditorium, followed by burial at Woodland Park Memorial Cemetery, the final resting place for a who's who of country music. The Ryman had seen its fair share of funeral celebrations for country stars including Bill Monroe, Chet Atkins, Waylon Jennings, and Johnny Cash but never, to anyone's knowledge, for someone in country music not front and center on the stage. Bobby wondered if the Nashville country elite would consider it a bit sacrilegious. He needn't have worried. It seemed to him that there were more big-name country stars at Eddie's funeral than at the CMA awards. All 2,363 pew seats were full, and there were enough flowers around the stage and Eddie's casket to cause allergies to flourish, even if you didn't have one.

Brad Paisley opened the services with his rendition of the old Southern gospel song "Farther Along," and later Crystal Gail sang "Amazing Grace," which Bobby hated only because he had to fight back tears each and every time he heard it. Bobby had been asked to say a few words, and he was nervous because public speaking wasn't his strong suit. He told the story of how they met, how good Eddie was at his job, and some funny stories of things Eddie had done to get what he wanted, like the time he was locked in a battle for Vince Gill with another recording company. He'd hired an impersonator to call up the head of rival label pretending to be Gill and telling them he had made up his mind to go with Eddie and Sidewalk. Gill, who attended the services, yelled out that he had never known that which was met with uproarious laughter, only to be topped by the duped record label executive, who yelled out that he never knew it either. Bobby continued.

"I'm not going to lie and say Eddie was perfect. He wasn't. In business, he'd rob you if he thought he could. Frankly, there were times he could be a real asshole. But for those who are familiar with both of us, you know Eddie was certainly more perfect than me and many of us. Most importantly, he was my friend, and although there were times I didn't realize it, he was as good a friend as someone could have. Tennessee Williams once said, 'Life is partly what we make it, and partly what is made by the friends we choose.' In my case, Eddie certainly is the most critical component I chose for my life, and I love him for it."

Vince Gill closed the services with Johnny Cash's "Life's Railway to Heaven."

It was windy and raining at the cemetery, and the oversized crowd tried vainly to squeeze under the canopy. After the brief ceremony concluded, Bobby offered his final condolences to Cathy and stayed behind, standing in the rain staring at the coffin buried under the flowers that had been tossed onto it. Two burial ground custodians waited patiently nearby, hoping this stranger would leave so they could finish the job and get back to the dryness of their truck. Bobby, now soaking wet, was lost in thoughts of Eddie's life and his own. Bobby had not cried or hardly grieved since Eddie's death. Maybe it was the shock of it all, or maybe there was just so much to think about and do that he hadn't had the time for it. But now he did, and he sobbed uncontrollably. After a few minutes, someone nudged his arm. It was one of the custodians, a Black man in his sixties. The custodian nodded and handed Bobby a shovel. After a moment, Bobby went over to the pile of dirt and started to fill the grave. Soon the custodians joined in. Not a word was spoken until they finished. Bobby handed the shovel back with a low thank you. The life and death of Eddie Fontana, God of the Salesmen, was complete. Although Bobby would occasionally send flowers to the gravesite, he never visited again.

CAREFUL WHAT YOU WISH FOR

The night of Eddie's suicide, Lauren was scheduled to have dinner with Taylor Swift, courtesy of Larry Loggins's invite. Granted, for all intents and purposes, Swift had turned her back on country and was now full-blown pop, but she was the biggest star in music—country, pop, or otherwise. If you were a rabbi and got invited to dinner with the pope, you would go.

The traffic heading into downtown was heavy, and Lauren was nervous she was going to be late getting to the restaurant. To calm down, she reached into her pocketbook on the passenger seat for her bottle of Adderall. She scrounged around for it, glanced inside her pocketbook, finally saw the bottle, and grabbed it. With one hand on the wheel, she put the bottle between her legs and twisted off the cap with the other hand. Sticking a finger into the bottle, she was able to pinch one of the white saviors and pop it into her mouth. As she looked down to put the cap back onto the bottle, a Mercedes in front of her stopped in the traffic; unfortunately, Lauren didn't. As she plowed into the shiny blue vehicle, the orange plastic bottle went flying, scattering pills inside the car, and her airbag deployed, slamming into her face. When she recovered from the shock of it, Lauren grabbed the bottle off the floor, shoved it under her seat, and picked up as many of the pills as she could until someone came to her window and asked if she was all right. She nodded yes, shoved the pills inside her bra, and got out of her car.

The driver of the Mercedes, a suit and tie executive from Bridgestone Tires, was less than thrilled. "Christ! I only had the car a week. Didn't you notice we were in traffic, lady?"

Lauren began apologizing profusely, albeit a little incoherently. The executive calmed down when he saw how upset Lauren was. Shortly thereafter, a police officer pulled up to the scene. He was so young that both the executive and Lauren paused for a moment in quiet astonishment. After Lauren told him what had happened and admitted her guilt, he asked for identification from both of them so he could write a police report. He took the executive's information first and then Lauren's.

"I thought I knew you from somewhere, Ms. Culiver," he said, looking at her license. "My girlfriend and I love your album!"

In a different scenario, Lauren would have been appreciative, but considering she had likely blown the dinner of a lifetime, all she could muster was a polite thank you. The officer apologized for giving her a ticket for reckless driving. After the parties exchanged insurance information, the officer told the executive he was free to go. Lauren begged to go as well, but the officer replied that was impossible because of the air bag. He got into Lauren's car and drove it to the side of the road, then walked over to Lauren and handed her the empty Adderall bottle.

"You might want to do something with this," he said. "It would make a judge mighty unhappy."

Lauren thanked him again and slipped the bottle

into her pocket. As the tow truck pulled up, the officer asked her if she needed a ride. She doubted the officer would believe her, but she said she'd been on her way to have dinner with Taylor Swift. Before she could say another word, the officer had her in the back of his squad car, siren blaring on the way to Rodizio Grill. During the ride, the officer pulled out a pen and asked Lauren for her autograph. In exchange for the ride and the ixnay on the pills, Lauren thought it more than a fair request.

By the time the officer dropped Lauren off at the restaurant, she was coming to the conclusion that taking the Adderall had been a bad idea. Her heart was pounding, she was out of breath, and her mouth was dry. Sweat dripped down her face, and her hair was in disarray. She could feel the melted Adderall tablets on her breasts. Wiping her face, pushing back her hair, and taking a deep breath, Lauren entered the restaurant and told the host why she was there. Lauren followed the host upstairs, where two beefy security guards were standing outside a doorway. The host departed, and one of the security guards opened the curtain so Lauren could enter. The other just looked at Lauren and shook his head.

With a mix of remorse and terror, Lauren entered the room. Loggins and Swift were seated at a table, two empty plates and an almost empty bottle of wine between them. Loggins, showing a hint of annoyance, stood up and introduced Lauren to Swift. Lauren began to apologize, telling them about the accident, but Swift cut her off.

"About time you made it," Swift said. "I just about have to leave to feed my cats."

For a moment, Lauren thought she might fall to her knees. Seeing Lauren's distress, Swift got up laughing, walked over, and gave her a hug.

"I was only kidding! I hope you're OK! I am thrilled to meet you."

Both Lauren and Loggins smiled in relief. Swift ordered another bottle of wine and insisted that Lauren have dinner. After a rather hastily finished glass, Lauren calmed down, and the stress of getting there faded into a distant memory. Lauren and Swift talked for well over an hour, with Loggins chiming in now and then. In the end, Swift gave Lauren her phone number and told her to feel free to call if she ever wanted to talk. Wrecked car notwithstanding, on her way back to her apartment in an Uber, Lauren was on cloud nine. She would tell that story many times over the years, sans the auto accident and its repruccussions.

The next morning, Lauren was supposed to meet with Bobby, but his assistant called just before she left her apartment to share the news about Eddie and to let her know Bobby had cancelled all of his appointments for a few days. Lauren had learned a lot about Bobby's relationship with Eddie over the past few months. She tried to reach Bobby on his cell phone to offer condolences, but there was no answer. She didn't leave a message.

Lauren attended Eddie's funeral, but Bobby was preoccupied, and as dozens of people approached him afterwards outside the Ryman, she just gave him a brief wave from afar. She was tired and thought she could use another Adderall. Problem was, she'd lost them all in the car accident. She called up Jimmy. "Hey, do you have any more of the stuff?"

"What stuff? You mean the A?"

"Yeah, I could really use some. The funeral was a bummer."

"I just gave you a full bottle the other day. What happened to it?"

"Lost it in the accident," Lauren said. "Jesus, Jimmy, what's with the third degree?"

"Lauren, I'm not a drugstore. I can get you some, but it'll take a bit of time. Get a big cup of coffee or something. I'll see what I can come up with later today."

"OK, sorry to bother you." Lauren attempted to lighten the mood and ease the tension. "Can't wait to see you later."

Jimmy took a deep breath. "Ditto."

Outside the Ryman after the funeral, Bobby was approached by Kevin Murphy, Eddie's attorney. Murphy suggested that Bobby come see him as soon as possible, and they agreed to meet in the lawyer's office the next morning. The office was downtown in the Pinnacle Building, one of at least a dozen skyscrapers built in Nashville over the last decade. The twenty-nine-story building had a mirror like sheen, giving it the feel of a fortress: we can see you, but you can't see us.

Murphy brought Bobby into a conference room where documents waited on a table. In short order, Bobby learned that Sidewalk Records had grown to be one of the largest independent labels in the country, with the last year's revenue topping $105 million and the current year on track to do even better. A private equity firm in Chicago owned 30 percent, but Eddie, and now Bobby, owned the rest. Murphy explained that the private equity firm would be hands off if the profits remained steady. Last year's profit was $32 million. Bobby knew Sidewalk was getting big, but he had no idea it had gotten that big. Murphy asked Bobby how well he knew Sidewalk's CFO, Judy Komanski. Bobby replied he had no idea who she was. Murphy showed Bobby a picture of her on the Sidewalk website, and Bobby realized it was the woman who had an office down the hall from Eddie's. The fact was, even back in the day, Bobby hadn't been the numbers guy. Not that he couldn't do it, but it just wasn't his thing. As the early relationship with Eddie grew, Bobby had focused more on client acquisition and production while Eddie focused on the books. Bobby felt he barely had enough time to do what was needed for Lauren and the band; how was he going to run a company this large? There was a stack of documents on the table almost two feet high. Murphy said they were the various contracts with Sidewalk's artists. Bobby nervously wondered if he was expected to know the details of each. There was another stack of contracts almost as high for Sidewalk's vendors and banking relationships. "I guess we'll have Judy K. deal with those," Bobby said. Murphy, seeing Bobby's anxiety, nodded.

Bobby left Murphy's office with a mixture of emotions. Anyone would be excited about a financial boost, and this was more like a financial moonshot. Not even a year ago, Bobby was fighting with Nashville Electric about his chronic late payments, and now he could afford to light up all of Broad Street. But Eddie was the one who'd been responsible for Sidewalk's success for years, and the fact that Bobby waltzed in after being away from the business for so long left him kind of nauseated. He wasn't sure how he felt about having his life defined in large part by someone else's success. There would always be a question mark about his role at the company. He did not want a tombstone that read: "Here lies Bobby Linder. His life was fairly mediocre until the generosity of another made it a lot better."

Bobby texted Lauren after he left the lawyer's office and asked if she could stop by Sidewalk. She said yes even, though she was a bit frustrated that Jimmy had not been able to come up with any Adderall. "I'm working on it," was all he said when she asked.

In Bobby's office, Lauren was finally able to offer her condolences. Bobby gave a polite thank you but quickly moved on. He had made a decision at the cemetery, in the rain, shoveling dirt onto his former partner and friend, that he needed to put Eddie's passing aside for a while. It made him too emotional, and Bobby was afraid it would become all consuming. At least for a time, he would not bring Eddie up in conversation and would just listen politely when someone else did.

"I've been thinking about the songs you've recently written. I'd like to bring the band members in, and maybe we can toss around some ideas."

"That would be great," Lauren said.

"Good. I'll forward the lyrics to the band so they'll have an idea of what we're working with." Bobby leaned back in his chair. "By the way, I heard you had a little fender bender a few days ago?"

"Who told you? Loggins?"

"Nope. You are not a nobody in this town anymore, Lauren. Stuff like that can be bad publicity. Let's just say we have a special relationship with the boys in blue."

"What's the big deal? It was just an accident. You had one a few months ago."

"But I'm a behind-the-scenes guy. Fans and the media don't give a hoot about me. But they want to know every detail about you. The accident was one thing, but the bottle of pills is another. If that got out, it could be bad news for a rising star."

"I suppose you found that out from the police as well."

"We're not going to do them favors if we don't realize we need to, now would we?"

"Jimmy gave me that bottle a few weeks ago. He was pulling a lot of all-nighters working on an album, that's all. I didn't take any of them."

Bobby nodded, but he was doubtful. "Look Lauren, I agreed to stay out of your personal life, and I am. The only thing I will say is I went down that road, and it's a really bad trip."

Lauren was anxious to change the subject. "Thanks, Dad," she said jokingly. "I value your sage advice. Now can I show you two more songs I am working on?"

The initial rehearsals with the new songs went well. Everyone agreed that the lyrics were strong, and now that they had more cash, they could afford to do more, production-wise, on the second album. They considered bringing in horns for one song, two drummers for the most upbeat number, and female backup singers on another. Previously, Wyatt had told the band during about the $24,000 fiddle he'd seen at The Violin Shop. At their second rehearsal, Bobby surprised Wyatt with it. "Maybe that will help you sound better," Hanson quipped. Wyatt said he was going to sleep with the fiddle. No one in the room realized it at the time, but that wasn't a joke.

After the band spent a week tinkering with the songs, the skeleton of the future album began to take shape. But Bobby feared he was getting stretched. The top artists at Sidewalk wanted to make sure they didn't lose their place in the pecking order now that Eddie was gone. Other artists saw Eddie's death as an opportunity to improve their standing at the label. The phone calls, messages, and surprise visits were nonstop. Judy Komanski was in Bobby's office first thing every morning to go over sales figures, growth estimates, contract renegotiations, and other things Bobby had little interest in. The good news was that Komanski was a consummate professional, notwithstanding her butch wardrobe and haircut.

Jimmy's main supplier of Adderall was a big fan of Slow Bourbon. Jimmy had been trying to reach him for a few days, but he wasn't answering his phone. Through the grapevine, Jimmy learned the guy was in jail on a charge of sale and distribution of amphetamines. Jimmy was concerned that his relationship with the dealer might come to light, but that didn't prevent him from trying to score elsewhere. Lauren was harassing him for more, and his schedule was so hectic, he could use some himself. Jimmy called up a club manager who was a well-known connection for a lot of local bands. The manager said Adderall had been in short supply, but he could get his hands on some good meth. Jimmy hesitated. He'd tried meth a few times, and he didn't think he was the type to get addicted, but he didn't want to push his luck either. The manager went on to say he thought the Adderall drought was a short-term situation. Jimmy decided he needed to be flexible in the meantime, so he went ahead and bought some crank.

Lauren was skeptical. "Meth, Jimmy? Really? Don't you think that's a little over the top?"

Jimmy was frustrated. "I searched all around town for Adderall. This is all I could get, and it's basically the same thing. No one is forcing you take it."

"Damn it!" Lauren lay back on her couch. She knew she was going to a place she shouldn't be going, but she didn't really have the control to say no. Within a few short weeks, she'd gotten to the point where she had trouble getting through even a few hours without Adderall. She knew it was bad, but it felt so good. She sat up and held out her hand.

"OK, I'm in."

Jimmy reached into the plastic bag, took out a white pill, and placed it in her hand. Lauren wondered why the number 115 was stamped on it. She grabbed the can of Pepsi she'd been drinking and swallowed the pill. Jimmy joined her. Within a few minutes, she was not just alert but exhilarated. Jimmy made a move on her, which Lauren more than welcomed. In the bedroom, she smiled as Jimmy climbed on top of her, although her mind was in so many other places.

YOU CAN'T ALWAYS GET WHAT YOU WANT

It was just a few short weeks before Bobby realized that the day-to-day running of Sidewalk just wasn't for him. Yes, it was great connecting with all the stars on their roster, and yes, it felt good to suddenly be getting calls from anyone who was anyone in the business—producers, promoters, writers, even competitors. Also the money was astronomical, and he was not one to begrudge it. Komanski handed him his first monthly check—almost three quarters of a million dollars. Bobby had yet to cash it; he was almost embarrassed to do so. He wished he were one of those executives who lived under the illusion that they were actually worth the ridiculous amounts they were paid.

One morning after his briefing by Komanski, Bobby announced he was giving her a promotion to president. He would remain as chairman but made it clear that she would be responsible for the overall operations of the company. In truth, he wanted to focus on Lauren and the band; there was a lot of unfinished business to attend to before he could walk away. More importantly, it was what he loved doing. The challenge of identifying raw talent and bringing it to its full potential was what kept Bobby's blood flowing.

"What about my CFO duties?" Komanski asked.

Bobby reached into his desk, pulled out his uncashed check, and handed it to Komanski. "Hire one."

Slow Bourbon was opening their tour at the Classic Center Theatre in Athens, Georgia. Jimmy had rented an RV for the band and himself and as well as a truck for the small crew and the equipment. Lauren agreed to go along with Jimmy to see the show and planned to rent a car to drive back to Nashville while Jimmy and Slow Bourbon continued their tour. The band was more than a little excited and already partying hard. Unlike Lauren's band, in which cannabis was usually the hardest drug around, Slow Bourbon's RV could have been mistaken for a traveling pharmacy. Percocet, Adderall, and cocaine were laid out on the small kitchen table like appetizers at a picnic. Lauren helped herself to an Adderall, and at the suggestion of the guitarist, she also accepted a pill of ecstasy, which he said would enhance her experience later that night at the show.

The group pulled up to the theater midafternoon. After unloading the equipment, the band headed back onto the bus to continue the festivities. The four band members were going to stay in the RV that night while Jimmy booked a room for Lauren and himself at the Indigo Hotel, just off the campus of the University of Georgia. The crew would leave right after the show with the equipment for the following evening's gig at Daily's Place in Jacksonville.

After checking into the hotel, Lauren had Enterprise deliver a car for her trip back to Nashville the next day, and then she and Jimmy took a walk around the university. It was warming up in the late Georgia spring, and the pink flowers of the campus magnolias were in full bloom. The couple were quiet as they walked, enjoying a peacefulness they were not accustomed to over the past few months. They stumbled across a large, open field in the middle of campus. In the center was a circular fountain. They sat on the edge, and Lauren commented on how good the mist felt.

Jimmy did not seem to hear her. "Well, I guess this is as good a time as any."

"As good a time for what?"

Jimmy stared into Lauren's eyes. "I was going to wait until after the show, but this view is so nice." Jimmy motioned to the fountain and the area around them. Then he reached into his pocket and pulled out a small, blue box. Getting down on one knee, Jimmy smiled at Lauren. She was caught totally by surprise. She put her hands over her mouth and felt her face flush. When Jimmy asked the question, so many thoughts rushed into Lauren's head at once. On one hand, it was only a few months ago that they agreed to get back together and supposedly take it slow. On the other hand, Lauren no longer questioned Jimmy's commitment to the relationship. But what about her career? Things didn't seem like they would slow down anytime soon. Could she give both her marriage and her career the attention they deserved? Although questions continued to whip through her mind, she heard herself say, as if she were on the other side of the fountain watching the couple, "Yes!"

On the way back to the hotel, they joked about telling Lauren's mother and hoped she wouldn't be too shocked that Jimmy was not actually a doctor.

"She might be able to get past the fact you

aren't an MD," Lauren said, "but once Louise finds out you're in the music business, we might need a defibrillator."

After dropping Lauren off at the hotel, Jimmy went back to the theater to prepare for the evening's show. Lauren picked up the keys to her rental car, which had been left at the front desk, ordered dinner, and planned to meet Jimmy a bit later. Alone, Lauren wanted to tell someone the exciting news, but who? She owed it to her parents, but that was a call that would need some planning. She managed to get her friends Amy and Kayla on the phone, and they seemed genuinely happy for her. She was running short on time, but she thought she owed Bobby a call as well. Now that it was going to be the three of them, Lauren wanted to get the relationship between Bobby and Jimmy in as good a place as possible.

"Hi, Bobby, it's Lauren."

"Hey, I was just thinking of you. I had a teleconference with Larry Messina today. He's been putting some great venues together around the country. Wait until I show you the lineup."

"That's awesome, Bobby."

"How's Georgia?"

"Athens is very pretty. I'm going to Slow Bourbon's show in a bit, but I wanted to call you before I head out because I have some pretty big news."

"Are you going to tell me, or are we going to play twenty questions?"

"Jimmy and I are engaged!"

Bobby tried his best to hide his disappointment. He could have done better. "Well, that came out of nowhere!"

"I know. We were walking through campus when Jimmy just popped the question. At first, I was shocked, but then I thought to myself, why am I spending so much time with this guy if not to start a life together?" Lauren waited for Bobby to agree. "Aren't you happy for me?"

There were so many things Bobby wanted to say, but he went with what was expected. "Lauren, if you're happy, I'm happy."

Lauren smiled. "Thanks, Bobby. We'll celebrate this and the tour plans when I get back."

"Absolutely. Be safe, Lauren. Again, congrats to the both of you!"

After hanging up, Bobby sat alone at his desk staring at, but not really seeing, a picture of Lauren on his office credenza. The photo had originally appeared alongside a story in the Los Angeles Times the day after the show at the Staples Center. The headline read, "New Country Artist Electrifies the City of Lights." The reviewer had gushed over the band's performance, and Bobby had the picture printed to remind him of the destiny the article seemed to promise. The picture was taken from the side of the stage and showed the band intently focused on the music while Lauren stood singing at the edge of the stage in the outfit Becca had purchased for her. Her legs were spread apart, her back was straight, and she was staring into the far reaches of the arena. The faces of the fans in the first few rows showed a mixture of surprise and pure joy.

Bobby felt bad that he wasn't thrilled for Lauren, but what could he do? Jimmy just gave him a bad vibe.

Lauren arrived at the theater about an hour before the show. Backstage she found Jimmy not in the best of moods. Apparently, the theater manager had told Jimmy that only about two thirds of the tickets to the show had been sold.

"We're playing this gig for a percentage of the house," Jimmy said. "The guy guaranteed me over the phone that his marketing team would have the place sold out."

"Well, you'll probably get a lot of sales at the door."

Jimmy turned to go. "I didn't see a line out there last time I looked. Did you?"

A moment later, the guitarist who had given Lauren the ecstasy walked by and asked if she'd taken it. She'd actually forgotten about it and was planning not to drink much in hopes of a romantic evening with Jimmy to celebrate their engagement, but that no longer seemed likely. Thanking the band member for the reminder, she scrounged around in her small pocketbook until she found the pill and chased it with a bottle of beer.

Lauren found Jimmy and told him that instead of listening backstage, she was going to grab a seat in the theater to get a better feel for the band. Jimmy shrugged and moved onto other business. Lauren sat about thirty rows back from the stage. Looking around, she thought the house manager had been exaggerating the crowd size; the place didn't seem even half full. She remembered playing to a lot of empty seats during her first shows with Faith Hill and made a mental note to remind Jimmy of that. She began to feel hot and became anxious about the effect of the drugs. She hoped it wasn't too much for her. The band came out to play, and Lauren had a hard time focusing. But after a few minutes, she began to feel much better; a warm sense of well-being floated over her body, and her attention to the music went from sporadic to hyper focused. She felt like dancing and stood up, moving to the music in front of her seat. The warmth of her body started to mix with renewed energy, and she did not want the music to stop. A song or two later, a stranger, at least fifteen years older than Lauren with a dark mustache and a crooked smile, started dancing next to her. She smiled back and continued as her euphoria reached a level she'd never experienced. A few minutes later, the music suddenly stopped, and Lauren was confused by a commotion on the stage. She would later learn that the guitar player had taken too much of what he had given Lauren, and after trying to fight off a dizzy spell, had fainted. He was taken backstage, where he went in and out of consciousness as Jimmy and a young medical student from the crowd tried to revive him. Once the medical student learned the cause of the problem, he called 911, and the remainder of the show was cancelled.

There was almost a riot as the manager attempted to convince the crowd that enough of the show had been performed that refunds were not in order. He was still at the microphone when a Payday candy bar purchased at the concession stand struck him on the forehead. This was followed by a shower of popcorn and cups of beer. He left the stage and sent his assistant out to inform everyone that refunds were being issued at the box office, or requests could be submitted via the website.

Jimmy was now completely distraught. They'd lost money on the show, and the band had been mediocre even before the guitarist collapsed, which added an additional dose of humiliation and bad publicity to the mix. In addition, the manager was furious at Bobby for the band being under the influence and unable to complete the show, and he threatened to sue Jimmy for the lost revenue. Lauren, still feeling the effects of the molly, tried to lift Jimmy's spirits, but she was rebuffed. "Jesus Christ," he said, "you are all messed up right now. I wish you'd just leave me alone!" Taken aback, Lauren said nothing. Her recent feeling of peacefulness shattered, she left in quiet anger.

Back at the hotel, Lauren sat on the edge of the bed and stared at her reflection in a framed photo of peaches in a wooden bowl. She had never witnessed that vibe from Jimmy in their previous arguments. Granted, he had worked extremely hard to bring his band to this moment, and it must have been awfully frustrating and disheartening to see the evening unravel. But what had she done other than try and be helpful? Most importantly, hadn't they both, on this very same day, made the biggest commitment of their lives?

Lauren couldn't sleep, and the fact that Jimmy hadn't returned to the room didn't help. At around three-thirty in the morning, she heard the click of the door. There was a loud noise as Jimmy tripped over the luggage rack. "Fuck!"

Lauren sat up and turned on the nightstand light. Jimmy was sprawled on the floor. "Jimmy! Jesus, are you OK?"

Jimmy lifted his head off the floor. He was having difficulty getting up, and it was clear that at the very least, he had been drinking. It took a few tries before he made it to his feet. "Do I look like I'm OK?"

"No. No, you don't. Why don't you take your clothes off and come to bed? You'll feel better in the morning."

"Ah, she's clairvoyant now!" Jimmy went to the minibar fridge and pulled out a nip of Tito's vodka.

"Jimmy, do you really think that's a good idea?"

"Hey, I'm not driving, am I? Just sitting in my room minding my own business. Can't a guy enjoy a drink in his own room?" Jimmy opened the plastic bottle and drank it.

Too exhausted to deal with the flurry of emotions flowing through her, Lauren got out of bed and took Jimmy by the arm. "It's almost four o'clock. Let's go to sleep."

"You go to sleep." Jimmy pushed her in the direction of the bed. Lauren fell, and her face hit the wall. Her body slumped to the ground. Jimmy stumbled over, mumbling an apology, and tried to help her up.

"Get away from me, Jimmy!" Lauren held her nose, which was bleeding all over her oversized Patsy Cline T-shirt. Lauren got up, rushed into the bathroom, and locked the door behind her. She splashed cold water onto her face as Jimmy pleaded for her to let him in. In the mirror, Lauren checked to make sure her nose wasn't broken. A pink mix of blood and water flowed in tiny rivulets down the drain. Lauren sat on the toilet, tilted her head back, and held a wet washcloth to her nose. Twelve hours ago, she would never have guessed how this evening would play out. But sometimes that's the way it works. In high school, Lauren kept getting bigger roles in the school play. In her senior year, the school was to perform Beauty and the Beast, and everyone thought she'd get the role of Belle. As luck would have it, about two weeks before tryouts, a new student from New York, a sophomore who'd had a few minor child roles on Broadway, transferred into her school. Within thirty minutes of auditions, the new girl got the part. Lauren got the role of Babette. As Lauren cried at home, her mother was less than sympathetic. "Sweety, you can't change the facts. You can only deal with what is. Like the song says, 'You can't always get what you want.' Your job now is to go out there and be the best feather duster you can be. No more and no less." Lauren guessed it was time to accept the role of feather duster again. Once her nose stopped bleeding, she cleaned her face with a damp towel, dried herself off, took a deep breath, and opened the door, only to find Jimmy sitting in a chair he'd pulled over from the desk. His head was tilted back against the wall, and Lauren realized he had fallen asleep. Just as well. Lauren took off her bloody T-shirt and put on a pair of jeans and a sweater. She combed her hair and threw the brush onto the bed. She didn't pack anything but the clothes she was wearing. Who wanted the memories anyway? She grabbed her car keys, and a few minutes later, she was on Route 78 West heading back to Nashville.

A LITTLE CHAT

Bobby gave Miguel a call and asked if they could meet because he had a few things on his mind and wanted some advice. Miguel said he was cooking some pork ribs on the grill, and Bobby should stop by. On the patio by the pool, the pair drank beers as the scent of seasoned pork from the smoker sweetened the air. Cynthia had already set the table outside and was inside talking to a contractor about redoing the kitchen

"She just had it redone two years go," Miguel said. "She's a great woman, but sometimes I feel like I live in a never-ending construction zone."

"Don't make one of my mistakes. In every good marriage, sometimes it pays to be a little deaf."

Miguel nodded in agreement. Bobby mentioned that he wasn't feeling good about things lately. Miguel was surprised, considering Bobby was now the majority owner of Sidewalk Records and was producing the fastest rising act in country music.

"Don't get me wrong," Bobby said. "I've been blessed. A year ago, success for me meant getting a free round at Edgefield's. Now I'm back in the game. But not so long ago, Eddie told me the business had changed, and even if I was able to adjust to the changes, I wouldn't like it. I thought he was just blowing smoke up my ass, but he was right. The business has changed, and I don't like it. I've always understood the top priority is to make money, but I never thought it was the only priority. That's why Eddie and I worked so well together. He handled the money side; I took the lead on the creative end. Back then, there was room for both. It worked. Today, I'm not so sure. When I first took over Sidewalk, the meetings I had with the lawyers, the accountants, and our CFO would make your head spin. You could go weeks without hearing anything about artistic quality but not a day without a report on expenses and revenue. And on the creative side, so many people have their hand out that it limits the label's ability to take risks. Just too expensive. That's why ninety percent of the top hits are by the same artists, year in and year out. Don't get me wrong—they're good, but we both know there are people hustling tables in this town that but for the grace of God would be just as good if given the chance."

Miguel nodded in agreement and got up to check the ribs on the smoker. "So why don't you make Sidewalk into the label for the talented unknown?"

Bobby let out a short, low laugh. "I don't think the private equity firm that owns a good-sized chunk of us would appreciate that. Plus, Sidewalk is in too deep now. We have just about half the big-name acts in country. That's our bread and butter. When I brought Lauren in, Eddie didn't even want a piece of the action. She wasn't worth the time and attention. He had another dozen acts whose albums sell millions."

"But look at what you've done with Lauren and Nash. They're well on their way to doing the same thing."

"It's a lot of work, though. You know that. Easier to steal a rising star from a smaller label than to bring one from the ground up."

Miguel came back from the smoker and sat

down. "But that's what you like to do, my gringo friend. We're on about the fifteenth hole of life. Not many shots left. Who cares about those private equity guys? Worst they could do is pay you to leave, and you start your own indie label, if that's your thing. But my bet is they'll see your success with Lauren as being worth the gamble."

Just then Cynthia came out to the patio wanting to know when the ribs would be ready as she had some baked beans, mac and cheese, and collard greens to bring out.

"Honey," Miguel said, "cooking ribs is just like when we make love; you can't rush a good thing."

"So," Cynthia said, "two more minutes?"

During dinner, they continued to talk about Bobby's dissatisfaction with his current role. Cynthia agreed with Miguel that Bobby should do whatever he wanted to do.

"You want to cash out of Sidewalk and start an indie label, I'll go in with you," she said. "I'm not sure Miguel told you this, but I was a talent scout for Curb records when I met my first husband at some industry convention. He was a plodding midlevel executive at Capricorn. I must admit, the jerk swept me off my feet. Anyway, before we married, he got me a scouting job with Capricorn. Shortly afterwards, I told him I had seen this guy play at a barbeque, and I thought he might have something. The guy had a gig at a bar in Germantown the following weekend, and I told my ex we ought to check him out. We did, and my ex flipped over him. The next day, my ex brought the guy into the office to play a few more songs and signed him on the spot. That was the beginning of Kenny Chesney's career and the beginning of my ex's rocket ship ascension. He eventually landed as the CEO of Arista Records."

"Wow," Bobby said, "that is a good story."

"And not the only one," Miguel added, sucking the meat off a rib bone.

"Yes," Cynthia said. "You can add my discovery of Brad Paisley and Toby Keith to the list, but those are stories for another day." Cynthia took a long sip of her white wine. "So, if anyone complains about me getting half the son of a bitch's money, I'll tell them he made out like a bandit."

"Sure sounds like it," Bobby agreed.

"I think the point Miguel and I are trying to make, Bobby, is that you should never feel like you're locked in. Miguel said you are the straightest shooter he knows. If you want our help, we're here for you."

Bobby nodded in thankful agreement and asked Miguel if he wouldn't mind putting a few more ribs onto his plate.

When Jimmy awoke in the Athens hotel, it wasn't his best of mornings. He vaguely recalled some back and forth with Lauren in the room and knew whatever it was, it wasn't good. He had no idea where she was since all her clothes were there, and the only thing that appeared to be missing was her pocketbook. Jimmy guessed that she probably went to the lobby to grab a cup of coffee. He called her cell phone, but there was no answer. Expecting her back shortly, he gave his guitar player a call to see if he had been released from the hospital. A fellow band member answered and told Jimmy the patient had been diagnosed with a severe irregular heartbeat, was undergoing more tests, and was not likely to leave the hospital anytime soon. Jimmy had to call up Daily's Place in Jacksonville to apologize that they would have to cancel the show the following night. Jimmy said he would follow up to reschedule, but the Daily's Place manager said don't bother; he had heard about the debacle in Athens. He also said he would be sure to send Jimmy a bill for his share of expenses for the marketing and the cost of refunding the tickets. Now Slow Bourbon's next show wasn't for another five days in Charlotte. Already bleeding money, Jimmy decided that to preserve cash, they would head back to Nashville and make the six-hour drive to North Carolina the day of the show. As for the guitarist, Jimmy reasoned that he got himself into this mess, so he could figure out how to get back to Nashville on his own. Jimmy was thinking about replacing him anyway. But where was Lauren? Jimmy called her again. This time Lauren answered. From the background noise, it was clear she was in a car.

"Hey," Jimmy said, "where are you?"

"About twenty-five minutes from home," Lauren said.

"Nashville?"

"Last I heard, that's my home," Lauren snapped.

Jimmy began to inquire about the prior evening, but Lauren was having none of it. "I am driving right now, and I am not getting into it. When I'm ready to address the situation, I will reach out. In the interim, stay away from me. I'm dead serious, Jimmy. That means any and all contact."

"Lauren, are you for real?" Jimmy asked, but

she'd already hung up.

The atmosphere in the RV back to Nashville was quite different than the trip into Athens. "I am only going to say this once," Jimmy said. "Anyone who can't go on with a show because they drank too much or took something they shouldn't, I want you to know that you are not going to the hospital. No. What I will do is take you backstage, find a private room, and then I'm gonna kill 'ya."

About an hour later, Jimmy got a text that the show at the Uptown Amphitheatre in Charlotte was cancelled.

Bobby was late for work following the long evening at Miguel and Cynthia's. As he walked into Sidewalk, the receptionist told him that Lauren Culiver was waiting for him upstairs in his office. He didn't remember scheduling a meeting, and his assistant confirmed that he hadn't. She said Lauren had been in his office about ten minutes and didn't look very well. It was an understatement. Lauren had dark circles under her eyes, and her nose was swollen. Her hair, which she took great pride in, was disheveled, and she was slumped on the couch as though she were about to slide off.

"Jesus, Lauren," Bobby said. "What happened to you? Run into a wall?"

With one hand over her eyes, Lauren said, "That's exactly what happened."

Bobby's tone grew more serious. "Coffee?"

"Please."

Bobby yelled for his assistant to bring two coffees. "What's going on?"

With a bit of difficulty, Lauren sat up straight. "Well, about twenty hours ago, I was on top of the world. I was thrilled to get engaged to Jimmy. Then last night we had a terrible fight back at the hotel."

"Did he hit you?"

"No! He just gave me a little shove to push me onto the bed, but he was drunk, and I fell." Lauren put her head down and began to cry.

Bobby came over and put his arm around her shoulder. "I cannot imagine how tough this is on you, and I don't want you to think I am sugarcoating the situation by what I am going to say."

"Like what, that my black eyes won't last long?"

"Nope." Bobby smiled. "You might be out of luck on that one. I assume you're here and feeling like you do because you're having second thoughts about your future with Jimmy, and I know that must be tough. But consider this. What if this had happened after you were married? Or even worse, after you had a child? I am not going to tell you what to do. But whatever you decide, I know it will be the right thing for you."

Lauren wiped her eyes and nodded. "Thank you," she whispered.

"Now may I suggest you go home and get some rest? I don't even want you driving. We'll call you a car and have somebody bring yours over later."

After Lauren left, Bobby called in his assistant, Mary Baker, who had been Eddie's assistant for nearly twenty-five years. Bobby told her to cancel all sessions with Lauren and Nash over the next week so she could rest and sort things out. "Mary, years ago I remember Eddie used to have a guy he called when somebody was stalking or harassing one of our clients. Is he still around?"

Mary came back with a name and number written on a piece of paper.

Jimmy decided it best to honor Lauren's wishes and leave her alone for a while, although he sent her flowers most every day and wrote her a long letter saying he was sorry, loved her more than ever, and would wait patiently for her return. In the meantime, Jimmy was furiously trying to salvage the Slow Bourbon tour. The guitar player was released from the hospital and made his way back to Nashville. In a discussion with Jimmy, he said he had found Jesus, and drugs were now a thing of the past. Jimmy was able to stop the bleeding of show cancellations, and the group planned on starting out again in a little over a week.

At the end of a long day, Jimmy decided he needed to let loose a bit and stopped at the Third Base Strip Club & Car Wash, a box-shaped bar on Church Street in midtown that offered specialty auto cleaning in the parking lot during the day. Once inside, Jimmy sat down and ordered a beer. Sipping his drink, he melted into the loud music and the multi-tattooed girl dancing around a silver pole on a small, mirrored stage. It felt like it was the first time in recent memory that his brain had turned off. He was interrupted by another dancer who asked him if he would like a lap dance. Jimmy thought she couldn't be older than twenty, with pale blue eyes that didn't convey much worldly experience. He nodded and handed her twenty dollars. She put her legs over his and, but for an occasional smile, stared into a black light on the ceiling as if all the answers to the universe were contained therein. Five minutes later when it was over, Jimmy tipped her another twenty but hinted that would be enough for the evening. Jimmy ordered another beer and watched a new dancer onstage do her thing to Guns N' Roses' "Welcome to the Jungle." Not long after, the toll of a busy day started to seep into his bones, and it was time to leave. Outside, he saw that it had begun to rain and cursed his luck. He hurried to his car and was opening the door when he felt a sharp object in his back.

"Shut the fuck up and close the goddamn door."

Jimmy did as he was told. "Hey, man, no problem. My wallet is in my back pocket. It's yours." He started to turn around, but the man slammed his face into the top of the car.

"I don't recall asking you to turn around, fuck nut."

"Sorry man, sorry."

"Now turn the hell around."

Jimmy did as he was told, feeling as though cement had been poured into his shoes. The stranger in front of him was no youngster. Tall with a stocky build, his long white hair was pulled into a ponytail, and it was clear he wasn't a big fan of shaving. There was something about his eyes that caught Jimmy's attention. Even in the dark parking lot, they had a haunting, mean shine that hinted at a bad past; he looked as crazy as a rabid mountain lion.

"Good boy," he said, folding the knife and putting it into the pocket of his black leather jacket. "Now let's have a little chat, shall we."

"About what?" Jimmy asked.

The answer was a sharp blow to his stomach.

Jimmy bent over and caught a knee to his face, causing him to fall to the pavement.

The stranger leaned over him. "I am sorry if I confused you. By chat I meant I talk, you listen. Now I heard that your girlfriend had a little accident because of you. Big man, eh?" There was another kick to Jimmy's stomach. He gasped for air and thought he might pass out. He finally was able to catch his breath and vomited. The stranger knelt and put his face inches from Jimmy's. "Now I am only going to say this once, so I want you to pay attention. Are we clear?"

Jimmy slowly nodded.

"You lay another hand on that girl, even if it's to comb her hair, and this little visit will seem like we just had a nice brunch together. And if she happens to ask what happened to your pretty face, you simply tell her you got into a fracas with a drunk tourist on Broadway." The stranger got up and put his boot on Jimmy's head, pressing it into the vomit. "Are we clear, my friend?"

Jimmy tried to nod, but it was impossible; he let out an unintelligible whisper.

"What was that? I couldn't hear you."

With all the strength he could muster, Jimmy yelled, "Yes! Yes!"

"OK, then." The stranger grabbed Jimmy's arms and helped him to his feet. Then he brushed off Jimmy's sweater, pulled out a handkerchief, and wiped some blood off Jimmy's nose. He opened the driver's side door of Jimmy's car as if he were the on-duty valet and motioned for Jimmy to get in. "I am so glad we had this little chat."

Jimmy slowly got into the car. The stranger shut

the door and gave him a smile and a thumbs up through the rain-soaked window. A white Mercedes GLS pulled up, the stranger climbed in, and the SUV disappeared into the Music City darkness. Jimmy drove home, lay on his bed with an ice pack on his face, and stared at the ceiling until early morning.

MEN

Toby was in his apartment lounging on his couch eating a chicken salad sandwich and reading Peter Massie's book on Frederick the Great. His cell phone rang, and he didn't recognize the number, so he let it go. So many nuisance calls. Except the caller left a lengthy voicemail. It was Lauren, and she wanted to know if he had time to grab a beer or a coffee later that afternoon. Lauren had never called Toby before, and their interactions had involved only their work in the band. Toby hoped he wasn't getting booted out. He called Lauren back and suggested they meet at The Villager Tavern, a hole-in-the wall bar in the West End known for a friendly, subdued clientele and cold beer.

Toby arrived first and grabbed a stool at the end of a long table that abutted a brick wall adorned with hundreds of photos of people drinking beer out of a dog bowl—a birthday tradition at the bar. When Lauren arrived, Toby stood up and nervously asked her what she'd like to drink.

"Just a beer, thanks," Lauren said.

Toby soon returned with two Shiner Bocks.

"Thanks for meeting me, Toby."

Toby nodded but didn't say anything. Lauren thought that a little odd.

"Is everything OK?"

Toby just nodded again.

Lauren shrugged it off, and after some small talk—mostly hers—she got to the crux of the matter.

She confided in Toby that she was having a hard time with Adderall and was getting desperate to quit because it was becoming all-consuming, causing severe mood swings and difficulty sleeping. She was afraid to tell Bobby and thought Toby could keep her confidence. "In short, I need help. You're a smart guy, so I thought you might have some ideas."

The conversation caught Toby off guard, but he felt a wave of relief that he wasn't getting kicked out of the band. He could see the fear on Lauren's face but was reluctant to ask about the fading black eyes visible under her sunglasses. "Gee, Lauren, I'm sorry to hear this, but no worries on me keeping this between us. I'm certainly no doctor, but what I've read about most addictive drugs is that after a while, the chemical makeup of your brain changes, so it's best not to just go cold turkey. The side effects can be really rough."

"You're saying I should just try and take a little less each day?"

"No, I'm saying it's probably unwise to do this on your own. If you could have stopped by yourself, I think you would have by now. Addiction is awfully tough."

Lauren shook her head. "But I can't do that. This town has no secrets."

"I bet Bobby could find someone. You certainly aren't the first country star to have this issue."

Lauren smiled. "Thanks, but I'm not a country star, and I can't tell Bobby. Let's just say it's complicated."

Toby sipped his beer. "Well, if I may make a suggestion, there's this cousin of mine. We were close growing up in Kansas City. Now he's a doctor at a big-time hospital in St. Louis. I can give him a call and see if he has any advice. Without naming names, of course."

Lauren thought Toby's idea was a good one; she relaxed a bit and even suggested they have another beer. In the end it, was four or five beers, and Lauren found herself amazed at how much this fiddle player from Kansas City knew about a lot of things.

It had been a week since Jimmy's run-in at the Third Base Strip Club & Car Wash. The day after, he'd gone to the doctor, who told him that yes, his nose was broken. He really didn't have much time to dwell on that. The disastrous start of the Slow Bourbon tour had put him in a deep financial hole, and he was busy trying to salvage what was left of it. The band was leaving for a show at the Palace Theatre in Louisville the following day, which would begin a string of twelve shows over fifteen days through Kentucky, Missouri, Oklahoma, Louisiana, Texas, and Mississippi. Other than the flowers and the letter, Jimmy hadn't reached out to Lauren, but since he was going to be gone for a while, he thought he should at least text to let her know. Much to his surprise, she texted back about an hour later: "Let's talk. Parthenon. 2 p.m.?" Jimmy said yes and made a silent vow to himself that with the restart of the tour and this reconnection with Lauren, his messing up days were over.

The Nashville Parthenon was a replica of the original in Greece. It was located in Centennial Park on Twenty-Fifth Avenue North in the West End and was built to celebrate the one hundredth anniversary of Tennessee's admission into the Union in 1796. Due to its popularity, the original wooden structure was replaced with a more permanent cement and steel structure in the 1920's, but it wasn't patronized by any of Nashville's Black residents, who were prohibited from visiting the park until passage of civil rights legislation in 1964.

There was a hint of a Nashville summer right around the corner as Jimmy stepped into the park. With just a few clouds in the sky, the warmth of the afternoon sun enveloped his nervous limbs. Walking across the expanse of grass, he could see Lauren sitting on the steps just below the eight columns adorning the front of the replica. She was casually dressed in a short sleeve pink shirt, white shorts, and sandals. Jimmy gave a brief wave, and Lauren responded in kind. As Jimmy approached the stairs, Lauren could plainly see the injuries to his face. His right eye was red from a broken blood vessel, and his nose was tilted to the left side of his face, which appeared swollen.

"Oh, my God, Jimmy! What happened to you?"

Jimmy smiled. He reasoned some concern was better than none. "A bus hit me."

"No. Seriously?" Lauren stood up and took a closer look at Jimmy's face.

"A couple of hicks jumped me late one night coming out of the recording studio. They wanted my wallet. I said they would have to fight me for it. And they sure did."

"Jesus Christ, Jimmy. Not too smart."

"I know. I haven't been thinking straight lately. I miss you."

Lauren sat back down on the steps and motioned for Jimmy to sit next to her. After thanking

Jimmy for coming on short notice and some small talk about his imminent tour, Lauren got to the point. "I know you are aware by now that I was extremely upset over what happened in Athens. On my way back to Nashville, when you called, I said I would speak to you about it when I was ready." Lauren looked down at the ground, took a deep breath, and continued. "Well, now I'm ready. So much has been going through my mind. Not just about you, but my problem with Adderall, my career, and frankly, my spiritual well-being. If I were happy, why would I be taking drugs that put me outside my real self? Doesn't really make sense, does it?"

"Are you suggesting I'm to blame for you getting hooked on the stuff?"

"No, I take responsibility for that. I'm a grown woman. But let me ask you this. You enjoyed taking stuff from time to time, right?"

"Sure, especially if I was tired. But I guess I don't have an addictive a personality."

Lauren forced a brief smile. "Would you recommend it to your mother if she were tired? Or let's say if you had a teenage daughter?"

"Come on, Lauren. Those are ridiculous questions."

"Are they?" Lauren looked out across the park. "Don't rattle your brain too much with those questions, because that's not why I asked you here. When I came back, I did some soul searching, you know? I figured that since you were my boyfriend for quite a while, we needed to take the next step. I mean, that's the way it's supposed to go, right? That's what I've been hearing for my whole life. I got really focused on that. Even when you did dumb things, like the time I saw you at

Edgefield's on Halloween, or heard you were out with some other girl, or some other stupid stuff. But I put it aside because, after all, we were serious boyfriend and girlfriend. It would pass, I told myself. When you asked to marry me a few weeks ago, I was so happy. Or at least I thought I was. I mean, I got the guy I loved. But when I got back here, I thought to myself, did I really? I mean, when we first met, I was working at the boot store, trying to get any gig and just trying to survive. You helped me with my music, and I want you to know I appreciate that more than you can imagine. Then we became lovers. But you know what I appreciate you for more than anything?"

Jimmy had no idea where this was going. He took a flyer. "For sticking with you no matter what?"

Lauren laughed. "That's your answer? Sticking with me?" She shook her head. "Oh, that is priceless. But no, that's not it. I appreciate you most for what happened in Athens, and I'm not talking about our engagement. I'm talking about what happened at the hotel that night. You saved me from the biggest mistake of my life—marrying you." Lauren stood up and wiped the dust off her backside. Jimmy could only stare at her. "When I looked back on it, I realized you haven't treated me right since the beginning. It's called respect, Jimmy. I realize now it is the foundation of any relationship."

"But that was in the past," Jimmy said. "We agreed to move on."

"People in close relationships don't offer each other drugs, Jimmy. I'm not excusing my role, but if you wouldn't offer drugs to members of your family, you certainly shouldn't have offered them to me. But rest assured, I am hell bent to beat it. People in close relationships also don't try to cause dissent in their partner's business relationships. They don't cheat or flirt with other people. They don't treat their partner with disrespect in public, and they certainly don't put them in harm's way. I walked around for a week with black eyes, you asshole." Lauren reached into her pocket, pulled out the engagement ring, and handed it to Jimmy. "I need someone I can respect and who respects me. I wish you all the best. Please respect my decision if you can't respect anything else."

Jimmy just shook his head. "You need someone you can respect? Really? Like that manager you have?"

Lauren stood to leave. "He has nothing to do with this."

Jimmy stood up and moved closer to Lauren. "Oh really? Well, my face certainly does."

Lauren backed away. "You said some hicks jumped you."

Jimmy opened his arms wide. "Oh, did I? I guess I'm still confused from the stitches in my head. Actually, your Mr. Wonderful heard about our little tiff in Georgia and sent some friends to pay me a visit."

Lauren forced a laugh. "You're lying."

"Oh, am I? I have friends in the underbelly of this town, too. Shall we go ask him?"

Lauren was ready for this to end. "We aren't going to ask anyone. Goodbye, Jimmy."

Lauren turned and walked away, her mind a thicket of thoughts. Behind her, Jimmy yelled, "I helped you when we first met, and now you are returning the favor. Thank you! I almost married an ignorant, newly stuck-up little bitch."

Lauren was tempted to turn around and kick him between his legs, but then she realized he had just proven her point. Respect. She smiled and continued walking away.

Jimmy was still yelling as she got into her car and drove off. She was relieved that was over, but what Jimmy had said about Bobby gnawed at her. It seemed ridiculous, but she wanted it out of her mind. She drove to Sidewalk Records. Lauren was escorted into Bobby's office by Mary. Bobby, who was on the phone, smiled at Lauren while signaling to her to have a seat. A few seconds later he was off the phone.

"There she is. You look a lot better than last time I saw you. Are things working out?"

"I'm getting there."

"Good, glad to hear it." Bobby came around to the front of his desk and sat on a corner in front of Lauren. "What's up?"

"I broke up with Jimmy today."

"I'm sorry to hear that," Bobby said. "Is this a permanent thing, or do you think you guys will work it out?"

"If death is considered permanent, I would say this is as well."

"Well, to be honest, I think you did the right thing. As you know, I was never good at hiding the fact that I didn't like the guy."

Lauren looked straight into Bobby's eyes. "He accused you of having him beat up."

"Me?" Bobby was at a loss for words. Lauren simply nodded and waited for clarification. Bobby wanted to deny it. It would make everything so much easier. He had never lied to Lauren before, and she would have no reason to doubt him. Compared to Jimmy, he was Thomas Aquinas. Plus Jimmy was now out of the picture. Why create waves when the floating is so peaceful? In the end, though, he couldn't bring himself to lie. "Lauren, if a man hits a woman, it's only the beginning. We wanted to make sure you were safe. No one told him not to see you again. It was just a suggestion not to get physical again."

Lauren stood up, angry. "'We' wanted? Who is 'we,' Bobby? Could 'we' just be you? And you just gave Jimmy a suggestion? Looked like more than a suggestion to me. He could hardly see out of one eye, there were stitches in his head, and his nose looked broken." Lauren shook her head. "Both of you are just too much. Like I need either one of you to make decisions for me. I never asked, Bobby. You can't seem to grasp that. You promised you would stay out of my personal life, and now you go around beating people up in my name? How did you even know if I loved him or not? What if I were moving forward with him?" Lauren waited for an answer, but Bobby didn't know what to say. "That's good, Bobby. Don't say anything, because there really is nothing to be said, is there?"

Bobby was ashamed. "No," he said, his voice barely audible.

Lauren turned around and left his office.

Arriving home, Lauren thought she would have a good cry but didn't. She'd just broke up with the man she thought she would marry, and now she needed to rethink her relationship with another man she thought she could trust. She felt surprisingly good but angry. An Adderall would have made her feel better, but

Lauren called Toby instead.

"Hi, Toby, this is Lauren. I think I'm ready to take up on your offer."

"You want me to call my cousin in St. Louis?"

"No, I want you to drive me there."

REHAB HIDEAWAY

Bobby was rather concerned that he hadn't heard from Lauren in five days following her discovery of Jimmy's beating. Out of the blue, Toby paid him a surprise visit at the office. He nervously informed Bobby that Lauren had asked him to take her to St. Louis to deal with her addiction and that she was going to be at a rehab facility just outside the city for a few weeks. Bobby was furious at Toby for not coming to him first.

"But Bobby, she really wanted to keep it confidential," Toby stammered.

"Well, that's very considerate of you. But I guess you forgot that your checks come from Sidewalk Records, not Lauren Culiver. A lot of people, including you and I, depend on each other. Secrets don't help the team. I could have gotten Lauren help right here in Nashville rather than having her shipped out to god knows where with no one to look after her. I have weeks of things scheduled for her and the band that now need to be rearranged. No sweat off your back though, right?"

"I'm sorry. It's just that when a friend asks me to keep something confidential, I can't dishonor that. And I thought that since we probably won't be doing much until Lauren gets back, I'd go to St. Louis to check up on her from time to time until she's able to come back here ready to go."

Bobby stared at Toby for a moment, and his

anger began to dissipate. Toby was caught between a rock and a hard place and was just trying to do what he thought was right. Toby was the Abraham Lincoln of Nashville. Bobby called Mary into his office and told her to cut a check for $10,000 to Toby for travel expenses. He told Toby to stay in St. Louis until she completed rehab.

After Toby left, Bobby sat quietly at his desk, thinking of a lot and thinking of nothing. He had never experienced a panic attack but now felt sweaty; his heart was racing, and he was struggling to breathe. He felt as though he needed some air and went out onto Music Row. He walked northeast on Music Square West, turned right onto Roy Acuff Place, and passed RCA Studio B, the former recording studio for Elvis Presley, Willie Nelson, Waylon Jennings, Dolly Parton, Chet Atkins, and just about anybody who was anybody in country music from the mid-fifties to the mid-seventies. Bobby loved the building because it was the birthplace of the Nashville sound, a smoother, more sophisticated country music than the honky-tonk sound that preceded it. The Nashville sound followed a philosophy that country music was not static and needed to evolve to remain fresh. It was a philosophy Eddie and Bobby lived by, and it was more responsible for today's Nashville music scene than any one artist, writer, or producer. Bobby stopped and stared at the building, a temple to all that he worshipped. The meaning of country music life.

Arriving on Music Square East and still feeling out of sorts, he strolled past the guitar shaped pool built by Webb Pierce, the biggest country singer of the fifties; it was located right next to the former Spence

Hotel, which was initially built for Elvis Presley and would be the short-term home for many a country music star and a few U.S. presidents. Bobby then walked into Owen Bradley Park and sat on the piano bench next to the statue of the park's namesake, a legendary record producer and one of the godfathers of the Nashville sound. Bobby studied the bronze Owen, one hand on the piano the other raised with its palm to the sky, a big smile permanently etched upon his face. "You should be smiling, Owen," Bobby whispered. "You got yourself on top quick and stayed there. Good for you." Bobby felt a bit dizzy and sat for a while before he proceeded past the park, where the street ended with the Buddy Killen roundabout encircling the Musica sculpture. Bobby had not visited the sculpture in a long time. He got up close and touched the leg of one of the giant bronze figures. It was warm from the sun and felt good on his hand. It was a bit difficult to see the women with the tambourine being held high by some of the figures because the sun was directly in Bobby's eyes. As he stepped back, the dancing figures actually seemed to begin to move, slowly at first but with steadily increasing energy. Bobby could hear the tambourine jingle, which was followed by the distant sound of orchestral music growing louder. Bobby recognized it as Beethoven's "Für Elise." It was beautiful, and he smiled. Five of the figures held hands and danced in a circle while three in the middle began to dance in the opposite direction, still holding the tambourine woman aloft. Bobby had to fight the urge to get naked and join them.

Bobby's serenity was broken by the arrival of a German tour group. The dancing stopped. The

Germans circled around and snapped a lot of pictures as a local tour guide dressed in a cowboy outfit fed them some garbage about Garth Brooks being discovered while playing his guitar underneath the statue. Bobby left in disgust.

Barnes Jewish Hospital Drug Rehab did not permit visitors for the first ten days, so Toby spent most of his time at the DoubleTree Hilton or at the medical library at nearby Washington University reading as much as he could about drug addiction.

At rehab, Lauren was being weaned off Adderall. They said it would take seven to fourteen days, but after five days, she said she'd had enough. By the look in her eyes and the sound of her voice, the doctors were not about to argue. She attended several sessions that delved into the causes of her dependency. In the end, they could find no reason other than the fact she'd been offered the drug to help with her exhaustion, she'd taken it, and she was thereafter off to the races.

The rehab staff also coached Lauren on lifestyle changes to battle her fatigue. Meditation, better eating habits, exercise, and alternative sleep regimens were proposed. Lauren progressed rapidly, and after ten days, Toby was allowed to visit. The pair took a walk through nearby Forest Park, and Lauren thanked Toby for hanging around. "It felt good knowing someone I know was around, even though I couldn't see you until now," she told him. Lauren told Toby that she was going to tell the doctors when she got back to the center that she was ready to go home. Toby cited statistics on the increased chance of relapse for those who leave rehab before the recommended time. She agreed to give it a few more days.

The following day, Lauren was in a group meeting with a few recovering addicts. She found it a bit embarrassing when they introduced themselves and a younger member of the group asked for her autograph. The counselor opened the meeting by asking where they wanted to be a year from now. An older woman who seemed to have the beginnings of Parkinson's said she hoped she'd be allowed to see her grandchildren again. The autograph seeker responded that he wanted to be a video game tournament champion. When it was Lauren's turn, she said she hoped to continue to grow her success in her career. The counselor asked if that would make her happiest. Lauren responded that it would certainly make her happier than she was now. The counselor said, "But Lauren, that's not what I asked. If I were in ICU in a hospital and was moved to a regular hospital room, I'd be happier, but I don't think I'd necessarily be happy."

Lauren thought for a moment. Finally, she replied, "I get it. A little extreme maybe, but I get it. I'm not sure I can answer that right now."

But the meeting did get Lauren thinking. Even though it seemed she was making it big in music—her lifelong dream—she realized that some of her saddest moments had been during the same time period.

The next day, Toby came for a visit, and they went to lunch at a French brasserie in a nearby hipster area of the West End. Over a plate of pate de foie gras and toast points, Lauren told Toby about the group meeting the day before. Toby said that inner peace was what made him happiest. "I mean, I love playing with the band; don't get me wrong. But there were times on the road and during practice and in the recording studio that were stressful."

"But isn't that part of the experience? If everything were la-de-da all the time, wouldn't that be kind of boring?"

"Yes, but stress does affect us. Some of us drink or smoke or take drugs."

Lauren raised her hand in acknowledgement.

Toby continued. "We lose sleep. It affects our relationships."

Again, Lauren with the raised hand. "So, what do you suggest, Mr. Wizard?"

Toby blushed. "I think you can't be happy until you know yourself. There are probably a lot of ways to get to that point. I think some people get there sooner than others, and some people never do. Mahatma Gandhi once said, 'Happiness is when what you think, what you say, and what you do are all in harmony. I know for me, meditation helps. It clears my mind, reduces my stress, helps me focus, and lets me think about things I would never think about."

"Like what?"

"I don't know. The makeup of the universe, or why crumb cake is so delicious."

"They talked about meditation in rehab. I guess I should take some lessons when I get back home."

"No need; I can help you. I'm a certified meditational instructor."

Lauren leaned back in her chair, shook her head, and smiled. "Mr. Keyboard Man, you are really starting to impress me."

Lauren insisted on getting some meditation instruction right away. Back in Toby's room, he taught her comfortable beginner's positions and some basic breathing exercises. Twenty minutes into the instruction, Toby, seated crossed legged with his eyes closed, felt a hand on his leg. The meditation lesson was over, and Lauren would get reprimanded for reporting back to rehab much later than scheduled.

Bobby was really having a hard time with the Lauren situation. He thought he might have suffered a panic attack after discovering Lauren went into rehab, and in retrospect, he seriously doubted that the Musica figures had actually been dancing. So what was going on with him? He was relieved when Toby finally called to say he'd seen Lauren and she seemed to be making a lot of progress. Bobby asked Toby to call him every morning with an update.

Hanson and Wyatt stopped by Bobby's office unannounced. They wanted to know if the rumors were true about Lauren having a nervous breakdown. Bobby was always amazed how supposedly confidential matters turned into half-truths in this town.

"No she didn't have a nervous breakdown, for Christ's sake. She just had a personal issue she had to work through. Mentally, she is as sharp as us three combined. I have Toby keeping an eye on her in case she needs anything."

At the mention of Toby's name, Bobby worried Wyatt might get jealous, given his past longing to be more than just the fiddler in the band to Lauren. But unbeknownst to Bobby, the groupie following Wyatt around the tour had grown on him quite a bit and was now properly known by her birth name; Margarita had moved in with him a few days ago. She was an heiress to the largest Mexican liquor producer, had a strong love for American country music, and an even greater predilection for blonde haired fiddler players.

Hanson and Wyatt told Bobby that they were available if he needed anything. Hanson also wondered if he could have an advance, as his luck had been less than stellar on a recent trip down to the casinos in Biloxi, Mississippi. Bobby shook his head and wrote Hanson a check.

Bobby decided to meet with Henry Taylor and Hope; he didn't want them to feel like they were the only ones out of the loop. Hope came in first, dressed as though she were going to meet some teenagers in a park for skateboarding and cigarettes. She was totally nonplussed by the news that Lauren needed to take care of a personal issue; she said that she would take the extra time to visit her parents back in Memphis. Turning his attention to Henry, Bobby realized the two of them hadn't had any one-on-one time in quite a while. When Henry came in, Bobby apologized for not reaching out sooner and explained the reason the band had not been getting together recently.

"She didn't have a nervous breakdown?" Henry asked.

Bobby just looked up at the ceiling, shook his head, and said no.

"Ah, that is so good," Henry replied in his Jamaican Rasta accent. "I have been praying for her."

Although not religious himself, Bobby always had a certain respect, if not envy, for those who were. At least those who were and didn't throw it in your face as though you were a leper if you did not conform. "Henry, can I ask you a personal question?"

"Of course."

"As a Rasta, what is it with the long hair? I have nothing against it, of course, but when you don't have your hair under your hat, it almost goes down to your knees. I had hair down to my shoulders in the old days, but I think it would bother me now. Is it a brotherhood thing? Do the chicks like it?"

Henry laughed and took off his stocking hat; his thick braids fell below the chair, nearly touching the floor. "It is from the Bible, the Old Testament, Leviticus 19.27: 'You shall not round the edge of your head nor shall you destroy the edge of your beard." Henry smiled a big, toothy grin. "And yes, the chicks like it."

THE BREAK

A few days after their first meditation lesson in Toby's room, Lauren signed herself out of rehab. She wanted to go back to Nashville but keep it confidential until she was ready to let people know she was back. Lauren tried to get Toby to cover for her, but the fact Bobby had asked him for an update every morning created an awkward situation. Toby told Lauren he was a terrible liar, and Bobby would see right through him. Lauren relented and called Bobby's assistant, Mary. She told Mary that she was coming back to Nashville, but the doctors told her she needed to rest for a few days, so Bobby should not try to contact her.

When Mary told Bobby the news, he wasn't happy. "She said what?"

Mary repeated the message as requested in a monotone voice. Bobby pointed her to the door.

Toby was packing his bags when his cell phone rang. He had less than no desire to answer. "Hi, Bobby."

"Toby, what the hell is going on?"

"Uh, Lauren is leaving rehab today. We're heading back to Nashville."

"I know. What's with the no contact? Did the doctors really say that?"

"I would assume so, if that is what Lauren said."

"Toby, don't fuck with me."

Toby could feel his face flush, but he held his

ground. "I'm sorry, Bobby, but I think you should speak to Lauren about it."

"How can I? Goddamnit! She supposedly can't be contacted!"

Toby wasn't sure how to respond, so he opted for a strategy that ensured the interrogation would end. He hung up.

Toby was a bit surprised at himself but also relieved. His phone rang again. He put it in his pocket, finished packing, and went to pick up Lauren.

As Bobby tried again to get Toby on the phone, he felt a tightness in his chest. He hung up and sat down. He called Mary into his office. She took one look at him, grabbed the phone off his desk, and called 911.

Miguel was relaxing at home listening to some old Deford Bailey music while reading Edmundo O'Gorman's Mexico el Trauma de su Historia, when Cynthia came running in with the phone. It was Mary, reaching out to let him know that Bobby had just been taken to the hospital. Mary apologized, saying she didn't know who else to notify. Miguel grabbed his keys and was on his way.

Miguel hated hospitals. When he was a teenager, his mom developed breast cancer. As it progressed deep into stage four, Miguel visited her every day in the hospital. Miguel would later describe it as "my daily trip to hell." Watching his mother's pain grow worse, her body rattled with fatigue and weight loss, he hated himself for wishing it would just end. Miguel wasn't particularly religious but found himself praying out loud while driving, afraid of what he would discover when he arrived at Vanderbilt Hospital.

When Miguel arrived, he was led into an emergency room area where Bobby was already in a bed partitioned off with a curtain. Before going in, Miguel spoke to a nurse who told him that the preliminary diagnosis was a panic attack. Jimmy was surprised to see Bobby drenched in sweat but alert; he was attached to a few machines that bought back some dark memories. Bobby acknowledged him with a weak wave.

Miguel smiled back. "Kemo Sabe, what happened? Sounds like you are going to be OK?"

Bobby replied in a weak voice. "I thought I was going, man. Could hardly breathe."

It was the greatest news Miguel had heard, but knowing it was a panic attack and not Bobby's heart brought some relief. He was not about to take a return trip to the dark side. Miguel looked at Bobby and could still see a mix of fear and shame. "Hey man, this shit happens. You got a lot on your plate. You've been burning the candle at both ends. When we get you out of here, we have to figure a way to give you some Bobby time."

Bobby just shook his head and closed his eyes. Miguel sat on the one uneven plastic chair in the cubicle and watched him sleep. About six hours later, when the doctors were confident of their diagnosis, they said Bobby could be discharged. A young emergency room doctor told him that panic attacks don't necessarily stop on their own, and he should see a doctor for treatment.

When they left the hospital, Bobby said he was hungry, so they stopped at the Pelican and the Pig, where they sat at a small counter overlooking the kitchen. Miguel ordered the braised rabbit over gnocchi and Bobby the short ribs. They split a Silver Oak cabernet. After some small talk, and once Bobby seemed somewhat replenished, Miguel broached the subject. "So, what do we do about this situation? You going to listen to what they said at the hospital and see a doctor for treatment?" Miguel already knew what the answer would be.

"Well, it certainly scared me, I can tell you that much. I need to think about what the best course of action is. Right now, my mind is a muddled mess."

Miguel decided not to push Bobby; the day had enough stress already. He poured them each another glass of wine and ordered a piece of strawberry short cake.

Lauren had been back in Nashville just over a week, and she felt good. She hadn't touched a single pill since being home, although the urge was surely there from time to time. Toby continued to teach her meditation techniques, and now they were actually doing the lessons. She had called up the Commander a few days earlier because she felt a strong urge to perform. Tonight was the night, and it would be a secret until The 5 Spot put it on their social media. Bobby got wind of the gig and felt a mixture of anger and resignation. For the moment, he decided to let her be, as requested, until she felt good enough to return to the nest.

Lauren was not scheduled to go on until eleven, but the crowd started lining up late that afternoon. The Commander sent a car to pick her up and sneak her in the back door. By the time Lauren arrived at around ten, bouncers were telling the angry line stretching down the block that no more people were going to be allowed inside.

Lauren greeted the Commander in his office. He walked over and gave her a hug. "So great to see you. I heard you were out of town for a bit. Hope everything is OK."

For a moment Lauren was surprised, but then she recalled what the Commander had told her. "I know. You're in the Nashville club business. It is your job to know what's going on."

"Now you got it."

The pair spoke for a while, and Lauren thanked him for the opportunity to perform. She told him she needed to clear her head, and this would help a lot.

"Anytime," The Commander said. "It's not hurting my finances either."

A few minutes before eleven, Lauren stood alone in a short hallway, steps away from the small stage. Peeking out, she saw the stage contained only a microphone and a stool. She realized that she hadn't performed alone in quite some time. It wasn't an arena, just a few hundred hometown folks. Without a band, there was no cover. Just you alone. Lauren took some comfort in that. No one was counting on her to make good. No Bobby, no Jimmy, no Toby or the rest of Nash band. Just her own need. Lauren closed her eyes and rubbed the side of her guitar, which was slung over her shoulder. Tonight, she wasn't even going electric.

The Commander came out of his office and walked up to Lauren. "Do you mind if I do the honors?"

She smiled and nodded.

Onstage, the Commander bellowed into the microphone. "Folks, we have a very special guest here tonight."

The crowd cheered, and the Commander signaled for them to pipe down; to his surprise, they ignored him. "Back in her hometown after a remarkably successful national tour, please welcome back to The 5 Spot, Ms. Lauren Culiver!"

The crowd clapped, whistled, and hollered as Lauren crept onto the stage. Between the stage lights and the dense crowd, the antiquated air conditioning was no match for the rising heat. It took her a moment to find her voice. "It's so good to be home."

Lauren opened with "Waiting on a Song" by Dan Auerbach. She then played most of the songs off her first album, interspersed with some works in progress for the second. When she finished her set, the audience was so appreciative that the Commander asked her to go back for one more song. Forty minutes and half a dozen audience requests later, she finally closed with Chris Stapleton's "Starting Over."

Sweating and breathing hard, Lauren sat on a chair alone in the Commander's office. She felt a wave of exhilaration overtake her body, and she smiled to herself. The Commander, who had struggled to get through the crowd, walked in. He handed Lauren a bottle of water. "Mrs. Culiver. My, my, you have come a long way, girl. Now you know I ain't one for overdoing compliments, but that was the finest performance I have seen in here in a long time."

"Thanks." Lauren stood up and gave him a hug.

The Commander went to his desk, opened the top drawer, and pulled out a checkbook. "Now I know we never agreed to anything, but I want to give you a piece of the action. It was a big night."

"That's OK, Commander. You have no idea how I have been paid back tonight."

"You sure, girl?"

Lauren nodded as she put her guitar back into the case. "Can you get me a ride back to my place?"

"I'm so proud of you, I'm going to drive you myself."

The next morning over coffee, Bobby read a review of the show in the *Tennessean*. The first paragraph read:

If you are lucky in life, you may experience a musical performance that you know is unique and incredibly special. Like the folks who listened to Hank Williams when he was a teenager live on WSFA radio in Montgomery, or Bob Dylan in the clubs of Greenwich Village, or Bruce Springsteen at the Stone Pony in Asbury Park, New Jersey. Last night, Lauren Culiver played a surprise solo acoustic show at The 5 Spot. It was there I saw something special and unique for myself. I saw the future of country music.

I saw it first, Bobby thought. On one hand, he was happy for Lauren's recognition and the fact that she seemed to be well on her way to returning to music. On the other hand, the suspense of not being able to reach out to her was getting worse by the day. He had just received word that Lauren and the band would likely be up for the Country Music Association Best New Artist of the Year as well as Album of the Year. Shouldn't she know about this? The message was, she needed a few days. Hasn't it been more than a few days? Bobby decided that if he didn't hear from Lauren by the end of the day, he would go see her tomorrow. There was just too much to do to play hide and seek.

The next morning, Bobby met with Judy Komanski at her request to get a sign off on a new record contract for Kenny Chesney. It was a big one. "Is he worth it?" Bobby asked.

"Looking at all his past record sales, Chesney couldn't miss charting in the top ten if he was a mime."

After the meeting, Bobby was getting ready to take a ride over to Lauren's apartment when Mary announced that Hanson had stopped by to see him.

Slightly frustrated, Bobby asked, "Do we know what this is about?"

Mary shook her head.

"OK, OK," Bobby said. "Send him in." Bobby smiled as Hanson entered the office, and Hanson forced a weak one back. "Take a seat. Are you OK? You look a little perturbed."

Hanson said thanks as he sat down. He put his right foot over his left knee, and his boot rocked back and forth nervously.

Bobby sat behind his desk. "I hope you don't think I'm rushing you Hanson, but I was just about to head out to Lauren's place."

"Ah, so she told you then."

"Told me what?"

Hanson rubbed his forehead. "Oh, man. I came to say I'm sorry. I thought you knew."

Bobby leaned forward. "As a friend, I hope I don't have to ask you again. Know what?"

Hanson looked at the floor for a moment and then made eye contact. "Lauren is going over to Sony. She told us last night."

It took Bobby a moment to process what Hanson had just said. He stood up and came around his desk in front of Hanson. Still confused, he asked, "She told who?"

"The band. Me, Toby, Wyatt, and Hope. I'm sorry, Bobby. I thought you knew. I just came by here to thank you for everything."

"You don't have to thank me, Hanson. You were one of the first to step up when I was putting Nash together. Tell the band not to worry. I'm sure I can talk Lauren out of this crazy idea. Worst case scenario, even if I can't, let the band know that I will find them other spots. We can always use great musicians at Sidewalk."

Hanson looked like he wanted to say something.

"What is it?" Bobby asked.

"Some of the band is going with her, Bobby. Hooking up with someone like Lauren is a once in a lifetime gig. You know that as well as anybody. Toby, Hope, and I agreed to go. Wyatt and Henry have opted out. Wyatt said he would feel too guilty since you surprised him with that expensive fiddle, and Henry said he would like to but didn't have the heart to leave Sidewalk."

Bobby could almost feel the blood drain from his face. "And I guess it doesn't matter about the guy who brought you all into the gig, eh?"

"Bobby, I came here as your friend. I am sitting here face to face. And does it really matter to you? I mean, you own most of this record company, with more than a few names who bring in more revenue than Lauren."

Bobby was too agitated to reply. "I need to get

to the bottom of this," he said to no one in particular, stalking out the door. Hanson called out to him but to no avail.

Lauren had just put her hand on her doorknob to head out when Bobby knocked. Opening the door, she was not totally surprised. "Oh, hi. I was literally just coming to see you."

"Seems to me a bit late, no?"

"Please come in."

Bobby walked to the middle of Lauren's living room with hands in his pockets. "So Hanson came to me this morning and hit me with the news."

"I am really sorry. I didn't know he was going to do that. I intended to be the first one to talk to you about it."

"Lauren, it seems I am far from the first person you've talked to."

"I don't want to have a fight here, but I do want to talk through it. Can we do that?"

Bobby sat down on the couch and nervously held his hands out. "I am all ears."

"Thank you." Lauren sat down on a chair across from the couch. "I have been going through a lot, and I don't want you to think I made this decision lightly. You know, you and I are a lot alike. We love music. It's even more than that; our very beings are intertwined with it. Maybe when you first saw me play in the park, you figured you could help me get a little better. But neither of us expected it to get this big, this fast. And even if it hadn't, I'd still be doing what I do. I'd still be playing those park gigs even if you never came up and introduced yourself. I know that.

"But Bobby, I was in a bad place. Everyone is always telling me what I should do and what I shouldn't. My mother, Jimmy, you, a host of others. Not that I don't want advice; I do, but there never seemed to be any boundaries. I can't tell you how good the Adderall made me feel. It didn't just help with the exhaustion; it helped me tune all the bullshit out. But in the end, I realized it was a total copout. Putting aside the fact that it might have killed me, I should have been able to stop the bullshit on my own. I am a grown woman."

Lauren stood up and paced the room. "Toby convinced me to get some help." Lauren smiled. "By the way, that boy is one smart cookie. Anyway, when I cleared my head, I came back to Nashville and realized that deep down I was unhappy. Even with all the success we've had, I was awfully unhappy. I was sad, you know, and I blamed myself, thinking I must be self-absorbed to be blessed with so much and not appreciate it. I hadn't performed in a while, and I needed an outlet, so The 5 Spot gave me a slot. I really didn't know what to expect. I mean, I hadn't played to an intimate audience in a while. It was just me and my guitar. I didn't even have a playlist. To say I was nervous would be an understatement."

Lauren walked up close to Bobby. "But Bobby, it was wonderful. I just got into a zone. I ended up playing for over two hours but felt like I could play all night. It was just me and my guitar up there on a closet of a stage wearing the same old clothes I had put on that morning. When I got home, I was so ramped up, I couldn't sleep. No Adderall, just my own adrenaline. And I got to thinking. I never had a clean break. I mean,

I never had a time in my life when I called my own shots. There was always someone perched on my shoulder telling me what to do. Remember the great review we got in the LA Times after the show? I emailed it to my parents. I got an email back from my mother wanting to know if Jimmy, who she thought was a doctor, was still in the picture. We blew the roof off the Staples Center, and she was concerned about me messing up a relationship with a doctor who didn't even exist! I am forever grateful to you for everything you've done, but you could never totally let me be me. You are in this thing too deep. I need the clean break, Bobby. From everything."

In the silence that followed, one could hear customers in the parking lot coming into the Lipstick Lounge for lunch.

"You have anything to say?" Lauren asked.

Bobby stood up and turned away from Lauren before speaking. "You're probably right,. I am in this deep. To be frank, I hardly give any thought to anything else going on at Sidewalk. All I care about are you and the band. I don't know if it's because you brought me back from the brink or what, but you're right. I get it. I'm having a hard time with it, but I get it."

Lauren stood in front of Bobby and gave him an embrace. "Thank you. I know we never even got around to signing a contract, but whatever you want from me, I am sure we can work it out. As for the band, that was the toughest thing. I love those guys but believe me when I tell you I didn't hard sell. Sony said I could come with or without. I just asked the band what they wanted to do and told them I understood if they wanted to remain at Sidewalk, because I knew you would get them new gigs. They said they would think about it and get back to me."

Bobby nodded. "When Hanson told me this morning, I literally wanted to hit him. In retrospect, that was pretty sad of me."

"No, I would be upset too. I should have been the first to tell you."

"Why Sony? They're a bigger than us. Do you think you can get a clean break there?"

"I don't know. They offered a five-record deal. I told them I wanted to start with just one."

"You do realize that most artist vie for a longer contract?"

"I know it's risky for me, yes, but if they don't give me the freedom I need, I can get out."

"Record companies are experienced sharks. Do you have a good attorney?"

"Toby has a friend over at Bradley Arant."

"Of course he does."

"Are you going to be OK?"

Bobby forced a smile. "Nothing a bottle of bourbon won't cure, at least temporarily. You took some time to clear your head; I think it may be time for me to do that as well."

"Well, speaking of lawyers, I have to be at Sony offices in an hour to sign some papers or something."

Bobby stood up. "OK, then. I don't know what else to say. Good luck, I guess?"

"I totally understand if you are terribly angry. I also get it if you don't want to remain friends, but hopefully after the dust settles, we can talk about things."

Bobby opened the door to leave, paused, and

turned around. "Lauren, I know even if I wanted not to be friends, I could not get myself to do that with you."

Bobby left Lauren's and drove aimlessly for a while until he ended up near the Belmont University campus. He needed some air, so he parked the car and began to walk through campus. He was now glad that Miguel had persuaded him to take a call from a doctor acquaintance of Cynthia's who prescribed him some Zoloft. With this Lauren news, Bobby prayed it would work. Being in-between semesters, the campus was quiet. He walked through the main quad to the Bell Tower and Carillon. It was his favorite structure during his brief time on campus as a freshman. Bobby opened the narrow wooden door and went inside. The first floor contained a small chapel on the left and a cast iron staircase to the right. Bobby didn't think it had changed at all since the last time he was there, almost fifty years ago. He went up the stairs past the second floor, which housed a library, and the third floor, which contained a practice carillon. On the fourth floor, Bobby saw the keyboard control mechanism for the bells on the level above. It reminded him of what a time machine might have looked like in a 1950s sci-fi movie. Finally he reached the fifth floor, which was half open to the elements and held the bells, all forty-three of them. Bobby ascended an iron ladder, forced open a small hatch, and climbed out onto the roof. From there he could see the office of Sidewalk Records on Music Row and beyond that downtown Nashville. It was amazing how much the city had grown over the years. Canvassing the skyline, Bobby noted at least a dozen tower cranes. While Bobby was getting older, the city was getting newer every day.

Bobby thought about the conversation he just had with Lauren. It made him sad. Everything had been working so well with Lauren and the band, the whole concept of starting from nothing and bringing them into stardom. It was what had been making him tick. It had him happily working late into the night and rushing to the office before anyone else arrived. Why couldn't he be happy with all he was given? He could go back to his office right now as head of a major record label and be busy from morning to night and still be smack in the middle of the country music scene with all its benefits.

No. He realized Lauren had gotten it right. She paused, did some introspection, and fixed what she needed to fix. He just kept driving at a hundred miles an hour without paying attention to any flashing yellow lights. During the last conversation, Lauren, more than thirty years younger than he was, had been the adult in the room. Bobby could almost see her inner peace, and he was envious. He was uncertain where to even begin. He sat down on the roof and let his mind drift. Hours later, a security guard interrupted his trance, telling him he couldn't be up there. Shaking his head without speaking, Bobby got up and climbed down the tower, quite sure that things were going to change but having no idea how.

REDUX

On a Sunday four months after his last conversation with Lauren, Bobby was finishing his second bourbon at Edgefield's. He didn't come there much anymore. It wasn't because he no longer liked it. Nor was it because he'd finally cut down on his drinking—he had given up on that. Rather, he'd taken some of his money from the sale of his portion of Sidewalk Records to the private equity company, and he had bought a penthouse apartment in one of the new condominium buildings in the Gulch. Edgefield's was quite a ways across town now, and he had at least twenty bars within spitting distance of his new place. Lucy teased him with a nickname, Trendy Bobo. Bobby bought the condo thinking that if he had a cool place in Nashville, it might convince his daughters to come visit. It didn't work with Jessica, but Emily had come out a few weeks earlier. Bobby decided the purchase was worth the price. But from time to time, Edgefield's still offered him a comfort he couldn't find anywhere else, like the old flannel shirt you just can't throw out.

Miguel had been pushing him to consider starting a new independent label with Cynthia, but he just wasn't sure if he wanted the headaches or, at this stage, if he even had the desire. Bobby did manage to convince Wyatt and Henry to take the gig with Lauren. He told them there was a distinction between loyalty and common sense. Hanson was right. Gigs like that were once in a lifetime. Too clear his mind, he had taken a spur-of-the-moment trip back to Paris and was happy to see that his favorite patisserie still made delicious lemon tarts. When Bobby returned home, he wrote some songs and gave them to a few producers and musicians to see if anyone was interested. He hadn't yet heard anything back. He ordered another bourbon and looked at the TV, which was broadcasting impeachment hearings of the president. Both parties yelling at each other, throwing insults, and accusing the opposing side of lying. Bobby thought the scene made the music business seem like summer school and whorehouses like monasteries. "Hypocrites and phonies," Bobby said to no one in particular.

"Would you like me to change the channel?" Lucy asked.

"No thanks, NP, I'm just going to finish up here." Bobby drank the last of his bourbon and placed some money on the bar.

"OK, Trendy Bobo, thanks for coming. Don't be a stranger now. Contrary to what they think in the Gulch, we do take a bath around here once in a while."

Bobby smiled. "I'll try and convince them that is true."

It was midafternoon as Bobby got into his car for the drive back to the Gulch. Outside, the trees were beginning to change color. After parking in the garage of his condo, he decided to walk around while it was still light. During his stroll, he passed by the Nashville Boot Co., which he hadn't visited since he purchased the pair from Lauren. Bobby looked down at his boots. He could use a new pair. He decided to wait and maybe give Boot Country or French's Shoes and Boots downtown a try.

A few blocks later, he passed The Station Inn, a longtime bluegrass venue that hosted bluegrass and country gospel music every Sunday afternoon. Bobby thought he could use a dose, so he paid fifteen dollars and went inside. He grabbed a draft beer at the concession window and found a worn chair. The musicians onstage were a hodgepodge of longtime Nashville professionals, a group that changed from week to week and often included well-known players and singers. On this day, they were doing a lot of traditional gospel songs including "Green Pastures," "Daniel Prayed," and "Will the Circle Be Unbroken." Bobby felt comforted. Toward the end of the show, they introduced a young woman who had been in the back manning the sound equipment. She seemed almost too shy to sing a song, and it took some doing to get the microphone adjusted to her short stature. Her short blonde hair looked like she might have cut it herself, but she was cute in a one of those difficult-to-articulate ways. The lead fiddler introduced the song "Something in the Water." Seconds in, Bobby was mesmerized. It seemed as though her voice went right through his body rather than into his ears. When the song was over, she bowed to a raucous ovation and sheepishly left the stage for her original post in the back of the room. Her heart was beating fast as she tried to refocus on her sound duties. She did not see the man approach her, and at first she was a bit startled when he said, "Hey, that was really great!"

ABOUT THE AUTHOR

Daniel Scavone is the author of *The Last Autumn*. A native of Brooklyn, New York, he holds B.A., J.D. and MBA degrees. Currently living in Belle Mead, New Jersey, he is president of a consulting company and a lecturer at Rutgers University.